𝕽𝖎𝖓𝖌 𝖔𝖋 𝕾𝖙𝖔𝖓𝖊

To Julie

Hugh McCracken

𝕳𝖚𝖌𝖍 𝕸𝖈𝕮𝖗𝖆𝖈𝖐𝖊𝖓

BeWrite Books, UK
www.bewrite.net

Published internationally by BeWrite Books, UK.
363 Badminton Road, Nibley, Bristol. BS37 5JF.

© Hugh McCracken 2002

The right of Hugh McCracken to be identified as the author has been asserted in accordance with sections 77 and 78 of the Copyright, Designs and Patents Act 1988. The right of Hugh McCracken to be recognised as the sole author is further asserted in accordance with international copyright agreements, laws and statutes.

British Library Cataloguing in Publication Data.
A catalogue record for this book is available from the British Library

ISBN 1-904224-61-X
Digitally produced by BeWrite Books, UK.

Also available in eBook and CD-ROM formats, from www.bewrite.net

This book is sold subject to the condition that it shall not, by way of trade or otherwise, be lent, resold, hired out or otherwise circulated without the publisher's consent in any form other than this current form and without a similar condition being imposed upon a subsequent purchaser. No part of this publication may be reproduced, stored in a retrieval system, or transmitted in any form by any means electronic, mechanical, photocopying, recording or otherwise without the permission of the publisher, BeWrite Books, UK.

This book is a work of fiction. Any similarity between characters in its pages and persons living or dead is unintentional and co-incidental. The author and publishers recognise and respect any trademarks included in this work by introducing such registered titles either in italics or with a capital letter.

**EXCLUSIVE COVER AND INSIDE ARTWORK
BY ALAN GELDARD © 2002**

"They hanged both of them, but cut them down when they were still alive to bring them round, wide awake before their bellies were slit and their guts pulled out."

"I don't want to hear the rest," Jo said.

"They flogged each twice before they hanged them again," Henry said. "And again, and again ... they've got the heads in sacks in the barn. Want to see? The sergeant let me look."

"Those swine deserve their fate," the judge said. "But it was too quick. One justice I heard of hanged a peasant twenty times. Once in each of the towns, villages and hamlets he visited. Before death, the pig was cut down and revived and kept healthy for the next occasion. By the last time, his neck was so stretched and weak he could not hold up his head. It flopped about like a straw doll.

"He had a collar of leather made to support the neck and head on their travels so that it wouldn't break and the man escape the real torture later."

While the judge laughed at his own story, Rick muttered: "And you're surprised the peasants revolted; you're surprised they behaved as they did with such sadistic justices?"

Hugh McCracken has lived in Canada since 1967 with wife, Lyn. They have two sons and three grandchildren and, for thirteen years, he was principal of a junior/senior high school.

The family and workplace experiences might account for Hugh's magic touch when it comes to stories for children and young adults and a rare ability to introduce historical fact so subtly the reader hardly realises he's being educated as he's entertained.

Also by Hugh McCracken:

Rules of the Hunt
Grandfather and The Ghost
Return from the Hunt
The Time Drum
BeWrite Books, 2002

Kevin and The Time Drum
Electric E-book Publishing, 2001

A Time Check From Hugh McCracken

The ribbon of time is endless, but do we travel only on one side with our past, our present, our future; our before, our now, our after? Unable, forbidden to cross over the edge?

What is on the other side? Another time line? An alternate universe? Could we get from our time, our universe to the other without crossing an edge? If we did, could we get back?

The Möbius Loop – a simple loop of ribbon with a single twist discovered by the 19th Century German mathematician and astronomer August Ferdinand Möbius shows us – generations before Star Wars – how we might easily pass from one side of reality to the another.

Puzzled?

… try this …

◊Take yesterday's newspaper and a pair of scissors and cut yourself a long strip, maybe one foot long by a couple of inches wide.

◊Make a hoop but don't fix the ends to each other yet.

◊With us so far?

◊Now … make a single twist in the paper and join the ends with tape or a staple.

◊Doesn't look much does it?

◊Mark a cross with a felt-tipped pen on one side of the paper and a circle on the other side directly opposite.

◊Hold it in one hand, then gently run the forefinger of your other on the inside of the loop …

⟨⟩Notice anything strange? Of course you do! Your finger stroked the 'inside' AND the 'outside' of the Möbius Loop without crossing an edge – you got from the cross to the circle without going over the edge.

⟨⟩You have just proven to yourself that you can traverse dimensions, that our idea of space and time might be ... well ... out of the loop.

This is how your friends in my books might be shifted through the centuries. A simple twist in time and space. Before you tried your experiment, you may have thought this sheer science fiction ... but what do you think now that you are dangling the evidence in your hand? Show your folks, show your friends – see what they think of your first REAL adventure into the ultimate paradox!

Your friend – Hugh McCracken

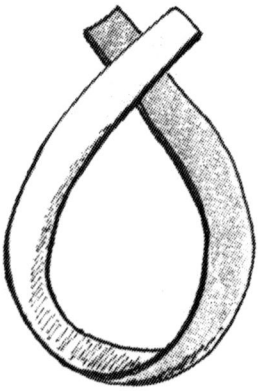

To my wife,
for her patience while I researched and wrote this.

Alan Geldard was born in Stockport, England in 1963. He still lives and works in the Cheshire city. He honed his natural skills with study and practice to the extent that he produces stunning images like those reproduced here. Alan – also a keen, prolific and talented author – is happily married to Alison. They have four children; Debbie, Vicky, Jo and Amy.

Also illustrated by Alan Geldard:

Rules of the Hunt
Return from the Hunt
BeWrite Books 2002

King of Stone

Book One

Chapter One

Rick could still feel his ears ring when he sat up. Odd, the moon had gone. Covered by a cloud, perhaps? No, above him, he could see the sky was brilliant with stars. The smell of explosives hung in the air.

Chris lay curled up beside him, very young and vulnerable. Malcolm lay, one of two black shapes, stretched out close to one of the perimeter stones. While Rick watched, Malcolm stirred, sat up, and held his head in both hands.

"God. I'll never drink that stuff again, what a kick, what a head."

"Are you all right?" Rick said.

"I've been better. What the hell happened?"

"See to Chris, will you? He's still out."

Malcolm knelt beside the boy and gently felt him all over.

"There's no sign of any external damage. I think he's coming round. Just playing possum, weren't you?"

Chris sat blank eyed for a minute. When he saw Rick beside him, he huddled against Rick who put an arm round his cousin's shoulder.

"I had an awful dream. It started okay, but the end frightened me." He sat back and gazed round him. "It was a dream wasn't it?"

"Maybe not," Rick said. "Anyway, you're fine now."

Other dark shapes groaned and moved.

Chris tugged at Rick's sleeve.

"Have you looked round? Wasn't there a full moon? What's happened to the town lights? We could see them from here before, and the bay prom lights."

"I don't know. You know as much as I do."

"Come outside the stones, you lot," Arthur's voice shouted.

Cautiously, Rick, Malcolm, and Chris moved out of the circle to join Arthur. Three other shadows converged on them at edge of the grassy mound.

"The pack we left outside the circle has gone," Arthur said. "The lot. I've checked everywhere I planted stuff. There's a strong smell of explosives, but there's no trace of an explosion any place: not in the ground, nor on the stones, nowhere. Something has happened to the town lights. They aren't there any more."

Their eyes adjusted to the starlight, they stared at each other in silence. Arthur scowled at Malcolm.

"Why the hell did you jump me?"

"How was I to know it would set your damn bomb off?" Malcolm said. "I'm a medical student, not a bloody demolitions expert. Why the hell did you bring explosives? Why involve us?"

"Oh, come off it. We didn't ask you along. Anyway, it was your fault the frigging stuff went off when it did. If you had scarpered when I said to, we'd have been clear before the bang."

"Cut the chat, you two," Dennis said. "There must be a power failure in town, that's all."

"A pretty big one," Malcolm said and waved his arms around. "It put the moon out too."

"There must be some simple explanation. A cloud maybe?" Dennis insisted.

Arthur laughed, a short bark devoid of humour, and pointed at the star-filled sky.

"Face the evidence," Arthur said. "No moon, but fifteen minutes ago it was full and high in the sky. No town lights. No bay prom lights. No traces of any explosion, except the smell, and yet we all damned well heard and felt it. The stuff we left outside the stones has all gone."

"That stone," Chris pointed, "doesn't lean as far over as it did, and aren't there more stones standing now?"

Arthur shrugged. "See how dense and thick the wood is, it didn't grow in fifteen minutes."

"Well, what the hell do we do now?" Dennis said.

"We wait here till daylight," Arthur said. "Since we don't have any frigging idea what's out there, we can't risk getting separated in a strange forest."

Rick looked at Arthur's other two companions. They could be brothers, he thought. Both had jet black hair, very pale complexions, and white even teeth. The bigger of them had his arm round the smaller figure's shoulder.

"We'd better introduce ourselves, hadn't we? I'm Rick, he's Malcolm, and this is my cousin Chris."

Malcolm and Arthur snorted, but one figure said: "I'm Pete, and this is Joe, short for – "

Joe's elbow rammed into his midriff and he gasped.

"It's short for Joseph," Joe said.

Malcolm laughed. "My, how original."

Chapter Two

Was this a dream? Rick wondered, or was earlier tonight the dream?

He stumbled over roots in the darkness of the wood and Chris bumped into him again.

Me and my big mouth, Rick thought. How did I talk myself into this, and why did I bring the kid along?

Chris pressed close against him when they saw the standing stones on the mound through the last of the trees. The clouds parted and the light of a full moon flooded the scene making shadows even inkier.

The stones grew, the closer they got, till they towered over them. The wind, hardly noticed in the trees on the hill below, became a monk's chant, with a backing of stiff brushes on drums. Waves broke on the beach below the cliff and stirred the weeds to send them the incense of the sea.

The boy stopped. "Something moved."

"Come on, you two. It's only shadows," Malcolm said, himself a lumbering, shaggy bear. "Let's get right into the circle and put up our banners."

Although the stones looked hacked into shape, they felt smooth and worn with age, especially on the side facing the sea. Some stones stood straight, but most leaned at odd angles and there were gaps with dips in the mound where others had been.

Two lay flat. One in the circle had fallen over; the other perched on two low slabs almost at the centre had to be an altar, Rich thought. A sacrificial altar? Its top was smooth, with a hollow the length and breadth of a large man.

This was my destination in the circle of standing stones, eight years ago; I was only Chris's age now – thirteen.

I came up here on a dare on Halloween. I sprinted the last leg and in the dark stumbled into the altar stone. I stopped to draw breath, the moon came out again and across the bay I saw a whole castle, not the ruins I knew. Its walls gleamed white; its towers stood tall with a small town nestled round them. I turned to face the altar and I saw a naked man on the fallen stone, belly down, head turned to one side, legs dangled over the end, he struggled, his mouth open in a soundless scream...

Nothing has changed in eight years, Rick thought. He was older and bigger, but the stones were still huge and seeing the circle in the moonlight, being right there again, the hair on his neck bristled.

"Come on, Rick," Malcolm said, "give me a hand with the banners, this was your idea after all."

"No it wasn't. I only said this was common land, and they'd no right to keep it fenced. It was you that wanted to bring our banners up."

"You agreed we should re-establish the right-of-way."

"I'd had a couple of beers too many, and I didn't want to look stupid in front of the two yobs in the pub."

"Who are you calling frigging yobs?"

Chris shrieked at the sight of four shadows that separated themselves from the dark side of a stone to their right. When the shadows approached, he darted away from them to the centre of the circle. Rick and Malcolm ran after him, closely followed by the four dark shapes.

At the flat centre stone Rick caught Chris and the three of them turned to face their pursuers. Rick peered over the top of Chris's head and recognised two figures: Arthur with the pasty, ferret face, and lank, black hair that drooped over his forehead, his yappy terrier's voice aggressive when it wasn't whining; Dennis, Arthur's sidekick, a wolf at rest, with eyes that saw and assessed everything, his voice quiet; the two yobs from the pub in the evening. The other two were new to Rick and one wasn't any bigger than Chris.

"Arthur, what the hell are you doing here?" Rick said.

"You were so frigging eloquent at the pub earlier, Dennis and me decided to come up ourselves, right, Dennis?"

"Yes, very persuasive you were. Now, let's go. There isn't much time."

"It's only some lads Rick and I met earlier at the pub, Chris," Malcolm said.

Arthur gripped Malcolm's arm and pulled.

"Hey, cut out the rough stuff," Malcolm said. "We'll all go when we've put up our banners, okay?"

"No, there isn't time."

"Don't be stupid."

Arthur tugged and Malcolm pushed.

"Christ, stop the damned clock," Dennis said.

"Clock, what clock?" Malcolm said.

Arthur shook himself free and ran, with Malcolm in hot pursuit, to the edge of the circle. He knelt, fiddled with something in the shadows, and half-turned to face Malcolm.

"What are you up to? Let me see."

When he dodged back to avoid Malcolm's grasp, Arthur's hands, one wire in each, came together. Rick saw a bright spark against the gloom. Thunder roared and the earth erupted round them.

Damn it, Rick thought, they both feel real. Will we all wake up in the morning... When Rick woke his back was cold. Half asleep, eyes still shut tight; he groped for the covers.

"Chris, you little brat," he muttered, "let go of the covers. I'm freezing."

His hands first touched Chris's anorak, and beyond him, Malcolm. All at once fully awake and aware, Rick opened his eyes. The sun was up and dazzled him when he tried to sit. The figures outlined against the sun were not his companions.

"No, Master Gerald."

"Carry on, Sergeant."

The sergeant snapped an order. Two soldiers jerked Pete to his feet. They hustled him over to the fallen stone that lay almost flat. The soldiers untied Pete's hands and pulled off his anorak. When they tugged at his sweater, he started to struggle, but at a snap of his fingers from the sergeant; one of the pike men stepped forward and hit Pete hard on the head. Pete slumped, dazed. They stripped him to the waist, threw him face down onto the stone, and drew off his boots and socks. When his belt prevented his jeans from passing over his hips one of the soldiers simply sliced through the belt and jeans' waistband with his short sword. Naked, Pete lay still on the slab.

"What are they going to do to him?" Chris whispered. Rick glanced round. The guards, engrossed in the events at the stone, ignored them.

"I don't know. Whip him?"

"Will they do that to all of us? I'm scared."

Rick inched closer to Chris and felt the boy lean against him.

Pete stirred.

"Ready, Sergeant?"

"Yes, Captain."

"Proceed."

At the sergeant's signal, two soldiers grabbed a leg each and pulled Pete back along the stone till his hips were level with the edge. Two other soldiers pulled Pete's arms out to the side and pinned them to the flat top of the stone. Belly and chest flat on the stone, head turned to one side, legs dangled over the end, Pete struggled. His mouth was open, but Rick heard no cry. A fifth soldier jumped onto the stone and sat astride Pete's back, facing his legs. The soldiers who held his legs pulled them apart, and gripped tightly.

Three soldiers picked up a long pole that tapered to about an inch and a half at one end.

"Christ Almighty," Malcolm said. "They're going to impale him."

"They don't impale here. There's no historical record of it being done," Rick said.

"Shit. Bloody hell..." Arthur's voice trailed into a dumbstruck silence

They watched, horrified, while the soldier who sat astride Pete grasped the tapered end of the pole and positioned it between Pete's legs. He turned to Master Gerald.

"Is the end smooth and round and the pole well greased?" Master Gerald called.

"Yes, Master."

"Carry on."

The soldier nodded at the four at Pete's limbs. All four gripped hard and pressed the limbs against the stone, and the three with the pole pushed and twisted.

Pete gave a shriek that faded to a loud moan. Joe fell in a faint across Rick's legs. Pete screamed when the three soldiers pushed again.

The sergeant stepped forward to examine the pole and spoke to the soldiers. Those who had held Pete down, now supported him. They carried him and the shaft to the hole they had prepared, inserted the free end, and pushed Pete in the air. When the pole grounded abruptly, Pete's arms and legs flailed wildly. He gave another ear piercing scream before he lapsed into unconsciousness, and his limbs twitched.

"Clumsy, Sergeant, very clumsy. You should have tied his legs."

With a smile, Master Gerald added: "If I ever get the chance to impale you, Sergeant, I will chose my men with great care. It should be done slowly, lovingly. Each step should take forever. If the culprit faints, you stop till he comes round. Properly done, a strong man should last a week. This one will be dead within the hour."

Chris sobbed and leaned against Rick as hard as he could. Joe shuddered, and struggled to sit up, but, after a glance at Pete who jerked spasmodically on his pole, slumped back down against Rick's legs.

"Kick, Pete," Malcolm muttered. "Kick hard and end it."

Glassy eyed, Dennis simply sat and stared, while Arthur swore steadily in a monotonous voice.

Chapter Four

"A disappointing performance," Master Gerald said. "No finesse."

"The sergeant was clumsy," the captain said. "However, we can leave an example without the necessity of a guard."

"Make no excuses for the sergeant. He knew what he was about. It wasn't carelessness or clumsiness, but insubordination. Come, we will leave him to bring these varlets back to the castle."

The captain talked briefly with the sergeant before he and Master Gerald cantered off. The officer gone, the soldiers lounged for a short time and virtually ignored their prisoners, before the sergeant started giving orders for the return.

Malcolm and the others were hauled to their feet and lined up. Joe kept his eyes down. He refused to look at the figure twitching on the pole. The sergeant stared up at Pete, stroked his jaw with one hand, half turned away, stopped and snapped an order. Rick watched two soldiers walk over to Pete and wondered what was to happen now.

"Are they going to let him down?" Chris said. "Will he be all right?"

"Christ Almighty. Shut up can't you," Malcolm said.

The soldiers took hold of a leg each and jerked down hard. Pete gave a loud scream, then slumped, motionless and soundless. Joe was promptly sick, and Chris started to cry again.

"You bastards. You frigging, rotten bastards," Arthur shouted.

"Sergeant," Malcolm spoke loudly. "May I examine my friend before we leave? I give you my word not to escape while in your custody."

The sergeant nodded and a soldier started to lead Malcolm to the pole.

"I need my hands free, please. You have my parole."

Malcolm rubbed his hands and forearms while he walked to Pete. He felt for a pulse at the ankles and at Pete's groin, before he turned back to join the group.

"He's dead."

Joe sobbed.

"Could you untie the boys at least?" Malcolm said. "They won't run without me. You have my word not to escape, or you can tie me again."

The sergeant looked over the group. "Very well, free these." He pointed to Rick and the two boys.

Untied, Joe, Chris, and Rick rubbed numb wrists and hands. Joe stood, his shoulders slumped, and Rick put an arm round him.

"Come on, Joe. There's nothing we could do, or can do now. Was Pete an old friend?"

"He's my brother." Joe wailed, and buried his head in Rick's shoulder.

"Let's move."

The sergeant made no objection to Rick walking with Chris and Joe, and the three of them set out with Rick in the middle.

Arthur and Dennis stumbled along; hands still tied behind them. The sergeant walked with Malcolm.

"Sergeant, thank you for what you did for Pete."

"You're a smarmy frigging bastard," Arthur spat out. "To thank the bugger for killing Pete."

"Shut up, Arthur. You know nothing about it. If the sergeant had done it by Master Gerald's rules, it would have been slower, one hell of a lot more painful for longer, and just as sure."

"But the last bit."

"You'd rather Pete struggled like a bug on a pin for hours, if not days? They pulled his legs to make sure an internal organ ruptured, so he'd be unconscious and bleed to death internally, quickly. As it was, the pole must have hit his heart for him to be dead when I examined him."

The sergeant eyed Malcolm.

"If I hadn't done it, Master Gerald would have. And he would still be toying with the first stages. An execution should be a hanging or a beheading. I don't hold with this way."

"It's not common around here, then?" Rick said.

"No. No one but Master Gerald uses it. I saw it done in the Holy Land, in many ways, when My Lord and I fought there."

Once off the mound, they were immediately in the trees. No long open stretch of hill between as existed when they made their way up. The wood seemed wilder to Rick, with older trees and fallen, decaying trunks. They didn't seem to be on a trail, but simply headed downhill, taking the path of least resistance. When they finally cleared the wood the riverbank was right there with no sign of the chain-link fence or the bridge to the town side of the river.

Rick shook his head. Why had he expected to find them?

The sergeant marched them upstream before he led them over a knee-deep ford. On the other side, a cart track, where the main road should be, led off towards the town two miles away.

"Rick, I've got to go," Chris whispered.

"Sergeant," Rick said, "could we relieve ourselves? You surprised us this morning before we had time."

At the sergeant's nod, Rick and the two boys stepped behind the hedgerow. Joe took off to one side to some bushes. Rick and Chris zipped up, and Joe reappeared fastening his belt.

"Your shirttail's hanging out," Chris said, and Joe tucked himself in and blushed furiously.

While they waited for Arthur and Dennis, the sergeant turned to Malcolm.

"You aren't a bandit, are you? You're a learned man, perhaps even a doctor? I'm sorry I must again tie you and the boys. I accepted your parole, but my captain wouldn't approve."

Malcolm said: "Could my men be tied less tightly? They haven't had the time out of bindings the boys and I have had. Their blood is being slowed in the veins."

This time, the loop round each of Rick's wrists was tight, but not the circulation stopping tightness of before. The little slack between the hands meant less strain on his upper arms and shoulders.

"What gives, calling us your men?" Arthur whispered.

"Just play along. If they think we are vagrants or bandits, they'll whip us out of town at best, or we'll end up like Pete. Doctors did sometimes drift around in the Middle Ages didn't they, Rick?"

"Yes, I think so, but I don't know what date we're at. Did you see the castle?"

"Line up. Escort to position. Forward."

They were much more obviously and formally prisoners now. Malcolm and the others formed a single line headed by Malcolm, with Dennis and Arthur at the rear; the order set by the sergeant. Their escort formed a file on either side of them. The sergeant marched at the head, those with short swords next, the pike men to the rear.

Rick didn't remember his hometown ever having a wall, but there it was, three or four tall men high with towers spaced along its length, about half a football field apart. The track lead directly to an arched gateway set in a double tower. Two bored looking soldiers at the gate stared curiously at them when they passed through.

Inside, urchins attached themselves to the parade, and aped the soldiers, but took care to keep out of reach. The street was narrow with buildings made from twigs, crudely cemented together with mud – wattle-and-daub, leaving little room for their three columns. They reached a small, open square and turned right. A ramp led up to the castle gate and Rick gaped at the massive white, lime washed walls stretched on either side of the immense towers flanking the entrance.

Inside the castle gate, they stopped and waited while the sergeant reported.

"What will they do with us?" Chris said.

"Whatever they like by the looks of it," Arthur said. "Don't we have any frigging rights here?"

"That depends on what they think we are," Rick said.

"What's the point?" Joe mumbled. "What does it matter? Nothing matters."

After the sergeant reappeared and gave his orders, they marched to the left, along the outer curtain wall to a corner tower.

"In here."

It was an empty room or cell about fifteen feet in diameter with two narrow, unglazed window slots. The door clanged behind them.

"Do you think they'll feed us?" Chris asked.

Rick glanced at Malcolm and said: "Don't jump him. He's only a kid."

"It's all right. Sorry I snapped up at the circle. Yes, I think we're all hungry now, but I don't know whether they'll feed us or not."

The door opened and they all looked warily at the four soldiers who entered. Two had drawn swords. While the armed men watched, the other two untied the group, and, still in silence, they left.

"That's a little more hopeful anyway," Malcolm said. "Since we're going to be together for some time, whether we like it or not, we should know about each other."

The silence stretched and Chris shuffled while Arthur and Malcolm glowered at each other.

"Okay. I'll start," Malcolm said. "I'm a medical student, in my fifth year at university. My grandfather left a trust fund for me. I live on that and the grants. My father's a doctor. I'm a pacifist and a green. Rick and I are AWOL from the university to come here for the protest march against the new poll tax. Everyone in the country shouldn't have to pay the same amount no matter how much they have or earn just for the privilege of being alive."

Arthur snorted.

"Good for you. Just what we needed, two more frigging academics."

"I'm in third year Arts, studying history," Rick said. "What the grant doesn't cover, Dad picks up. I never really thought about the environment and rights-of-way and so on till I met Malcolm. Chris?"

Chris giggled. "I'm Rick's cousin. I live with his mum and dad. I came along because Rick did."

Arthur and Dennis looked at each other.

"Oh, what the hell," Arthur said. "It doesn't matter a damn now anyway. We're never going to get back. Dennis and me, when we left school, got into one of the youth opportunities programmes. It was good at first. A job in the building trade. We learnt a lot, but when the grant ran out, so did the job, and we couldn't go again."

Dennis went on: "No one would hire us because they could get Youth Opportunities kids cheaper. We managed to fiddle a second go round at a different job, but shortly we were out on our ears again. We got involved in some street stuff. It was something to do.

"At one of the shindigs, it was National Front and Socialist Workers Party, I think, this geezer said he liked our style. He got us sent to a camp where they taught street fighting and handling explosives, urban guerrilla stuff, for the class struggle to come. Shit, what had we to lose? They paid us. Anyway, it was better than hanging about with nothing in our pockets. We got sent out: sometimes to guard, sometimes to hassle, sometimes to start a fight, or to stir it up a bit if it was too quiet. We got to travel all over."

"Agents provocateur. Rent-a-mob," Malcolm said.

"Yes. I suppose," Arthur and Dennis said.

They all looked at Joe.

"You lot make me sick," Joe said. "A rich layabout who'll forget all this student nonsense once he's a doctor, an upper middle-class tagalong, and two working class traitors, in it for what they can get. Fighting for whichever side paid them best. Pete trusted you two. He really believed in what he was doing. He thought the march against the poll tax was part of a real struggle for the people – and he's the one that's dead."

Joe burst into tears, lurched to his feet, and retreated to rest his forehead against the rough stone wall. The others looked at each other, and Malcolm with a glance at Rick jerked his head in Joe's direction.

With a sigh, Rick got up.

"Pete was Joe's brother, you know," he said and moved to stand with Joe. He put an arm round Joe's shoulder. Joe's first reaction was to shrug him off, but instead in a torrent of tears, Joe clung to Rick who stood rather uncertainly and patted Joe's back.

"Well, I suppose that clears the air a little," Malcolm said. "Regardless of what we think of each other, we're all we've got. We must stick together. Agreed?"

Arthur and Dennis nodded, but didn't look too enthusiastic.

"We really did mean it about the right-of-way stuff," Dennis said. "We wouldn't be here now if we didn't."

"Bugger the right-of-way," Joe said, and wailed louder than ever.

"Shut up, Dennis," Arthur said. "You're not helping any."

Malcolm cleared his throat.

"Because of the beard, I look the oldest."

"You *are* the frigging oldest," Arthur said.

"I know enough medicine to play the part here. The sergeant is half convinced already. Just play along. I'm a doctor. Rick is my assistant. Joe and Chris are pages or apprentices. Arthur, you and Dennis are mercenaries, hired bodyguards. So was Pete. Bandits or robbers chased us into the circle. There was thunder and lightning. When we came to, the sergeant and his men were tying us up. All right?"

"Think they'll buy that crap?" Dennis said.

"Will they buy what really happened? Would you?" Malcolm countered. "It's an easy story for us all to learn. If we all stick to it, we'll be fine."

Arthur and Dennis whispered briefly.

"Yes. We'll go along. We've nothing to lose," Arthur said.

"Okay by Chris and me," Rick said, and led Joe back to the group.

Joe, still tearful, nodded agreement.

"But, if I get half a chance, I'm going to kill that bastard, Master Gerald," Arthur said.

Chapter Five

They had been in the cell for some time when the sergeant came in.

"I have spoken to my captain about you. I think I could persuade My Lord to see and question you himself. Master Gerald wants you turned over to him for questioning. That would mean torture and certain death for some of you."

"Why do you care what happens to us?" Rick said. "Why should we trust you?"

The sergeant shrugged.

"I have asked myself the same question. I don't know why I care, or even if I do. Master Gerald is set on having you and I like to thwart him when I can, and when it's safe. Anyway, do you have a choice?"

Malcolm laughed. "Yes, you're right, we appear to have little choice. Thanks for your kind interest."

"Good. I have some more suitable clothes for you. The way you were dressed will interest My Lord, but if you appear before him in your outlandish garb, Master Gerald might win the day."

The sergeant banged on the door and two soldiers entered, arms full of clothing.

"The long robe is for you, doctor. Change now. I'll be back for your clothes after I've spoken with my captain again."

They sorted through the pile dumped on the floor: six shirts of some coarse material, one long robe like a priest's cassock, five tunics, six sets of coarse linen breeches, a bundle of long stockings or hose with leather soles, a jumble of assorted lengths of cord or rope.

"You're the historian, Rick. How do we wear this stuff?" Malcolm said.

"Chris, you strip off," Rick said.

"Why me? Why not Joe? Or you?"

"Strip, or we'll strip you."

Down to his underpants, Chris stopped.

"These too?"

"Those too."

"Right, the smallest breeches."

While Arthur and the others watched Chris dress under Rick's instruction, Joe had collected his clothing and withdrew to one of the alcoves where he quickly changed, faced away from the others into the corner.

The other four changed with many jokes about the style. Rick showed them how to adjust the length of the tunic with the girdle rope tied round the waist on the outside.

"Much better," the sergeant said when he returned. "My lord will see you at his afternoon audience."

"We look a proper set of berks," Arthur said, and they laughed, even Joe.

"Much more presentable," the sergeant commented.

"How should we address your master?" Rick said.

The sergeant glared at them for a moment.

"He is Sir Harold Fitzwilliam, Lord of the Manor. You will not speak to him, except to answer a direct question. You will address him as you would your own lord."

"Patience, please," Rick said.

"We are in shock," Malcolm interrupted, "both from the events of the night and Pete's death."

"We have been travelling with Malcolm, the doctor, and have seen many strange customs," Rick said. "Remind us, please, of how those of our assumed rank should behave in your master's court."

"Aye, you are odd. It would be a pity to offend My Lord and end in the tender hands of Master Gerald."

When the sergeant had rehearsed them several times and satisfied himself they could behave with enough decorum not to endanger him, he banged the cell door.

Chris fluttered his eyelids at the sergeant and said: "We haven't eaten since last night."

The sergeant looked at Chris and Joe and laughed.

"Aye, growing lads do get hungry. I'll do what I can."

Immediately the sergeant had left, Malcolm turned on Arthur, who had snorted in derision when the sergeant referred to him and Dennis as followers.

"For God's sake play along. This is our only chance. If you won't cooperate, I swear I'll throw Rick, Chris, Joe and myself on the mercy of this lord. I'll tell him you're part of the bandit gang that chased us into the circle."

"Fat chance he'll believe that."

"I'd say we were too afraid to say earlier. By the time Master Gerald tires of playing with you, I'll have worked out a story for the rest of us." Malcolm paused. "Is it worth so much to prove you're macho?" Arthur glared at Malcolm. "I mean it. I'll ditch you for the National Front lout you are. Who do you think the lord will believe?"

"Shit. Even here it's the same. The frigging nobs will stick together. Okay, Dennis and me are your bloody bodyguards. We'll do as you say … for now."

Chapter Six

The door opened and a jailer walked in carrying a small sack.

"The sergeant said to feed you. This is all there is for now."

He dropped the sack on the floor and left.

Chris pounced.

"Whoa, there," Malcolm said. "Let's see what there is and share it out. Here, sit down and hold out the front of your tunic, like an apron."

"Hey, this floor's cold on my bum."

"Shut up or we'll warm it for you, kid," Arthur growled, but then, deadpan, winked at Chris.

Chris smiled hesitantly and glanced at Rick, but beamed when Arthur grinned and winked again.

The sack contained small loaves of dark bread and some lumps of cheese. Malcolm divided the food as evenly as possible and handed it round.

"I don't want anything," Joe said and turned away.

"Take it, Joe," Arthur said. "We don't know when we'll eat again. Not eating won't help Pete now."

"He's right," Malcolm added. "We're all sorry about Pete, but a hunger strike isn't going to help you or us – or him."

"This bread's stale," Chris said, "and there's greeny-blue stuff on the cheese."

"If you don't want it, kid, pass it round," Dennis said. "This isn't the Ritz."

Chris clutched his bread and cheese to him. "No, I'll eat it."

They munched in silence. Chris finished first, and glanced round at what each of the others had left.

"That was good," he said.

Joe barely nibbled at his share, and stared black-eyed at the wall before him.

"Keep your beady little eyes and thieving fingers off Joe's share," Arthur said. "Here, if you're really hungry and need some more, have a piece of mine."

"I shared it out evenly," Malcolm said. "We agreed we all need it."

"What I do with my share is none of your frigging business, Mr Doctor. I'll keep my end up, never fear."

With Malcolm's mouth open to reply, Chris said: "Please, don't fight. It doesn't matter. I've had enough."

Chris got up, but when he passed Arthur, Arthur grabbed his wrist and pulled him down.

"Aow. My wrist. The floor's all cold again."

"Here, never you mind what Dr Jerkyl says. It's mine."

Chris grinned and took the chunk of bread and cheese Arthur handed him.

"Thanks, Arthur."

He wolfed the food down, after a quick glance at Rick and Malcolm.

"He's only trying to bug you," Rick whispered. "The hard man has a soft centre. I think he really wants what's best for the two youngsters."

"Maybe," Malcolm muttered. "But he's bloody irritating nonetheless."

"I need to pee," Chris said. "Where's the bathroom?"

Rick laughed.

"It's not funny. I'll burst. Sitting on the cold stone did it."

"Chris, I think at this time prisoners used a corner of the cell."

"God, this place'll reek to heaven in no time," Dennis said.

"Let's see what happens if we bang the door first," Malcolm suggested. "What would you call it here, Rick?"

"The garde-robe, or the necessary, I think."

Malcolm banged the door. After some time, the small barred window in the door opened.

"What's all the noise?"

"Can we use the garde-robe?" Malcolm said.

"I need a pee," Chris wailed.

The spy hole clanged shut, and they heard the guard laugh.

Chris danced from foot to foot and clutched at himself, before the door opened.

A rather surprised looking guard said: "The sergeant says you can use it. One at a time. Who's first?"

When the door re-opened, a much-relieved Chris bounced in.

"It's only a bit cut into the castle wall. There's a ledge to sit on with a hole cut in it. If you look down, you can see the ground outside. God, what a stink." He wrinkled his nose.

While they waited for the sergeant to return to take them to the audience, time stretched endlessly. Joe sat slumped against the wall and stared into space. Chris couldn't sit still for more than five minutes and constantly prowled the cell.

When the door opened, they all scrambled to their feet except Joe.

"It's time," said the sergeant, and Malcolm and Arthur pulled Joe to his feet.

Outside the tower they blinked in the daylight while the sergeant looked them over.

"Quite presentable," he said. "Doctor, you first followed by your assistant and the pages, and lastly your men. Follow me."

Only two pike men escorted them on their walk from the tower through the outer ward to the gatehouses and through the inner gatehouse to the inner ward.

Rick looked round. It was difficult to orient himself. Yesterday, he'd shown Malcolm the ruins of the tower in the park on the promontory. It was hard to believe of all he could see now, there would be only one ruined tower left. The inner ward was almost square, about a third of a football field on a side. They walked diagonally across the courtyard and into a small room.

They came to a halt and Chris said: "I thought we were going to see the lord."

"This is the antechamber, boy. You wait here till the majordomo calls for you. You all know how to behave?"

They nodded and the sergeant gave some quiet orders to the escort and left.

"Are we all clear on the story?" Malcolm said. "Arthur? You agree?"

"Yes, Doc. Dennis and me will go along."

After another long, boring wait, a soldier came for them. They walked in the order set by the sergeant. The hubbub round the hall continued unabated when they entered, although the crowd parted to form a passage when they and their escort walked in.

The escort halted and the lead pike man grounded his spear. As rehearsed, Malcolm dropped to one knee, while the others knelt behind him on the rushes that covered a stone flagged floor. Heads bowed, they waited. Rick realised they had halted a pace behind where the sergeant stood.

"Are these the men from the circle?" a voice said from somewhere ahead of them.

"Yes, Sire."

"Have them approach the dais."

Malcolm rose, and the others made to do so also.

"On your knees," the sergeant whispered.

They advanced several feet, before they again stopped.

"They look like other serfs to me. What is there special about them that should see them in audience?"

"Sire, they aren't simple serfs. Their leader," the sergeant gestured at Malcolm, "is a physician. They were set upon by brigands and their possessions stolen. The way they were dressed when taken shows their strangeness. I thought they might amuse My Lord."

"Where are these strange clothes? They seem ordinary to me, unfashionable, if they're not serfs, but certainly ordinary."

Some of the onlookers laughed.

The sergeant snapped his fingers, and a guard produced one bundled anorak. The sleeves untied, the contents tumbled onto the floor. Sir Harold and his brother examined the clothing one article at a time. Each piece handed up by a guard.

"Let us see one dressed in these."

The sergeant turned to Malcolm. "Look at the clothes, doctor. Who should put them on?"

Malcolm raised his head, and made to turn to the others, but the sergeant snapped: "Point to one, doctor."

Malcolm pointed to Chris. Two soldiers lifted Chris to his feet and ushered him to the dais, and forced him to his knees again.

"Are these your clothes, boy?"

Chris looked.

"Yes, Sire."

"Put them on."

When Chris made no move, the voice went on: "You may rise and dress."

"Up here?" Chris squealed.

The others heard the sound of a slap and Master Gerald's voice said: "Address My Lord Brother as Sire."

Head still bent, Rick risked a glance through his eyebrows at the dais. Chris, bright red, stripped and quickly put on his own clothes.

"Very strange indeed. Were the others similarly dressed?"

"Yes, Sire."

"In some ways not unlike the new French style showing the full leg, but the material and colours are drab. A strange fastening ... cunningly made ... strange." Sir Harold zipped Chris's fly down then up again. He shrugged. "Later. What's your name, boy?"

"Chris. Christopher, Sire."

"A good honest name. You may dress properly again. Put him back with the others."

Sir Harold stepped down from the dais and stopped in front of Malcolm.

"You are the one my sergeant calls the Physician?"

"Yes, Sire."

"You may rise. My brother Gerald says you are brigands or magicians. He would put you all to the question."

"Sire. We are neither. We are travellers. I am a doctor with an assistant and two pages who joined us when their parents died. We had three mercenaries with us as guard companions. One of them Master Gerald had impaled this morning."

"Yes. Perhaps we should turn your other mercenaries over to my brother. Their protection was not very effective."

"Would we have come off better if we had resisted, Sire?"

Sir Harold glared at Malcolm.

"No, probably not. Sergeant, you were right, there is something of interest here. Take them to my room and stay there with them till I come. You may withdraw."

Chapter Seven

"That didn't do much for us," Arthur grumbled.

"You jest surely," the sergeant said. "You are here in My Lord's chamber and not in a cell awaiting Master Gerald's call."

"Thank you, Sergeant." Rick scowled at Arthur. "We do appreciate your interest and guidance. Arthur had simply not thought the matter through. Do we kneel again when Sir Harold comes in?"

The sergeant had barely nodded when the door opened and Sir Harold strode in, followed by a boy about the same age as Chris. They dropped to their knees.

"No ceremony here," Sir Harold said. "Stand, and let me see your faces if you be honest men."

Sir Harold removed his belt, wrapped it round his dagger scabbard, and handed it to the sergeant, who placed it on top of a large campaign chest. He stretched and paced briefly, before he sat on the stool by the fireplace and turned to look at Malcolm and the group. The stool was the only place to sit in the room apart from the ledges in the window niche and the bed. The boy stood behind and to one side of him, and gazed at each of the group in turn before finally staring steadily at Chris.

"Despite your present appearance," Sir Harold said, "you don't carry yourselves like serfs. You seem like men accustomed to being free men."

The sergeant cleared his throat.

"Doctor, tell My Lord your story."

Malcolm told the story they had agreed on.

Sir Harold raised his eyebrows and looked round at the sergeant.

"Is there a whiff of witchcraft here?"

"It is strange, My Lord, but I think they are innocent."

"Perhaps we should release the physician and his assistant, maybe the boys too, but let Gerald have the men?"

"Sire," Malcolm said. "May I speak?"

At Sir Harold's nod, Malcolm went on: "Your Lordship is, of course, the final judge, but I couldn't accept my release if Arthur and Dennis are to be imprisoned, especially if they are to be tortured. I willingly give you my parole. If any of us acts against Your Lordship's law or word, then punish them and me, but don't separate us without cause."

"I thought you were a physician, not a lawyer." Sir Harold laughed. "What do you think, Martin?"

"Release them, Sire."

"Very well. They can stay in the castle, as my guests, till I make up my mind. Find some more suitable clothes for the physician and his assistant. Dress more suitable to his station."

"My Lord, what about the boys? The clothes I found were for serfs. I can dress the men from my store, if My Lord permits."

"By all means, you clothe the men. My lady has been overseeing new garments for Walter. One of these boys may be dressed in his old attire."

Sir Harold turned. "You, boy, Christopher, stand beside Walter. Yes, you are about the same size."

When Sir Harold turned away from the boys, Walter nipped Chris's thigh hard and hissed: "Smelly, stinking serf."

Chris yelped, turned on Walter who was bowled over almost instantly, and leapt on him. Sat astride Walter's chest, Chris pummelled him, while Walter did little more than squirm and try to shield his face.

Arthur and Dennis jumped to pull Chris to his feet and away from Walter. The sergeant pulled Walter rather roughly to his feet. When Walter made a move towards Chris, the sergeant held his arms.

There was a tense silence during which the two boys glared at each other.

Malcolm, the sergeant and Sir Harold all spoke at once.

"My Lord, I apologise for the actions of my page."

"Sire, Walter did start – "

"They are certainly not serfs."

They all stopped and Sir Harold continued: "As I said, they are not serfs. No born serf would ever dare attack a member of our house. Boy, are you even aware that I could have you flogged, or hanged, for what you have done?"

"No, Sire. He started it."

"Silence, boy. Kneel. You two also," Sir Harold pointed to Arthur and Dennis, "while I think."

The sergeant let go of Walter who shook himself and glared, first at the sergeant, and then at Chris.

"He should be flogged, Sire, at the very least," Walter said, and faltered into silence under Sir Harold's scowl.

"If they were serfs, I would have the boy flogged within an inch of his life for an attack upon you. Fetch my rod."

Walter grinned, ran to the chest beside the bed, and came back with a peeled, springy wand about as thick as a thumb.

"Stand, Christopher, and bend over."

Sir Harold gave six hard strokes of the rod on Chris's buttocks. Chris stood; his tunic fell back to cover him again; tears trickled down his cheeks; and he rubbed his rump.

"Is that all, My Lord?" Walter said.

"You may judge for yourself, and tell me later," Sir Harold

said. "Didn't you hear me say to the sergeant that they were to stay as guests in this castle, *my* guests?"

Walter's expression changed.

"My page should be polite to my guests, and you may not fight with their page, especially in my presence. Bend."

The six strokes that fell on Walter's stretched breeches sounded every bit as hard to Rick as those Chris had received. When Walter stood, he was no less red eyed than Chris.

"Is the punishment enough or do you seek more?"

"No, My Lord. Thank you."

"Shake hands like sons of gentlemen," Sir Harold said, and the two boys touched hands reluctantly and very briefly. "Take them to the seneschal, Sergeant, and see to their clothing. Ask the seneschal to come here, and, when he has more appropriate garments, bring the physician back."

"Yes, Sire."

They followed the sergeant's lead, when he bowed to Sir Harold, and bending low, walked backwards to the door and out.

Through the closed door they heard Sir Harold's angry voice. "You may not disgrace me, boy, in front of strangers. You are far from ready to become a squire. I doubt seriously if you ever will be ready."

There was the sound of a blow and a muffled cry. Chris looked very warily at the sergeant and silently moved closer to Rick and Arthur.

Chapter Eight

"How am I supposed to provide clothes for them?" the seneschal grumbled at the sergeant.

"I simply pass on My Lord's instructions," the sergeant laughed. "You two men come with me."

Arthur and Dennis shrugged and followed the sergeant.

The seneschal led the others to a wardrobe and a large wooden chest. He glanced at Malcolm's six foot, well-developed frame, and rummaged through the contents of the closet.

"This might fit. His lordship's last physician was also a large man before his death."

After many muttered comments to himself, the seneschal had both Malcolm and Rick fitted out. They now each had a white, collarless, linen shirt, and white linen, ill-fitting breeches like boxer shorts. A tunic worn over the shirt, and long, leather soled hose, the top of which tied to the bottom of the tunic through slots. Mid-calf length robes, like a priest's surplice, of a much finer material than the one the sergeant had given Malcolm earlier, completed the picture.

He stood back to examine them.

"Sober respectable clothing, suitable for a physician. Most gentlemen now have moved to the short tunic and two-legged hose worn very tight, and boots with very long points. The more sober elders still prefer the long robe, and doctors should, of course, dress moderately and seriously, as befits their calling. I suppose you can't pay me for this courtesy?"

Rick smiled, and spread his hands.

"No, Master Seneschal, I'm sorry, we have no money. We appreciate we have used up your store of My Lord's cast off clothes, which is, of course, yours by custom to sell. We will repay, and are now under an obligation to you. It can be useful to have a physician in your debt, can't it?"

The seneschal smiled. "The sergeant said you were not serfs. He is a sound judge. I shall place you above the salt tonight. You may yet be My Lord's physician."

Rick bowed and fractionally later so did Malcolm.

"Let me see if I have suitable girdle belts for you, gentlemen."

After a brief hunt, the seneschal produced two leather belts with dagger scabbards and pouches.

"I have no daggers to give you. The sergeant may be able to provide you with those. We understand each other, gentlemen?"

Rick nodded. "We are indebted to you."

"I can provide the fashionable short tunic and cote-hardie for only one of your pages."

"You have them, Chris. I can wear a longer tunic," Joe said.

After a glance at Rick who nodded, the seneschal handed Chris the page's outfit and he changed.

The under-tunic or shirt barely reached his hipbones and the breeches were like badly cut, slightly baggy jockey shorts. The tunic, or gypon, as the seneschal called it, came a little farther down, but not much. Chris pulled one leg of the hose on and tried to fasten it to the girdle of his breeches as before.

"No. No, boy. Here."

The seneschal pulled at the hose to stretch it tight on Chris's leg and wrenched it round to fit tightly into Chris's crotch and up the crease between thigh and abdomen, to cover one leg fully at the back.

"Tie your points through the eyelets in your gypon. God's Blood, have you never dressed before?"

With both legs of the hose on, Chris stood uncertain. The hose now covered his rump, over the breeches, joined but not attached at the back, but he obviously felt exposed at the front.

"The codpiece, boy."

Chris squirmed with embarrassment while the seneschal helped him fasten the triangular piece that covered the front fork of the hose to the hose with laces or points.

"It's a different colour from the hose." Chris wailed, and the seneschal nodded.

"Now the cote-hardie."

The final article barely covered Chris's hips and fitted tightly, fastened down the front by a series of small buttons.

"God. This tunic barely covers my bum," Chris said.

Malcolm laughed.

"The style is positively indecent, but it is how Walter was dressed. It doesn't leave anything to the imagination."

While they concentrated on Chris, Joe had found a tunic of a fine material that fell to slightly above his knees.

"Can I have this, Master Seneschal?" he said.

The seneschal nodded. "Yes, it would be quite appropriate."

"Look, Joe. This bit in front makes me look like I've got a hard on, doesn't it?" Chris laughed, and squirmed, his face scarlet.

Joe blushed, and said: "It's no worse than some tight jeans I've seen."

The sergeant reappeared with Arthur and Dennis, now dressed more or less as the soldiers had been at the circle in the morning.

"Much better," the sergeant said. "Now, Master Seneschal, My Lord wishes to see you. Doctor, would you and your assistant come with me?"

Arthur laughed and pointed.

"Is that all you, Chris? You have grown since this morning."

Chris blushed.

"What about us, sergeant?" Arthur said.

"You are free to do as you please, within the castle."

On their walk back to Sir Harold's room, the sergeant commented: "You have dressed them well, Master Seneschal. His Lordship will be pleased."

Walter opened the door at their knock and they entered, with low bows.

"Much more suitable," Sir Harold said.

He and the seneschal withdrew to the window niche where they talked in low voices for some time. When the seneschal left, he nodded to the sergeant, but bowed to Malcolm and Rick, with a murmured: "Masters," before he turned, bowed low to Sir Harold and backed out of the room.

"You may leave, Sergeant. Walter, stand outside. I don't want to be disturbed."

Sir Harold walked round Malcolm and Rick, before he finally sat on the stool.

"Yes, Martin was right, you are not serfs: I haven't decided yet exactly what you are. I thought Martin was protecting you simply to spite Gerald. That may still be so, but you pique my interest. You were all born free, even your mercenaries. I would guess merchant or trade families for you and the boys?"

"My father was a doctor, Sire," Malcolm said.

"Ah, just so. You are called Malcolm?" Malcolm nodded, and Sir Harold turned to Rick. "What is your name?"

"Rick, Sire. Richard, really."

"The same as our young lord, the King. A good name indeed. Now, Malcolm, are you really a physician?"

"Sire, I have studied medicine all my life, I think, under my father and under several other learned doctors."

"And the sciences?"

"Yes, Sire."

"My last physician died, of some flux, about Easter, and if you are sufficiently skilled, you might take his place." Sir Harold smiled. "Martin was right, but we must remember Gerald may also be thought right by some and, of that, you and your followers could die. The doctor had a house outside the castle. Some nonsense about being able to treat the people of the town and country. Perhaps, Master Malcolm, you and your followers could have it. I will consider the matter.

"You should avoid my brother. He has been here already to complain of my generous treatment of you. Had Gerald been here earlier, your page would certainly have paid long and painfully for his attack on Walter.

"You may go. I'll decide what's to be done with you before sunset tomorrow."

Chapter Nine

"Well, Doctor?" Arthur said, when they all met in the courtyard. "You and the other frigging nobs settled what's to happen to us peasants?"

Malcolm flushed red, but before he could reply Rick cut in: "Come on, Arthur. It's not Malcolm's fault we're here."

"I suppose you think it was my fault?"

"Oh for Christ's sake. I don't know how we got here. Does it matter? We're here. We've landed bloody lucky so far," Rick said.

"Except Pete," Joe said. "You all forget Pete."

"I'm sorry, Joe," Rick said. "We don't forget Pete. You've every right to mourn him and to be angry, but it's like a battle, a war. We can't stop till we're safe."

"Yes, I'm sorry too," Dennis said. "None of us ever really got to know Pete. He was so quiet. Hardly said a word most of the time. We didn't even know he had a brother."

"The sergeant has given us daggers," Arthur said. "Here's one for you Rick, and this one's for my master, his holiness, the physician."

Arthur handed them each a dagger. Malcolm's had a slightly more ornate handle.

"Apart from poor Pete," Malcolm said, "we *have* landed lucky. If the sergeant didn't have it in for Gerald and hadn't somehow guessed I might be a doctor, we might all have ended like bugs on pins."

Joe's face drained of all colour, and he turned to rest his forehead against the stone wall.

"Sorry, Joe," Malcolm said. "At best we'd be in some dungeon waiting for Gerald to send for us. Sir Harold would never have seen us. At least this way we're free, in the castle anyway."

"Malcolm's right," Dennis said. "We still have a chance to help ourselves."

"What the hell do you know?" Arthur snapped. "When have you ever done anything but follow orders? From me, or from one of the frigging nobs?"

"This isn't any use," Rick said. "Do we want to stay alive?"

"Well..." Arthur started.

"No. A straight yes or no," Rick interrupted. "One at a time."

All, including Joe, said, yes.

"Right then. As free men or serfs or bondservants?"

All said, Free.

"Fine. If you and Malcolm want to screw up and fight later, you can. For now, let's work with what's going for us. Agreed?"

There was a silence.

"Come on, Arthur," Rick said. "Call a truce. Malcolm's not trying to be the big man or boss you. Let's stick together till it's safe to fight. You fancy yourself as a realist. What advantage is there in us all getting killed or enslaved to spite Malcolm? Will it help the serfs here?"

Arthur grinned. "With some coaching you could be in politics."

"Or one of those speechmakers they were training at the camp. Remember you called them the provokers, Arthur?" Dennis said.

"Agents provocateur," Rick said.

At Arthur's scowl, Rick hastily went on: "Right, we all work together. For now we play the parts the sergeant and Sir Harold have given us?"

There was general agreement.

Malcolm said, "Rick have you any idea when in history this is?"

"What does it matter?" Arthur said, and Rick hurried to answer.

"It's difficult to be exact, but Sir Harold said my name, Richard, was the same as the King. Richard II came to the throne in 1377. How long they'd still think of him as our young lord is difficult to say. He was fourteen in 1381 at the time of the Peasants' Revolt. So I'd say we are sometime after 1377, but before 1390. The way the upper classes are dressed would agree with that too."

"Can they do what they like to us?" Dennis said. "Are there no laws? What about Magna Carta and all the tripe we learnt at school?"

Rick closed his eyes and recited:

"No freeman shall be taken, or imprisoned, or outlawed, or exiled, or in any way harmed, nor will we go upon him, nor will we send upon him, except by the legal judgement of his peers, or by the law of the land.

"That what you mean?"

"Yes. I suppose so. How can you spout a screed like that?"

"It's a knack. The psych. prof at the university says I've got unusual auditory imagery. I can remember word for word pieces I've heard or read."

"Sorry I asked."

"The villeins, the serfs, didn't get any political or civil rights out of it. They were the majority, but they were property. They belonged to the lords who forced King John to sign the Charter to protect their rights, not the rights of their serfs. Common freemen didn't get a hell of a lot out of it either. If I'm right about the time, the Black Death – the plague that killed a large percentage of the population in the fourteenth century – has forced some lords to free their serfs, to rent the land they worked, but we're still a hell of a long way off common people like us being protected by the law."

Arthur applauded, and Malcolm scowled.

"By God, you'll make a good communist yet," Arthur said. "We've no protection here but our wits. Much as I dislike saying so, Malcolm's right: we've got to stick together. Should we get you a soapbox, Rick?"

Rick laughed. "Unless you've got very powerful friends, the law isn't much protection. If we all vanished, who would there be to make a fuss?"

"What *is* our standing?" Arthur said.

"Well, we're, quotes, guests, close quotes, of Sir Harold. Really sort of privileged prisoners, I suppose. No one will touch us without his say-so, but if he loses interest, or drops us before we've found our feet … it's goodbye Charlie. Can you really carry off the doctor bit, Malcolm? That's the key."

"Yes, I'm sure I can. I was on wards. I know at least as much as the barefoot doctors in China."

"Even if Sir Harold thinks we're runaway serfs from a different manor," Rick said, "if we're useful to him, a useful addition to his town, he'll let us stay. Serfs who stayed free for a year and a day in another manor or town were free."

"Watch it, here's what's-his-face," Chris said.

Master Gerald and the page, Walter, strolled into the corner of the courtyard. Rick turned towards him and whispered to the others: "Face him and bow. Follow me."

"Amusing is it not, Walter? Swine, in My Lord brother's cast off finery, sunning themselves."

"Yes, Master Gerald. That one's dressed in my old clothes, he's the one who attacked me."

"Indeed." Master Gerald pointed at Chris. "Approach, boy."

Chris turned to Rick for guidance and instruction, and Master Gerald snapped: "At once, boy. Here, I am your master's master.

"He fills your cast-offs well, Walter. Show me what you did before he attacked you."

With a grin, Walter reached out and nipped Chris's rump, hard. His behind already tender from the rod, Chris yelped, and clenched his fists. Arthur's hand flew to the hilt of his dagger.

"No. Chris, stand still," Rick shouted. "Arthur put your hand down, slowly."

"Very wise advice," Master Gerald said with a sour smile. "I was in no danger, but even My Lord brother would have condemned you for drawing on me. A pity, I would have enjoyed the distraction. For your sake, *soi-disent* physician, I hope you are as proficient in your skills as your assistant is with his tongue. In My Lord brother's absence or illness, I rule here."

He turned. "Come Walter, there is naught of interest to gentlemen here. Ah, here comes My Lord brother's watchdog, snarling to protect his litter. Do you seek me, sergeant? What is amiss?"

"No, Master Gerald. I see naught amiss. I see three gentlemen in conversation in the sun, pages and men close by. Walter, our master seeks you. If you intend to sit, or even lie with any degree of comfort tonight, I would run to him."

Walter and Master Gerald left, Walter at the trot.

"Sergeant," Malcolm said, "did you see Master Gerald encourage Walter to hurt Chris again? Would his lordship approve?"

"Yes, Master Malcolm, I saw, but if I were to report it, I would also have to report that Arthur almost drew on Master Gerald and that Chris almost hit Walter again. It is better I saw naught. Boys get worse beatings daily and survive. I would swear this pert youngster has had his share."

The sergeant clapped Chris's shoulder and Chris grinned at him.

Chapter Ten

"There's little love lost between Sir Harold and his brother," Rick said to the sergeant.

"Sir Harold was nine and already a page with a neighbouring lord when his mother died during the Death," the sergeant said. "The older brothers died too, as did all of my family. His father remarried within the year and Master Gerald was born the year after. Master Gerald was ten when his father finally died and Sir Harold took the castle. There was no time lost in sending him off to be a page, I can tell you."

"If you're so well in with Sir Harold, why aren't you a knight, or at least the captain here?" Arthur said.

"Sergeant," Rick jumped in, "Arthur means no offence. He sometimes does not think before he talks."

"No offence taken. Arthur is, as I was, a common soldier unused to the niceties of court talk. Like me, he will learn, in time, to guard his tongue." The sergeant laughed. "A low born such as me could never hope to become a squire, let alone a knight. The captain of the guard is a squire. A poor relative of My Lord's who could not afford to become a knight. I was given to Sir Harold as a child, to be his body servant. Unlike many, I was well treated and we grew up more like brothers than man and servant."

"God. No frigging difference. Rank and privilege. When did it all start? You're a thousand times the man that shit Gerald is."

The sergeant frowned and chewed at his lower lip. "You are not followers of the hedge priests, I hope. My lord would flay me alive, and rightly so, if I have brought such into his house. You are very free with each other despite differences in station. Oh, I pray you are not of John Ball's persuasion."

"No, we are not with John Ball," Rick assured him.

"Who, and what, are the hedge priests?" Arthur said, so quietly Rick almost missed it.

"I'll fill you in properly later," Rick said, "but Ball was – is? – a peasant priest whose sermons about equality stirred up the peasants and upset the nobles."

Chapter Eleven

Chris had watched, open mouthed, the bustle in the courtyard. The gate of the inner ward was open, and through it the main gate to the outer ward and the lowered drawbridge could be seen. Two soldiers apparently lounged inside the inner ward gate, but no one entered or left that they did not see.

Part of the courtyard was paved and the rest was hard-packed earth. There were ladies and gentlemen in their finery taking the air after the recent audience. They mingled with tradesmen from the town and surrounding country, who made deliveries to the castle. There were two peddlers, each with a little wooden tray in front of him, suspended on a leather strap from his neck. Some ladies crowded round one, and fingered ribbons. The other had more men round him, and from time to time bursts of raucous laughter peeled out.

Chris's nose twitched. There was a heavenly smell of cooking.

"Does no one ever eat here? I'm starved."

The sergeant laughed. "Supper will be at sunset, but you did miss dinner, didn't you? You two boys come with me. I'll see if the kitchen will find you aught to hold you till supper, with your permission, Master Malcolm, Master Richard."

"I'm not hungry," Joe said.

"I am," Chris wailed. He trotted off happily after the sergeant, in search of food.

"Does no one else notice the smell?" Joe said. "This place stinks."

"It is a bit ripe," Malcolm said. "There's a stable over against the far wall."

"See the hens pecking over the courtyard. The dogs ignore them," Dennis said. "Most of the time," he added when one dog got a little too close to a hen that ran off squawking furiously.

"It's a mixture of barnyard, stable, dogs and unwashed people," Rick said.

Joe wrinkled his nose. "Yeough."

"Let's walk round a bit," Rick suggested, and they strolled out of their corner. On their approach to the open gate, one of the soldiers hefted his pike and moved towards them.

He bowed to Malcolm and said: "I'm sorry. My orders are you and your people are to stay within the inner ward."

"We are not about to leave. We are merely strolling," Rick said.

The second peddler sold pomanders.

"Mm. Those smell nice," Joe said. "I read about pomanders in history, but I couldn't really understand why you would need one. But here ... Wow."

"Smell my herbs, young sir. They are a sure protection against all ills. With one of these you could safely walk through the stews of London Town itself. My Lord of Lancaster buys from me. I sold to him in his Palace of Savoy on the Thames not many months since. Come, masters, buy a sweet pomander, and one for the pretty page."

"Malcolm," Rick said, "I can place us now. Richard came to the throne in 1377. The Savoy burned to the ground in 1381. Lancaster was John of Gaunt."

"You're a real fund of useless information, aren't you?" Arthur said.

"I thought you once said no information was useless. You just have to be smart enough to know how to use it," Dennis said, and Arthur flushed.

"Got you there, hasn't he?" Malcolm grinned.

Arthur ignored Malcolm and turned back to Rick.

"You know a bit about this time?"

"A fair bit. It's the period I've done one hell of a lot of work on."

"What about this lord, Harold?"

"Nothing very detailed about bit players. Harold is a Saxon name, so the chances are his mother was Saxon. He's more Saxon than Norman in looks, I think. Gerald is a Norman name, so Sir Harold's father's second wife was probably of Norman stock. Sir Harold and Gerald don't really resemble each other do they, in spite of having the same father?"

"I bet Gerald will play that card, if he gets a chance," Malcolm said.

"Sir Harold wasn't the oldest son of his father's first family," Rick said. "That could be one more angle for Gerald to needle at, especially if Gerald is the only son of the second wife."

"Well, none of that's much use to us unless we wanted Harold out and Gerald in. We're better off with Sir Harold in charge than Gerald," Arthur said.

Malcolm nodded. "I'm glad we're agreed on that point."

Arthur continued to ignore Malcolm. "What about more general stuff? The hedge priests the sergeant talked about, for instance. What about them?"

Rick glanced round carefully.

"Don't talk about them here. If anyone seriously thought we might be with the hedge priests, Sir Harold couldn't save us from being questioned, even supposing he wanted to."

"Tortured, you mean?"

"Yes, tortured. Let's leave that subject till we're on our own somewhere safe. John of Gaunt, supported, supports, Wycliffe. Although he's powerful right now, he's not popular. Let's not declare ourselves until we know how matters stand with Sir Harold, and any others in control here."

"If I knew what the hell you were talking about, it might make some sense," Arthur said. "These names mean nothing to me. But, okay, we lie low till it's safe. You can give us a history lesson later, Prof."

"Don't knock Rick's information," Malcolm said. "It's like having a chart."

"Look mate," Arthur said, "you might want to chart a safe course so you can live the easy life here. I want to know what happened at this time, so I'm not knocking Rick's info, but you're not bloody well telling me how to use it."

"If you two can't talk without shouting at each other," Rick said, "maybe you'd better not talk to each other at all. It was you two arguing in front of the sergeant that made him think of the hedge priests. We don't want anyone else to wonder."

"Hi, you lot."

Chris grinned cheekily at them.

"The sergeant got me some grub. The cook wanted to chase me, but Martin grunted at him and I got a chicken leg, some kind of meat, and some black bread. I managed to grab a fresh loaf when no one was looking. Want some?"

Chris produced the loaf with a flourish from his tunic.

Arthur laughed. "Yes, I'll have some since you ate half of my bread and cheese."

Chris grinned at him, tore the loaf apart and handed pieces around.

"Do you know they only eat twice a day here?" Chris said. "About ten, they have dinner, and supper is at sunset."

"That's right, Chris," Rick said, "and up at sunrise."

"What about breakfast?"

"No breakfast," Rick said, and laughed at the expression on Chris's face. "You'll need to get used to stuffing yourself at dinner and supper. As pages, you and Joe have to serve us. You get to eat the leftovers."

"How's your bum, kid?" Arthur said. "That was some whacking Sir Harold gave you."

"I haven't tried to sit down yet," Chris said, "but it was frigging sore."

Rick cuffed Chris's ear.

"Aow. What was that for?"

"We don't use that word."

"Arthur does, and you don't slap him."

"He frigging knows better," Arthur growled. "I'd break his face. But, Rick's right. If he doesn't like it, don't use it. You're to be with the gentry, so don't copy me."

Joe sighed. "I wish you lot wouldn't fight."

There was a shout followed by a scream from the kitchen area. A boy in rags ran from the door, followed by an adult brandishing a long wooden spoon. The boy paused, blinked in the daylight, and peered round him before he dashed across the courtyard. His pursuer shouted: "Stop him. Stop that boy."

The ladies and gentlemen interrupted their stroll to watch the diversion.

"A crown the boy makes it to the gate," one called.

"Taken," came several replies.

The crowd laughed and watched the boy run, scant yards in front of the panting cook. He darted between the spectators, who drew back to avoid contact. The boy saw a gap leading towards the gate and sped up. He passed the two laughing guards and was only steps from the gate when Walter appeared and stuck out his foot.

The boy tripped and fell heavily on the paving. There was a crack, a scream, and the cook was on him. With a grip on one arm, the cook tried to pull the boy to his feet, belabouring him about the head and shoulders with the wooden spoon.

"Give it to him, cook," Walter said.

The boy didn't struggle, or even try to get his feet under him, but hung limp from the cook's hand.

"The boy's hurt," Malcolm said. He pushed his way through the laughing throng, followed by his group.

"Stop it. Stop at once I say," Malcolm shouted.

In mid-blow the cook stopped. Accustomed to obeying any reasonably dressed and authoritative sounding man, the cook lowered the hand with the spoon, but kept a tight grip on the boy's upper arm. The boy moaned and struggled to put his feet under him. The other arm dangled, with an extra joint between elbow and wrist.

"Arthur, Dennis. Quick. Grab hold of the boy. His arm's

broken. A hand in each armpit and hold him up."

The cook scowled when Arthur and Dennis moved to follow Malcolm's orders.

"This is only one of the kitchen slaveys, sirs. No need for you gentlemen to concern yourself. I intended to punish him for the theft of one of the loaves when he ran."

"Right, cook. Haul him back to the kitchen and beat him on the table the way you did last time," Walter shouted.

"The arm is broken, I say," Malcolm insisted.

"He's only a turnspit. He can use his other hand," the cook said.

"No. The arm must be seen to," Malcolm said. "Anyway he didn't take the loaf, Chris did."

"A fair exchange, cook. Let them have the slavey, and you take the other stinking serf. I'll come in and watch you beat him." Walter laughed.

Chris bristled and faced Walter.

"You don't smell so good yourself, pig. Maybe you should take his place. It was your fault he fell."

Walter went white and slapped Chris's face hard. Without hesitation, Chris drove his fist into Walter's solar plexus, and, as before, within seconds Walter was on his back with Chris astride him, pummelling his face.

Rick and Joe grabbed Chris and pulled him to his feet. Walter gasped for a few seconds, before he struggled to his feet and drew his dagger. He lunged at Chris. A riding crop snapped down and caught Walter's arm above the wrist, and the dagger clattered to the ground.

There was an instant silence. The hand holding the riding crop was Sir Harold's.

"What means this disturbance? Cook, let go of the boy and return to your duties."

"Yes, Sire, but what of my turnspit?"

"Have someone find another boy. Now, go."

Sir Harold examined the boy's arm briefly and nodded.

"It is broken. We have no bonesetter here. Release him. He may go. He will be of little use in the kitchen now."

"Sire, if the arm is not set he will never be able to use the arm again," Malcolm said. "He may even die."

"Yes," Sir Harold shrugged, "probably. As I said, he is of little use to us now." He paused. "Are you also a bonesetter?"

At Malcolm's nod, Sir Harold said: "You may have him, if you wish. First we must deal with these two pages. My lesson earlier was disregarded."

Sir Harold stared at the two boys.

"Christopher, you must learn you may not attack my people. Luckily for you, you did not draw, or you would hang. Walter, did I not say these gentlemen, and their followers, were my guests? Since when do we attack or insult guests?"

Walter, clutching his right arm in his left hand, scowled at Chris and blurted out: "Master Gerald said they are peasants, and that you are foolish to…" His voice tailed off.

Red-faced, and with a vein pulsing at his temple, Sir Harold said quietly: "You are impertinent, boy, and much too familiar with my brother."

Every word carried clearly in the silent courtyard.

"Sergeant, two men. Here, now."

The sergeant ran up followed by two soldiers.

"Have your men make a back for the boys."

The sergeant stood a soldier in front of Walter with his back to him. Standing behind Walter, the sergeant raised Walter's hands over the shoulders of the man. The soldier braced himself, and gripped the wrists tightly. Sir Harold handed the riding crop to the sergeant.

"Give him six. Lay them well on, on the buttocks."

Walter struggled and shouted: "Sire. Not in public. Not by a common soldier. Master Gerald would not permit it."

"Damn Gerald. He is not master here. I am," Sir Harold shouted. The onlookers shuffled, and started to move away.

"Stay, and watch. Sergeant, start now."

The soldier bent forward, which stretched Walter and lifted his feet clear of the ground. The six strokes given, the soldier lowered Walter. At a nod from the sergeant the man supported the boy while his legs trembled. Walter pushed the soldier away with an oath.

Sir Harold said: "Walter. Sometime you will learn the self-control of a gentleman. Stand still or I will have another six on your naked body. Sergeant, beat the other boy."

Rick winced with every stroke, but was glad Chris made no more outcry than Walter had. When the sergeant stopped, and the soldier lowered Chris off his back, Chris staggered. The soldier put out a hand to steady him. Chris, with a wan smile, gripped the arm and said: "Thanks."

Sir Harold gave Chris a wintry smile and glared at Walter.

"Now, Doctor, do you wish to try to set the boy's arm, or shall we leave it?"

"Oh no, Sire. It must be set. I require a table and good light."

Sir Harold snapped his fingers. The two soldiers with the sergeant ran to the great hall and came out with two trestles and a plank tabletop. They set it up in the courtyard, and Malcolm had Arthur and Dennis lift the boy, to lie on his back on the table. The boy kicked and struggled, but when he moved his arm he squealed.

"Gently, boy, gently."

Malcolm smoothed back the boy's greasy locks.

"Sergeant, I need two pieces of wood about the thickness of the boy's arm and the length of elbow to finger tips, and linen binding strips."

Malcolm drew his dagger and leaned over the boy who almost squirmed off the table.

"Hold him. Hold him still. Quietly, boy, I only want to remove your shirt."

The shirt was little more than a rag and Malcolm slit it from waist to armpit on the boy's left side.

"Pull it away, Rick. What's your name, boy? No, lie still. They're holding you to stop you from hurting your arm more."

"Todd, master."

"How old are you, Todd?"

"Nine, master, ten maybe. I don't rightly know."

"Will these do, Master Malcolm?" The sergeant said.

Malcolm tried the splints for size along the thin forearm, and nodded.

"Arthur, hold his other shoulder and arm down. Dennis, put a hand on each side of his pelvis at the hips. Joe, hold his legs. Rick, you hold this shoulder. When I say hold, hold hard for all you're worth."

Malcolm smiled down at Todd.

"I'm going to fix your arm. This will hurt, not because we want to hurt you, but because I can't do it any other way. Chris, stand here and hold these splints ready for me."

Slowly and gently, Malcolm moved his hands and ran his fingers over the boy's forearm.

"Both bones broken about halfway between elbow and wrist. I can't feel any splintering. Now, hold hard."

Malcolm grasped the thin arm in both hands and pulled and twisted. The boy screamed and slumped.

"Good. He's fainted."

Working quickly, Malcolm manipulated the bones.

"Okay. That's the best I can get it by feel. God, what would I give for an X-ray unit now. Right, Chris put the splint there, under his arm. Fine, now the other on top. Great, you hold tight while I bind. Well, it's not perfect, but it'll do, I think. Sergeant, I need a square of cloth for a sling. You lot can let go now."

The boy moaned and moved on the table. Malcolm leaned over him, and again smoothed back his hair.

"It's all right now, Todd. It won't be so painful now, and your arm should be okay in a few weeks."

"Well done, Doctor," Sir Harold said. "Neatly done. Wouldn't you agree, Sergeant?"

The sergeant grinned. "Yes, Sire."

"What's to be done with Todd now, Sire?" Malcolm asked. "I wish to observe the progress of the healing."

Sir Harold shrugged. "He is yours. Do with him what you will."

Todd stood rather shakily while Malcolm fitted the sling.

"The turnspit has peed himself," Walter sneered.

Both Malcolm and the sergeant turned to Walter and the sergeant said: "You show your ignorance, Master Walter. I have seen seasoned warriors, good warriors, do as much and more when a bonesetter worked on them. Perhaps we will someday have the opportunity to watch how well you stand up to such pain."

"Enough," Sir Harold said. "Walter, go to my room, and wait there. Do not visit my brother first. Am I quite clear?"

"Yes, Sire."

When Malcolm bent over Todd to pull off the rough breeches the boy wore, he wrinkled his nose.

"Wow, You don't half stink, Todd. Sergeant, is there a tub we could bath him in? Can you find some clothing about his size? Oh. I'll need a fine bone comb. His head's alive."

The sergeant had one of the soldiers show Malcolm where the common tub was, the one used by the soldiers. Malcolm used his dagger to hack Todd's hair into more or less a pageboy style.

"God. What's the hell is that?" Malcolm said when the sergeant handed him a flagon of a pale, straw-yellow liquid.

"Mare's urine, Master Malcolm. As you know, it's a sure specific against lice."

Malcolm sighed.

Todd had allowed Malcolm to strip him with no protest. He watched wide-eyed while Malcolm removed his own clothes, to stand in nothing but his short breeches.

"Right, Todd. Eyes tight shut. Hold your nose. Here we go. Christ. What I do for science."

The dousing with mare's urine Todd endured stoically, but when Malcolm tried to lift him into the tub, he started to struggle furiously. The sergeant leaned over and slapped him hard.

"Do what the gentleman tells you."

Todd quivered when Malcolm lowered him into the tub. When Malcolm soaped him with the coarse soap, he calmed down and even allowed Malcolm to rinse and lather his head several times by the simple expedient of dumping a bucket of water over him. At first, Malcolm tried to keep the cloths holding the splints on dry, but soon gave up. Finally, Malcolm lifted Todd out.

"I could have done with some help, you lot," Malcolm grumbled.

"That's not an act you expect from your guards, Dear Doctor." Arthur laughed. "Stay in role, remember?"

"I'll help," Rick said. "What do you need?"

"It's a bit late now," Malcolm said. "He's one of your downtrodden proletariat, Arthur. I'd have thought you would be interested."

Arthur snorted. "If he was a she, and about six years older, you couldn't have kept me back. I'll leave the little boys to you and your assistant."

Malcolm flushed and started to rub Todd dry with the rough cloth the sergeant had provided.

"Hey, come and see this."

Now his skin was more or less clean, they could see the boy's body was a mass of bruises, some old, some new. About the only places free of bruises were the soles of the feet, which had skin like leather, and the abdomen and groin.

"The abdomen doesn't show bruising easily," Malcolm said.

"Shit. Some bastard has been beating up on this kid for ages. Look at him," Arthur said.

The sergeant shrugged.

"He's only a kitchen slavey, a serf. He's probably beaten at least once a day by someone. Sir Harold probably wouldn't let even him be beaten to death, but it's not unusual."

"Right. We keep him with us?" Malcolm said. Each nodded in turn till Malcolm came to Chris.

"What do we need a kid for?" Chris mumbled.

"You're jealous you won't be the baby any more?" Joe teased.

"Come on. I know you're sore after the two whackings, but see this kid. Have a heart," Arthur said.

"Yeah, okay then," Chris said. He and Joe started to help Todd dress in the clean clothes the sergeant had brought.

"Interesting, Master Richard," the sergeant said. "Why did Master Malcolm not simply tell you Todd was his? Even Chris, the youngest page, had to agree?"

"No," Rick said slowly. "Not exactly, but we find it works better for us if we can agree, all of us."

"Will Master Malcolm do anything for Chris?"

"What can he do, Sergeant?"

"Cold cloths, well wrung out in vinegar, placed on the boy's buttocks, will reduce the pain and any swelling. Master Malcolm will know that. He can use my quarters. Chris knows where."

All the clothes were obviously cast-offs and well worn, the hose darned at the knee, but Todd's style of dress was now similar to what Chris and Walter wore.

"Look at me," Todd said. "I'm like a lord."

They laughed.

"No, Todd. You're one of us," Arthur said, "and don't you forget it."

"Stay with me, Todd, and out of bother," Joe said, relaxed and smiling easily for the first time since morning at the circle.

"We will all meet here at sunset before supper," Malcolm said. "The sergeant has given us permission to use his quarters to doctor Chris. We'll see if we can make him a little more comfortable."

Chapter Twelve

Rick, Malcolm and Chris joined the others in the courtyard at sunset. It grew dark, and two servants appeared with flambeaux that they set into holders on either side of the door. The door opened and people began to stream into the great hall. Rick gazed round him. When they'd been in the hall before, he couldn't see much from his knees with his head bowed except the rushes on the floor. Now, he could see it was about a hundred feet by eighty, with a low platform or dais at one end. Plank trestle tables lined the two long walls making a U-shape with the open end of the U at the kitchen end of the hall.

"How are you doing, kid?" Arthur said to Chris and took a pretend punch at him. "It's a good job pages don't get to sit down, eh?"

"Oh, it's not so bad now," Chris said. "Rick and Malcolm put some stuff on it that made it feel better."

"I'll bet they did." Arthur leered at them. "God. Malcolm, straighten your face. It's a joke. I know how you feel, kid. I remember it hurt like hell when they birched me."

Todd could hardly control his excitement. He bounced up and down beside Joe, who put a restraining hand on Todd's good arm.

"Simmer down. It's only supper and we get to serve," Joe said.

"It's so grand, with lights and all. I've never been in the great hall."

"We're not in yet. You worked in the kitchens, didn't you? You must have seen the great hall," Joe said.

Todd snorted. "I turned the spit. I scraped pots and platters. I sometimes got to eat what I could scrape. I slept in a corner, if cook or the older skivvies let me. I fought the hounds for scraps.

"Oh. There's cook. Hide me."

Like an eel, Todd wriggled round to put Joe between him and cook.

Cook's gaze came straight at him, past him, and cook wiped his greasy hands on his apron and turned back to the kitchen.

"He didn't even recognise you, all cleaned up and in your new clothes," Arthur said, and clapped Todd's shoulder.

"See. I said I looked like a lord," Todd crowed, and again danced with excitement.

Inside the great hall a servant held a basin of water on each side of the doorway. Most guests dabbled the first finger joint, or at most two, in the water and shook them before they wiped their hands on the cloth held by a second servant beside each bowl. A few dipped most of the hand in, before they rubbed their hands together and dried them.

"There's no soap," Chris whispered, "and they're all using the same towel. Aunt Sheena would have kittens."

Rick grinned. "Wouldn't she just."

When they entered, the seneschal bustled up.

"Master Physician, if you and your assistant would follow me. My lord has given orders to seat you above the salt. Your two men may sit with My Lord's men. The sergeant will see to them."

"What does 'above the salt' mean, Rick?" Chris whispered.

"Salt is expensive here ... now. The salt on the table divides people with some rank or position from the nobodies. The farther away from the salt in the direction of the high table the higher your position."

The seneschal had already turned on heel and they followed

him up between the long trestle table and the wall. About half way between the salt and the high table on the dais, the seneschal stopped and pointed with his staff: "Here."

There was no space. Malcolm and Rick stood, uncertain what to do. Impatiently the seneschal thrust his staff between two seated gentlemen.

"Make space. Our lord Sir Harold wishes his guests seated here."

With much grumbling, the lower man, the one nearest the salt, shuffled down the bench and Malcolm and Rick squeezed in.

"I'll sit on your right, Malcolm," Rick whispered and the seneschal nodded approvingly.

Rick and Malcolm's seats were on the right of the head table. There were four high-backed chairs at the table on the dais, one with a higher and more ornate back than the others. Everyone else had long, backless wooden benches.

Rick started, aware the man on his right, the one they had displaced, had spoken.

"Sorry, I was elsewhere. You spoke, sir?"

"Yes. Weren't you at the audience today, dressed as serfs?"

"We were attacked by brigands. When Master Gerald found us at the standing stones this morning he had us arrested."

"I hear one of your party was killed."

Rick nodded and his neighbour went on: "Was it someone of consequence, or simply one of your servants?"

"A guard, Master Gerald had him impaled."

"Master Gerald can be hasty at times. Impalement is a nasty habit he picked up in his travels in the East. I saw your master set the bone on the scullion's arm. It was neatly done, but I was surprised he would lower himself to do the work of a bonesetter, and on a scullion at that."

"Master Malcolm wouldn't see anyone suffer needlessly, lord or scullion."

"If he treats sickly serfs, he will have little time for anyone else and little money. Ah. Here comes Sir Harold, we will eat soon."

The major-domo grounded his staff on the edge of the dais three times and announced: "All rise for Sir Harold and the Lady Eleanor."

Walter limped in after Sir Harold and Lady Eleanor, followed by Master Gerald and his lady.

A second series of thumps from the major-domo brought quiet again while a priest, almost opposite Rick on the other table, mumbled grace. After a flurry of hands as they crossed themselves, the hall erupted in a babble of conversation and everyone sat down to grab at bread. Servants scurried in with platters and large jugs, entering the open end of the U to deposit them along the tables. Daggers plunged into the meat on the platters to bring back slices onto the trencher bread, the knives flashed in the flickering light

"I hope this isn't the table we had Todd on to fix his arm," Malcolm said. "His hair and clothes were alive before I washed him."

The jugs contained a thin, sour beer. Malcolm drank, turned to Rick and screwed his nose up.

"I'd rather have last night's brew."

"Do you see Arthur and Dennis?"

Malcolm peered across the hall at the men seated on the far side below the salt.

"Yes, there they are. Down close to the end on the far side."

Malcolm pointed and Rick scanned the opposite table. Arthur raised his mug and Malcolm brandished his mug in reply. Out of the corner of his eye Rick saw Chris's hand wave. Arthur had saluted Chris, not Malcolm and him. With a mental shrug, Rick decided against commenting on this to Malcolm.

A group of three jugglers performed during the meal. Todd pushed his way between Malcolm and Rick for a better view. He turned with an oath when Chris punched him hard between his shoulder blades. Malcolm grabbed Chris's arm and Rick pulled Todd back roughly.

"Let them fight, master. They might be more entertaining than these inept jugglers," Rick's neighbour suggested, and turned back to the jugglers to throw an end of hard bread at them. In an instant there was chaos, with a barrage of scraps launched from both sides. Sir Harold seemed oblivious to the riot, engrossed in conversation with his lady, but a flick of a hand in signal to the seneschal resulted in three sharp bangs from the major-domo's staff, and the troupe withdrew in some disarray.

Two musicians with lutes replaced the jugglers, and started to play a low plaintive melody, while one sang. The audience settled down again, and the level of conversation dropped.

After a glance round, Rick grabbed some of the fowl from the platter in front of him, and passed it back to Joe.

"Here, Joe. Share this out."

"You spoil your pages." It was Rick's neighbour again. "They eat well enough of the leftovers when we finish, before the servants clear. The turnspit should not be here. He is a serf and no page."

Malcolm heard the last comment, and leaned across in front of Rick to say: "Sir Harold gave the boy to us. He is what we say he is, and he goes where we say he goes."

Rick's neighbour shrugged. "You may know physic, Master Physician, but I know serfs. He is a serf born and bred. Perhaps you can train him to be a house carl, but I doubt it."

"He is ours. We will do with him what we will."

"Yes, you have the right, given you by Sir Harold. I simply say he will take it much harder when you tire of him, as you will, and send him back to the kitchen. Kinder perhaps to slit his throat now and save him the bother."

Malcolm glared and his hand tightened on the handle of his

dagger. Rick saw the instinctive reaction on the part of his neighbour and gripped Malcolm's wrist tightly. Rick smiled at his neighbour.

"You are probably right. However, Master Malcolm, like all good physicians, is pledged to preserve life. He sees good in all men, even the meanest serf. Let us not quarrel."

The man scowled for a moment, before he relaxed and grinned.

"Boy, charge our mugs. A toast, sirs, to your health and prosperity here." Malcolm and Rick raised their mugs in reply. "Let me know when you find the good in Master Gerald."

The man beside Malcolm choked on what he was drinking. Malcolm pounded his back. Red faced, he leaned forward and croaked: "Have a care, Jack. You will speak your mind once too often before the wrong men."

Rick broke in quickly: "You misheard, sir. Master Jack was toasting Master Gerald ... to the good Master Gerald."

Jack scowled.

"You are indeed lucky, Master Physician, to have such a smooth tongued assistant. A word to the wise; if you debate with anyone else, keep your hand clear of your dagger when the cutting of the food is finished."

He turned his attention back to the musicians.

"Malcolm," Rick said quietly, "you must be very careful. In this time, even adults behave in what we would think of as a very juvenile way. You almost started a knife fight there by grabbing at your dagger."

"Don't be silly. You know me. I'd no intention of using a knife."

"Then don't grasp it the way you did."

"I was annoyed. I clench my fist when I'm annoyed. A bad habit maybe. The dagger just happened to be in my hand."

"I know this period better than you do. What you did was very dangerous, for all of us. Take my word for it. It was a signal, body language – a challenge to fight."

The musicians finished and bowed deeply to the high table, and to the audience in general, in response to the applause. At a gesture from Sir Harold, the major-domo beckoned the singer to approach the dais. There, the major-domo handed him a small leather purse that gave an encouraging clink. Lady Eleanor whispered to Sir Harold, who leant over the table to talk to the singer. With a broad smile, the singer nodded and mounted the dais. He bowed to Sir Harold and Lady Eleanor, before he half turned to face the audience and started to speak.

The audience, for the first time since supper began, fell completely silent.

"What was that?" Malcolm sounded surprised. "We did Chaucer at school, but I couldn't understand a word of it. The poem he recited, I understood it. It sounded like ordinary English. How it be?"

"Yes, really odd isn't it," Rick said. "I wondered about that. They must all speak the local dialect here, because they all sound the same. When we came through the Gateway, somehow we must have acquired Middle English. I suppose it's no stranger than us being here at all."

"The sergeant did say we spoke English with an odd accent. I didn't think about it till I heard the poem."

"Sir Harold must speak French too, but it'll be medieval French. I wonder if we got medieval French too?"

Malcolm laughed. "If we did that will be a real miracle. I couldn't speak or understand a word of French at home."

"How does it sound in your head?" Rick said. "Any different from in our own time?"

"No, not that I can see, or hear I should say. It sounds exactly like always, but it must be coming out in the local talk since everyone understands us."

"Yes, it's really odd. They talk to us in Middle English, but apart from the odd turn of phrase from time to time, we hear it in our heads as our own brand of English."

The recitation ended to tumultuous applause and the musician grinned at the reception. He bowed deeply, and grinned even more widely when Sir Harold threw him a second purse.

Sir Harold and Lady Eleanor rose and everyone stood while the head table left the dais. The instant the dais emptied, the hall was a Babel of voices. Everyone sat down and again grabbed for their mugs. Below the salt became very noisy and the sound of voices raised in anger was heard.

The seneschal touched Malcolm on the shoulder.

"Sir Harold wishes you to join him, if you would follow me, sirs."

Rick and Malcolm stood, and Malcolm was about to stride off after the seneschal when Rick tugged his sleeve. Rick bowed to their immediate neighbours, and Malcolm followed his example.

"I thank you for your company and your courtesy, Master Jack, sir. I hope we will have the pleasure of dining with you again."

The two men rose in their places and bowed back, and Malcolm and Rick hurried after the seneschal.

Rick was unsure if the pages should accompany them, but decided to bring them. They followed the seneschal not to Sir Harold's own room in the tower, but instead to the building at right angles to the great hall, on the opposite side of the inner ward from the stables.

The seneschal led them up two flights of stairs. Finally he knocked, or rather hammered, on a solid wooden door. A very sullen looking Walter opened it.

"Master Malcolm and Master Richard," the seneschal announced, stepped aside, bowed and withdrew.

Rick and Malcolm took about three steps into the room and bowed, but Rick almost fell over when Todd bumped him from behind. Joe and Chris had stopped and bowed, and Chris took the giggles at Rick's half stagger.

There was laughter, quickly suppressed, before Sir Harold's voice said: "Enter and welcome, masters. My Lady, may I present Master Malcolm, a physician, and Master Richard, his assistant? Masters, my good wife, the Lady Eleanor."

Lady Eleanor inclined her head and held out her hand. After only a brief hesitation, Rick stepped towards her, bowed, placed the back of his hand under hers, and bent to touch his lips to her hand. The effect was spoilt when Todd, for some reason determined to stay close to Rick, again walked into Rick's protruding backside and knocked him off balance. There was no question now of who had laughed before, as Lady Eleanor laughed aloud, and her three ladies discreetly covered their mouths with their hands.

Rick tried to apologise, but Lady Eleanor waved his apologies aside and extended her hand to Malcolm who successfully followed Rick's example.

Sir Harold smiled and said: "That is the boy whose arm was broken, My Lady. He obviously needs some training in manners."

Todd by this time had retreated behind Joe and clutched his belt, trembling.

"Come forth, boy. Stand before the Lady Eleanor. No one intends you any harm," Sir Harold said.

Warily, Todd edged out and, still clutching at Joe, came forward.

"I remember my ladies altering those clothes to fit Walter, some five years past."

Lady Eleanor turned to her ladies. "Strange isn't it, clean and dressed like this, who would guess this is only a kitchen boy, a potboy?"

Todd bristled. "I was turnspit."

He hid behind Joe again.

One of the ladies laughed.

"Until he spoke, or showed his manners, that is, My Lady."

"Come, boy. Stand here, I want to look at your arm," Lady Eleanor said. Todd again emerged.

To Rick, Lady Eleanor was professional in her examination of Todd's arm.

"Was there much displacement? There isn't much swelling or bruising," she said.

"It was a clean break of both bones, My Lady. I couldn't feel any splintering and the ends fitted nicely. He should be fine."

"We must have a talk about herbs and potions. I know a little about medical matters."

"I am at your service, My Lady," Malcolm said.

"Walter, some wine for the gentlemen," Sir Harold said, and Walter, reluctance in every movement, stepped to a side table to pour wine. He carried the goblets to Malcolm and Rick, and gave each a very slight bow.

"My lord hunts tomorrow, masters," Lady Eleanor said. "My ladies and I will not join him this time. I will send for you before dinner."

Rick and Malcolm bowed, and the conversation turned to the recitation after supper.

"Did you enjoy the recitation, masters?" Lady Eleanor said.

"Yes, My Lady," Rick said, "I thought it well done. It was an English translation of part of Le Roman de la Rose wasn't it? Chaucer, perhaps?"

Lady Eleanor clapped her hands and laughed aloud.

"Martin is either very wise and perceptive, or very lucky," she said. "He is right, you are not serfs. It would have been a great pity to have you butchered by Gerald. There are too few gentlemen, other than clerics, who know anything of the niceties."

"Have you met Chaucer?" Sir Harold said.

"No, My Lord," Rick said. "But we have heard of him, and I have read some of his works."

Lady Eleanor smiled and nodded.

Sir Harold crossed to the door, clapped his hands once, and a servant appeared.

"Send the major-domo to me," he said, and turned to Malcolm. "We will meet again tomorrow, when I return from the hunt. My Lady Wife will meet with you during the day."

The major-domo knocked and entered with a bow.

"Find my guests some space in the great hall. A window niche perhaps, where they, their pages and men might sleep. Good night, masters."

Malcolm and Rick signalled the boys to bow and leave. The major-domo grumbled on their way back to the great hall.

In the great hall, Rick spotted the sergeant in one of the window alcoves, and the sergeant waved to them.

"You should be able to sleep here," he said. "I have cleared this space for you."

"Thank you, Sergeant," Rick said, and the major-domo nodded.

"Excellent, exactly as My Lord instructed. I will leave you now, masters, good night."

Chapter Thirteen

"I thought we were going to our bedrooms," Chris whispered to Rick.

"No, Chris. This is it. There will be some rooms in the wing Lady Eleanor has her chamber in. The garrison, the soldiers, have barracks above the stables. You've seen those. In many castles they would sleep in the great hall. Everyone else beds down here, or else where they work. Todd used to sleep in the kitchen, remember?"

"There may be a straw pallet or two not yet taken," the sergeant said, "but I doubt it. Good might, masters."

"Good night," Rick and Malcolm bowed.

When he moved past Chris, the sergeant clapped the boy on the back.

"Rest easy, Christopher, and avoid Walter tomorrow if you can. I don't particularly want to beat you again."

Chris grinned.

The sergeant gone, Malcolm turned to Dennis.

"Where's Arthur?"

Dennis shrugged.

"After you left the hall, it got pretty wild for a while. Arthur almost got into a fight with one of the soldiers. He made some crack about Pete's dancing, sorry Joe, and Arthur nearly clocked him one. Anyway, they drank some more and staggered off

85

together. The soldier made some mention of tumbling serving wenches in the stable."

The tables had been taken down and stacked along the walls. Around the hall, people began to settle down for the night. Some had thin pallets filled with straw or sweet herbs, but others simply pulled rushes together, wrapped themselves in their cloaks, and lay down. In the dim light of the dying embers of the fire and the few remaining flambeaux guttering in their wall brackets, it was an eerie sight. In their window niche, Malcolm pulled open the shutters.

"What do you think," he said, "do we sleep on the seat ledges or on the floor? It might get cold during the night. It was, last night, and none of us have cloaks."

Todd had already settled the issue for himself, curled into a ball in one corner.

"I've got to go," Chris said. "Where is it?"

"Dennis," Malcolm said, "you, Chris and Joe go to the garderobe first. I think there's one in the wall outside the hall before the corner tower. Rick and I will hold our spot here till you get back."

When they settled down for the night, Chris crept over to lie between Rick and Malcolm who talked quietly over his sleeping head.

Rick looked round and noticed Joe had moved to lie with Todd and both were sound asleep. Todd's head nestled in the crook of Joe's arm.

Malcolm commented: "These rushes are probably alive with fleas. I got most of Todd's livestock earlier, I hope. We'll need to check each other over carefully. It's going to be bloody difficult to keep clean and vermin free here."

Chapter Fourteen

The floor was hard through the rushes, and Rick thought he would not sleep. It had been a long, tiring day. There were sounds around the great hall Rick could not quite place, some human, some not.

He moved and shivered.

Damn, I knew I wouldn't sleep.

But he realised others in the hall were stirring, and there was a faint pre-dawn glow in the sky. He had slept after all. By the feel of his muscles and bones, he must have lain like a log. His movements disturbed Chris, who moaned in his sleep and wriggled closer to Rick, following the warmth.

"You awake, Rick?" came Malcolm's voice. "You two slept okay."

"God, I'm stiff," Rick said. "I wonder what today will be like. Did Arthur find us during the night?"

"No," Malcolm said. "He didn't appear while I was awake, and that was most of the time."

By now, there was a general stir in the hall, and shouts from outside, from the direction of the stables. They stretched and scratched while they collected in the window niche.

"Let's go out to the trough, or to the tub outside and wash up," Malcolm said.

They picked their way out of the hall. Immediately they reached the courtyard, Todd slacked the points on his codpiece and started to relieve himself against the wall.

"Todd," Joe said, "go to the garde-robe."

"Why? I'm done. Anyway, the servants and the soldiers would kick me."

"You're not a turnspit or a kitchen boy now," Joe scolded. "In future, you go to the garde-robe."

Todd shrugged, shook himself, and grinned at Joe.

"Last night was good. Nobody kicked me, and I got to sleep all night, nice and warm."

They splashed their faces with cold water, rubbed wet hands together, and flapped them in the morning air to dry.

"Here's Arthur," Chris said.

"Where have you been all night?" Malcolm asked.

Dennis laughed. "Tomcatting, I bet."

"This place might not be so bad after all." Arthur grinned. "I was in the hayloft beside the stables. You wouldn't believe the girl Thomas found for me."

Arthur moved his hands in the air before him.

"Boy, what a night. I'm bushed."

Dennis laughed.

"Tell us about it. Look at Joe, blushing like a girl."

"What's the matter, Joe?" Arthur said. "Never had a girl? I'll get you one tonight."

"What about me?" Chris said.

Arthur grappled playfully with Chris.

"Not yet. It would be a waste of time from what I've seen. You've a way to go yet. You wouldn't even know what to do with a girl."

"How wouldn't he know what to do?" Todd said. "I seen them humping in the kitchen, and the fields."

"Todd," Joe said, "don't talk like that."

"I know what to do," Todd insisted, "how wouldn't Chris? What I don't know is why. It doesn't look like much fun to me."

They all laughed, Joe included.

"Time enough yet, Todd," Malcolm said.

"Well, it looks like plenty of R and R, free for the taking," Arthur said.

"What about VD, Malcolm?" Dennis said. "How do they treat it now?"

"It's not here yet, I think. Unless one of us brought it," Malcolm said. "Do you know, Rick?"

"A character in Canterbury Tales, the Cook, I think, had what sounded like a syphilitic sore on his leg. Chaucer wrote it after 1387. So if Arthur brought it, it would have had time to spread by then."

Arthur scowled. "Why should you think I would be the one to bring it? Your fancy friend here, The Doc, is as likely to have the clap."

Rick laughed. "Okay, Arthur, okay. I vaguely remember it didn't get here for a couple of centuries yet. No AIDS either, unless one of us brought it."

"Count Dennis and me out on that one. We're not frigging AC/DC."

"Heteros can pick up AIDS too," Malcolm said. "Don't be so smug. Anyway, none of us here is gay."

"Hey, look at Joe," Dennis said.

"Brother Pete neglected your education?" Arthur said, and Dennis poked at Joe's chest with an extended forefinger. Dennis's mouth was open to speak, but Joe, furious, landed a stinging slap on Dennis's face. A slap, which sounded like a pistol shot, rocked Dennis's head back on his shoulders.

Fists clenched and raised, Dennis stood his ground.

"What the hell was that for? Can't you take a bit of teasing?" Dennis snarled. "Come on, put your fists up and fight like a man."

Arthur gripped Dennis's arm and pulled him back.

"Leave it, Dennis. He's maybe younger than we think from his size. He doesn't even have any peach fuzz. Leave it. It's not worth the hassle."

While Arthur spoke, Todd looked from one angry face to the other. Before anyone could stop him, he drew his knife and leapt at Dennis and shouted, "You leave Joe alone. Touch him, and I'll cut your balls off."

The knife lodged in the flesh on Dennis's right side. Malcolm and Rick grabbed Todd and pulled him off. Arthur let go of Dennis and advanced menacingly on Todd.

"I'll wring your neck, you little fart."

Joe put his arms round Todd and glared at Arthur and Dennis, while Malcolm moved to see to Dennis.

Rick put a hand on Arthur's arm and was roughly shaken off. In the momentary distraction, Todd had seized Joe's knife. He stood now and glowered at Arthur, tensed to use the knife.

"Hold fast. Put up your blade, boy."

It was the sergeant's voice. Rick pushed Joe aside and pinned Todd's arms behind him.

Todd squealed and struggled.

"Rick, you'll hurt his arm," Joe shouted.

Arthur snarled: "Let me at him. I'll break his other frigging arm."

"Dennis is down," Chris said.

"Shut up, all of you," Malcolm said. "Help me with Dennis."

Rick whispered in Todd's ear and shook the boy. He squealed again, but nodded and Rick let him go. Promptly, Joe pulled Todd to him and, with a frown at Rick, started to fuss with the splints.

Arthur turned to Dennis now stretched on the packed earth.

"If the fighting is over for the moment, you can take him to my quarters," the sergeant said.

"I want the knife in place till I examine him," Malcolm said. "He'll lose less blood that way. Arthur, Rick, carry him carefully to the sergeant's."

When they laid him on the sergeant's bed, Dennis was fully conscious again. Malcolm cut the shirt to extend the slit on either side of the knife, and eased the material out of the way. The sergeant appeared with some linen cloths, and at a snap of his fingers a servant entered with a basin and a ewer of water.

"Wring out two cloths. Now fold them into pads about three or four inches square. Right. Rick, you hold one against one side of the knife. Arthur, you hold one on the other side. Press in and against the blade while I pull it out."

Malcolm grasped the hilt and pulled. He motioned Rick and Arthur to lift their pads, and peered at the wound. Dark blood oozed out. Carefully pulling the edges of the wound apart, Malcolm tried to peer in. There was more blood.

"He didn't touch an artery, or we'd have more blood spurting out. It would be brighter red too. Nothing vital touched either. Breathing is okay. Pulse is a shade rapid, I think, but okay in the circumstances. A clean puncture. He'll be fine. Help him sit up and lean over, Arthur. Rick, take his other side."

Malcolm took the basin and placed it on Dennis's lap.

"I'm going to make you bleed, Dennis. I've no disinfectant, and God only knows what would be on Todd's knife. The best bet is to make it bleed some."

The sergeant nodded.

"I know not what disinfectant may be, but bleeding him some is best. Wounds bound and closed too quickly can trap evil humours within."

After a while, Malcolm pressed a fresh linen pad over the wound and bound it on by wrapping strips of linen round Dennis's chest.

"God, what I'd give for some adhesive tape. Right, lie back Dennis. May he lie here a spell, Sergeant?"

The sergeant nodded and they went back out to the courtyard.

"Doesn't it need a stitch?" Arthur said.

"What the hell would I stitch it with? It's not very big."

Malcolm turned to the sergeant.

"What's Todd likely to have used his knife for?"

"Meat, bread, picking his teeth. He'd probably clean it well with earth and grass."

"Yes," Arthur said, "and Christ knows what might be in the scabbard."

"Take not the name of the Son in vain," the sergeant said.

"Has Dennis had an anti-tetanus shot lately? Do you know?" Malcolm said.

Arthur's face lightened. "Yes, he has, a month or so since. He cut his foot on a bottle on the beach."

"Fine, we'll hope for the best."

"We have to decide what to do about Todd," Rick said.

"You're not going to do anything to Todd." Joe pulled Todd hard into him.

"He stabbed Dennis." Arthur glared at Rick and Joe.

"May we go up to a quiet corner of the wall walk, Sergeant?" Rick asked.

In an angle sheltered by a corner tower, Rick had them stand in a small circle. Malcolm and the sergeant stood together, and Rick, Chris, Joe, Todd, and Arthur completed the circle. Todd shook and clung to Joe, who had one arm round him.

"Master Sergeant," Rick said, "the facts are not in dispute: Dennis teased Joe, and prodded him. Joe slapped Dennis. Dennis challenged Joe to fight. Todd jumped between Joe and Dennis and stabbed Dennis."

"You don't say that Dennis is a freeman while Todd is only a serf," the sergeant said. "It has a bearing."

"No, Sir Harold gave Todd to Malcolm to do with as he wished, before the whole castle. When Todd joined us, he ceased to be a serf. He is as free as Dennis, as free as any of us is. He is one of us. Arthur himself said Todd was one of us now.

Remember, Arthur?"

Reluctantly, Arthur nodded.

"Who speaks for Todd?" Rick said.

"I will," Joe said. "Todd was wrong to stab Dennis. He thought he was protecting me. Remember how he's been living till now. He's only nine or ten, but he stood up to Dennis to defend me. Give him another chance."

"A chance to do what? To stab me?" Arthur said.

"Give him a chance to learn about us and our ways, a chance to grow up free. You, of all people, should agree. Arthur," Joe said.

"Todd. What have you to say for yourself?" Rick said. "Did you really think Joe was in danger?"

Todd shuffled, and looked at the ground. Joe shook him gently.

"Speak up, Todd."

"I wanted to frighten Dennis. Joe's smaller than Dennis. He couldn't fight without having the shit knocked out of him," Todd mumbled, head down. He raised his head to stare straight at Arthur and added, "I only nicked him. If I'd wanted him dead I could have belly ripped him, or torn his throat out, easier than I stuck him in the side."

Arthur snorted. "Dennis wasn't expecting a pipsqueak like you to knife fight him. You wouldn't find him, or me, so easy next time."

"Shut up. That's not relevant," Rick said.

Rick drew Malcolm out of earshot and talked with him briefly, before they returned to the circle.

"Todd must learn he cannot draw on, and wound someone in this kind of quarrel," Malcolm said. "We could disown him. Send him back to the kitchens. Abandon him to the streets of the town."

Vehemently, angrily, Joe said, no, and both Arthur and Chris shook their heads. Rick made no comment.

"We could simply reprimand him and hope he would learn the lesson," Malcolm said.

Joe grinned, hugged Todd and said: "That's the ticket."

Arthur scowled. "No frigging way. He stabbed Dennis. A ticking off would let him off too lightly."

"It would probably not satisfy Dennis either," Malcolm said. "I'm sorry, Joe. With Todd's background he would think he had escaped free and would learn nothing, or the wrong lesson. We're left with a beating. Agreed?"

Arthur nodded. Chris rubbed his rump and thought for a minute.

"Yes, if it's that or send him back."

Joe, in tears, said: "It wasn't Todd's fault. I'll take the beating for him. It's not fair. He thought he was helping me."

Todd shook slightly and, white-faced, said: "I don't want to go back. I want to stay with Joe, and all of you. I won't stick anyone again, honest – unless Joe says it's all right. Can we do it now? Waiting is worse than the beating."

"Sergeant," Rick said, "what do you think? Is the decision just and reasonable to you? If so, I saw some birch rods some place yesterday. Can we use those?"

"Yes, Master Richard, it is a fair judgement. Lenient, perhaps, but he is only a boy, and Dennis's injury is slight. You still have Todd for further punishment if Dennis dies. Christopher, come with me to fetch the rods."

While they waited, no one spoke. Joe sat in one of the crenellations, and pulled Todd beside him.

Chris returned with half a dozen birch rods.

"Martin had work to do. He says, will these do?"

"How many? And who does it?" Arthur said.

Malcolm glanced at Rick and said: "Twelve, and you do it, representing the injured party."

"Chris, stand here," Rick said. "Todd, stand in front of him. No, face Chris. Bend over and touch your toes. Chris, grab his waist and pull him tight to you. Arthur, here's the rods. Set to."

Rick handed Arthur the birch rods and Joe moved over to kneel beside Todd.

"Joe, pull his hose and breeches down, and his shirt and tunic up," Rick said. "The birch should be on his bare backside."

Joe protested, but followed orders, and Arthur took his place behind Todd.

The small, thin, bare buttocks were startlingly white in the early morning light. Scars and bruises from previous beatings were clearly visible from mid-thigh to lower back.

Arthur raised his arm and Todd tensed, only to have Arthur lower his arm without striking. Again Arthur raised his hand and again Todd tensed. The moment stretched.

Joe suddenly shouted: "You're a sadistic bastard, Arthur. Do it and get it over. Don't torture the kid."

Arthur drew the rods down hard, and thin red weals sprung up on the white flesh. Todd gave one involuntary yelp.

"Shit. I can't do this." Arthur snarled, threw the rod down, and stamped off along the wall walk.

Rick picked up the rod, and turned to Todd.

"Right, Todd. You can stand up now. That's it, Todd. Arthur represented the injured party. Since he's satisfied, it's over."

"Can I stay with you? Please. I'd rather get a full beating from Arthur than be sent away."

He jumped at Arthur's voice.

"For better or worse, you are one of us now, Todd. Behave in future, or I will beat the shit out of you. Chris, do you want to come with me and see Dennis?"

"Can I come too?" Todd said.

"Sure, why not. Here's your knife."

Todd examined the blade closely, spat on it and rubbed it vigorously on his gypon sleeve.

"Now we know. The blade was clean and sterile," Malcolm said. "You keep your knife clean, don't you, Todd?"

Todd nodded solemnly, grinned, and ran off after Arthur and Chris.

"After all that, he ran off with Arthur," Joe grumbled, "the one who was going to beat him."

"But didn't," Rick said.

"You're a crafty one, Rick," Joe said. "You knew all along, didn't you, Arthur would be too soft on kids to beat Todd when he saw him naked."

Rick laughed.

"I gambled. I think he'd have watched one of us beat him, and enjoyed it. He might even have done it himself if Todd was covered. The naked little backside covered in bruises was too much for him. Remember, he told Chris he'd been birched himself."

"It cleared the air too," Malcolm said. "Arthur and Dennis can't say we weren't prepared to discipline Todd. The sergeant can also vouch for it, if any of the castle people saw the incident and want to pursue the matter."

Chapter Fifteen

No one raised any objection to their being on the wall walk of the inner ward or strolling on it, so they walked slowly along.

Joe moved away from Rick and Malcolm, and leaned against the parapet looking out over the outer ward and the town.

Rick made to move to him, but Malcolm shook his head.

"Leave him. Let him cry in peace. There's damned little privacy here for him to grieve. He has to have some time."

"It was maybe lucky for him he had Todd to look after last night. Perhaps it took his mind off Pete a bit."

"What do you think are the chances of us being allowed to bury Pete?" Malcolm said. "I'm sure Joe would like us to."

"I don't know. We can ask Sir Harold, but remember this age is a lot different from ours. Did you see the head on the pike at the gate when we came in?"

"No, thank God, and I don't think the others did either. I'm glad you didn't point it out."

"Christ," Rick said, "look."

He pointed. From where they stood, the view was out over the bay. They could see, through a gap in the trees, the stone circle and the tiny figure of Pete on the pole.

"Let's keep Joe away from here. Walk back towards where we left him," Malcolm said. "How old do you think he is? He is taller than Chris, but a lot more fine boned. As Dennis pointed out, he has no facial hair to speak of. Have you ever seen him stripped?"

"No. It's funny. We've changed to the skin twice now since we got here. Each time, Joe has managed to change while we were all busy arguing, or all concentrated elsewhere."

They walked back to where Joe still gazed out over the ramparts.

"Are you all right?" Rick said.

Joe sniffed and dabbed his eyes with one sleeve.

"Yes, I'm fine. Thanks."

Chris and Todd ran up the stairs to the wall walk, laughing and whooping.

"I take it you found Dennis well," Malcolm commented.

Chris moved over to Joe and giggled.

"You should have seen it. Dennis lay there, with his eyes shut, but he looked fine. Todd went in on tiptoe, and stood beside the bed with his knife out."

"When I spoke," Todd said, "Dennis opened his eyes and saw me and the knife. He almost peed himself. It was lucky for me he was lying down."

"He still managed to land one on Todd's face," Chris giggled, "before Arthur stopped him."

"That was a dreadful stunt to pull, Todd," Joe said, and Todd's mouth turned down and his eyes lost their sparkle.

"Yes, it was bloody silly. You probably started him bleeding again," Malcolm said. "I'd better go and check on him."

"Don't blame Todd," Chris said. "It was Arthur's idea." He giggled again and prodded Joe. "Come on, if you'd seen it you would have laughed. Even Dennis laughed when he cooled down."

"Let me see your face, Todd," Joe said. "You're going to have a black eye."

"I'm fine. I've had worse. Dennis and me are even now. He won't go after you again."

Todd beamed at Joe, when Joe ruffled his hair and said: "I

suppose no harm's done, but it was a cruel joke."

"What the hell are you doing?" Malcolm shouted, when Arthur appeared on the stairs with Dennis close behind him. "I told you to stay put."

"And I told him to move," the sergeant said, a step below Dennis on the stairs, one hand at Dennis's back. "It's naught more than a pin prick. Many a man has fought a whole day with more."

Dennis smiled, a little white, but otherwise well.

"Sit here in the archer's loop in the sun," Malcolm said, and took Dennis's wrist. "Pulse is fine. How do you feel?"

"A bit light headed."

"Well, that's normal for you," Arthur quipped.

"I'm sorry, Dennis, about earlier," Joe said. "Todd really thought he was helping me."

"Arthur told me what happened. Todd's only a kid. We're all a bit uptight right now."

There was a silence, finally broken by both Rick and Chris speaking together.

"Sergeant, would Sir Harold let us bury Pete?"

"Martin, can we get out of the castle today?"

"I don't know, Master Richard, but I will ask My Lord when he returns from the hunt. No, Christopher, not until Sir Harold grants your freedom to live at liberty in his domain."

"Is he likely not to?" Malcolm said.

"Much depends now on the Lady Eleanor. If she speaks for you, My Lord will listen. If not…" the sergeant shrugged.

"If not, what, Sergeant?" Arthur said.

"Master Gerald would still like to charge you with witchcraft or brigandage."

"How could anyone believe such charges?" Malcolm said.

"Your confession would suffice."

"Why would anyone confess to something so stupid?" Dennis said.

Rick shivered. "If we are charged, we can be put to the question; tortured. It's part of the legal system, like helping the police with their inquiries in our time."

"The Holy Church itself sanctifies judicial torture," the sergeant said. "Carried out in accordance with its rules, naturally."

He glanced at the sun and the shadows in the courtyard.

"I must be about other business. A bell will sound for dinner. Follow the directions of the major-domo. With the hunt, there will be few to dine."

He bowed and they bowed back.

Chris and Todd wandered off along the wall walk. Joe drifted off to stand again by himself, and stare out over the outer ward and the town.

"What now?" Dennis said. "Think we'll ever get back?"

"We don't know how we frigging got here, so how the hell are we to find our way back?"

"The stone circle and the explosion had something to do with it," Malcolm said.

"So what do we do? Stand in the bloody circle like fairies, and wait for lightning to strike?"

Rick laughed. "No, Arthur. Even if we knew what the trigger is, we've no idea which direction the circle would take us in. We might well end up sometime worse than this."

"So you think we're stuck here?" Dennis said.

"Yes. What we have to do is work out how to survive."

"The sergeant would take Dennis and me on as part of his outfit, I think. He's already hinted as much."

"Do you want to join up?" Malcolm said. "It would put the two of you clearly under Sir Harold's protection, wouldn't it, Rick?"

"Yes. You wouldn't have much freedom of action or movement though; you'd be part of this system."

"Bugger that, I don't think much of this frigging system so far. How do we support ourselves? There's no dole here."

"If Sir Harold loses interest in us, we're on our own," Rick said. "Do you and Dennis know enough about the building trade to work at it?"

"Sure," Arthur said, and Dennis nodded.

"We might have some problems with the local guilds, but maybe the sergeant and Sir Harold could help there."

"Do you have some plan?" Arthur said. "Or are you just breaking wind?"

"Sir Harold mentioned yesterday a house in the town his doctor used to use. If we can persuade him to give us that to use, we can all live there, but Arthur and Dennis could maybe find some work outside too."

"So we'd get to work as wage slaves, while you two live like bloody lords? What have you in mind for the boys? Rent them out to Master Gerald?"

"Stow it," Malcolm said. "Rick's already said it's to give you some freedom of action and movement."

"Relax, Malcolm. God, you're so easy to annoy, it's not very much fun any more."

"Hello, the wall. Is one called Malcolm the Physician there?"

"Here," Malcolm shouted. "Who calls for me?"

A servant appeared on the stairs and approached the group.

"Lady Eleanor requests the presence of Malcolm the Physician and of one Richard the Scribe," the servant said, and bowed.

"Arthur, will you see to the boys?" Rick said. "We'll join you before dinner."

"I'm sorry, masters, I do not wish to contradict, but my lady will dine in private with her ladies today. She expects you to join them."

"Have the boys eat with you, Arthur, okay?" Rick said. "Try to keep Chris and Todd out of mischief."

"That's like asking a dog with fleas not to scratch, but I'll do what I can, masters," Arthur said straight-faced, but with a wink at Rick.

Chapter Sixteen

Malcolm and Rick followed the servant back to the wing where they had visited the Lady Eleanor the night before. This room was bigger and had three large windows set in alcoves along one wall. The centre window actually had glass; stained glass, Rick noticed. It must be the solar, he realised – the private quarters of the owner of the castle.

The servant announced them and they bowed deeply.

"Welcome, masters. Please join us," Lady Eleanor said from the centre alcove. She sat on a stool with her back to the window, an embroidery frame before her. Her ladies were also sewing, but they worked on more utilitarian articles. Lady Eleanor noticed Rick look at the window.

"You admire my window?"

"Yes, My Lady. It is most attractive."

"I had window openings in the other manors specially rebuilt. This window goes with me when we travel to our other houses. Margaret has been reading to us, but the work really needs a man's voice. Would you read for us?"

Hesitantly, Rick took the book from Margaret. He wondered if his ability to hear and speak Middle English would extend to being able to read it fluently. Certainly, he had studied Middle English and French of the period, since he needed it to read contemporary documents. Could he sight-read it well enough for the Lady

Eleanor? The book was beautifully hand crafted and, to Rick's relief, the script was clear.

Rick cleared his throat and started to read. It was one of the interminable poems of courtly love. Full of events which, if they happened in real life, would result in challenges and in mutilation and probably death for the participants. Rick remembered one of his professors described these poems as the soap operas of the Middle Ages; equally unrealistic, but equally popular. Some passages were decidedly ribald, and Rick could feel himself flush while he read them. Malcolm shuffled his feet from time to time and fiddled with his girdle belt. Rick was glad he had his back to the window and the ladies were viewing him against the light.

Lady Eleanor held up her hand and Rick stopped.

"You read well. Perhaps My Lord will prevail on you to read for us some evening at supper. Are you familiar with this poem?"

"No, My Lady. Not at all."

She nodded.

"Martha, you may tell the major-domo we will eat now."

Servants scurried in and set a trestle table in the solar. The ladies set down their sewing and moved their stools to the table. Lady Eleanor clapped her hands.

"Fetch stools for my guests," she said.

Two servants ran to get stools for Malcolm and Rick and set them in place with mumbled apologies.

Lady Eleanor waved Malcolm and Rick to sit. Each had a pewter plate, but the ladies still took a piece of the trencher bread. Each lady took a small satchel from the pouch that hung at her waist and produced a small, bone-handled knife.

Rick gaped at the healthy appetites the ladies showed. No small, genteel, ladylike portions here. As the night before, Rick and Malcolm helped themselves using their daggers and ate with their fingers.

Lady Eleanor smiled. "These knives, Sir Harold had specially made for my ladies."

"Margaret, in the chest by the door, there are other knives My Lord had made that I would not have as they are big and clumsy. They would not be out of place in the hands of these masters. Fetch them."

Margaret smiled when she handed the knives to Rick and Malcolm.

When the meal ended, Malcolm made to leave the knife on the table for the servants to clear. Rick nudged him. The ladies all wiped their dining daggers on pieces of trencher bread before returning them to their satchels. Rick and Malcolm wiped theirs and sheathed their daggers, but were uncertain what to do with the smaller dining knives.

"Margaret, there should be sheaths for these knives in the chest. Get them."

Lady Eleanor waved aside their protestations.

"My lord would wish you to have them. Now, Master Malcolm, I have enjoyed my talk with your assistant. He is obviously a man of culture. I would relish having him stay here. We must now talk of herbs, and potions, and salves."

Lady Eleanor and Malcolm stepped into one of the other window alcoves, where Lady Eleanor sat on a bench at the open window while Malcolm stood.

Margaret smiled at Rick.

"Have you travelled far?"

"Yes, Lady Margaret, and for a long time."

"I think Sir Harold is likely to wish Master Malcolm to settle in his town."

"Will Lady Eleanor approve?"

"We will soon know." Margaret smiled again and waved her hands towards Lady Eleanor and Malcolm. "I think she will."

"What will Master Gerald have to say?"

"Hush, sir," Margaret placed a hand on Rick's arm and drew

him slightly apart from the others.

"Lady Gwenne," she said, "is Gerald's wife. So much the worse for her, but don't say anything about Master Gerald in her hearing."

"Why is Master Gerald against us? We haven't done him any harm."

Margaret shrugged. "Master Gerald trusts no one. Lord John of Gaunt or Wycliffe didn't send you, did they?"

Rick hesitated. This could be thin ice.

"No, My Lady. We know of these gentlemen, of course, but they didn't send us."

"Master Gerald suspects you may be in their pay, if you are not witches. Either way he would put you to the question, if he could persuade Sir Harold that he had grounds."

"You must not keep our guest to yourself, Mistress Margaret."

The speaker was Lady Gwenne, and Margaret bobbed a half curtsy before she replied. "No, My Lady. I asked him how the page Christopher was today, after his beatings. How is Walter's backside, My Lady, or should the question be more properly addressed to your lord husband, Master Gerald? I'm sure he will have examined him carefully."

"You are impertinent, mistress."

Margaret, eyes wide, a picture of injured innocence, said: "I, My Lady? Surely not. I meant only your lord husband is well known for his kindness and consideration. What other interpretation is possible. Is it not so, ladies?"

Margaret turned to the others; hands parted, palms up. She raised her eyebrows. The other ladies tittered, but one moved to stand protectively beside the Lady Gwenne.

"We bore our guest with this chatter," she said. "You must not keep him to yourself, Mistress Margaret."

"Your mistress has already said so, Mistress Mary." Margaret smiled. "She is not quite so old that she needs someone to speak for her."

Lady Gwenne and Margaret stared at each other and it was Lady Gwenne who looked away first.

"What are the latest fashions in London?" one of the other ladies asked in the silence.

"Alas, I know nothing of London fashion," Rick said. "We have not been there for a long time."

"Where have you been?" Lady Gwenne said.

Rick hesitated. They had not discussed an answer to this question. Where would it be safe to say?

"Master Malcolm and I have travelled in France as far south as Avignon and north into Flanders. We have visited Canterbury and Oxford, and have wandered in the north and in Wales. A physician is welcome most places."

Lady Gwenne sniffed. "These are the journeys a spy might take."

"You have perhaps some experience in such matters," Margaret said, "but to me they are the travels of two scholars and gentlemen learning of the world."

"Where do you come from?" Mary said.

Before Rick could think up a reply, Margaret interrupted: "It is hardly polite to ply this gentleman with personal questions, questions that should properly be asked by Sir Harold. If he is satisfied, who are we to pry? Wouldn't you agree, My Lady?"

Lady Gwenne, lips pursed, nodded. The ladies drifted back to the stools the servants had replaced in the centre alcove. Margaret remained with Rick in the centre of the room.

Mary's voice, low pitched and quiet, came to them.

"It is strange to me that a poor physician would have such an educated assistant and travel with three soldiers and two pages."

A second voice said: "Perhaps one is a great lord travelling incognito?"

"Or a scion of a great house sent on his travels?" another said.

"It is not unknown, and they are gentlemen despite one being a physician and the other so bookish."

There was general laughter and a voice said: "Master Gerald might regret his haste at the circle. The man he had killed could well be the servant of the bastard son of some great house, even perhaps of the Lord of Lancaster?"

In a sudden silence, Lady Gwenne raised her voice. "Master Richard, will you not join us? Margaret, could you persuade the master to read for us again?"

Rick was aware Margaret had watched his face closely during the low voiced conversation.

"Shall we join the others?" She smiled when Rick held his right arm out to her, and rested her left hand on his arm, while they walked back to the centre alcove.

"I will find you another book to read. My Lady Eleanor would not wish to miss any of the present piece," Margaret said, and left him in front of the glass window.

The book Margaret handed him was older than the previous one and when Rick opened it, he saw it was in French. He glanced up and caught Margaret's amused glance, and almost laughed when she raised one eyebrow. Rick glanced through the first page, cleared his throat and started to read.

As the first phrases rolled off his tongue, Rick caught, out of the corner of his eye, Lady Gwenne's start of surprise and her gasp when she pricked herself.

When he finished a section, after reading for some time, Rick looked up to see Lady Eleanor and Malcolm together outside the alcove. Lady Eleanor smiled.

"*Continuez, je vous emprie, Maitre Richard,*" she said. "*C'est bien fait, n'est ce pas, Maitre Malcolm?*"

Malcolm flushed.

"I'm sorry, I don't speak French at all well."

"Perhaps Master Richard would continue in English?"

Rick swallowed hard and turned back to the book. Now he read more slowly, translating as he went.

God, this is worse than an exam at school, he thought. What he was putting out wasn't poetry.

At the end of the next section, Rick stopped for breath. Lady Eleanor said: "That was well read. I do not agree with all of your translation, but we must allow for some poetic license, mustn't we? Margaret, will you ask the major-domo to send in some wine before the masters leave?"

Obviously, the audience was over, so when they had drained their goblets, Rick bowed to Lady Eleanor and said: "With your permission, My Lady, we will now withdraw."

With deep bows to Lady Eleanor and Lady Gwenne, Rick and Malcolm walked backwards to the door. With a final bow to the ladies, they left the solar.

Chapter Seventeen

"How did your interview go?" Rick said.

"Her ladyship certainly knows her medicinal herbs."

"Do you? That's more to the point. Will she accept you as a doctor?"

"As a good ecology buff, I took a hard look at homeopathic medicine when I was doing pharmacology. Lots of the old folk medicines work. I held my own, and even suggested some herbs she could try."

"It sounds to me as if we might have Lady Eleanor on our side."

"You were very cosy with her lady-in-waiting. Margaret, wasn't it?"

Rick blushed. "We have to watch out for Lady Gwenne. She's Gerald's wife and apparently she's as much against us as he is."

They walked round the inner ward as Rick filled Malcolm in on what he had said of their travels. The others were not in sight. In fact, the courtyard was strangely quiet. As they approached the gatehouse, a guard stepped forward.

"Masters, the Sergeant said to inform you that your people are in the outer ward with him. You may pass through should you wish."

The outer ward circled the inner ward completely. A cobbled road led from the outer gate to the inner gate, but apart from that, there were only paths of beaten earth. A whitewashed picket fence kept the ever-present horde of cats, dogs, and chickens out of Lady Eleanor's herb garden.

"A nice southern exposure and sheltered from the wind," Malcolm said.

As they rounded one of the corner towers of the inner ward, they saw a small crowd and heard Chris shouting.

"God. What now?" Malcolm said, as they hurried.

Malcolm and Rick forced their way through the circle where they saw Joe and one of the soldiers squaring off in the centre. The soldier held something in his right hand as if it was a dagger. Closer, to Rick's relief, he saw it was only a short stick. The soldier tossed the stick from hand to hand.

"Come on then. Scared this time? Now you've got a real man against you?"

Joe stood, looking quite relaxed.

"You heard me tell the others. I won't attack."

The soldier leapt forward and lunged with the stick. Quicker than Rick could follow, Joe moved, and the soldier sailed through the air to land with a thump on his back. The onlookers gasped. Several crossed themselves. Joe moved to the fallen man and extended a hand to help him up. The soldier grasped the hand, then, with a laugh, tried to pull Joe down. Quickly, stepping over the extended arm, Joe turned, twisting the arm, and threw himself back. The soldier screamed an oath as Joe's legs made a fulcrum of the soldier's elbow. His own weight provided the torque as long as he held Joe's hand.

"You'll break my arm."

Joe, scarcely breathing hard, said: "No. You'll dislocate your own shoulder or elbow, if you struggle. Let go of my hand."

Released, Joe quickly scrambled clear. "Enough?" he said.

The soldier nodded as he sat massaging his arm and shoulder. "I know not how you did it, boy. But it was, as agreed, a friendly fight. No harm intended. You caught me by surprise. It would not happen again."

The soldier stood, put out his hand to shake, and when Joe took it, clamped him in a bear hug, arms pinned to his side. The soldier laughed and started to squeeze.

"Go to, Jude. Squeeze the seeds out of him."

"Press him till his eyes pop."

Joe went limp, and Jude slackened his grip for an instant. Joe's knees rammed up into Jude's groin. Jude let go. Joe danced back, but as Jude, slightly glassy eyed and gasping, advanced on him, Joe darted forward. His hands moved, too fast for Rick to see exactly what they did, and Jude crashed on his face to the ground. He lay motionless.

In the startled silence, several of the onlookers again crossed themselves. The Sergeant stepped forward.

"Tournament over. Get back to work."

The spectators drifted off, talking in low voices.

Chris and Todd capered round Joe shouting in excitement. Spotting Rick, Chris ran to him.

"You should have seen it, Rick. One of the soldiers tried to push Joe, and when Joe pushed back, swung at him."

"Joe did something, a magic word, and the soldier flew through the air," Todd said, breathlessly.

The sergeant joined the boys. "I have seen such fighting by the infidels in the Holy Land, but never by a Christian."

"The Sergeant stopped the men. Some were going to mob Joe. Some were going to run away," Arthur said. "He made them all come out here and asked Joe if he was willing to fight, one on one, with any that wanted to try their luck. Jude was the third."

"I did not do wrong, Master Richard, did I?" the sergeant said.

"No, Master Sergeant. It was probably the best way to stop anyone getting hurt."

"Except Jude, that is." Malcolm commented from his position

beside the soldier. "I think he's broken his nose. I've set the nose as best I can, but without tape I can't be sure it'll hold that way."

"I didn't stick anyone." Todd said, and tried to squirm away as Arthur held him and tickled.

"Only because I grabbed him," Arthur said. "He was all set to jump the first soldier."

Squeaking, Todd, eel like, wriggled free and ran laughing to Joe.

"Will you teach me how to fight like that? Will you? Will you?"

"Me too," Chris said. "It was great."

"Is he alright?" Joe said. "I didn't really mean to hurt him. I sort of lost my temper at the last bit."

Jude lurched to his feet and looked at Rick and his group. He bowed slightly to Rick.

"Master, to have such skilled retainers that even your page can best a skilled warrior, you must indeed be of a great house." He turned to the Sergeant. "I am glad I was not of the party that impaled the other. Great houses protect their own, and exact retribution, even for their bastards."

Before the Sergeant could speak, Rick said: "We absolve of all blame or guilt those who in ignorance simply followed orders."

"All but Master Gerald," Joe growled.

"All but Master Gerald," Rick agreed, and scowled at Arthur. "And him we leave to a higher judgement. We will not act against him while we both eat of Sir Harold's bread and salt."

Jude held out his hand to Joe, who looked very wary.

"Nay lad, by my oath, in friendship. It was a friendly tussle. We both grew a little overheated at the end."

Joe shook hands. "I am sorry about your nose, Jude."

Jude strode off with the sergeant.

"Where did you learn Judo, Joe?" Arthur said. "How far on are you?"

"Black belt," Joe said. "They taught it at my school. I've been at judo since I was eleven or twelve."

Arthur laughed. "Maybe it's a good job Todd stabbed Dennis. Dennis is only a beginner and I'm only a yellow."

"I can teach judo. I've been an instructor for over a year."

Chapter Eighteen

The group moved back to the wall walk.

"What's all this rubbish about a great house?" Arthur said. "It's all over the frigging castle. They've pegged Rick as the bastard of some bloody nob. You're his keeper, Malcolm, gossip says. We laid our story on a bit too thick. Believe it or not, we're too strong a group to be what we claim. Someone says Rick even looks like this nob's family."

"He has a few bastards, and he's owned up to all of them," Dennis said.

"Acknowledged, is what they say here," Rick said, absently.

"Well, acknowledged." Dennis shrugged. "He paid all the mothers and had the boys brought up as gentlemen. After, he pays to send them abroad. We fit the kind of group they go in."

"Does this help, or make matters worse," Malcolm said.

"We're less likely to be given over publicly to Gerald, I think, but it's probably more likely he'll have someone slide a knife between my ribs."

Todd listened intently to the exchange.

"Are you really a lord, Master Rick? What should I call you?"

"Don't be stupid, Todd, he's my cousin…" Chris's voice tailed off. "That would make me a lord too."

Arthur reached out and gripped Chris by the neck.

"Don't let it go to your head, kid. Swollen heads can be cured by enough force on the bum."

Chris wriggled free, grinned at Arthur and stuck out his tongue. Arthur, deadpan, winked at him.

"There are no lords here, Todd," Arthur said. "We are all free men and equal; you too. For a while we'll play the game of lords and ladies, but we know it's only a game. Someday, the game will end, and all men will be free and equal. There'll be no more serfs, or lords and ladies."

"A nice speech," Malcolm clapped his hands slowly. "But it could get us all killed very messily. The lords and ladies you so despise still rule, and will, for centuries yet. Don't get us all slaughtered for spite."

"Keep your damned hair on, Doctor Malcolm. I'll play the game. I want to live as much as you do, but I want to see it better for everyone, not just safe and comfortable for me."

"Do we act any differently?" Dennis said, while Malcolm, red and angry, shrugged and turned away.

"No, we keep them guessing," Rick said. "Keep on as we've been doing. If we try to claim something we aren't, we could run ourselves into a pile of trouble."

A shout from the top of the gate tower attracted their attention.

"Hello the gate. The hunt returns."

The sergeant appeared out of the gate to the inner ward.

"Guards. Stand to," he shouted, and half a dozen pike men clattered out to line up inside the outer gate.

Rick and his group watched the horsemen riding in. The sergeant ran forward to take the reins of Sir Harold's horse, while grooms ran to hold the other horses. Walter rode immediately behind Sir Harold, and swung out of his saddle to move forward to hold Sir Harold's rein as well as his own.

"A good hunt, My Lord?" the sergeant said.

Sir Harold dismounted and laughed.

"Yes, Sergeant. It was very fair. We got a boar and a deer. One of the huntsmen was gored. They are carrying him back. See what can be done for his comfort. Have the priest here for his arrival."

Sir Harold started towards the inner gate, but turned back to the sergeant.

"Oh, some fool of a peasant got in the way of the hunt. Almost cost us the deer. He had no right to be there. He must have been hunting in the King's preserve. Hang him."

"The men on foot are here now," Chris said.

This group of hunters appeared much more tired and bedraggled than the mounted gentry did. The injured huntsman, face bone white, hands twitching, lay on a board carried by two men. One rope round his ankles and the board, and a second round his chest stopped him rolling off. At the end came an unkempt bloodstained man whose arms were tied behind his back. When he stumbled, a soldier who held the halter round the man's neck jerked it sharply.

Malcolm ran, and shouted to the others to follow him.

"Sergeant, a table in good light. Lay him on it gently and remove his clothes. Cover him with a clean linen cloth."

The sergeant snapped his fingers. "What are you waiting for? Jump to. You heard."

"Boil water," Malcolm shouted and followed the huntsman to the inner ward.

In the gateway they met the priest who ran in answer to the sergeant's summons.

"Not yet, Father," Malcolm snarled when the priest started on the last rites. "Not yet. Let me see him."

Malcolm lifted the rapidly reddening cloth and stared at the figure on the table.

"Christ, what a mess, where the hell do I start?"

Arthur gazed at the bluish purple, pulsating mass protruding from the man's abdomen.

"Do they have surgical needles and so on now?"

"No, not that I know of, anyway," Rick said. "God, Malcolm, can you do anything?"

"Malcolm, the urban guerrilla course Dennis and me were on," Arthur said. "They said you could use animal tendons or boiled gut for stitches. They've got a fresh boar and a deer."

"Arthur. I could kiss you."

"No frigging way. I leave that to you and Rick."

"Sergeant," Malcolm shouted, "did they bring back any of the lights?"

"Yes, of course."

"Good. Get a length of intestine about a foot long. Clean it thoroughly. Make one cut along its length to open it up. Parboil it; use a very sharp knife to cut it into very narrow strips; the narrower the better. I need fine needles, curved like sail maker's needles, but much smaller."

"The armourer can make those from stock used to make and mend chain mail," the sergeant said.

"Right. Everyone move."

Malcolm dipped linen cloths into boiling water, using a stick to hold them, and wrung them out as hard as he could, the instant he could touch them. Gently, he started to pack the cloths into the abdominal cavity to soak up the blood, and to staunch the bleeding.

"The gut itself isn't cut," Malcolm said. "There's no smell of bowel gases. So there'll be no contamination from bowel contents. That would kill him now for sure."

"Could you cauterise some of the small bleeders? The gut'll be much too coarse."

"God, Arthur, you're a genius."

In minutes Arthur was back with a small brazier of hot coals from the armourer, and lengths of fine rods, pencil thin, some hammered to a point.

"Chris, take these hand bellows and pump like crazy. Keep

these coals white-hot."

Malcolm started to move his hands around the opening and touched the red-hot point to the flesh each time he met a small bleeder.

"Where's the damned gut?" Malcolm roared. "There's one bloody big vessel here I can't cauterise."

"Here, Malcolm," Arthur said. "And here are your needles, all boiled."

Malcolm threaded the gut through the needle with some difficulty while Rick watched, and stitched across the vessel about an inch back from the torn end. When he pulled his stitches tight, the blood stopped.

"Christ. It might work at that," Malcolm said. "We're in luck. There was only one major vessel cut; a vein, thank God, not an artery. The others were all minor, and with the gut stuck through, it applied pressure on the vein and slowed the bleeding there. I'll close now."

Malcolm carefully felt round the cavity for the blood soaked linen pads. Satisfied, he pushed the pulsating bluish black gut into place and started to stitch the inner layers.

"Whatever did this, didn't damage much more muscle than I'd have to cut to remove an appendix. It tore rather than cut."

Malcolm stitched steadily, and mumbling to himself, finally closed the skin and placed a fresh linen pad on the wound.

"Can someone bind this in place?" he said. "I want to check on how he's doing."

Lady Eleanor, Sir Harold and Master Gerald watched the entire procedure. Malcolm ignored them while he checked the pulse and raised each eyelid in turn to peer at the eyes. When he bent over, his ear to the huntsman's chest, Malcolm became aware of the priest chanting in Latin.

"Christ, man. He's not dead yet. Let me listen. Shut up, will you?"

Sir Harold gestured and the priest faltered into silence, and Malcolm pressed his ear against the patient's chest.

"He'll live. I think. He must have the constitution of an ox to survive this far. Right, Sir Priest. A prayer for the living, if you please. Say one for him and for me. The man is in deep shock. Sergeant, I want him kept warm, and inform me when he wakes, no matter the hour. Unless poisoning sets in from the tusks, he should live."

"Sir Priest," Sir Harold said, "you have other business before supper?"

"Yes, Sire. I must confess and shrive the poor wretch to be hanged."

"Frigging hypocrisy," Arthur said. "You hang a man for nothing, but you give him a priest first."

Sir Harold scowled. "We would not endanger his immortal soul by sending him out of this world unshriven, no matter what his crime."

"He did Pete," Joe protested and pointed at Master Gerald. The others nodded.

Sir Harold slowly turned to stare at Gerald. Their eyes met and after a brief time Gerald looked down.

"Why was the man not shriven?" Sir Harold thundered. "Our house is dishonoured by this."

Gerald coughed. "The priest was not free to come to the circle and I thought…"

"You are incapable of thought beyond your own advantage, sir. May the sins of he who died unshriven, by your hand, be on your soul. He should have been brought here if you had no priest with you. It was not a battle."

"My Lord," Rick said. "May Pete be given Christian burial, and not left to rot on his pole?"

"Tomorrow at first light, we will go out and bring him back for burial. You, Gerald, will walk, barefoot and bareheaded in a penitent's robe."

"Sire, he died unshriven with his sins on him," the priest said.

"Pete and I were at confession and absolved the afternoon of the day before his death," Joe said. "I was with him from then on. He had no occasion for mortal sin before he died."

"Enough?" Sir Harold said.

The priest wilted under Joe's glare and said: "Yes, My Lord. I will bury him."

"Good. See to the peasant. It is almost sunset."

Chris and Todd followed the priest and the sergeant to the outer ward.

"Shit. Let's see if we can stop the sergeant hanging the poor peasant bugger," Arthur said.

They stood, uncertain what to do. Todd and Chris tumbled down the stairs and ran across the hard packed earth towards them.

"There's a hook on the outside of the wall," Chris said. "They tied the rope to that and pushed him off the wall."

"He only kicked once or twice." Todd sounded disappointed. "The last time, they let the man down slowly. He twitched and kicked for ages."

Joe pulled Todd to him.

"Don't let it upset you, Todd, or you Chris. Like with Pete, we couldn't do anything about it."

"I've seen better hangings," Todd said.

Joe slapped Todd hard, and, in tears, would have slapped him again had Rick not stopped him.

"Easy, Joe. He doesn't know any better. This is his world. It's not his fault."

Chapter Nineteen

Tonight when they entered for supper, Malcolm and Rick received courteous bows and a muttered, Masters, from those below the salt. Dennis and Arthur joined the sergeant.

Malcolm and Rick headed for the same place as the previous night, but before they could sit the seneschal bustled up to them.

"If you would follow me, masters, I have other instructions from My Lord."

The seneschal marched them to within two places of the high table before he peremptorily pushed his staff between two guests.

"My lord's physician and his honoured companion sit here, by My Lord's command."

No grumbles tonight, Rick noticed, as those below them moved to make space. The smaller bone handled knives they used instead of their daggers did not pass unnoticed. When Sir Harold and Lady Eleanor rose, the seneschal tapped Rick on the arm.

"My lord requires that you and your people join him in the solar. The sergeant will bring your men."

Sir Harold and Master Gerald were talking to Lady Eleanor when the group entered the solar.

"Walter, wine for our guests," Sir Harold said. "Master Malcolm, that was indeed interesting this afternoon. Will the huntsman live, do you think?"

"I think so. I hope so, Sire. He lost a fair bit of blood. If he comes out of shock, however, he should live."

The sergeant entered followed by Arthur and Dennis. When the sergeant was about to leave, Sir Harold said: "Stay, Martin. You have a part in this. Brother Gerald, you have questions before I announce my decision?"

"Master Richard," Gerald said, and both Rick and Walter started. Gerald had not been so polite to the group before. "A physician so obviously skilled as Master Malcolm would not wander the country aimlessly. He would be in the employ of some great lord. Are you and your page Christopher related?"

Rick glanced at Sir Harold, who smiled and nodded.

"Our mothers are sisters and our fathers cousins."

Gerald nodded. "That would not be uncommon. You claim to be the bastard of John of Gaunt…"

"My Lord," Rick turned to Sir Harold, "I make no such claim. My father would be angry at the very thought. Malcolm, my friend and companion, is a physician, as you have seen…"

"I still think it unlikely a physician would have such an entourage."

"Enough, Gerald," Sir Harold said. "Lady Eleanor concurs. Master Malcolm may have the house occupied by my late physician. He and his people are under my protection, but free of all restraint. Do you accept, Master Malcolm?"

The question was directed at Malcolm, but the raised eyebrows were for Rick.

"May we consult briefly?" Rick said.

They talked quietly in an alcove for a few minutes before they returned to Sir Harold. Malcolm stepped forward, and looking Sir Harold straight in the eye said: "I, Malcolm the Physician, accept your offer of protection in this time and this place. I will, with thanks, use the house you offer. I, in turn, offer you my services as physician, and swear I will truly and faithfully serve you in that capacity without reservation. I cannot speak for Richard and

Christopher."

Sir Harold nodded and turned to Rick.

"I, Richard, a freeman of this realm, place myself and my cousin Christopher under the protection of Sir Harold Fitzwilliam. We will defend his honour and the honour of his house as if it were our own. There is no conflict between any allegiance we may owe another and this pledge. I so swear."

After a short silence Sir Harold said: "That will be satisfactory, masters. Martin, Walter, you will treat these masters as gentlemen of my household. I will provide servants tomorrow, after the burial, to see to your residence. Tonight you may sleep here in the solar. The centre alcove should suit."

"May I say something else?" Rick said, and at Sir Harold's nod went on: "Arthur and Dennis are free men. They have not been paid, and they are free of any obligation to us. If they wish to remain in our service, we will be pleased to have them, but they are free agents. Joe will remain with us until he is of age to make his own choice. He came with his brother, and we are his family now."

Sir Harold turned to Arthur and Dennis. "You are free, but have no means of support. Will you stay with Master Malcolm, under my protection, and bound by his oath?"

Arthur scowled. "We will stay with Malcolm and Richard until they settle here."

"Sergeant, you may go. Master Malcolm's men may be more comfortable with you. They are excused. Walter, invite my lady's ladies to join us."

"Brother, Sire, shouldn't we insist on a more binding oath? Can we trust them?"

"I'm sure we have nothing to fear. To ask for a more binding oath would be an insult to this house, if not to Master Richard. I am content.

"Ah, the ladies are now seated. My lady tells me you read

exceptionally well, Master Richard. Would you read for us now?"

"If you wish, My Lord."

When Rick finished reading, Malcolm asked permission to go to examine the huntsman.

Sir Harold nodded. "I would like to see this miracle myself. Lady Eleanor and I will come with you."

The entry of Sir Harold and Lady Eleanor, with Malcolm and Rick at this hour, created consternation in the stable where the huntsman lay. The huntsman tried to struggle up and Malcolm quickly but gently pushed his shoulders back down.

"Lie still. Do as the doctor says," Sir Harold said.

"Your belly muscles are cut," Malcolm said. "It will be some time before you regain your strength. I will not remove the bindings tonight. How do you feel?"

"As if I'd been kicked in the belly by a bull, but hungry."

"Nourishing broths, Master Malcolm?" Lady Eleanor said.

"Yes, My Lady. For the next day or so anyway."

"Come, Walter. Todd, you know where everything is in the kitchen, come with us."

By the time Lady Eleanor returned with the broth, Malcolm had the huntsman propped up on a small bale of straw, and was checking his pulse.

"Has he any fever?" Lady Eleanor said.

"No, My Lady, no fever yet. His breathing is fine."

"Has he peed yet?"

Malcolm's mouth dropped open at the blunt question.

"No, not yet. I will, of course, monitor kidney function, but I am not worried about it. Although renal involvement and failure is certainly a possibility."

"You mean bloody water, or no water, in plain words?"

"Yes, My Lady."

"Then say so."

"Huntsman, you owe this master your life," Sir Harold said. "I wouldn't have wagered on your being alive after tomorrow with that wound. Now, by *Corpus Dominus*, you should live to show your children the scar and tell them the tale."

"My Lord," Malcolm said, "with your permission, I will remain here with my patient tonight."

"As you wish, although I don't see why. Do you require anything else?"

"Perhaps Todd would stay here with me, in case I need a runner?"

"Todd and I will both stay," Chris said. "Okay, Rick?"

Rick was reluctant to split the group up, but he could see why Malcolm wanted to stay, and why he might need at least one boy. If Sir Harold had not offered them the solar to sleep in, he might have been tempted to have them all sleep in the stable. Would Sir Harold be offended if they spurned his offer? Obviously not many were allowed to sleep in the solar. In some castles only the owner and his family slept in the solar and used it during the day when they wished to be private.

"Right, Malcolm. You keep Chris and Todd here tonight. The rest of us will sleep in the solar. We'll be in the centre alcove."

Chapter Twenty

In the solar, Arthur grumbled. "Having Sir High-and-Mighty in the stable will put a real damper on the action there tonight."

"Oh, I don't know," Dennis said. "I didn't notice anyone being particularly shy in the great hall last night."

They each pulled some rushes together and lay down. After some time, Rick moved over and sat with his back against the wall. Arthur and Dennis were both sound asleep, but Joe stirred.

"Can I come and sit with you?"

"Yes, if you want to."

Seated beside Rick, Joe leaned against the wall and said: "I'm frightened. What's going to happen to us here?"

"You've got the valiant Todd ever ready to defend you."

"Don't try to jolly me along. I'm frightened."

"We all are. Only an idiot who couldn't understand wouldn't be frightened."

Rick put an arm round Joe's shoulder and Joe leant back against him. Not sure what to do to comfort Joe, Rick patted the boy's back. A short time later, Joe wriggled back against Rick's arm and chest. The arm no longer circled Joe's shoulder, but curved round his back, and Joe grasped the wrist to pull the arm tight round him. Slowly, Joe's other hand crept across Rick's lap to touch and to hold his hand, and finally to pull it to join the other, completely enfolding Joe in Rick's arms.

God, what am I, a scoutmaster?

First I had Chris to look after, then Joe, and now Todd. Although, Todd had taken a shine to Joe. God, Joe is thin.

Rick could feel the ribs through the robe and shirt.

"Don't, Rick"

Joe squirmed, and Rick made to take his arms away.

"No, just hold me. Don't tickle. Don't move your hands around."

"I wasn't…" Rick started to protest.

What the hell, he thought. His brother was being buried tomorrow. He was entitled to be a bit touchy.

Rick drifted off. His head jerked and he woke with a start.

"Let's lie down and get some sleep."

They slid down to lie on the floor, Joe still in Rick's arms, and Rick's hands slid up Joe's chest.

"Keep your hands to yourself, I told you," Joe said, and pulled Rick's hands down roughly.

"For God's sake, what did I do now?" Rick pushed Joe away. "Sleep by yourself."

To Rick's surprise, Joe burst into tears, turned to face him, and pushed back into Rick's arms.

"I'm sorry, Rick," Joe sobbed, head buried against Rick's chest. "You're the only one I would trust."

Puzzled and embarrassed, Rick hugged Joe back and patted his shoulder.

"It's all right, Joe. It's okay."

"I'm not Pete's brother."

'I'd rather not know this,' Rick thought, and felt himself flush hot and cold.

He'd nothing against homosexuals, but he'd rather not be quite this close.

"Well, what does it matter now if Pete wasn't your brother? It's all over now."

"Oh, Pete was my brother."

"But you said you weren't his brother…"

"Idiot. I'm his sister."

Rick was suddenly aware that the figure on the floor beside him was in point to point contact from head to toe, and he now had an erection.

Joe laughed.

"Well, in spite of what Arthur thinks, you're not queer."

Suddenly solemn, she said: "What do we do now?"

At Rick's gasp, she laughed again.

"No, not that, Rick. I mean do I still pretend to be a boy? Women, except ladies like Eleanor, don't seem to have much of a life here. I won't end up as someone's skivvy, and I don't intend to be raped."

"As far as I know, in peacetime it's not apt to happen. You're in more danger from the likes of Master Gerald."

"I'd kill him."

"How long do you think you can go on posing as a boy?"

"Did any of you suspect?"

"Well, Malcolm and I talked about you not having facial hair, and seeming younger than Chris, although everything else pointed to you being older. What age are you?"

"What a question to ask a lady. I'm surprised at you. I'm eighteen, nearly nineteen."

"Now I come to think of it, your fight with Dennis started when he pushed at your chest – your breasts."

"Luckily, I'm not very big in that department. It was fashionable at school to be very thin, so I worked at it. Exercise. Diet. I think it must have been all in the mind. Despite everything, I've eaten quite well here. I'm bound to get bigger if I start to eat properly, and my periods will start again."

At Rick's exclamation, Joe said: "Relax. I'm not pregnant. I can't be. Take my word for it. Periods sometimes stop when you diet too severely."

"What do you want to do?" Rick said, and could feel himself blush. "About telling everyone I mean."

"If there were some chance of us going back soon, I wouldn't tell anyone. If we're stuck here, it's bound to become obvious. We'll tell the others in the morning, all right? You think about how we tell Sir Harold, and *what* we tell him."

Joe turned her head up to Rick and pulled his mouth down to hers. They kissed. Rick pulled her hard in to him, but when one hand moved in a caress down her back, Joe drew her head back.

"No, Rick, don't. I like you. I trust you, but I'm not ready for anything else yet. I told you because I do trust you. Arthur or Malcolm would have been all over me like an octopus. Let's get some sleep."

She wriggled round, and, back to Rick, snuggled into him, and pulled his arms tight round her.

"G'night, Rick. Sleep tight."

Sleep tight indeed, Rick thought. I'm wound up tighter than a clock-spring. This was not how Malcolm would have handled the opportunity.

He could hear Malcolm's mocking voice in his head as he lay with Joe in his arms.

"Go on Rick, she doesn't really mean no. She only wants to be persuaded. God, you're soft."

Rick sighed. He wasn't soft, anything but.

Chapter Twenty-One

Rick woke, one arm numb from elbow to fingertips. What a crazy dream. He barely moved the numb arm and Joe moaned slightly. It wasn't a dream, he thought.

When Rick pulled his arm clear, Joe wakened and turned to face Rick.

"Good morning, Rick," she said, and kissed him.

They lay face to face in each other's arms.

"What is your name?"

"A fine time to ask, young man, having slept with me all night," Joe laughed. "It is Jo. That's what Pete always called me. It's short for Josephine"

"That's what he almost said two nights ago, isn't it?"

Jo sighed. "Yes, and I punched him and knocked the wind out of him."

"You two going to get married?" Arthur's voice said. "I bet I couldn't get a frigging thin penny between you. I thought more of you than that, Joe."

Arthur gaped at them when they moved apart, and laughed at him.

"Arthur, Dennis, I've something to tell you," Jo said.

"I think I know. You're another frigging fairy. I saw the pair of you."

"I'm not Pete's brother, Arthur…"

"Just his frigging pansy friend?"

"Shut up, Arthur," Rick said, "let Jo tell you."

"I'm Pete's sister, Josephine."

After a stunned silence, Arthur laughed. "Little Ricky got first go, did he? Here, give me a kiss, my turn next."

Arthur put a hand on Jo's shoulder to pull her to him. Jo grabbed his hand and Arthur fell to his knees. His other hand vainly tried to slacken her grip on his fingers. Jo's foot came up. A beautifully placed kick, Rick thought. Jo's instep connected and Arthur curled up in a tight ball on the floor clutching himself and moaning.

"You want to try for the jackpot, Dennis?" Jo said.

"No thank you. Your demo with the soldiers yesterday made the point quite well."

"Did you need to be so rough on Arthur?" Rick said.

"When you've been to as many rallies as I have, you get to know the type. Anything in skirts is fair game. He'll be fine. He'll go after easier pickings now. We'll be friends, till next time he forgets. Let's go and see how Malcolm and the boys made out with his patient."

When Jo and Rick started to leave, Arthur sat, leaning against the wall.

"She knew she'd be safe with him, the little pouf. He couldn't do anything if he tried," Arthur said.

Rick flushed and clenched his fist, but Jo laughed.

"Sour grapes, Arthur. Rick's no more queer than you are, less maybe. He is a gentleman. He waits till he's invited, or at least till he's welcome. Come on, Rick."

They emerged into the early dawn light and started across the courtyard towards the stables. Todd stumbled out and rubbed his eyes. He yawned and turned to relieve himself against the stable wall.

"Todd. I told you to use the garde-robe," Jo said.

Todd turned, shook himself, and ran to Jo.

"Good morrow, Joe, Master Richard."

Jo ruffled Todd's hair and they walked into the stable arm in arm.

"Hi, you two," Chris said.

"How's your patient?" Rick said.

"He's fine, thanks," Malcolm said. "No fever to speak of. I'm about to check the wound. He passed a good night."

Chris wandered out of the stables and, when Todd followed him, Jo said: "Malcolm, I'm Pete's sister, not his brother. I'm a girl."

Malcolm grinned. "So Joe wasn't short for Joseph. What do we do now, Rick? Hello, what's happened to Arthur?"

They turned when Dennis and Arthur came in. Arthur walked as if his legs wanted a divorce.

"The shock of finding that Jo was a girl went right to my vital parts. And I forgot the little display she laid on yesterday," Arthur grinned ruefully. "It's criminal to teach girls judo. Where the hell did you learn to fight, Jo? Girl's borstal?"

"No. A much tougher school. I was at an all-girl boarding school for years."

"Rick, you tell the boys," Malcolm said, "then we'll discuss our next move."

With a sigh, Rick moved out of the stable.

Rick will look after the kids, he thought, nothing changes.

"Chris, Todd, come here," Rick called. "I need to talk to you."

"We were going to see if we could scrounge some food," Chris said.

"I've something to tell you, boys. Just between us, not to be passed out of our group. Understand?"

"Sure, fine," Chris said, and Todd only nodded.

"Joe's a girl. She's Pete's sister."

"Right. Can we go and scrounge some food now?" Chris said.

"I know," Todd said.

"How could you know, Todd?" Rick said.

"I felt her up, when she was asleep the night before last. I wasn't going to let anyone make any moves on me, and she kept touching me and patting me. I wondered."

"Come on, Todd," Chris said. "Let's go."

Rick shook his head and rejoined the others.

"Well, what do you suggest," Malcolm said. "You're the storyteller."

"We wait till after the funeral. Then I'll try to talk to Margaret, Lady Eleanor's lady-in-waiting."

"The one that took a shine to you?" Malcolm said.

"What's the story?" Arthur said.

"Jo is Pete's sister. She travelled dressed as a boy for safety. We all knew, but didn't say till we were sure how things were here. We may have to place Jo under Lady Eleanor's protection."

"What would that mean?" Jo said.

"Dressing as a girl, behaving properly." Arthur jeered. "No more assaults on innocent bystanders who look sideways at you. How's your embroidery?"

"Fine, as a matter of fact. How's yours?"

Chapter Twenty-Two

They had washed to the best of their ability when the sergeant called them together.

"We will move out soon. I have horses for you, masters."

Sir Harold strode across the courtyard to them.

"How is the huntsman, Master Malcolm?"

"He is doing well, Sire."

"Good. Good. I may see him when we return."

"My Lord, may I speak?" Rick said, and at Sir Harold's nod went on. "We appreciate your consenting to Pete's burial. It is most gracious of you. May I suggest that Master Gerald need not accompany us?"

"No, master, you may not."

"But, Sire. We don't wish to humiliate Master Gerald or further antagonise him."

"I have spoken. It has nothing to do with you. He dishonoured my house by his act. To send a soul unshriven into the beyond, except in the heat of battle, is dishonourable. Do you and your group forgive him the act itself?"

Rick hesitated. "No Sire. We do not."

"Sergeant. Are all assembled?"

"Yes, Sire."

"Inform Master Gerald and the priest. Mount up."

A groom made stirrups of his hands and heaved Malcolm and

Rick in turn onto their mounts.

"You all right up there, Rick?" Chris laughed. "I didn't know you could ride."

"Slack off your reins," Jo said, and moved to the horse's head.

"What the hell do I hang onto, if I slack the reins?"

Jo laughed. "You sit relaxed. I'll lead him. Nobody'll gallop off today."

She fondled the horse's head, and it nuzzled her as she led it through the inner gate.

The group assembled was the same as those who had been at the circle two days before. The soldiers lifted a plain wooden coffin to their shoulders when Sir Harold appeared. The priest stood at the head of the column with the captain, and a barefoot figure, in a plain brown robe tied round the waist with a length of rope, stood behind them.

Sir Harold moved to the head of the column, and the sergeant indicated that Rick and Malcolm should ride behind him. Jo shook her head and stayed with Rick's horse when the sergeant said the others should fall in behind the horses. The procession wound slowly from the castle gate to the town gate. Curious townspeople stopped their early morning activities to watch them pass.

They paused before they forded the river. Rick leaned forward to speak to Jo, and almost slid off the horse. He grabbed for the saddle.

"I'm fine, Rick. I'll be okay up at the circle. Just don't you fall off your horse."

Rick glanced back. "Some penitent. Look at his face."

When they approached the circle, the wind blowing toward them carried the sweetly sickening smell of death; the smell of a body decomposing.

Jo shivered and moved to place Rick's horse between her and the circle.

Sir Harold reined in his horse, and the company stopped.

"Sergeant, you may proceed. Master Gerald will assist."

Gerald glared at Sir Harold. His look was full of venom.

"Come, Brother Gerald. It was your haste that led us to this. You will help."

The soldiers heaved the pole out of the ground, and Gerald, disgust plain on his face, helped lower the body to the ground.

"Someone must hold the body while the pole is removed," the sergeant said. "Perhaps you and the priest would hold him, Master Gerald?"

Gerald's fierce look, Rick thought, would have cowed many men, but the sergeant smiled.

Rigor mortis was well past, and the body flopped like a rag doll. Rick noticed the crows had been at the head. The bitter taste of bile flooded his mouth and he swallowed hard. Jo stared at the ground trembling but did not look up after one quick glance. Rick hoped she had not seen Pete's face too clearly. It would stay in his dreams for some time to come.

Stony faced, Arthur watched the proceedings, his scowl fixed on Master Gerald, his hand clutching and unclutching his dagger handle. Dennis was almost green, swaying slightly. Todd edged closer for a better view, but Chris, after dashing to the edge of the circle to be sick, backed up to Rick's horse and held Rick's ankle. Malcolm sat impassive on his horse staring blank-eyed into the distance.

At a snap of the fingers from Sir Harold, the soldiers hurried forward with the coffin. The Priest and Gerald with some difficulty lifted Pete's flaccid, uncooperative body into the coffin. A soldier nailed the lid down. Heads bowed, the group waited while the Priest said two prayers. Four soldiers hoisted the coffin onto their shoulders and the procession started back down the hill through the wood to the ford and the town trail.

They did not turn in at the town gate, but continued past, on a path parallel to the wall.

About quarter of a mile farther they came to a cemetery. Two labourers, leaning on their shovels when the procession arrived, touched their forelocks to Sir Harold and crossed themselves when the coffin passed them.

They placed the coffin on two boards spanning the grave. Sir Harold dismounted, and Rick and Malcolm quickly followed his example; Rick much less gracefully than the other two.

The priest intoned the words of committal while the soldiers lowered the coffin into the grave.

"Sir Priest." Jo stepped forward. "You have not said anything of absolution and you have not spoken my brother's name."

"Young sir, the Lord already knows his name and state of grace."

"I want to hear the words, Father. My brother was murdered in broad daylight for no reason. I will not have his immortal soul damned for ever, that would be like murdering him twice."

"Joe, masses will be said for the repose of your brother's soul, daily, for as long as the priest feels it necessary to ensure your brother's passage through purgatory," Sir Harold said. "A requiem will be sung on the morrow. Gerald will pay for the masses."

"There should be a stone bearing my brother's name."

"It shall be. At Gerald's cost."

"Peter Thomas D'Arcy of Oxford should be on his stone, with the date of his death. Age twenty-one years and four months."

Jo knelt at the graveside, crossed herself and threw a handful of earth onto the coffin lid. Each of the others in turn cast earth into the grave.

Sir Harold, impatient now, remounted. Malcolm and Rick again in the saddle, Sir Harold nodded curtly at them and cantered off. On impulse, Rick held out a hand to Jo, who promptly pulled herself up behind Rick. She pulled herself hard against Rick, and whispered: "Put the reins in my hands. You hang onto the saddle and grip tight with your knees."

At a flick of the reins, the horse cantered off after Sir Harold. Having Jo cling to him as she was doing was very pleasant, but the movement of the horse under him and the feeling he was about to fall off at any instant, Rick found decidedly less pleasing.

In the courtyard, Jo sprang from the horse unaided, but Rick more or less slid to the ground.

"So much for a girl's dreams of a knight racing to her rescue on a charger," Jo said. "You'd be more comfortable on a bike."

"That's the first time I've ever been on one of those damned beasts. The first time in years I've been so close to a horse." The horse whinnied. "Oh, shut up. Don't you laugh too."

Malcolm cantered in and swung off his mount.

"We'll need to teach Rick to ride properly," Jo said.

Rick rubbed his rump.

"I've got to see if I can get to speak to Margaret on her own, to explain about you, Jo. I'm not really sure whether in this age I can be alone with her."

After some searching, Rick located the seneschal and asked him if he could arrange a private meeting. The seneschal smiled, winked at Rick, and touched his forefinger to the side of his nose.

"The Lady Margaret has so far managed to avoid any marriage plans since her husband-to-be, arranged by her parents before they died, died himself in France. I will do what I can. Wait here."

In a short time the seneschal returned.

"The Lady Margaret will meet with you in the chapel, Master. She will have a maid with her. She says you should have a page with you. The maid and the page can stand in plain sight, but out of earshot."

Rick ran to get Jo and they both hurried to the chapel.

Margaret and the maid stood inside the door.

"Joe, you will wait here with Martha. Master, we can talk in the Lady Chapel. Come." Margaret took Rick's arm and led him across the chapel.

"Well, what is so important we had to meet in this fashion? Sir Harold was very angry when he returned from the burial. Poor Lady Gwenne made some comment, and he snarled at her. Something about Lady Gwenne's idiot husband, Sir Harold's imbecile brother, choosing to kill, in that fashion, a man with a name. He wondered why such a man would be foot soldier to a doctor. He was sure a great house must be involved. He actually damned Sir Gerald!"

"We are not quite what we appear to be, but we do hold Sir Harold and Lady Eleanor in high regard. They have been good to us and have nothing to fear from us or ours, I do assure you. I sought this meeting on another matter. I must explain: Jo is Pete's sister, not his brother. She travelled with us, dressed as a page for her protection. With her brother dead, and us here for some time, it may become difficult."

"Joe is a girl?" Margaret studied Jo and Martha at the chapel door. "Yes, now you say it, I can see the possibility."

She stood silent and thoughtful for some time.

"I will talk to Lady Eleanor. We could perhaps have Jo as a maid?"

Rick shook his head and Margaret frowned.

"No, I agree, perhaps a lady-in-waiting?"

Margaret strode to the entrance and said: "Come, Jo. We must find Lady Eleanor."

Interlude One

Rick's Journal

Day Three

Sir Harold's scribes reluctantly parted with some of the precious supplies of parchment and ink they had prepared for themselves, but only after a direct order. Quills I had to sharpen for myself from goose feathers. So now I am all ready to start my journal. What date should I put on it?

This is surely Autumn, Fall. Richard II is on the throne so it's after July of 1377. The Savoy Palace burnt down in June of 1381. The peddler today implied that the palace was still intact, so it's before December of 1380. I suppose we'll find out soon enough.

If I'm right, it's strange the marchers in our home time were protesting the imposition of the poll tax – a flat tax per head simply for being alive – and here we are on the eve of the biggest poll tax protest of all time: the Peasants' Revolt.

By dinner today attitudes had changed. Lady Eleanor and her ladies did not appear. Nor did Jo. Sir Harold was rather formal and stuffy, and after dinner in the solar, he and Lady Eleanor confronted us.

In their story, Pete was a younger son of minor landed gentry owing allegiance to my father's house. His parents, or mine, had assigned him as companion to me. I was the bastard son of a nobleman. Jo was in danger and was with us on our travels disguised as a boy.

Groups such as ours were apparently not uncommon and would not excite too much attention. For Sir Harold, the clincher was that Jo could read and write, spoke French, and was obviously a lady. Although her judo exhibition raised some eyebrows, apparently some young ladies were trained in the arts of war. Even Chris's fights with Walter fitted their scenario. As my cousin, Chris, not accustomed to insults, had not been able to sustain the role of low born servant when Walter offended him. Malcolm is my doctor, appointed by my father to supervise my wanderings. Poor Arthur and Dennis are still mercenary guards.

Is our real story any more believable? Theirs at least is home grown and fits the facts as they see them.

Sir Harold said rather frigidly that he would not press for the names of our families. He would, until we chose to confide in him, assume the wardship of the Lady Jo, and guard our secret. I assured him we trusted him implicitly, and our problem would in no way involve him in any conflict with any great house or person. This satisfied him, or at least he nodded.

As promised, he had the physician's house prepared for us. He dispatched us with the major-domo and the seneschal to see the house and settle in. Jo and Todd stayed at the castle.

The house is typical of this time. A wood frame filled with wattle-and-daub. The ground level is one large room with a beaten earth floor. A loft room, reached by a rough wooden ladder, extends halfway across the house. In the centre of the main room is a hearth slab with a hole in the roof directly above it. The servants swept up the old rushes which smelled of damp and droppings – Chris was horrified to see beetles and other insects flee across the earth floor thus exposed. They sprinkled some water on the floor to kill the dust, swept the loft room through the spaces between the boards and over the edge, swept the main room out through the front and rear doors, and laid fresh rushes. The furnishings are standard for the time: a rough wooden trestle table, some stools, a backless bench, and a few iron pots and ladles hanging on one wall.

When our eyes became accustomed to the gloom, we saw a large wooden chest on wood blocks to keep it off the ground. A second chest stood on end on what could be a crude, campaign desk.

The chest on the floor held clothes about Malcolm's size. The second chest opened into two halves. In one half was a collection of iron implements, each item lovingly wrapped in oiled linen; several small pottery mortars, one iron mortar; and a variety of pottery and iron pestles. The other side contained a range of glass bottles and vials, each carefully labelled in Latin.

Malcolm, for once, had no immediate comment.

He examined the chest in silence, and told us it was an apothecary/surgeon's chest and one of these in this condition in our time would be worth a fortune. I would suspect it is probably worth a lot right now, and I'm surprised it's still here.

The back door opens out into a paddock. All overgrown now, but Malcolm thinks it may have been the physician's herb garden.

We returned to the castle for supper, and the major-domo oversaw the issue of some provisions for us. When we were about to leave, the seneschal appeared with a young woman, Mary, and a small boy, Robert; servants. Arthur objected furiously. He didn't want us to have servants, but Malcolm overruled him and we returned to our house. I noticed, objections or not, the boy and young woman carried Arthur's share of our load of provisions.

Arthur thinks I'm stupid not to know what day and date it is, but it's not all at simple. He says we should ask, but we're strange enough already, without appearing stupid too.

Malcolm grumbles when I waste one of our few candles on my scribblings. Chris is already sound asleep in the loft room. Malcolm and I will sleep there with him. Dennis and Arthur have chosen to sleep in the main room where the servants will also sleep.

Day Four
I wakened this morning to Arthur's curses, and thought the place was on fire. Mary or Robert had lit the fire and the place was full of smoke. I don't know what Arthur was so mad about; the main floor wasn't bad, but the attic where we slept was thick with choking fumes. Gradually, as the fire caught, the smoke cleared.

Day Seven
Today is a Sunday. We heard the town church bell toll and when we asked Mary why, she said it was for Sunday mass. I dragged everyone out to mass. It is important we should not be seen to be too different.

Immediately mass was over, Mary and Robert scurried back to the house. We took a more leisurely walk around the town. It's not big. It takes about half-an-hour, I think, to walk round the wall. It's odd. I don't remember that our town ever had a wall.

The meals Mary prepares are adequate, but certainly don't match the castle kitchen.

Monday, Day Eight
We made a mistake the past few days. We spent them at our house and around the town, so as not to impose ourselves on the castle. After dinner today, a messenger arrived from the castle commanding our attendance at supper. Sir Harold made it very clear he expected his physician to present himself at the castle each day. We should also have been at mass in the castle chapel. Oh well, we live and learn. Malcolm, Chris and I, at least, are to be at

the castle for supper unless explicitly excused.

Monday, Day Fifteen

Today, the seneschal summoned us to dinner at the castle and mummers and players appeared after. That was most unusual for dinner. Jo says it's All Hallows Eve, October thirty-first. It was strange to see adults duck for apples in a wooden tub. Even Sir Harold took part. When Gerald's turn came, his brother crept up behind him and pushed his head under water. When Gerald surfaced I'm sure if it had been anyone else but Sir Harold, All Hallows' Eve or not, there would have been bloodshed. No one dared laugh, except Chris and Todd.

All sorts of bizarre and macabre stories were told this afternoon, but come dark everyone was shut up safe indoors, and wouldn't have opened up for anyone. We had supper at home for once in order to be indoors by sunset.

Tuesday, November 1, All Saints' Day

Arthur intends to build a fireplace of stone. Apparently, he suffers from bronchitis. The smoke is bad for him.

He and Dennis were out tonight when we got back from the castle. We were late. This being All Saints Day, there were fires lit in various places. Sir Harold even allowed one lit in the outer ward.

Chris and Todd were out with the children of the town. They went from house to house singing,

> *Soul, Soul for a soul cake,*
> *Pray, Mistress for a soul cake.*

The women gave them tiny cakes baked specially for this day. The cakes remain uneaten till tomorrow, All Souls Day. Walter was very scornful of Chris for running with the children, but Chris ignored him. Sir Harold was not pleased to hear Todd had been begging cakes in the town streets. Obviously, a member of his household should not take part in these public events. Jo interceded and Sir Harold laughed when Todd, miming the penitent in search of absolution, offered Sir Harold a tithe of the soul cakes.

I had to explain to Chris that a tithe was a tenth part, and the church taught that is was your duty to hand over to the church a tenth of your income. Chris was appalled at the very idea.

Wednesday, November 2, All Souls' Day
Arthur and Dennis arrived back well into the night. Feeling no pain by the sound of it. Shortly before dawn there was some sort of commotion outside, and a thud against the wall, a thud that shook the house. When Chris went out to the street at dawn, he found a huge flat stone leaning against the wall.

Neither Arthur nor Dennis was a cheerful companion this morning. Their language when the church bells tolled for the souls of the town's people departed this life was a bit ripe. Dennis looked positively green when Chris offered him some soul cakes. Robert and Chris tucked into them.

With much swearing and bad temper Arthur and Dennis finally managed to manhandle the slab into the house and into a hole they had dug for it against one wall. It was, at last, levelled to Arthur's satisfaction. That done, they took off with the neighbour's donkey.

Thursday, November 10
We've been here a little short of four weeks. Malcolm, Chris, and I have settled into a routine.

In the mornings Malcolm sees patients either at our house, or at their homes. Chris and I are usually with him. I'm the assistant, and to my surprise I'm actually learning some medicine. Dinner we have at home at the usual time here, around ten a.m. In the afternoon we go to the castle. There, Malcolm sees any of the castle residents who might need his attention, and otherwise we spend the afternoon much as the other gentry do.

I have started to teach Todd and Chris French and Latin, and Todd arithmetic. Sir Harold discovered this and added Walter to my class. He is not a willing pupil.

Wednesday, November 16

Arthur had managed to charm mortar out of the local masons, as well as the hearthstone. He and Dennis had collected stones and finally thought they had enough to start building. Chris was keen to help, but there really wasn't enough room for three to place stones. So he and Robert washed and sorted the stones, and under Dennis's watchful eye mixed mortar. Today the chimney reached the thatch and Arthur cut a hole through.

The fireplace finished, Arthur closed off the other smoke hole and we had a ceremonial fire lighting. It draws well, and it will be a relief not to have the house filled with smoke all day, every day.

Monday, November 21

Shortly before dawn a noise wakened me. Chris lay on his face, and squirmed, at the edge of the loft floor. At first I thought to ignore it. If he's at that stage, there's little enough privacy. However, it was obvious some article or action below had his attention, and I moved to see what it was. My movement wakened Malcolm too, but Chris, engrossed, didn't hear us.

In plain view on the floor below was Arthur and Mary locked together.

"Christ. The bugger is raping the girl."

Malcolm swung out onto the ladder and down.

At Malcolm's shout and sudden appearance, Arthur and Mary pulled apart. Mary scrambled to her feet and pulled her shift down. She quickly slipped her robe over her head, walked over to where Robert lay, and with a prod of her toe told him to get up and tend the fire.

Arthur laughed at first, but became angry in response to Malcolm's anger. They stopped short of blows. Malcolm accused Arthur of rape, and he said Malcolm was jealous. Mary set about her chores and ignored both of them. Malcolm stormed out and did not return until dinner.

This afternoon, after my class, Chris and Todd ran off, and I could see them, heads together, giggling on the ramparts.

After supper, in the solar, I talked to Jo. I was shocked. Jo had heard of this morning's incident from Todd and laughed.

"Rick you're a real innocent and a prude to boot. Arthur wouldn't be Mary's first by a long shot, nor her last. She's at least seventeen and has been in the castle as a bondservant since she was thirteen. It's the way life is here."

Jo puzzles me. After her speech, I must have smiled. She said: "Just wipe that grin off your face, Rick. I've no intention of getting into bed with you or any of the others. What happens with the poor bond servants and serfs is one thing, but the quickest way for us to drop to their level would be for me to behave as they do."

When we reached home I overheard Robert ask Chris what all the fuss was about. It happened all the time with servants in the great hall and hallways at night. He, Robert, had watched Arthur and Mary every morning since the first day in the house.

Monday, November 28

The fireplace does not impress all of our visitors. The most common comment is, it will be hard to store fish and meat, which usually hang from the rafters and become smoked more or less in the constant wood smoke. Arthur had ignored such comments for a while. Today, however, it got through to him and he stamped out in a temper.

He was back quite soon and sat at the fireplace apparently entranced by the flickering flames for a long time.

Tuesday, November 29
Arthur is at it again. He and Dennis, with Chris in tow, vanished early this morning. By noon they were back with timber. They are building in the paddock, but won't say what. They cleared an area, and dug a trench about two feet wide and six feet long by about six inches deep and have erected an A-frame over it.

Thursday, December 1
The A-frame is complete. They actually used very expensive planking, sealed the gaps with mud daub, and left only a small vent all along the top of the frame. This they covered with a plank roof ridge with a gap of about an inch all along between the roof ridge and the A-frame proper. Chris could not keep quiet any longer and announced they had built a smokehouse.

Friday, December 2
Chris isn't so keen on the smokehouse today. Arthur had him gut fish to smoke. He had been to the harbour soon after the fishermen returned and had bought a load of fish.

Monday, December 5
The smell of smoking fish has tantalised us since Friday. Arthur today declared them ready, and much to Chris's annoyance said he would get more fish tomorrow. In the meantime Chris and Robert were sent to chop more of the oak into the size Arthur decreed necessary for the smoking process.

The fish were a huge success. Malcolm insisted we present the first lot to Sir Harold, and we had smoked fish served as part of supper tonight. Arthur and Dennis were there, the first time at supper in the castle for ages.

Monday, December 12
Arthur has been smoking everything he could lay his hands on. He and Malcolm had a row when Arthur announced his intention of lowering our street shutter to sell the smokies. Malcolm gave in finally.

None of Malcolm's patients find it the least bit odd to have Arthur selling fish on the other side of the screen behind which Malcolm sees them. The fish sell exceptionally well. We are making money hand over fist.

The castle people Malcolm sees, of course, and the town notables have him call on them. Many pay cash, but others pay in goods or services. Although, much to Arthur's annoyance, Malcolm will treat even those who cannot pay, between Arthur's enterprises and Malcolm's practice we have paid back the seneschal and the major-domo, and are laying some money aside.

Tuesday, December 20
I knew it was too good to last. The Fishmongers Guild has complained to Sir Harold of Arthur's activities. Arthur is to appear at the Manor Court tomorrow, or rather *we* are.

Wednesday, December 21, 1379
It is 1379. I saw the Court title on the clerk's parchment,

"...held on Wednesday this twenty-first day of December in the Second Year of the reign of Our Sovereign Lord, King Richard II."

I had forgotten most documents would use regnal years. I had cursed the convention heartily as a student of medieval documents.

My head still spins from the wine after supper at the castle.

In the Manor Court, Sir Harold himself heard the fishmongers' case and not the seneschal who often presides for him.

The fishmongers simply said they had a monopoly and that we

were breaking the tradition. End of case.

I argued that the fishmongers most certainly had a monopoly to sell fresh fish to the public. However, Arthur and Dennis did not sell fresh fish, but smoked fish, a different item altogether. The fish they had smoked were surplus to the requirements of the Fishmongers Guild and the fishermen would have dumped them overboard. I called the head of the Fisherman's Guild and he testified their sales to the fishmongers had not declined. Arthur and Dennis were smoking extra fish.

Sir Harold thought for some time before he ruled the Fishmongers' Guild did indeed have the exclusive right to sell fish, all fish regardless of its state, to the public. The fishmongers looked very smug. They were congratulating each other when Sir Harold cleared his throat, and went on to grant our group the exclusive right to smoke fish commercially. The fishmongers would need to buy the smoked fish from us. It had become very popular.

After supper the seneschal privately suggested he would find the money to allow the group to build a larger curing shed or a series of smaller sheds for a percentage of the profit. Arthur asked for time to consider the offer. He and Dennis went off to drink with the sergeant, while Malcolm, Chris and I joined Sir Harold in the solar.

Saturday, December 24, 1379, Christmas Eve

Over the last few days, there has been a steady stream of arrivals at the castle. The weather has been cold and dry, so the roads are passable. The castle is crammed to capacity. Some of the retainers of guests lodge in temporary canvas-covered lean-to structures in the outer ward.

Arthur vanished this morning after dawn as he has done regularly since Wednesday. When he returned at dinner, he announced the Fisherman's Guild would be part of a co-operative to smoke fish. They would accept the seneschal's money, and the use of the land near the harbour belonging to the Manor, and build several curing sheds. If Malcolm wanted to, he could chip in too. Much to my surprise, Arthur offered me a share of the enterprise in my own right, if I would set up the constitution and rules of the co-operative and keep their books.

I suggested one of the town lawyers might be better, but Arthur assured me lawyers were not at all popular and both he and the fishermen would prefer me. He rather spoilt the effect and reduced my swollen head, when he went on to say I would be cheaper and easier to supervise.

"If you try anything, I'll kick the effing shit out of you," he ended.

I have some time to work matters out. No work or business will be done in the twelve days of Christmas.

Thursday, December 29, 1379

Today, we had some respite from the holiday festivities.

The supper on Christmas Eve was restrained. It was a fast day, so there was no red meat, but plenty of fish, plus our smokies, and fowl, plus fruit pies as dessert. After supper, everyone took part in decorating the great hall and in the ceremonial lighting of the Yule Log.

The feast after the morning mass on Christmas Day was spectacular. The menu included: hare and rabbit; roast goose and chicken; roast beef; pork, venison and savoury pies of all sorts. Jellies, fruits in syrup, fruit pies and tarts, and cakes followed, all accompanied with copious quantities of ale. Chris and Todd made little pigs of themselves. By the end of the meal the noise was incredible.

Servants cleared the tables, took them apart, and stacked them along the walls.

Two of the garrison put on a mock fight, while everyone sat on the benches, burping and, exhausted with eating, leaned back against the walls and the stacked tables.

After their fight, they challenged the audience to find a champion. Much to my alarm, Malcolm lurched to his feet and into the centre of the hall. Drunk or not, Malcolm was remarkably light on his feet and fought like a trained swordsman. His opponent made mistakes and Malcolm disarmed him. Malcolm bowed to acknowledge the cheers, then slumped exhausted. Before he fell asleep, he muttered: "Not quite like sabres at the varsity fencing club, but close enough."

Somewhat rested, the guests played Hoodman Blind. It was a riotous version of the game Blindman's Buff, roughly played, even with Sir Harold as 'It'.

While the guests rested and caught their breath, they listened to the minstrels' ballads. When they retired, a pipe and tabor started and the guests danced and sang. In the middle of this, the mummers arrived. When they finished their play a cry went up: "Clear the Hall. To the walls. To the walls."

We all lurched out of the great hall and in a long chain, like a group dancing the conga, wound our way out of the hall, through the inner ward and inner gate, out to the outer wall, and up onto the wall walk. It was a minor miracle no one fell off the unguarded walk into the outer ward. As it was, I'm sure there would be many bruises next day. Somewhat sobered by the exercise and the cold, the company wound its way back to the great hall.

When we stumbled back in, the tables were set for supper, and it all started again.

The succeeding days were, fortunately, somewhat lower key. Guests played games like chess, draughts, and backgammon – games brought back to England by men returning from the Crusades – or simply talked or dozed between dinner and supper. After supper, minstrels performed. Yesterday a hunt set out shortly after dawn, and returned only an hour or so before supper. Sir

Harold asked me to read for the company after supper, between performances by the minstrels. The audience was very appreciative, although Arthur said it was only because after the hunt everyone was too tired to throw anything.

We have slept at the house each night, or at least Chris and I have. Arthur, Dennis and Malcolm have been less regular. I commented on this to Jo. Her reply was not very helpful. She said that not everyone was cut out to be a monk. If only she knew, my thoughts about her are decidedly not monkish, but I cannot see myself in the one-night stands the others enjoy, and despite Arthur's jokes I have no designs on or desire for Chris or Todd.

Thursday, January 5, 1380, Twelfth Night
Another big blow-out at the castle and Christmas is over. We arrived home tired. Mary and Robert were with us for the first time since Christmas Day. It hasn't been much of a holiday for the castle servants. They were on the trot from before dawn till long after sunset. I hadn't really considered Robert before. He can't be more than nine, but we gave no thought to how he worked for us. I suppose he's better off here with us than most others. When I said this to Jo, she scolded me and said: "Mary works harder than Robert, and you haven't given her a second thought."

I had to speak to Todd about Robert. Chris had spotted Robert a couple of days ago and had stopped to talk to him. Todd tugged Chris's sleeve.

"Come on Chris, he's only a servant, a slavey."

He was quite crestfallen when I pointed out to him that not so long ago he was in an even lower class than Robert, and he, of all of us, should have some understanding. He's only nine or ten too, and Jo is desperately trying to raise his sights and status.

Malcolm says I'm suffering from post festivity depression.

Tuesday, January 10, 1380
We held a council meeting at the house this morning. Somehow, Arthur and Dennis have managed to persuade the Masons' Guild and the Woodworkers' Guild to allow them to do the tests for admission as masters. They want to pay the substantial guild fees out of our communal war chest, hence, the council. I think we should consult with Jo. She is, after all, one of us, even if she does live at the castle. After some argument, we agreed it was to the advantage of all for Arthur and Dennis to be Guild members. Should we fall out of favour at the castle the guilds would be a good backup. They have some degree of influence and independence, especially the masons.

Wednesday, January 11, 1380
Jo agreed we should pay the Guild fees communally, and even suggested we should apprentice Robert and Chris to Dennis and Arthur as an added protection. The idea excites Chris and Robert. Robert, of course, sees it as a high road out of the servant class, and Chris, if we are here for life, will need some way to earn his daily bread. We'll see, when, and if, Arthur and Dennis become masters in the Guild.

Wednesday, January 18, 1380
Malcolm and Jo have been teaching me to ride, under the pretext of instructing Chris and Todd. I must admit the boys both learn a lot faster than I do, but I can now ride quite competently and am not likely to make a fool of myself as I almost did at Pete's funeral.

Today, for the first time, Sir Harold invited us to join the hunt. Todd was not at first included since the ladies were not hunting. To my surprise, I saw Todd behave more like his age than the miniature adult he usually plays. He pouted and stamped and almost, but not quite, cried. Jo led him off by one ear, and he did yowl at that. When they came back, Jo said she would dispense with his services for one day, if the gentlemen would guarantee to take care of him. I know Jo wanted us to say no, but neither Malcolm nor I could resist the appeal in Todd's eyes.

The hunt was very interesting and in Sir Harold's view successful. Personally, I could take it or leave it. Malcolm says it is not quite fox hunting, but he thoroughly enjoyed himself.

We started with hawking and after a fair number of birds had been caught, a forester had word of deer, and we were off. The chase really was exciting, but when the hunters brought down the first deer I rather lost interest.

Malcolm and Sir Harold had a conversation of which I only caught snatches. Malcolm later told me he had assured Sir Harold that we had both hunted before and had been blooded. Todd dismounted when told to and approached the deer. To my horror I saw it kick and struggle when the huntsman grasped its head to expose the throat. Todd drew his dagger and placed it against the neck. When he thrust the blade in to sever the artery, Todd smiled at Walter. Incredibly, there was a smattering of applause and a few bravos. The huntsman placed a hand in the spurting blood and smeared some on Todd's forehead and cheeks.

Instead of remounting at once, Todd stood for a second, and shifted from foot to foot before he walked over to Sir Harold, who had remained mounted, grasped his ankle, and gazed up at him. Sir Harold smiled and bent over in the saddle, one hand on Todd's head. They exchanged words no one could overhear. Master Gerald and Walter looked at each other and both scowled. There was a significant event here; some custom of the time perhaps that escaped me.

"The next one is yours, Christopher," Sir Harold called, and we cantered off, leaving some men behind to dress the deer.

We finally brought a second deer down. Chris was pale, and his hand shook when he cut its throat and had its blood smeared on his face. Sir Harold looked inquiringly at Chris, but only said: "Well done, boy," when Chris turned to remount.

On our arrival back at the castle, the blood on Todd's face upset Jo. At first, she thought he was hurt, but when she learned from a very excited Todd what had actually happened, she was furious with us. Malcolm tried to pacify her, saying she must have been blooded riding to hounds. Her reply was most unladylike.

We could hear Todd and Jo argue about his washing before supper while she led him off.

At supper, Todd had at least partially won his case. There was still a smear of blood on his forehead. Chris, face completely cleaned, scowled at me when Todd came into the great hall.

A deer's head was carried in on a platter and placed before Sir Harold who rose and walked round the table, collecting Todd as he went. In front of the table, at the edge of the dais with one hand on Todd's shoulder, he waited until the hall grew quiet.

"In this demesne," he said, "I, and only I, or one with me, may hunt the King's deer and live. Today, two boys were blooded at the hunt, Christopher, cousin and page to Master Richard, and Todd, page to Lady Jo of Oxford of My Lady Eleanor's household."

There was some scattered applause.

"There are those who say a base born such as Todd has no right to be blooded like a gentleman at my hunt. He is about the age of my son who died last spring..." Sir Harold paused, and crossed himself. He went on: "I, and only I, will say who has any rights here, and what those rights may be, but to make matters clear before this company, I declare Todd a freeman of this realm, and name him, for his minority, my personal ward. I accept his oath of fealty, made and accepted, freely and gladly, at my stirrup today in the forest."

Sir Harold kissed Todd on both cheeks and they returned to their places in a hubbub of conversation and speculation.

In the solar after supper, Master Gerald put in only a token appearance and Todd was unbearable. Walter stayed in the shadows and moved only when Sir Harold spoke to him.

Tuesday, January 24, 1380
Arthur and Dennis were out all day at their tests. They were both, for them, effusive when we got home after supper. The test had gone well, they thought. I could hardly get them to stop talking long enough to tell them my news.

Sir Harold's secretary is old and feeble. A new clerk, sent by the Bishop to replace him, is not to Sir Harold's taste. He has asked me. It is most unusual for a secretary not to be a priest in holy orders, but it is equally unusual to discover a layman who reads English, French and Latin, and knows his arithmetic. I have accepted, of course.

Wednesday, January 25, 1380
They passed! There's to be a Guild Feast next week and they'll be formally admitted to the Masons' Guild as Master Builders.

My job doesn't please Malcolm. He says it ties too many of us too closely to the castle. Strange; he and Arthur for once agree and have ganged up on me. Jo thinks I'm right to accept and Todd, the complete snob, is enchanted. Chris and Dennis have not offered any opinions, although Chris did shrug and say he supposed it was up to me. Very gracious of him, I'm sure.

Tuesday, January 31, 1380
This is a little different from what I expected. I have two full time scribes to call on. They do the actual final drafts. I draft letters and documents and check the final product before it goes to Sir H. for signature. I attend meetings with S.H. and take notes; minutes I suppose. Thank God for shorthand, and for my ability to remember a lot verbatim.

S.H. is pleased so far at how good my notes are, but there is some reserve. Several times since I started, he was on the point of speaking then stopped. Yesterday he asked me what I knew of Wycliffe's teachings, but stopped me before I could answer beyond saying I knew his publication 'Civil Dominion'. Today he asked my opinion of Wycliffe's thesis. When I said I understood his doctrine to be a philosophical and theological theory rather than a political concept, S.H. smiled and said he had chosen well, that Lady Eleanor and Lady Jo had advised well.

With S.H. quizzing me about Wycliffe, I've been thinking a lot about the hedge priest John Ball. He was made a peasant priest by John Wycliffe, but he seems to have gone way beyond Wycliffe's ideas for a reform of the church. I can't remember just when he said:

Good people, things cannot go right in England and never will, until goods are held in common and there are no more villeins and gentlefolk, but we are all one and the same. In what way are those whom we call lords greater masters than ourselves? How have they deserved it? Why do they hold us in bondage? If we all spring from a single father and mother, Adam and Eve, how can they claim or prove that they are lords more than us, except by making us produce and grow wealth which they spend?

When Adam delved and Eve span,
Who was then the gentleman?

But I sure can see why Martin the sergeant was nervous when he overheard Arthur and thought we might be followers of the hedge priests. I must tell Arthur to try to tone down any like comments; statements such as John Ball's must make the lords and ladies very edgy.

Wednesday, February 1, 1380

It still isn't clear if S.H. supports Wycliffe or not. His questions could point either way, and my answers are ambiguous enough for him to take them as guarded support for whichever side he favours.

Malcolm and I got a quiet, private, but stinging tongue-lashing today. Two days ago, S.H. had one of the huntsmen who tends the dogs severely whipped. Today, he is far from well: a frequent, intermittent high fever, followed by shaking chills, and his back is very red and angry along the cuts. Malcolm had not been aware of the whipping at the time or he would have washed and dressed the wounds. He commented publicly on the matter and I agreed with him. S.H. swept out of the great hall, and minutes later a grinning Walter came to summon Malcolm and me to the solar. There, S.H. sent Chris and Walter away and glared at us in silence for the longest time.

Finally, he really tore us off a strip and ended: "You, Master Malcolm, are my physician, and as such, I value your advice when I ask for it. You, Master Richard, are my secretary, and I hope, my friend. A good secretary, but still a secretary. You are obviously of good family to dare speak critically of my action, but have a care. You have been discreet in all else; remain so."

We apologised, of course, and S.H., all affability again, had us drink wine with him.

"You are young men and much as I was when I was young. A physician, I suppose, like a priest should be compassionate, but also discreet. Let us forget the matter."

When we saw the huntsman before we left for the night he was worse. Malcolm fears septicaemia and there's not any action he can take for it now.

Thursday, February 2, 1380

Tomorrow night is the big guild dinner. I've got a surprise for Arthur. He dared me to write a ballad for him. I've cobbled together a piece that goes to the tune Greensleeves, more or less. I've taught the tune and the ballad to the minstrels who are to entertain. To my surprise, it pleased them, and I didn't even have to bribe them to sing it for me. A pity none of us will hear it except Arthur and Dennis. On second thoughts maybe it's just as well.

S.H. sent Walter and Chris out when I arrived today. He told me, in future, some correspondence, which he would designate, should be handled only by me or Bertram, the older scribe. This would be personal confidential material. Staring straight at me, S.H. said if there was any reason why I could not swear absolute personal fealty to him, I should declare it now. Nothing would change except that he would find another confidential secretary.

I hesitated and Sir Harold frowned. Hurriedly, I went to on to explain that my hesitation was not because I couldn't swear absolute fealty to him, but because I felt he deserved now to be told the truth about us.

He listened to my tale of us all meeting at the circle of standing stones, of the explosion, of us waking up stunned and confused in another time, with a look of puzzled disbelief. I faltered into silence.

Finally, he shook his head, crossed himself, and said: "I would tell no one else of this. It smacks too much of witchcraft. Yet I did puzzle over how a group such as yours could appear in my domain so close to my castle without my hearing of you as you travelled. No correspondence mentioned you. No roaming peddler spoke of you, yet your band would be noteworthy gossip. All strangers who cross my domain are noted."

He sat, his head bowed, his chin cupped in one hand, for a long time, before he shook himself. "I believe in many wonders," he said. "This is but one more. You are here. You are flesh and blood. We will talk further of this later. Will you swear fealty?"

So I took the oath of absolute fealty to Sir Harold swearing on his bible.

I wish now I hadn't written Arthur's ballad, or I'd written a different one. Oh well, no one will hear it except the guild members and they'll soon forget it.

The condition of the whipped huntsman has Malcolm very upset. He is now comatose and, Malcolm fears, close to death. Septicaemia for sure, Malcolm says, and without antibiotics blood poisoning is certainly fatal.

Friday, February 3, 1380
Noon: Not my usual time to write. They sent for Malcolm and I sometime before dawn. The huntsman was dying. We were with him when he died, at dawn, in the kennels with the dogs. Malcolm cried. Tears of rage and frustration rather than grief, but the priest and the other huntsmen didn't know that.

Malcolm raged at me in private on the wall walk. He sounded almost like Arthur in his denunciation of the rich and his anger at the abject condition of the majority, the poor. I tried to calm him down a bit before we met S.H.

S.H. did not help much. Our news didn't interest him; beyond the inconvenience of having to have someone else trained to care for the dogs. When Malcolm tried to go on, S.H. said obviously an ill humour had affected the man. It often happened after an injury, and invariably the victim died, no one could think the worse of Malcolm for it. Malcolm had cared well for the man. The priest was with him when he died to hear his last confession and give him absolution. What more could a man ask for? Very pointedly, S.H. indicated the audience was over, the matter closed.

Malcolm stormed off. S.H. commented he was of a very choleric humour and should perhaps have been a soldier rather than a physician.

Dismissed, I spent the morning with the ladies. Malcolm was nowhere to be seen and did not appear for dinner.

Evening: Malcolm is in the guardhouse. Not arrested, only asleep. When he left S.H. and me, about an hour and a half before dinner, he had gone to the cellar. The cellarer had given him some ale: "to lift his spirits, and to speed the departed soul on its way". One led to another, and Malcolm got gloriously, uproariously drunk.

Malcolm reportedly tumbled two serving wenches; not rape, thank God, since he'd been with both of them before. He challenged two gentlemen to a fight, and fought their grooms who tried to restrain him. Having won his fight, he finally arrived back at the cellar, where he got into one of S.H.'s good wines.

It had taken six soldiers to get him out of the cellar to the guardhouse, and there he now lay snoring gently, smiling peacefully.

Without delay when I heard, I went to see him, and tried to apologise to S.H. on his behalf. S.H. roared with laughter and finally, tears in his eyes, he asked the sergeant if his men had hurt Malcolm. The sergeant grinned and said there were some loose teeth on his side and doubtless some welts and bruises on both sides, but nothing that would require the attention of the physician. At this, both S.H. and the sergeant dissolved in peals of laughter. When he could talk again S.H. said: "Leave him to sleep it off. He is after all a man and not a saint. By *Corpus Dominus*, I wish I had seen him at his height."

S.H. *does* support Wycliffe. Letters he dictated today, one to Wycliffe himself, and another to a lord in London, are clearly supportive. I wonder if I should warn S.H. that Wycliffe will deny the doctrine of transubstantiation this year and will thereby lose most of his noble supporters, and that he will be more or less discredited after the Peasant's Revolt in '81. Can I? Should I? Dare I? I'll discuss it with Jo.

Malcolm, Chris and I have invitations to the guild banquet, but Malcolm is in no condition to appear.

Saturday, February 4, 1380

The banquet was a riotous success. Arthur and Dennis were carried home, and dropped without ceremony in our ground floor. Even I was glad I had Chris with me to steer the way. The ballad was surprisingly well received, but will, I hope, be soon forgotten.

ARTHUR'S BALLAD

A man of the people Arthur was,
A stalwart son of the soil.
In his own time he saw the strong
Oppress the poor who toil.

On common ground, from common folk
Fenced off, the Gateway stood.
Return the land to common use,
Said the group, in sombre mood.

Thunder sounded, lightning flashed,
The group was much dismayed.
The circle, long disused by Man,
Fatal power displayed.

The castle lookout saw the light
And crossed himself in fear.
The sun was fully in the sky
Before the guard drew near.

As long as there is sun by day
And sacred moon by night,
Arthur will not forgive the cause
Of that most dreadful sight.

His friend, his patron, stripped and spread,
Held face down on a stone,
While smiling Gerald watched the pole
And listened to Pete moan.

A man of the people Arthur was,
A stalwart son of the soil.
In his own time he saw the strong
Oppress the poor who toil.

Wednesday, February 8, 1380

Apart from a fierce hangover, Malcolm was none the worse for his escapade. His reputation, strangely, is enhanced rather than damaged.

Jo has been in retreat for most of the week. Tomorrow is the final requiem for Pete. There will be a big turnout. S.H. had me put out the word quietly that only those on some vital duty would be excused and there is to be a special dinner in honour of Pete's passage out of purgatory.

So far S.H. has not mentioned hearing the ballad, or of it. Somehow I don't think he would be amused. Gerald for sure wouldn't be. Well, perhaps it will die a quiet death.

Interlude Two

Arthur's Reverie

Shit. Nothing changes. The days of chivalry indeed. I remember reading stories when I was just a kid about knights in shining armour and damsels fair. God, how I loved them. What an age to live in, I thought then. The knights were like the cowboys who wore white in the old cowboy movies Pop used to bore me with. The villains all wore black. In those stories it was always black and white, never shades of grey. The white knight always won.

I used to think that sometime in the past it had all gone wrong. The world had somehow taken a wrong road. If only we could backtrack and find the fork, and change direction. Like resetting railway points.

If ever the world was right, and like the lovely stories, it sure as hell isn't now. Oh, sure, there's lords and ladies here, but, Christ, it's nothing like the stories. They never talked of how the people at the bottom lived, of the filth and squalor. They never mentioned the casual cruelty and how everyone accepts it. Not the calculated cruelty of the bastard Gerald ... that happens in all times, but the way everyone treats those below them. The children sold to beggars who mutilate them to wring an extra coin from the sentimental passer-by.

Sir Harold's like a Mafia don. The one in the flick Pop liked so much, The Grandfather? No, the frigging Godfather, that was it. Someone else did all the dirty work a generation or so ago, and he has fallen into it. He can afford to be My Lord. He doesn't have to fight himself or dirty his clean hands to maintain his status. His lieutenants and his button men do that for him. As he does, or has done, for the next one up the line. What was it Pop used to quote from the damned flick? *Capo del Capo*? The Boss of Bosses. The frigging king himself, so far removed and insulated from all the dirty work that he is clean. But Sir Harold had best watch his back. His brother, the bastard Gerald, he has his eye on Sir Harold's place, and given half a chance will take it.

Someday I'll kill Gerald. Slowly, from the front, so he sees it coming, and knows who's doing it and why.

Sir Harold is a different story. All he does, the law allows, but who in God's name made the laws? Who made these bastards gods? A flick of the wrist, a nod of the head from Sir Harold is enough to hang a man or have him flogged, for walking in a bloody wood!

Everything's done in due form and as the law allows. Masses are said for the souls of the dead, but who gives a shit for the living left behind?

Todd's a funny kid. Look at him standing proud beside his Lady Jo. Who could see in him now the lousy, stinking, scrawny kid that ran from a beating and broke his arm? He's still a little imp of hell, but now he has some skim of manners.

We'll make Rick one of us yet. He has a real sense of justice and injustice, if only he'd stop feeling sorry for the frigging nobs.

But Rick's right, damn him, on one count anyway. Someday I'll kill that bastard Gerald, but I could not kill Sir Harold in cold blood; in heat of battle maybe, but never in cold blood.

God. Will this mass never end? I hope Jo got some comfort out of them.

Christ. There's the pax at last. I'll go and visit with the sergeant, while Rick and Malcolm chat it up with the bloody nobs.

Interlude Three

Jo's Reverie

Pete, I should be praying for your soul, but if it's not at rest by now it never will be. Anyway, I'm all prayed out. What had you done to deserve such a death?

Damn your foolish altruism, your naïveté. You really thought everybody was as sincere as you. God, you were an easy mark for the likes of Arthur. He knew what strings to pull to open your heart and purse. The money you poured out to help the poor and disadvantaged went instead to feather Arthur's nest. You thought men could live in peace and harmony and the voluntary surrender of wealth and privilege, by families such as ours, would bring the laying down of arms and the promised millennium.

"They are the people," you once said. "The simple unaffected yeomen of our land."

Balls, Pete. Arthur has his own agenda. Damn to hell the stupid teacher who filled your head with egalitarian nonsense. He'd no money of his own to spread around, but he encouraged you to give up all for the oppressed, the downtrodden. The people father called 'the great unwashed'. Was it perhaps the only way you could see to rebel?

So, here we are: you dead, six long centuries before your birth, and me marooned in time with strangers. A time in some ways not unlike our own: soaring inflation, increasing lawlessness, rising taxes, awakening of some sense of power in the common people. The pot coming to the boil, Rick says, a time of protest. As in our time, there's even going to be a heavy poll tax imposed next year. Rick wonders if the similarities are what fetched us here.

You would have liked Rick, Pete. He is in some ways like you, an innocent in need of a keeper. If he fell in a cesspool he'd come up clutching a rose, having seen nothing else. Without his knowledge of this time, we'd all be lost. God, funerals should always have someone like Rick on hand. The way he hung onto the gentle, friendly gelding ... If I hadn't ridden with him, the canter back would have dismounted him.

Oh, but it was good to feel him close to me the night I told him I was your sister. Arthur has him pegged all wrong. He's no fairy. He was as ready then as any man can ever be, but he is a gentleman. Too much a gentleman perhaps with the stupid middle-class primness and over gentility you don't find in either the lower or the upper classes. I could well end up in love with him, but he'd need to roughen up some edges first. Malcolm and Arthur strike sparks off each other. They are flint and steel, but which is which? His handling of the hunter showed Malcolm at his best, a thoroughly professional man. At other times, he plays the buffoon and drunken lecher. Now I'm a woman again, I wouldn't want to be alone with him.

Arthur reminds me of Frank the Groom, who taught you to ride, and listened to your tales of woe from school, and comforted you when father beat you. I think he even once took the blame for some mischief you had done. Yet, to our parents, he was a surly, uncouth peasant, who had been stealing from them for years. You told me once you met him when he got out of prison, but, by then, you were full grown, and, in his eyes, one of the enemy.

Todd acts older than his years, at least as our time thinks. His life's been bloody hard and cruel. If well instructed, Todd can rise far above his present station. He's bright. He speaks much better than the other skivvies do and learns very fast.

Saint Peter, head in the clouds, you didn't notice the rabble round us at those camps: the touchers, the gropers, the not-quite rapists. When I started dressing as a boy to go with you it was still the same. The cast changed somewhat. To you, all men were brothers. Only those of wealth or station who didn't give all to the poor and accept the shittiest jobs were beyond the pale.

These past weeks have been a strange experience. If I hadn't been so frightened, I'd have laughed fighting with the soldiers. I bless the day tiny Sister Teresa insisted that a proper lady must know judo – if only to stay proper. I really liked the sport and she was right. The nuns, in general, were more pragmatic than the straight-back, stiff upper-lip idiots you had as teachers. What a pity in this day and age a lady can't participate in such sport. The other ladies of Lady Eleanor's entourage either never heard of the incident, or it didn't click that it was me, but I still get some very wary looks from some of sergeant Martin's men. Sir Harold mentioned it once, saying the Saxons once had warrior queens, but he would prefer if such matters were now left to his gentlemen.

The daily masses for your soul have helped resign me to your death. I would not have credited this effect before, in spite of what the priests say, but it does exist. Maybe the simple, concrete faith of those around me now is catching.

Todd's arm, though healed, is not quite straight. The other ladies, Lady Eleanor and Lady Gwenne, could have pages, but don't. Sir Harold let me have Todd.

Now that Todd can read and write better than some years older than him, the ladies don't see the serf in him so much. His manners still lack polish, but he learns. He had the ladies in tears of laughter reading to them from a primer of instructions for small pages. He acted out the opposites as he read. Even Lady Gwenne laughed and clapped her hands at his antics. Only Master Gerald, who came in halfway through, stood stony faced. He stamped out with a scowl when Sir Harold applauded and threw Todd a coin.

"Better than the mummers in the Hall tonight." Margaret hugged me. "My lord has not laughed and played like this since his only son and heir died of a flux a year ago this coming spring."

If anything happened to Sir Harold, Master Gerald would take his brother's place, at least until the eldest daughter married. Rumour has it Lady Gwenne is barren, but, the ladies whisper, it's Master Gerald's fault, not hers.

The fashion here is courtly love. Love at a distance. A love of looks and sighs and downcast eyes. The poets and bards here write and sing about it. The ladies are married by their families for dynastic reasons, like mergers in our times. The woman is only a chattel, a brood mare to produce a sound male heir of undoubted parentage. Romantic love as we know it doesn't exist. The men have all the sex they want with serving wenches and women of the lower classes. Above a certain station, virginity in the female is highly valued. The household males zealously protect the market value of their trade goods. When some noble impregnates a lady of middling rank, if the father's rank is high enough, he may acknowledge the bastard, or at least have him raised as a gentleman. This is what they think of Rick.

Christmas has come and gone. We're now in deep winter. The guests have left to take advantage of the hard frozen roads, and get home before the thaw and rain of spring makes them impassable.

Pete, this is the final mass. Master Gerald had the masses dropped to weekly. The priest says for sure that you've left purgatory. Masses will be said for you, at Master Gerald's expense, on your birthday, not on the anniversary of your death.

There. The pax is given and everyone is about to leave. I will not give the pax to Master Gerald. Neither will Todd, and it bothers Sir Harold.

Good bye, Pete. I hope you find in the next life the peace you never knew in this.

LOVE – JO.

Book Two

Chapter One

Rick glanced round the chapel. Anyone who had any pretensions to being somebody was there. Arthur and Dennis stood with some guild members. Sir Harold had told Rick to put out the word to attend, but many would have come anyway. No one had known Pete, but they were here out of respect for the Lady Jo, and Pete's friends Arthur and Dennis.

The crowd in the chapel packed people even against Jo and Todd, but there was a perceptible space round Gerald, his wife, and her lady-in-waiting. It was not fear of Gerald this time, but a distancing from his act, in this, the House of God. After all, Sir Harold had been most insistent and punctilious about the observances for this unknown. If he feared possible repercussions or retribution, divine or otherwise, it was only sensible for lesser folk to have care.

After the pax, to everyone's surprise, Sir Harold emerged from the niche, in which he and his immediate family attended mass. He walked up to Jo and gave her the kiss of peace.

Jo looks great, Rick thought, when he met Margaret and Jo in the courtyard. Her hair had grown a lot since their arrival. Its dark frame around her face, pale with indoor living, really brought her face into focus. He wondered what she was thinking. She looked so serene and tranquil in the chapel; nun-like almost.

Oh God. I hope not, that would be the bloody end, he thought.

He hoped these masses had been good for her. Since she and Pete were Catholic, he supposed they might have helped.

Rick bowed. "Lady Margaret, Lady Jo, good morning."

"Good morning, Master Richard."

Todd grinned at Rick. "Our lesson will be late today. Our Lord has decreed a special dinner in honour of My Lady Jo's brother's passage."

"Todd, you little imp," Margaret said. "How did you know that? It was to be a surprise for Lady Jo."

"I'll act surprised, Margaret," Jo said. "Don't worry, Sir Harold is too kind a man to disappoint in such an event."

Chapter Two

The dinner went well, and Jo feigned surprise that it was a celebration in honour of Pete's passage. Rick marvelled at the contradiction between Sir Harold and Lady Eleanor's sophistication in some matters, and their innocent delight at Jo's surprise and pleasure.

The age's fascination with death and the macabre always interested Rick. Naturally, while a history student, he had read about it. Experiencing it was still a shock.

The mummers staged a morality play full of images of death, decay, and everlasting hell. The minstrels sang several lugubrious pieces. After the minstrels, servants ran in with platters of pancakes.

"That's what the gorgeous smell was," Malcolm said.

"It's Shrove Tuesday. Pancake Tuesday. That's what was different about the mass today," Rick said.

Rick's neighbour smiled. "Our lord is generous, but nothing pleases him more than being able to be frugal in his generosity. We would have had a feast and revels today anyway, perhaps a little less lavish with the beer is all."

As at Christmas, violent games and furious dances alternated with pieces from the minstrels and the mummers. The songs moved from solemn to decidedly bawdy.

Two men had a mock fight with short broadswords. After

which, instead of issuing a general challenge, they marched up to stop in front of Malcolm and directly challenged him. Malcolm lurched to his feet and stood, swaying gently. Rick tried to dissuade Malcolm, but he was adamant he could beat either or both of them. When Malcolm stumbled forward, Rick thought one of the men looked at Gerald, and Gerald gave an almost imperceptible nod.

The audience roared encouragement to Malcolm, whose bow to acknowledge them almost caused him to fall over. He hefted the sword he had been given and tested its balance. When they started to circle and test each other's defences, Rick glanced up at the dais. For the first time that day Gerald looked cheerful and even happy. He even leaned over and spoke to Walter, and they both laughed.

Rick turned his attention back to the fight. The swords were, of course, blunted with their points filed. They could still hurt, but would bruise rather than cut. Malcolm, drunk or not, was a good swordsman. He had already delivered several solid blows without exposing himself, when one of the serving wenches shouted encouragement. He glanced at her and momentarily lost concentration. The other swordsman lunged. The audience roared. Some in appreciation of a good stroke, and some in laughter at Malcolm's slip, but his sleeve on his upper left arm turned red.

For an instant both swordsmen stood frozen, before Malcolm roared and attacked. The fury and skill of his attack drove his foe back. A discarded piece of food caused his opponent to slip. Malcolm pounced, forced him quickly onto his back, and knelt with his sword to the man's throat. He seized the other's sword in his left hand and looked closely at it. Without a trace of drunkenness in his stance or voice, he stood and handed his foe his sword. He, hefting the other sword in his right hand, bowed.

"Shall we continue?"

The swordsman half turned towards the dais.

"My Lord..." he started, and Malcolm slapped his thigh with the flat of the sword.

"Fight, or die where you stand," Malcolm said.

"Gerald put them up to it. Watch the other one," Rick said. But

Arthur and Dennis had already faded into the crowd.

The audience was now silent; eyes riveted on the combatants. The only sounds were the gasps of the fighters, and the clang of their blades. A sword slid across the floor. Malcolm's foe backed off quickly and stooped to pick it up. Malcolm, wary now, retreated a few steps, a grin on his face.

"I shall take great pleasure in stitching you up before they hang you."

The end came quickly. While they circled, the other man stepped out of the crowd behind Malcolm, dagger in his hand. Malcolm heard the warning from the crowd and half-turned. His opponent lunged and left himself exposed. Malcolm sidestepped and thrust; his blade sunk in below the sternum. The second man fell, Dennis's dagger lodged in his ribs.

There was a moment's silence followed by uproar. Sir Harold's voice boomed out and cut through the noise.

"These revels now are ended. Sergeant, clear the hall. Assemble everyone except the gate guard here. I wish an accounting of these proceedings."

No one needed to be urged to leave. Rick glanced round. Dennis was at one end of the dais, drawn sword in one hand, a dagger in the other, his back to those on the dais. Arthur, at the wall at the other end of the dais, Gerald's end, watched both the dissolving crowd and Gerald. The Lady Gwenne and Jo had retreated to the wall. Todd and Chris, daggers drawn, stood in front of the ladies. Chris looked unsure and a little nervous, but excited. Sir Harold stood at his place at the table, but half turned so he could see Gerald and Walter.

Rick and Lady Eleanor were by this time examining Malcolm's left arm. He protested he was fine and would have to look at the other two.

Walter made some comment and laughed. Unfortunately for him, he was within an arm's length of Sir Harold, who floored him with a backhanded slap. Gerald, purple with fury, moved forward, hand on dagger handle. The sergeant was instantly between him and Sir Harold.

"You have some contribution to make to the discussion, My Lord Brother?" Sir Harold demanded, and Gerald, controlling himself with an obvious effort, sank back onto a bench.

Malcolm, his upper arm roughly bound, moved to where the two would-be assassins lay.

"Both are still breathing, My Lord, but not for long. They are both bleeding internally. Punctured lungs, I suspect."

"Do you or your men recognise them?" Sir Harold said, and prodded with his toe the one who had fought Malcolm.

"No, Sire. I don't," the sergeant said. "You men file past and take a good look at them."

"Sergeant, I've seen them," one of the men said. "I was on the gate when they came in. They were with the mummers. At least I thought they were."

"Did you not question them? Total strangers?"

The man quaked at Sir Harold's tone and scowl.

"Sergeant, all private quarters are to be guarded. Assign two men here."

He turned to the trembling gate guard. "We will deal with your carelessness later, soldier. In the meantime find the mummers and bring them here."

He turned back to the two men on the floor.

"Can we question these, Master Malcolm?"

One breathed noisily, bright red arterial blood frothed and bubbled at his lips, and on the other, blood trickled from one corner of his mouth: a red slash across a chalk white face. He twitched uncontrollably.

Malcolm shook his head, and the priest, at Sir Harold's nod, began the last rites.

The mummers shuffled in, and bowed low to Sir Harold. They

looked nervously at the two on the floor, one now deathly still, but the other still twitching.

"These men were with your company," Sir Harold said.

The spokesman for the mummers quickly replied: "Oh, no, My Lord. They were not. They joined with us some two days out, and travelled here with us. They said little, except they had business here. Important business they said."

The others nodded, huddled together.

Sir Harold stared intently at each mummer. Finally, he nodded.

"They may go, Sergeant, but they are not to leave the outer ward. I may want to see them again."

"It could have been a simple accident, brother," Gerald said. But Sir Harold stared at him, and he swallowed. "Such accidents have happened, My Lord. The man did appeal to you when he discovered the error, that the sword was sharp."

"He appealed to someone at the high table, My Lord Brother," Sir Harold said. "Not when he found the edge sharp, however. Only when he lost the blade."

"Sire, who would wish to harm the physician, and in such a public manner?" Gerald pleaded.

"Yes, My Lord Brother. Who indeed? And why? Whom would it benefit? We will adjourn to the solar. Sergeant, have these disposed of. They offend me. Arthur and Dennis, join us in the solar."

Chapter Three

"Lady Jo, I regret the abrupt end to the feast for your brother's passage," Sir Harold said when they gathered in the solar. "Walter, wine for everyone. Todd, Christopher, help pass the cups."

Sir Harold raised his goblet.

"Brother, masters, ladies. Peter D'Arcy of Oxford, now with his Maker."

"May light perpetual shine upon him," Rick said.

"May he rest in peace," Jo intoned.

"Now to business," Sir Harold said. "My Lady, would you examine Master Malcolm's arm again and clean it thoroughly? I will not have him fall ill. Master Richard, we have work to do. Arthur, Dennis, join us." He bowed to Eleanor. "Excuse us, ladies."

Sir Harold led the way to his private chamber.

"Walter, you and Chris wait outside. Alert us if anyone approaches."

He turned to face Rick and the others.

"Masters, I congratulate you, both on your appreciation of the situation, and on your timely and effective action.

"Master Richard has told me what he says is your true story. I see no cause to disbelieve him, though it is indeed a wonderful tale. It does lead to some interesting possibilities.

"Your background is obviously warlike. Malcolm, a physician, is a skilled swordsman, as he has shown on two occasions. You two acted with restraint, you allowed Malcolm to defend himself while the fight was even. When you judged it needed, you acted decisively and with deadly effect. Christopher, not yet a squire, will not be pushed. You all act in concert, a well-trained body. No two alike, but each part of the whole." Sir Harold paused. "You, Arthur, are the 'man of the people', the 'stalwart son of the soil'?"

Rick turned purple and took a coughing fit. Arthur pounded his back.

"Whoever wrote the ballad," Sir Harold said, "may well hang, deservedly, some would say. To my point. I have Rick's oath of allegiance. Malcolm is my physician and bound by his oath. These are unsettled times. Ever since the Death there has been unrest. It is more obvious here, in town, than in my other holdings. There are those who think me too lenient, a bad example for the burghers and serfs to point to. These lords feel my brother Gerald would be more to their liking as lord here. They will not act overtly, but they would not condemn Gerald either, provided he does not implicate them."

He paused and stood, silent, thoughtful.

"Sir Harold," Arthur said. "You've been straight and square with us, maybe for reasons of your own."

"My Lord," Rick interrupted, "Arthur does not intend disrespect..."

"We are private here. Plain speaking does not offend me. Continue, Arthur."

"Can we stop beating around the bush," Dennis said. They all looked at him in surprise. "We all believe Gerald set up today's attempt on Malcolm's life. We can't prove it. I think you suspect this too. Can you, will you, act against him?"

"He is my brother, my only male heir. I cannot cut off my line."

"Would you have allowed the attack had you known of it?"

"Have a care, Dennis. You are impertinent."

"No, My Lord. You opened the issue. Would you, will you defend us?"

"Yes, I would. I will."

"Then we are your men. If we cannot stand with you, we will serve notice. We will not allow any attempt on your person, or your house, that we can prevent."

"I accept that, Dennis. Arthur, you scowl, does Dennis not speak for you?"

Arthur scowled at Dennis.

"Yes, we are your men. Of life and limb, as Rick says, while we agree. Dennis doesn't know how to frigging-well bargain." He looked at Rick and Dennis. "It doesn't mean we bind ourselves unthinkingly to you for life. There are some things we won't do."

Rick opened his mouth to speak, but Sir Harold held up his hand.

"Your time must be strange indeed. You have the air of professional soldiers, but talk as if you think you should fight only for a cause in which you passionately believe. We need not love or even like each other, but we must trust each other's word."

"Once bought, we should stay bought, you mean?"

"Soldier's Code, Arthur. We have a contract? Not to be broken on either side without notice?"

Arthur put out his hand, and Sir Harold, after a brief hesitation, grasped it in his.

"What of Gerald, Arthur?"

"I will not let anyone else kill him. No harm is to come to Chris or Todd."

"Todd is my ward. Gerald would not be so foolish as to harm him. I suppose Gerald must look out for his own safety."

The door flew open and Chris almost fell in.

"You were told not to disturb us, boy."

The sergeant pushed in behind Chris.

"Don't blame the boy, Sire. I insisted." He turned. "Bring him in."

Two guards entered, between them someone covered from head to toe in a rough cloak. The hood thrown back revealed a dishevelled, bloodstained man.

They forced him to his knees before Sir Harold.

"One of the mummers," the Sergeant said. "He made to escape after we mounted the assassins' heads on poles over the gate."

"God. I didn't know they were dead," Rick said.

"They were when we put the heads on the poles." The sergeant laughed. "This man knew them, or at least of them."

He prodded the kneeling man.

"Tell My Lord what you told me."

"My Lord, Sire," the man babbled. "I know nothing of any great moment."

"My Lord will decide what is of moment. Repeat what you told me."

"When they joined our company, I recognised them."

"This is like drawing teeth," Dennis said.

"Should we try that?" The sergeant grinned and hit the man on the side of the head with the handle of his dagger.

"I know of them, but did not *know* them."

"You try my patience, varlet."

"Sire, they were Sir William's men, Andrew the Physician's lord. I saw them deep in conversation with Master Andrew when we played at Sir William's manor, perhaps a fortnight since."

"What business did they have there? If you know aught else, you would do well to say now. If I have you put to the question and you have hidden anything, it will go the worse for you."

The man became deathly pale, tore himself from the grasp of the guards, and threw himself on his face in front of Sir Harold.

"Sire, I tried to flee the castle because I feared to fall into Sir Gerald's hands. He would kill me for sure, or have me killed, if he knew of my knowledge of Sir William's men."

"What has my brother to do with these men?"

"They come at his bidding, or at least to do his bidding. Sent by Andrew, Sir William's physician. I heard them talk on our travels."

They waited and the sergeant, impatient, pulled the mummer back to his knees, and hit the side of his head again with the dagger handle.

"As a storyteller, you leave much to be desired. What was their talk about?"

The mummer squirmed.

"Andrew the Physician would like to be your lordship's physician, I think. I don't know if killing your physician was Master Andrew's idea or Sir Gerald's. They had discussed it and agreed – or at least those two said so."

"How was it to be done, varlet?" Sir Harold barked.

"It was to appear an accident, Sire, whenever it was possible. They were to try to enter your lordship's employ as mercenaries, but secretly to do the bidding of Sir Gerald. They were to watch the false masters from the circle and if possible trick them into some action for which they could be taken or killed."

The mummer shrieked when the sergeant threw him face down on the floor and knelt beside to pull his head up by the hair and place a dagger point at his throat.

"Should I slit his throat now?"

"No, not here, not in my chamber. Let me think."

He beckoned the sergeant to join him in the window alcove with Rick, Arthur and Dennis.

"Martin, are your two troopers reliable?" he said.

"They are your men to the death. I would also stake my own life on them."

"This is part of a plot to isolate me and finally place Gerald in my seat."

"Couldn't you just kill him?" Arthur said.

Sir Harold looked startled.

"You cannot simply kill a man of rank without due trial, without proof. He is my brother, guardian to my daughters, my heir. There is no actual proof he intends me harm. I cannot believe he would consent to my death. To kill him would be murder."

"He murdered Pete, and tried to have Malcolm murdered. He was planning to have us murdered," Arthur shouted.

"Keep your voice down," Rick said. "Remember your manners, the honorifics, when you address Sir Harold."

"Bugger the honorifics."

Sir Harold laughed. "We are private here. Arthur is a soldier with a soldier's bluntness. He reminds me of Martin when we were younger."

The sergeant grinned.

"Your bluntness does not offend me unduly," Sir Harold said. "But we simply cannot do it that way. The other lords would see my hand in it, whether I approved or not. I would have to hang the murderer. It would give me no great pleasure to have to hang you, Arthur."

"It would give me none at all, Sire," Arthur said. "Politics I can understand, and political action and inaction. I can wait. I'm used to waiting."

"Could you not exile Gerald?" Rick said.

"No. I prefer him here where I can see what he is up to, and whom he contacts. That way I can nullify most of what he tries to do."

"Sire," Rick said, "Gerald must be wondering if the two assassins can be linked to him, and what, if anything, you know. Until you are ready to act, would it not be best for him to think you ignorant?"

"Yes. It would."

"Martin," Sir Harold said, "bring in Christopher."

He stood drumming his fingers on the stone sill.

"Ah, Christopher. Where was Walter when the Sergeant brought in this man?"

Chris glanced at Rick, who nodded.

"Master Gerald came up a while ago, and said it didn't need two to stand watch. He took Walter with him. I was by myself when Martin, I mean the sergeant, arrived, Sire."

"Good. So Gerald does not know we have this mummer. Who saw you take him?"

"Only the guard on the outer gate," the sergeant said. "He saw him try to pass and called us. We caught him and brought him here in the hooded cloak."

"Return to your post, Christopher," Sir Harold said. "You have not seen this man.

"If we hold him, Gerald will hear of it and wish to put him to the question. If we hang him, Gerald will suspect he told us something before he died."

"We could kill him quietly," Dennis said, "and dispose of the body."

Sir Harold stood seemingly deep in thought.

"Sergeant, you and these two men take this varlet, cloaked and hooded, some way out of town and there release him. I do not wish ever wish to hear of him or see his face in any of my manors again. Do I make myself clear?"

"Sire," the sergeant said, and the mummer tried to catch the edge of Sir Harold's gown to kiss it.

"Dennis, you will go with them. Return by supper."

"Yes, Sire."

They bowed. Rick thought Dennis and Sir Harold exchanged looks before Sir Harold nodded to acknowledge the bows.

The sergeant tied the mummer's hands behind him, threw the cloak round him and covered his head with the hood. This done, they left.

Chapter Four

"Before the interruption," Sir Harold said, "I was about to say it is almost time our entourage moved to another of my manors. Master Richard and Master Malcolm will, of course, accompany us. Arthur, will you and Dennis supplement the sergeant's guard?"

"That's what it was all about," Arthur said. "I wondered. Yes. Dennis and I would like to see some more of the countryside."

"Good. Let us rejoin the ladies in the solar."

When they entered, Todd rushed over to Chris.

"Where have you been? You missed it all. They took those two out to the outer ward and cut off their heads and stuck them on poles."

"Todd, be quiet," Jo said. "Don't be so disgusting."

In a quieter voice, Todd went on: "One wasn't very messy, but the other moved I thought, and there was much blood. Aow. My Lady. Don't. I was being quiet. I was."

Jo pulled Todd's ear and he squealed.

"Why was Todd not kept here in the solar?" Sir Harold said, in a quiet, ominous voice, and the solar fell silent. "I repeat. Why was Todd not kept here?"

"My Lord. You gave no instructions," Lady Eleanor said.

"Since when have you needed instructions, My Lady, to do what is right and sensible? I had men posted to prevent access to the solar in case Malcolm was not the target, and there were other assassins. Todd was in danger."

"Sire. I sneaked out and watched from the inner wall walk. I was in no danger."

Red with anger, Sir Harold took Todd roughly by the arm and marched him into one of the alcoves. There was the sound of a blow and Jo ran to the alcove.

"Sire, he is my page."

"Madam, he is my ward and I will decide his discipline."

Rick was now able to see into the alcove and laughed. Todd was comical, looking from Jo to Sir Harold to try to gauge the situation.

"I throw myself on your lordship's mercy," he said.

"Good," Sir Harold said, and sat on a stool to pull Todd across his knee. One large hand rose and fell while the other held Todd firmly in position. Silent at first, Todd bellowed lustily before Sir Harold stopped and stood to spill the boy onto the floor.

"I will not have any of mine so thoughtlessly and needlessly endanger himself. He'll live, madam," Sir Harold snapped at Jo when she pushed past him to Todd. "He has survived worse."

"Let me go, Lady Jo. Let me go. He'll have Hubert flogged."

Todd, eel like, squirmed out of Jo's grasp and ran to Sir Harold and planted himself squarely in front of him.

"It wasn't Hubert's fault, My Lord," Todd said. "He did try to stop me. I told him not to be foolish. His job was to stop any stranger from entering the solar, not to stop a small boy, a page, from leaving. Don't flog Hubert ... please. If anyone is to be flogged, it should be me."

"Oh no. He's been punished enough," Jo said.

"Please, Mistress, Lady Jo, stay out of it," Todd said.

Sir Harold grunted.

"Leave this matter between us men, Lady Jo. You know my guards as well as I do, Todd."

Todd grinned. "Better, Sire."

Sir Harold looked furious for an instant. Then he smiled.

"I won't have Hubert flogged," he said. "But I shall have the sergeant whip him. He must learn to follow orders and not be swayed by a smooth-tongued boy."

Complacently, Todd let Jo fuss over him when she drew him back into the alcove where he had been beaten. After a short time, they emerged.

"Can I tell Chris about the heads now?" Todd said, and yelped at Jo's hard slap on his rump.

"Leave him be, Jo," Rick said.

Jo sighed and said: "Yes, go and talk to Chris."

"He's really a good kid," Rick said. "Considering all he's been through, he's remarkably well adjusted. He's not your son or even your brother, Jo. Don't try to over-civilise him."

"You must train Todd well. He cannot become a squire, much less a knight, but he can rise as a learned man," Sir Harold said. "He learns quickly. I regret only that I did not find him earlier."

"He was here for years, as a common slavey," Jo said. "He could have died for all you knew or cared. There are many such."

"He is here with us now and I treat him as I would my own. I am truly sorry your feast was spoilt. I had intended a more pleasant day for our last day before Lent."

Todd and Chris appeared in front of them and bowed.

"My Lord, Master Rick, My Lady, may Chris and I be excused?"

Sir Harold smiled. "Yes, boys. I think all is safe for the present, but stay in plain sight. Take Hubert with you, since he follows your orders rather my mine anyway. My Lady?"

"Yes, Todd. Go and play till supper."

"Come on, Chris. Let's go and see if the heads are still dripping."

Rick and Sir Harold laughed at Jo's sigh and at the expression on Chris's face.

Chapter Five

The next weeks were busy with preparations for the summer out of the castle. Lady Eleanor's window was carefully dismantled and crated. Wall hangings were removed from the great hall, the solar, and the private chambers. Chris commented this was how he had expected inside a castle to look.

If Gerald was aware one of the mummers had known of his plot he gave no sign, and the mummers left without comment. Dennis did not reply when Chris asked why the mummer had been taken to the chapel before being led off out of town.

Gerald was icily polite toward Rick, Malcolm and Jo, but he barely acknowledged Dennis and Arthur when they met. He ignored Chris and Todd as if they did not exist.

Walter was beaten for deserting his post on Shrove Tuesday, and accused Chris of telling on him. The three boys carried on their feud to all intents in a different world from their adults. Rick watched, a little anxious, but did not interfere; afraid he might make matters worse.

The smokehouses were now finished and in full production. It now being Lent – a month of fasting with no meat – there was great demand for the fish. As Arthur had predicted, the smokies were popular in their own right and not simply as a means of preserving fish. Arthur and Dennis spent time training the women and the younger fisher boys in how to prepare the fish for smoking and how to tend the fires and smoke houses for best effect.

Malcolm was busy with his patients and not at all sure he should leave them for a holiday in the country. When Malcolm tried to use them as a reason why he should not go to the country manor, Sir Harold was brusque. Malcolm was his physician, as Richard was his secretary. If he chose, where he went, they went.

"We must give some thought to marriage plans for Lady Jo."

Rick swallowed hard. He stood and turned to face Sir Harold. Engrossed as he was in the correspondence, he had not heard Sir Harold come in.

"Sire?"

"Lady Jo. She is more than of age for marriage. We must see what match can be made."

"Have you talked to Lady Jo?"

"Certainly not, I would not raise her hopes till a suitable match is in prospect."

"But…"

"She is my ward, my responsibility. It will not be easy. She has no dower, except what I might provide. A younger son of some minor house, perhaps. One of my subtenants who would see such an alliance advantageous, despite the lack of dower."

"Lady Jo might not accept such an arrangement made for her."

Sir Harold glared at Rick. "And pray, Master Secretary, why not? She is my ward. She is of my wife's household. By *Corpus Dominus*, I will not be defied in this."

"In our time…"

"She and you are here now, to live and die. I do not see Lady Jo an unmarried lady-in-waiting all her life. If aught should happen to me, lacking a husband she would be Gerald's ward, to dispose of as he saw fit. Have you thought on that? I will speak to Lady Eleanor. It will not be easy."

Rick opened his mouth to speak again, but Sir Harold stretched and said: "Have you no work to do?"

Back with his letters and accounts, Rick's mind raced. He had not expected this. He saw Jo most days, usually before or after lessons with the boys. They often strolled the wall walk with Lady Margaret and could talk in the solar after supper. There were very few times when they could have any real privacy. They had walked arm in arm, and Rick thought Jo had pressed back when he had squeezed her hand.

Damn, I'm jealous of Todd. He gets to see her in private.

Rick blushed at the memory of what young Todd had said when told Jo was a girl.

God. I should be more like Malcolm and Arthur. No, damn it, I don't want to be like them.

He wanted Jo. But not for a quick tumble in the straw. Would Sir Harold let him marry Jo? More to the point, perhaps, despite what Sir Harold thought, would Jo?

"Not finished yet, Master Richard?"

Again, he had not heard Sir Harold enter and leapt to his feet.

"Not quite."

"You are somewhat distracted and not quite your usual efficient self. Are you thinking perhaps of a poem for one of our ladies? In need of some release? Shall I have Martin find you a fresh servant girl? You are celibate, as the Church says our priests are. This is not good for a young man. You will fall ill."

"No, My Lord." Rick broke in to stem the flow. "I'm fine thank you. The accounts will be ready for your perusal in a moment or so."

Sir Harold walked round Rick looking intently at him, and Rick felt himself flush under the scrutiny.

"You are a well proportioned, manly, young man. You don't prefer boys, do you?"

"No! Certainly not."

"Your cousin page is an attractive youth, but he and Robert are by all accounts untouched."

"My Lord! I should hope so."

"Then consider it settled. Martin will find some suitable wench for you; a young girl, fresh from the country. I know or hear of who couples with whom, and I know you have not been with a woman since your arrival here. It is unhealthy for a young man."

"I have sworn an oath to remain celibate, chaste, till my marriage," Rick stammered.

"Your betrothed must be in your own time and she as dead to you as you are to her. You will live out your life and die here. Will you remain celibate? I am sure you can be absolved of your vow. Some suitable penance would suffice even without revealing your real circumstances. We will talk to Wycliffe of this when we meet him. He is a reasonable man. I will tempt not you till then. Are you finished now?"

Rick handed Sir Harold the drafts of the letters and quickly went over the accounts with him, before he fled to meet the boys.

Chapter Six

"There will be no lessons today," Rick said when he walked in. "Todd, find Lady Jo and ask her if I can talk to her privately. Return to me with her answer. Afterwards you and Chris can go."

"Chris, we can go into town. It's a long time till supper."

Todd grinned and ducked to avoid Rick's swing at him.

"I'm going. I'm going."

Just inside Lady Eleanor's herb garden, Margaret sat on the stone bench, and waved Rick and Jo on. When they strolled away, Jo said: "What's all this about? You've dismissed the boys and dragged me out here."

"Have you ever thought about getting married?" Rick said.

Jo stopped, and stared hard at him.

"That's not funny."

"I'm not joking. Sir Harold said today that he's going to look for a match for you. He was serious."

"He's not going to marry me off, that's flat. God, it would be some local yokel. No one of any standing would consider me in this time without a dower."

She shivered, or shuddered, and Rick put his arm round her.

"Are you mad?" she said and shrugged him off. "If you're randy, find some serving wench like the others."

"Christ, Jo. I don't want some serving girl. I want you."

The slap sounded loud in the quiet garden, and Margaret

looked up, smiled and turned back to her missal.

"I didn't put that well, did I? I didn't mean it the way you took it, the way it sounded."

"Then exactly what do you mean? I hope you're clearer with the boys. Are the boys safe with you?"

"Shut up, and listen. Can I ask Sir Harold if I can marry you?"

"Why don't you ask me first?"

"Damn it, I am asking you. Sir Harold will marry you off whether you want it or not. You'd be better off with me."

"It's not the most romantic proposal I've heard. Arthur and Malcolm are much more ardent suitors."

Rick stopped and grabbed Jo's arm. "Have those two been pawing you?"

"Rick. You're jealous. Let go of my arm. No, they haven't. Malcolm's like an octopus if he gets the chance, but he sticks to the serving wenches. They're accessible and there's no commitment. I'd break Arthur's arm if he tried to lay a finger on me. Your Margaret, at the house, keeps tabs on him anyway. She's not going to have him play the field."

"Well then?"

"You're impossible. You've never given any sign of any romantic interest in me, and now you expect me to fall over and say I'll marry you. What about Todd?"

"Oh God. Don't you start on that. What about him?"

"I want to see him with enough education to make his way up in life here. I can't let him slide back."

"Of course, Chris and Todd would stay with us."

"Fine. An instant family. One of yours and one of mine. Just what every young couple needs."

"Think about it, Jo, please. You could tell Sir Harold you won't marry till the anniversary of Pete's death. He'd take that as reasonable, but unless he's given the message we are going to get married, he'll go ahead and set up a contract for you."

"Stop, please stop," Jo laughed, but at Rick's woebegone expression hurried on. "I'm not laughing at you," she giggled. "Yes, I am. This isn't exactly what a girl has in mind when she thinks of a proposal. You sound like a lawyer. Your arguments are all sound and logical, and if that was all there was to it, I might say yes. I like you, but I don't love you, and you haven't said anything to make me think you love me."

"Jo! I do love you. I've loved you ever since the night we slept together in the solar."

"I didn't think you were the type to kiss and tell," Jo laughed again. She wiped her eyes and tried to match Rick's seriousness. "Yes, I remember. I was frightened and you were the only one I felt I could trust. There was Chris, of course, but he was too young. You were sweet.

"Remember your Dickens? 'Barkus is willing'? As I remember, you were both willing and able." Rick felt himself blush. "You were a gentleman. Gentleman enough to back off when I asked you."

"Stupid enough. Shy enough. Backward enough. Soft enough."

"Oh, no. You weren't soft. I can vouch for that."

"Jo!"

"You're a prude."

"You're the one who's always after Todd about manners and being uncouth."

"What the hell does that have to do with anything? He's a child. I'm trying to shift him from one social class to another. We are adults talking in private."

"I don't understand you. If you talked like that to any of the others, they'd think it an open invitation."

"The topic isn't going to come up with the others. I told you that night because I felt I could trust you not to take advantage."

"We're not getting anyplace. Don't say anything to Sir Harold about this. He'd skin me alive for telling you his plans."

"What about his plans for you?"

"What do you mean?"

"He's setting you up with one of the serving wenches, isn't he? It's been the talk of the solar for days."

"Do you mean the ladies have all been talking about my sex life?"

Jo giggled. "No. The lack of it."

At the look on Rick's face she struggled to be serious again.

"It's a bawdy age. The conversation in the solar would shock senseless a good middle class Victorian lady. Fortunately, living rough with Pete in the camps broadened my education. Anyway, the social circles I moved in weren't exactly lily white. Only the middle class has any pretension to gentility. It clings to what it thinks is proper. There isn't really a middle class here yet."

"How can I come into the solar without being embarrassed, knowing that?"

"Same way as Gerald does. Except that you haven't done anything to be ashamed of."

"This hasn't gone the way I hoped it would," Rick sighed. "Anyway, I told Sir Harold I had taken a vow of chastity till I married, so we needn't worry about some servant girl."

"I wasn't worried, Rick. I'm sure you could get a dispensation from your vow. It's done all the time."

"Damn it. I don't want a dispensation. Can't you get that through your thick skull? I want you. Not some servant girl. Christ, we're talking about this as if there really were a vow."

Jo took Rick's arm.

"Let's not quarrel. I like you, Rick. We're friends aren't we? Let's keep it that way. Come, Margaret's waiting."

Chapter Seven

Finally, all the preparations were complete. At dawn, the baggage train wound slowly out of the castle and through the narrow streets to the town gate. Rick, Chris, and Todd accompanied it to the road beyond the walls.

Grumbling pack mules ambled through the gate, followed by two ox carts creaking under heavy loads. Servants walked alongside and the young men carried stout staffs or cudgels. Most of the soldiers strolled with the younger serving girls. The majordomo, the only one mounted, rode at the head of the column.

"Wow," Chris said, "and I thought Mum used to pack a lot of stuff when she went on holiday. Is that as fast as they'll go?"

"Yes," Rick said, "about two miles an hour or so. They'll be lucky to cover fifteen miles in a day."

"When do we go? I thought we'd all go at once."

"No," Todd said, "we're going to Sir William's place for a few days to give the servants time to set up the country manor."

Dinner was early and very much a scratch affair, since the chief cook and many kitchen servants had gone with the baggage train. Soon the order came to mount up and assemble.

The courtyard soon filled with men and horses. The knights' stallions snorted, glared, and pranced.

"Move to the outer ward, gentlemen. Make space for the ladies and their mounts," shouted the sergeant, and all but the immediate family and entourage left the courtyard.

Robert arrived with the mule carrying Malcolm's medical chest and the group's clothing, to add it to the mule train assembled to carry personal goods.

Chris and Todd were mounted on horses, flushed with pride. Bright eyed with excitement, and totally incapable of standing still, Robert danced round Todd and Chris and their mounts.

When they prepared to move, Robert, excited, backed into Walter's horse and startled it. Although Walter was still firmly in control of his mount, he hit Robert with his riding crop and shouted: "How dare you touch me, you stinking serf."

Robert drew his head into his neck, covered his head with his arms, and tried to run. When Walter urged his horse forward after Robert and struck at him with the crop, Arthur's horse swung round, to trap Walter's leg between the flank of his own mount and the hindquarters of Arthur's. The forward momentum of Walter's horse twisted the leg and Walter went white, dropped the crop and clung to the mane.

Robert's flight from Walter ran him straight into Gerald's horse and Gerald lashed out with his crop.

"Clumsy oaf, I'll have you flogged."

Gerald's second blow slashed Robert's cheek, and immediately Dennis was there, his horse pushed between Robert and Gerald. Ablaze with anger, Gerald raised his crop to strike at Dennis, who, stony faced, stared at him. Gerald's horse whinnied and reared, and Gerald struggled to control him.

Todd sheathed his dagger.

"I didn't hurt the horse too much, I hope."

Dennis smiled grimly, and Malcolm vaulted off his horse to see to Robert's face. Cleaned, it did not look too bad and Robert was more frightened than hurt.

"Let me look at your leg, Master Walter," Malcolm said. "You are certain to have a bad bruise."

Walter refused and trotted his horse to where Gerald scowled and calmed his horse.

Sir Harold, who had watched the whole affair from the mounting block, rode to Rick and Arthur.

"A unit in action again, I see. You defend the servant boy as fiercely as one of your number?"

"He is one of us," Arthur said.

"And I? Would you defend me with such vigour?"

Arthur grinned, and, hand on his dagger pommel, glanced toward Gerald.

"Say the word, My Lord. Say the word."

"Move out, Sergeant," Sir Harold said, and the procession snaked out of the castle and through the narrow streets of the town.

Robert trotted up to Arthur and tugged at his foot. "Thanks, master."

Arthur grinned down, and extended a hand.

"Come on, kid. You ride with me now. Between them, Margaret and Malcolm must have picked you clean of fleas and lice. And anyway, what's a little livestock between friends?"

Chapter Eight

About two hours out, Sir Harold gestured to Rick to join him, and spurred his horse to canter out ahead of the column. Arthur fell in ahead of them and Dennis behind.

"We stop tonight at the convent and the ladies will sleep inside. There's a guesthouse outside for important guests. I shall sleep there. You will share my chamber. Dennis and Arthur will sleep in the corridor outside my chamber."

"Oh thank you, My Lord. My saddle sores can feel the comfort already," Arthur said, over his shoulder.

"Arthur. Sir Harold and I were having a private conversation," Rick said.

"Christ. I've told you before. You've gone frigging native. Servants, guards, retainers aren't deaf, and most are far from stupid. You'd never make that mistake in our time."

"Arthur is right," Sir Harold said. "I had never really thought about it before you came."

"For the most part," Rick said, "they don't listen, except for an order. A change of tone alerts them, like the dogs and the horses, to the fact this now concerns them."

Sir Harold said: "I sometimes dismissed Walter, when I had business I didn't wish Gerald to know of, but till recently I did not think of servants and others. It's most disturbing. Before I trusted everyone, now I suspect all."

"Balls," Arthur said. "You trusted them as you trust a dog or a horse – too stupid to matter."

"A short time ago I would have had you flogged for speaking thus to me."

"We are both being educated."

Rick glanced at Sir Harold and thought he looked dangerously flushed. The right jaw line twitched ominously.

With a shrug, Arthur, who had fallen back alongside Sir Harold, flicked his reins to take up his forward position.

"Hold, Arthur. We have not finished."

"What is there to discuss? I await Your Lordship's orders."

"I must understand what you mean."

"Your servants, your retainers are men and women, exactly like you and your good lady."

"This smacks of the hedge priests. Have a care."

"Crap. Don't just put labels on. Think, man. Open your eyes. These hedge priests may be right in how it should be, but they're frigging idealists, not realists. Man won't be ready for them for centuries after our time, if ever. There just aren't enough bloody saints to go round."

"That's not the party line is it?" Rick said.

"I'm a pragmatist. I don't follow any party line."

"You're a bloody opportunist," Dennis said. "I'm with Sir Harold."

"So am I, knothead. Listen, My Lord. Listen to me. Now you know your underlings think, what now? Like Rick says, most will be too apathetic, too shit scared, to do anything, but what about those who aren't? What about those who have absolutely damn all to lose?"

"They are bound to me by law and custom. They would not dream of doing other than obeying me."

"Dream on, dream on. There'll come a day when law and custom aren't enough. What you need then is personal loyalty.

How much can you expect from the family of the groom you had whipped to death? Or the family of the man you hanged for being in the way at your hunt?"

"What groom? I had no groom flogged to death."

"The huntsman, the one who looked after the dogs, your dog."

"Oh, that man. He died of an ill humour, not of the beating. All know that."

"He died of the bloody lash as surely as if you had hanged him. Hanging might have been kinder."

"What nonsense is this?"

"We're off the point. If your serfs had to choose between you and Master Gerald, they would take you, I think. Would they be loyal to you, fight for you, defend you against someone who promised freedom, even if he couldn't deliver?"

"Some would," Rick said. "They couldn't envisage any other order than the present one."

"Fine fighters they'd be. Build loyalty now, while you can."

"Let us not quarrel," Sir Harold said.

"I'm your servant, Sire." Arthur bowed in his saddle.

"Don't tempt me. One does not quarrel with servants. One flogs or hangs a servant. One can only quarrel with friends. Think on it."

Sir Harold spurred his horse and galloped on, followed seconds later by Dennis.

"What the hell are you trying to do?" Rick said.

"What does it look like, My Lord?"

"Sarcasm doesn't suit you. Are you really trying to help? To make Sir Harold more gentle, more civilised? I can't help thinking revolutions happen not at the height of oppression, but when it starts to slack off. Like water in a pot when the pressure eases."

Arthur grinned and spurred his horse.

"We could almost have been listening to the same lectures, Prof. Well, you pays your money and you takes your chance. I got to catch up on the boss."

Chapter Nine

Sir Harold glanced round the room. "We are going to be a trifle crowded I fear."

The room had one large bed, and a bench in front of an open fire. Todd had not been allowed to accompany the ladies into the convent and stood with Chris and Walter in Sir Harold's chamber.

"Walter, you sleep in the corridor with Arthur and Dennis," Sir Harold said. "Don't be out of their sight. Understood?"

Walter nodded, but looked both angry and miserable.

"Take my boots off, boy, before you go."

Sir Harold sat on the bench while the boots were pulled off, then bent forward from the waist. Walter gripped Sir Harold's outer robe and pulled it over his head. The robe folded, Walter helped Sir Harold struggle out of the chain mail shirt.

"Leave us now."

Sir Harold stretched and scratched before he sat on the bench and motioned Rick to sit with him.

"Our conversation today with Arthur…" he started.

"Sire?" Rick prompted, in the long silence.

"Arthur disturbed me."

"He disturbs many."

Sir Harold laughed. "True indeed, but not as he disturbed me. I do my duty on this earth in the station to which God called me. I expect others to do likewise. I am called to rule here; others are called to serve. I rule as I was taught to."

"You rule well and justly in this time."

"Arthur doubts the loyalty of those bound to serve me. The deer poacher knew the punishment for what he did. Any other lord would have done as much. To do less would weaken my rule. His family is provided for. I so instructed my steward. The huntsman's family is also cared for. It is the Christian duty of one in my station to his inferiors."

"Arthur is not aware of that. Indeed, neither was I."

"It was before you became my secretary. Even if you knew, why should Arthur? It is no concern of his, and it's not your place to tell him."

"No, My Lord. Aren't we in some danger at Sir William's manor? The assassins were his men. The mummer said so."

"No, he did not. Think back. He said he saw them there. They were with Andrew the physician. Sir William might, or might not, know of any plot."

"If they had been successful, would you have taken Andrew as your physician?"

"Possibly, I met him at Christmas."

"Would Sir William have let him go?"

"If I asked for him. We have strayed far from what I intended talking to you about this afternoon. I want Arthur and Dennis to listen carefully when we stay with Sir William. We need more information."

"May I ask a question?"

Sir Harold inclined his head.

"Which side are we on?"

"Your question has no meaning. I am the loyal servant of our young lord King Richard. I serve him with all my heart. He is ill advised perhaps. I hold my lands as vassal to the Duke of Lancaster."

"John of Gaunt, and he supports Wycliffe," Rick said almost to himself.

"I did not catch that."

"It was nothing, My Lord."

"Let's get some sleep."

Sir Harold stretched and turned to the bed. The two boys were lying on the bed fast asleep.

"Get them off the bed. I am tired."

"They're sound asleep, and are only boys. I can sleep on the floor."

"Yes, of course. So should they. I am the master. They are pages and should know their place. What are you laughing at?"

"Nothing, I'll move the boys."

With a sigh, Rick pulled some of the rushes together and lay on the stone floor beside the boys.

"Good night, My Lord."

Chapter Ten

At dusk on the second day they stopped at an inn. It was full, but Sir Harold simply ordered that a room be cleared for him and one for the ladies. As the night before he made no arrangements for Master Gerald, who obviously had to find his own accommodation.

"We should make Sir William's manor by nightfall," Sir Harold announced when they left the inn. He motioned Rick to ride alongside him. For most of the morning, Sir Harold quizzed Rick about the conditions of the serfs, the tenants, the servants, the burgesses of the town, the trades people and their apprentices. Rick answered as clearly and as honestly as he could, both from his knowledge of the history of the time and his personal observations since his arrival.

Sir Harold appeared to be genuinely surprised and even hurt by Arthur's views.

"My Lord, you support Wycliffe's teaching. Surely, he teaches rank and privilege are held of God in a contract to be good. Failure to be good invalidates the contract and hence the right to rank and privilege."

"The ballad again?"

When Rick started to reply, Sir Harold went on: "I do not wish to know, of a certainty, who wrote it. Hanging a friend can be very upsetting."

Rick swallowed hard.

"Wycliffe's thesis is theological, not political. You yourself have said so."

"Yes, My Lord."

They rode, silent, for some time.

"Many noblemen support Wycliffe, including the mother of the king herself, and My Lord of Lancaster."

Rick hesitated.

"Some say, My Lord, that Gaunt supports Wycliffe because he would seize church holdings for himself."

"They had best not say so in my hearing."

"No, but it has been said in many quarters."

Sir Harold brooded, and looked sideways at Rick from time to time.

"The Church has become greedy. My gentle friend Wycliffe would simply see it relinquish its temporal powers and return to its roots. The cure of souls. The preparation of man for his place in heaven. It should not be a feudal power. Where monasteries hold much land, there is much discontent. Even more than in the holdings of the most severe lords."

"St Edmundsbury and St Albans, for instance?"

"By *Corpus Dominus*, you astound me. There has been no talk, no report of any troubles at either abbey since your arrival. Yes, as at the Abbeys of St Edmundsbury and St Albans. My Lord of Lancaster would see such abuses ended."

"And the land? Who would get the land? The serfs?"

"Most of the land was at one time in the gift of the crown, and would, I suppose, become so again."

"Ah. Gaunt, I understand, is not popular."

"Master Richard, we are private here, but it ill becomes one of your station so to refer to My Lord of Lancaster. It would not do in public."

"I apologise, My Lord. But I repeat, Lord John of Gaunt is not popular."

"My Lord of Lancaster is a powerful man. Powerful men have many enemies and detractors. At court some have even spread the rumour he covets the crown for himself. Yet he works tirelessly for his nephew, our lord King Richard. He is a great lord and lives in great state. The commons of London don't like him and vilify him because he does not pander to them in the way some lords do."

Rick wondered how much of what he knew of Gaunt was fact and how much the distorted view of the partisan chroniclers of the time. Look at the press poor Richard III got from the successful Tudors and their propagandists, he thought.

Absently, Rick said: "Descendants of Lord John of Gaunt will rule this realm for many years to come."

"What was that? I didn't catch that remark."

Before Rick could reply, Todd rode up with Chris close behind.

Todd bowed in his saddle and said: "My Lord, Master Rick; may Chris and I ride on ahead a little? Everyone is too solemn for such a fine spring day. We crawl forward."

Sir Harold laughed and flicked his reins.

"Come on, we'll race these two to yonder rise."

He took off, with Todd and Chris whooping in pursuit. Rick trailed after them, with Hubert discreetly following.

Chapter Eleven

The sun was low when the sergeant turned in his saddle and shouted: "Riders ahead, My Lord. A fair company of men."

"Probably Sir William and some men come to meet us," Sir Harold said, but Rick noticed that all the men shifted in their saddles, stretched, and made sure their weapons were easily at hand.

Arthur and Dennis moved to either side of Sir Harold. Hubert, Rick noticed, came to Todd's right side and slid his short sword an inch or so out of its scabbard.

The company plodded forward, silent and watchful.

"Sir William," the sergeant shouted. "I can see him clearly, and six men."

Sir Harold moved forward to the head of the column, still flanked by Dennis and Arthur, but the men stayed on alert, poised for action.

Sir William cantered up, reined his horse in and swung out of the saddle. On foot he approached Sir Harold's horse, and one hand on Sir Harold's foot, he dropped to one knee.

"Welcome, My Lord."

"Thank you, Sir William." Sir Harold dismounted and extended a hand to William. "Please rise."

After a few minutes, they remounted and rode on side by side.

Sir William's men fell in ahead of and behind Sir Harold's

column.

At the manor Rick was surprised to learn that he and Chris were to sleep in a tiny anteroom off Sir Harold's room and that Malcolm was to lodge with Andrew the Physician.

"Is that wise?" Rick said.

"Master Andrew will be courtesy itself, as will Malcolm. We know nothing, suspect nothing. You all understand? Dennis and Arthur will also stay with Andrew."

The company here was much smaller than Rick had become used to. The great hall was less than a third the size of that at the castle. The head table held only William and Sir Harold, and their wives, plus a lady-in-waiting for each. Jo sat between Rick and Malcolm, with Arthur and Dennis flanking them.

After supper, Sir William made a long speech of welcome, before he pulled a small boy forward.

"My son, Henry. He joins Sir Harold this day as a page."

Sir Harold smiled.

Henry, after a push from his father, stepped forward to kneel in front of Sir Harold, who placed both hands on the boy's head. There was scattered applause.

"That's why Walter is there with those other youngsters and not waiting on Sir Harold," Rick said to no one in particular. "I wondered."

Sir Harold raised his hands for silence.

"Sir William, Lady Mathilde. I welcome your son Henry as my page. I thank you for your trust in me in placing your son and heir in my care till he is of age to train as a squire. Perhaps we may even revert to tradition and have him remain with me as a squire. He has many worthy men to emulate. Martin, my friend and sergeant, true companion since my youth in many a bloody battle, a stout and cunning soldier with much to teach. Arthur and Dennis who have only recently come under my banner. They are skilled warriors having trained and fought in the lands of the infidel and have much secret knowledge and wisdom."

The audience shuffled and whispered.

"My physician, Malcolm, is as skilled with his sword, drunk or sober..."

Someone guffawed, and after a startled silence, laughter rippled through Sir Harold's entourage. Sir William's people, for the most part, looked blank. Rick glanced at Andrew who looked uncomfortable.

"...as skilled with his sword as he is with his potions and his hands in the saving of life, where all others would simply give the last rites. Master Richard, my secretary, a learned and scholarly young man, but with a knowledge and understanding of the world not often found in a scholar."

When they retired for the night, Henry staggered and yawned his way along the corridor.

"I had forgotten how useless a young page, only beginning, can be," Sir Harold grumbled to Rick. "Take my boots off, Christopher."

Sir Harold sat on the bench and held up his foot. Chris reached for the heel of the boot.

"No, no, boy. They're much too tight to be removed in such fashion. Straddle my leg with your back to me, as Walter did in the convent, and grasp the boot in both hands."

Chris did so, and Sir Harold placed his other foot in the small of Chris's back and pushed. When the boot finally came off, Chris was catapulted across the room to the wall.

"Ahh. Now the other boot."

Bootless, Sir Harold stood and waited.

Rick realised Sir Harold expected to be helped to undress.

"Allow me, My Lord. Chris, we sleep in the anteroom. Off you go."

"What about the new kid?"

"God's Blood. Not again. Todd is with his mistress. I will not have the child in my bed. Christopher, there is a truckle bed under my bed. Master Richard, put the child on that. We must start his training tomorrow."

Chapter Twelve

Rick had not appreciated exactly how much work Walter did.

Servants appeared with a tub and buckets of hot and cold water that they set before the fireplace, and lit the fire.

"Master Richard, come in here at once," Sir Harold shouted.

Sitting up in bed, Sir Harold scowled.

"You boy. What is your name?"

"Henry," the boy quavered.

"Show Henry how to prepare my bath, Master Richard."

Rick poured the buckets of hot water into the tub, checked the temperature, and showed Henry how to add cold water and mix.

"This is impossible. He is much too small," Sir Harold grumbled. Henry held up a large linen towel, but even arms raised, on tiptoe, he barely covered Sir Harold's nakedness.

With a smile, Rick took the towel and raised it.

"Warm Sir Harold's clothing before the fire, Henry. I'll see to our lord's bath."

The sound of all the water pouring and splashing, and the excitement, was too much for Henry who squealed and dashed to find the chamber pot.

With a sigh, Sir Harold said: "Lady Jo must take him in hand. She is making a good job of Todd. He will join you for lessons with the other boys. I have told Sir William so."

"I was surprised," Rick said, "to hear Sir William's

announcement. I was not aware we were expecting an immediate replacement for Walter."

"Mmm ... I thought it best to have Sir William's son with us, in case he's inclined to support Master Gerald."

"You mean Henry is a hostage?"

"By no means. He is my page. Damn the boy. What's is he up to now? I smell singeing."

Clad only in his linen undershirt Sir Harold strode to the fireplace where Henry had sat on the bench to warm the clothing. Half asleep, the boy had placed the shirt too close to the fire.

He shrieked when Sir Harold shook him ferociously.

"I am not used to such a young page. Walter had been trained by my lady..." Sir Harold paused and scowled, "and by my brother Gerald, before he became my page. I have it. He is yours to train. You and the Lady Jo teach him. In the meantime, I shall take Christopher. He is more the age and size I am used to."

So far, Christopher had watched, a broad grin on his face, but kept a respectful distance from Sir Harold. At this announcement he backed off into the anteroom.

Sir Harold turned and shouted: "Christopher, come here. Come, help me dress."

"My Lord," Rick said quickly. "Christopher is, of course, honoured to be your page, but remember he is of a different time and customs. He may at times be slow and clumsy."

"He will learn. I will teach him."

"Be patient, My Lord."

"I am the very soul of patience," Sir Harold bellowed, "else, I would not be standing here in a shift, freezing to death while we talk. My clothes, Christopher."

Chapter Thirteen

"This really is quite a manor house," Rick said, when he joined the others in the great hall. "From my memory, very few in this period had guestrooms with fires."

Jo laughed and linked arms with Rick.

"You really can be a simpleton at times. Sir Harold has Sir William's room. Mathilde's room is jam-packed with Eleanor and her ladies and Sir William and his people are crushed into the solar. Our people slept in the great hall, or in the barn, or the corridors."

"That still makes it a big manor house. In many, the solar is the only private room for the family. I thought we'd all sleep here."

"Where's Chris? Why is that kid draped over you?" Arthur said. "We'll really have to keep an eye on him, Jo. He keeps acquiring small boys."

Arthur peered at Henry, and he pressed even closer to Rick.

"This is Sir William's son. You all saw him last night." Rick introduced the boy to the adults. "This is Todd, Lady Jo's page."

"Henry, why don't you let go of Master Rick, and show Todd round the Manor?" Jo said.

"But, My Lady…" Todd started.

"Chris is obviously not free now. Go."

Reluctance in both their faces, the boys left. Rick told the others of the events of the previous evening and this morning.

"God, Rick. If you keep finding new children at this rate, there won't be any room for any of our own," Jo whispered to Rick.

"Oh, Jo. Sir Harold just dumped him on me." What Jo had said sunk home, and he pressed her hand. "Do you mean what that sounds like?"

"Down, boy. Down. I was only commenting on your ability to attract small boys like flypaper attracts flies."

"How was it with Andrew last night?" Rick asked the others.

"He and his lordship here talked medicine," Arthur said. "I thought Malcolm was pompous and stuffy, but he can't hold a candle to Andrew. We got a chance to look round this morning."

"You mean, you and Dennis snooped around the house?" Malcolm said. "You were his guests."

"We were billeted on him by Sir William at Sir Harold's instructions," Dennis said.

"We're supposed to get as much info as possible, you idiot. It was you he tried to have killed, remember? Or were you too frigging drunk?"

"Did you find anything?" Rick asked.

"Master Andrew writes everything down," Dennis said.

"The bloody fool. In clear too," Arthur added.

Malcolm scowled. "I saw nothing lying around."

"No, it was in the chest."

"You didn't break the lock did you?"

"No, your lordship. I didn't break the bloody lock. I picked it. His book is back safe and sound, all locked up. He'll never know it was disturbed."

"If you moved it, he'll surely see it was."

"Give me some credit, Malcolm. Everything is back where it came from, even the dust."

"Nit-pick and quibble on your own time, you two," Rick said. "Was there anything there?"

"Yes, two leather bags full of gold coins. Relax. They're still all there. Some letters, Dennis read them, and a ledger or diary."

Rick sighed. "Dennis. For God's sake, was there anything in the letters or diary, before I kill Arthur?"

"There were three letters. I just skimmed them. Two were chit chat, more or less. The third mentioned Sir Harold by name. It said: 'by all means seek to become part of Sir Harold's household. My Lord of Arundel and His Grace Bishop Courtney continue to be interested in your news.' The signature was an unreadable scrawl."

"Richard of Arundel and Courtney of London are members of the King's Minority Council. They are both anti-Lancastrians," Rick muttered, then added aloud: "What was in the ledger/diary?"

"Well, that's a bit more difficult," Dennis said. "I started at the back. 'Sir Harold's physician, as stupid and oafish as I remember. A pity those idiots lacked the skill to carry out their mission.' Sorry, Malcolm, that's what it said."

"I'll kill the bugger."

"He had some uncomplimentary remarks about us too, but you don't need to hear them."

"I leafed back through to about the date the two assassins would have left here. There's a prescription, I suppose you could call it. I copied it down for Malcolm to look at. The book says '...requested potion for SG'sL, already paid for, dispatched this day...'"

"Are you sure of the initials?" Rick asked. "You said, SG'sL."

"Well, his writing is difficult. It was for sure S, G, two squiggles and an L. Here's the prescription, Malcolm."

"Anything?" Rick said.

Malcolm frowned at piece of parchment. "I'll need to study it a while."

"Do you think Chris will be all right with Sir Harold?" Rick said to the group in general.

"Yes, he'll be fine," Jo said. "Why shouldn't he?"

"He's a bit scared of Sir Harold, you know, and Sir Harold can be very impatient and quick with his hands."

"Chris needs toughening up a bit," Dennis said.

Arthur added: "He's a good kid, but the odd slap won't hurt him. Dennis is right. Chris can be a bit of a wimp at times. Sir Harold will be good for him."

"What do you think, Malcolm?"

"I don't know. There's something odd about it. Maybe Lady Eleanor can help me."

"What on earth are you talking about?"

"The prescription, of course, aren't you?"

Arthur laughed. "Always right up to the minute, aren't we, Doc?"

Chapter Fourteen

"The sergeant says Walter and another two boys will leave for a training castle in a couple of days," Arthur said, at dinner. "He said to be on the watch for any move from any of them against Chris or Todd."

"God, I'd hoped we were finished with all that now that Walter's out of Sir Harold's service," Rick said.

Sir Harold beckoned Rick to approach the high table. There, Rick bowed and said quietly: "I will have some news later, My Lord."

Sir Harold nodded. "We have other business to deal with too. We will meet in my chamber before supper."

At Sir Harold's signal, Chris rushed forward to refill his wineglass.

"Your cousin is a gentle, somewhat fearful boy, despite his temper, and his fights with Walter. Over gentle, I fear, for this time and place. I have decided to have him trained as my squire under Martin, and Arthur and Dennis, of course. We will start him on that when we reach our summer place."

Rick thanked Sir Harold, but was not sure, from Chris's expression, that the prospect pleased the boy.

Sir Harold raised his voice to be heard all over the hall.

"You have no sword fight for us today, I see, Sir William. Perhaps our two physicians would care to stage a fight?"

Malcolm grinned at Sir Harold from his place at a side table.

"With the utmost pleasure, if Master Andrew is willing."

Red-faced, Andrew bowed to Sir William and stammered: "As Your Lordship knows, I am more skilled at the saving of life than the taking of it…"

"Except by accident, of course," a voice said from somewhere in the hall, and there was laughter from Sir William's retainers.

"…I must decline," Andrew finished.

"A mere jest, nothing more," Sir Harold said. "Most excellent entertainment."

Walter advanced to the centre of the hall. "If Sir Harold wishes to see a fight, I will fight Christopher, page to Master Richard."

Sir Harold scowled at Walter. "Be silent, I will deal with you later."

"My Lord Brother." Gerald smiled. "Walter is no longer your page. Such a bout might well be entertaining."

"Indeed," Sir William said, "a friendly tussle between the two youths might well be an amusing diversion."

Dennis moved to stand behind Sir Harold. He tugged at his sleeve, and whispered to him. Sir Harold shook his head angrily, but Dennis persisted.

At Sir Harold's command Chris stepped close to him. They exchanged a few words and Chris chewed at his lower lip, but after a quick glance at Dennis, nodded.

With a grim smile, Sir Harold turned back to the hall and raised his voice. "As the challenged, Christopher has the right to choose how they shall fight…"

"My Lord Brother, this is simply a friendly match between two boys."

"No, Walter is about to become a squire. I would not permit a man of position to fight, publicly, a servant, or someone below his station. It would not be fitting. Christopher is now my squire-in-training. He can quite properly engage in formal combat, unless, of course, Christopher considers Walter, who is not now a page, and is not yet formally a squire-in-training, beneath his dignity."

Sir Harold looked at Chris, who grinned and shook his head. Gerald scowled, and Walter appeared both angry and confused.

"Were this a tournament and they both full grown, trained adults, Christopher would chose the poleaxe. This, I will not allow here. They will use padded quarterstaffs. No other weapons. Sir William, will you have your master-at-arms prepare the staffs?"

While they waited, the minstrels sang, but no one really listened. Walter stood with the other youths who were about to leave to train as squires, and Gerald joined them.

Worried, Rick said: "What on earth are you thinking of? Poleaxes, indeed. Do you even know what a poleaxe is and what it would do to you?"

Chris looked blank and Rick went on: "It's a heavy axe on a long handle with spike on the other side of the pole and sometimes a spike at each end too. The axe landing on top of your head would split it in half like a watermelon."

"Leave be, Rick, it's quarterstaffs," Arthur said. "Chris'll be fine."

He and Dennis pulled Chris to one side and stood talking seriously to him.

"My Lord," Rick said, "we cannot allow this."

"Silence, I have allowed it."

"Jo, what do you think?" Rick asked.

"Chris will be fine. A few bruises, nothing more."

Two of Sir William's men arrived with quarterstaffs: wooden poles about an inch and a half thick and five feet long. Both ends had padding tied on with leather thongs.

The sergeant carefully examined both staffs and bowed to Sir William and Sir Harold.

"There is no difference, My Lords. They are both well prepared. Christopher, choose."

Chris selected one and stepped back.

"Remove your tunics and undershirts. Arthur, will you check Walter for other weapons?"

"I will check Christopher," Gerald said.

Arthur frisked Walter thoroughly, and removed a small dagger from the top of his right boot.

When Gerald ran his hands over Chris, Chris squirmed.

"I would like the training of you, my lad, but perhaps it would have been best for all if I had chosen you instead of the other at the circle."

Chris looked at him with fear and loathing.

The boys took their positions, and slowly circled each other.

"A gold piece on Christopher, Brother Gerald," Sir Harold called.

"Done."

In no time, bets were placed on all sides. Rick was surprised at how calm and confident Chris appeared. He actually looked as if he knew what he was doing. Walter lunged and Chris parried very successfully. At first, Walter was his usual arrogant self, careless, almost contemptuous, but when Chris parried each stroke, and penetrated Walter's guard twice with comparative ease, he became wary.

"Shit, Dennis. It's the same as in training. He frigging well doesn't have the killer instinct," Arthur said.

"Have you two been teaching him to fight?" Rick said. "Why didn't I know?"

"Open your frigging eyes and look round sometimes. Come on, Chris. Attack. Don't wait for him. Take the frigging initiative."

But Chris continued to fight defensively, and the two youths Walter had been with grew restive. One stepped up behind Chris and pushed him. Someone in the crowd shouted, and Todd launched himself at the youth. Chris glanced over his shoulder and saw two youths jumping on Todd. One blow from Walter got through, then Chris was a blur of movement. Walter retreated under the onslaught. His pole spun out of his hand. Chris jabbed hard at Walter's solar plexus, and swung the staff to connect with an audible crack under Walter's chin. Before Walter hit the ground, Chris turned and advanced on the youths holding Todd. One look at Chris's face was enough, and they backed off.

"Well done, Christopher. By *Corpus Christi*, well done," Sir Harold shouted.

There was applause. Todd hugged Chris, and they capered round each other. While the others crowded in to congratulate Chris, Henry pushed through, open hero worship in his eyes, to pat Chris's back.

"Come here, Christopher," Sir Harold called above the din. "Brother Gerald, my gold piece."

Gerald fumbled in his purse and produced a coin and thrust it toward Sir Harold.

"No, my tribute to the victor."

Red with fury, Gerald flipped the coin towards Chris, but Todd caught it, and looking at Sir Harold, bit it. Sir Harold roared with laughter.

"A sound judge, eh brother?"

Todd and Chris both grinned, bowed to Sir William and Sir Harold and, less deeply, to Gerald.

"By your leave," Gerald said, "I will go and see how Walter fares."

"You should check Chris over," Rick said to Jo, "either you or Malcolm."

"Nonsense, you spoil the boy." Sir Harold slapped Chris's bare shoulder. "Get dressed, that was very nicely done. Arthur and Dennis have made a good start with you, even if it was without permission. I am well pleased with my new page, squire-to-be."

Later that afternoon, Rick knocked on Sir Harold's door. Chris answered.

"Master Richard, My Lord." He winked at Rick.

"Some wine before we set to business?" Sir Harold said.

"As My Lord pleases."

At Sir Harold's snap of the fingers, Chris leapt to pour wine. He slopped a little from the goblet he handed to Sir Harold.

"A cloth, boy, a cloth."

When Chris offered him a hand towel, Sir Harold scowled. "Do you wait till it stains my whole robe?" he said, and, when Chris dabbed at him, "God's wounds, boy."

Sir Harold snatched the towel, wiped vigorously, and slapped Chris hard with the towel, before throwing it in a corner.

"My Lord. Patience," Rick said.

"I am the most patient of men. A veritable model of patience. A less patient man would have him, and you, flogged. Leave us, Christopher."

With a grin at Rick, Chris withdrew.

"Really, how is the boy to learn anything if you constantly interfere? He is a good boy, and will be an excellent page and squire, but he lacks polish."

Rick told Sir Harold of Dennis's report.

Sir Harold rubbed his earlobe. "So, My Lord of Arundel and Bishop Courtney are in indirect correspondence with Andrew the Physician."

"Andrew obviously knew of the attempt on Malcolm, even if he didn't initiate it," Rick said, "and he did send a package of some description to an S G L."

"Who is S G L?"

"We don't know yet. This is how it was written."

Sir Harold squinted at the shape Rick had scratched in the ashes on the hearth, and almost to himself said: "The Lady Gwenne? Sir Gerald's Lady. Could it be? S, G, something, something L? What potion could she have need of that My Lady could not provide?"

"Perhaps Malcolm can provide a clue when he's deciphered the prescription."

"Are Andrew's activities for Gerald connected with his association with Arundel and Courtney, I wonder?"

"We shall be as observant as possible."

"Well, we have letters, and I wish to look over the accounts for this manor."

Chapter Fifteen

When they prepared to leave next morning, Henry's lower lip jutted out and quivered while he watched Todd and Chris mount up. Rick was about to lift the boy to ride with him, when a young manservant led a horse over at the trot. He grinned at Henry and made a stirrup for the boy with his hands. Mounted, Henry beamed round him. The servant turned to Rick and touched his forelock.

"I be Wilf, master. Sir William says I be part of your household while Master Henry is under your care."

When they were about to leave, Rick noticed Walter and the other two squires-to-be were also mounted. They travelled as a group till nearly noon. Sir Harold and Gerald rode a little away from the main group and argued, Rick thought, but he was too far away to be sure. Toward noon, Sir Harold beckoned Rick to ride up.

"My brother will ride with the youths to where they will train. I wish you to accompany him. Sir William has provided an escort."

"Does Henry go with me?"

Sir Harold rode silently for so long that Rick thought he had not heard the question. When he was about to repeat it, Sir Harold said: "No, I will not risk Henry in Gerald's hands."

"Then Henry *is* a hostage."

"No, but I would not have him become so by any fault or default of ours. Henry will stay with the Lady Jo. Take Todd with you, and Dennis."

When Rick dropped back to tell Jo and Malcolm of the change in plan, Dennis spurred forward to join Sir Harold.

"Take care. Don't let anything happen to you, please." Jo squeezed Rick's hand. "Don't trust Gerald at all, and look after Todd."

"Damn it, Jo. There you go again. I'm not a scoutmaster. It's always, 'look after the boys, Rick. It's all right, Rick will see to the boys.' I'm fed up with it."

"What's the Prof's beef now?" Arthur said, joining them. "Afraid someone will make off with Chris? A joke, Rick, a joke! I know Chris better than that, but for once, Rick's right. Todd, you look after Rick. Don't stick anyone I wouldn't, OK?"

Todd turned in his saddle to look at Jo and said: "Am I to go? Really? My Lady?"

"Yes, Todd. You do as our lord Sir Harold orders. We all do."

When the trail forked, the squires-to-be and Gerald drew off to one side. They were joined by four mounted men. When Rick, Dennis and Todd pulled off the trail, Master Gerald stood in his stirrups, and shouted: "We will now ride at a pace more appropriate for men. Any who cannot keep pace with us, travel on their own. Come, Walter, we have wasted enough time."

The initial gallop could not be sustained, and they soon settled to a steady pace; faster than that of the main group, but not one that presented any difficulty for Rick or Todd. Walter and Gerald rode at the head of the column, the youths and three of Sir William's retainers in the middle, and Todd, Rick, Dennis, and the fourth soldier breathed their dust.

At dusk, they stopped at a roadside inn. When Rick and the rearguard arrived, the innkeeper said: "I have only one room left. A good room with a large bed. It will take four full-grown men most comfortably."

"Fine, innkeeper. I will take it. You have sleeping platforms round your hall, I take it? That, or the barns, will do the others."

The main room of the inn was dark and smoky. A fire burned at one end, but there was no chimney, only a hole in the roof. Wool merchants ate at a rough plank table. They glanced up when Gerald strode in followed by Rick.

Gerald moved to the fireplace and glared at the young man who sat on the only bench. After only a brief hesitation the man rose, bowed slightly and moved away.

"Innkeeper. Mulled ale. And quickly," Gerald shouted, and sat.

"Sit, Master Secretary, sit."

Rick had been about to sit, anyway.

Boy, I'd better be careful, he thought. I wouldn't have seated myself without an invitation in Sir Harold's presence.

"Thank you, Master Gerald."

"Sir Gerald, I am a knight. It is only with my brother's household I am still Master Gerald."

"I am of you brother's household..." At Gerald's look, Rick's voice tailed off. "But we are out of Sir Harold's domain here. I understand, Sir Gerald."

"See you do. And your man, Dennis."

They sipped their mulled ale while Gerald stared morosely at the fire.

"The page of the Lady Jo's, Todd. What do you know of his history?"

"Nothing, really, Sir Gerald. He was a turnspit in the castle kitchen till Sir Harold gave him to us."

"Mmm. He learns too quickly to be a Saxon peasant, son of peasants. He must have some Norman blood. A by-blow of some lord, perhaps."

"So some of the ladies say."

"What age is he?"

"Nine or ten perhaps, but we really don't know."

"Innkeeper. More ale."

Rick was unsure if it was proper for him to initiate conversation. He had never been alone with Gerald before, and had never had anything even approaching a conversation with him.

"You have taught him," Gerald said. "He learns well? Better than Walter?"

"He is a more willing pupil than Walter."

"Be open and honest, Sirrah. He is of quicker intellect than my cousin Walter?"

Reluctantly, Rick nodded. This was potentially dangerous water.

"Is that a yes or a no? Answer me directly."

"Yes, he appears quicker than Walter. Already he reads better and figures more quickly."

"Appears? We are not diplomats to mince words. You are over careful. Is he or not?"

"He is, I think."

Gerald laughed out loud, and the two merchants looked over at them.

"By Our Lady, my brother has a good eye for a secretary. You are as discreet as you are competent, perhaps a shade too competent, competent beyond your apparent station. Nine or ten you say, and of the town?"

"No one really knows."

"Enough. Silence."

Gerald brooded, and muttered to himself.

"There were no notable lords I heard of at the castle at that time, unless incognito. Could these have been sent for him? Have I been wrong? They defend him as no man I know of would defend a mere turnspit become page. I wonder."

Rick strained his ears to hear what Gerald was saying.

"Innkeeper. More ale. Where is our meal?"

"We are almost ready, My Lord. A few more minutes only."

Gerald dismissed him with a wave of his hand.

"It is strange. The Lady Gwenne and I have no children. She has miscarried twice." He laughed, a short bark devoid of any amusement. "I have bastards, some I know of, doubtless others I do not know of, in many lands, but no legitimate heir."

Rick sat, unsure if the comments were meant for him or not, and not at all sure this was a particularly safe conversation.

"My brother has three daughters only, now his son is dead. Walter's father has proposed an alliance of Walter with Harold's oldest daughter. Did you know that?" Gerald snorted. "If my brother and I die without male issue, all goes to Walter or his father anyway. Marriage would simply bind it sooner."

Obviously no comment was required of Rick, and he sipped his ale.

"What of you? How many bastards have you?"

Rick blushed. He could feel himself go red all over, and hoped in the flickering light it would not show.

Gerald stared into the fire; he seemed lost in thought. Almost to himself he said: "Walter has a savage time ahead. I cannot be seen to offer any comfort or consolation now. It would make matters harder for him." He shook himself. "Damn the man. Innkeeper. My supper."

"At once, My Lord, at once."

"Set a table here, before the fire. Master Richard, sup with me. Todd will serve."

The others of the party sat at a trestle table down the room. The squires-to-be on one side and the escort and Dennis on the other.

Supper over, Gerald stretched. "To bed. We ride at first light. Master Secretary, join me in my chamber – and bring Todd."

They followed the servant with a candle up the stairs to the room.

"Our boots, boy."

Todd helped both of them out of their boots, pulled Gerald's over-shirt clear and helped him struggle out of his chain mail shirt.

"That will do, boy. We will sleep as we are now."

Gerald looked critically at Todd.

"Nine or ten. Mmm. Strip, boy, I would see all of you."

Surprised, Todd looked at Rick who shrugged, and nodded.

Stripped, Todd looked even smaller and more vulnerable. He shivered when Gerald took his arm and turned him.

"Hold the candle, Master Richard."

Even now, Todd's back and buttocks were still criss-crossed with scars, though faded.

Carefully, Gerald examined him from head to toe. With a shrug, Gerald said: "Could be, I suppose. Put your shift on, boy, and let's get to bed."

"Are we to sleep here?"

Before Rick could reply, Gerald said: "Yes, boy. You and your master may sleep on that half of the bed."

When they lay, Rick between Gerald and Todd, Gerald said quietly: "Relax, I do not find you appealing, and the boy is much too small."

Chapter Sixteen

Their destination when they reached it next afternoon surprised Rick. He had expected a castle probably bigger than Sir Harold's and had racked his mind to think of where it could be. The only castle ruin to survive to his time in this area was Sir Harold's.

Instead, they came upon a very large manor house. Rick thought it enormous by the standards of the day with countless barns and outhouses and servants everywhere.

When they clattered into the central courtyard a tall, blond, distinguished man met them. Gerald immediately dismounted and bowed low. Rick, Dennis, and Todd followed his example.

"Sir Gerald, I had not expected you to accompany these youths."

"My Lord, one of them, Walter my cousin, will be heir to our estate should my brother and I die without male issue. He is of value to our line and it pleases me that he will be under your tutelage."

"Here he is but one of fourteen squires-in-training and among the most recently come. He will have many hard lessons to learn, and some of the hardest may be from his fellow squires here already."

At a gesture, a massive and decidedly frightening looking soldier stepped forward. He grinned.

"Masters, dismount. Lead your horses after me. I will show

you your quarters and your duties."

One of the three boys did not bow the instant he dismounted and the soldier struck him.

"Manners, masters, manners. Bow to My Lord."

Lord Thomas nodded his head in curt acknowledgement before he and Gerald strode off.

A man bustled forward and bowed slightly.

"I am My Lord's major-domo."

"Richard, secretary to Sir Harold Fitzwilliam," Rick said.

"We shall find accommodation for you, your man, and your page. Come, Master Secretary."

At first light next morning, Rick was already awake when a servant peered at them in their corner of the great hall and stirred Todd with his toe.

"Up boy, rouse your master. Tell him Sir Gerald means to ride out soon. Your mounts are already saddled. I would not keep Sir Gerald waiting in his present humour."

In the courtyard, while they waited for Gerald, Rick saw figures move beside an outhouse building. In the dawn light, Rick could barely make out that one of the figures was Walter clad in nothing but a breechclout. He carried something and beside him a taller youth swung a stick.

"Damn. Where the hell has Todd got to?" Dennis stood in his stirrups and looked round. "There's Gerald making his farewells."

"I'm here." Todd ran over and scrambled into his saddle. "I only sneaked over to see what was happening. That's night soil from the squires' barracks Walter carried. He had to empty it in the cesspool." Todd wrinkled his nose and laughed. "Imagine, Walter doing slavey work. The man with him beat him there. Walter had to bow and say, thank you, after each stroke."

"You are not to chatter endlessly and giggle all day, boy," Gerald snarled.

Gerald mounted and galloped off. The other three had to spur hard to keep up with him, but soon they slowed to a trot and finally to a walk and plodded ahead in silence, with Gerald in the lead.

Dennis commented in a low voice to Rick on the absence of an escort.

An hour or more out, Gerald turned and waved Rick to ride beside him.

"I don't like this new style of training squires-to-be. A gentleman of quality should not be exposed before his inferiors."

He rode silent again.

"Isn't personal service to your lord or knight the accepted duty of a squire?" Rick said.

"Aye, but there you have it. You have bathed, dressed, and picked up after my brother as he would for his Lord of Lancaster or his grace the King. That detracts not from a man's rank, dignity, or pride. I have so served My Lord when a squire. Even as a knight I have attended closely on My Lord and seen to his needs and pleasures. I expect the same from those under me."

"Then…"

"Don't interrupt. Those youths have no personal knight. They are a pack under a Master of Hounds. Our whole system is in peril."

Rick made no reply and they rode for some time before Gerald said: "You are dull company. Fall back. Send Todd to ride with me."

"What should I talk about?" Todd said, panic in his voice.

"I've never known you short of words before," Dennis said.

"When I make the ladies laugh he scowls. He frightens me."

"Todd. Come forward. Now."

"I think leaving Walter has really upset him," Rick said.

"Couldn't happen to a nicer kid, but it won't improve his temperament any."

"Do you think it'll be really tough on him?"

"Medieval boot camp. As Arthur says, nothing changes. The

new squaddies get beaten and hazed by those one step above them. The real nasties, like Walter, when they move up enjoy passing it on. Those who survive will be damn tough buggers or totally cowed. Wasn't it about now that the noble ideal of feudal chivalry began to crumble?"

"I don't know if it ever really existed outside the romances. The knights weren't chivalrous to anyone below their station. After a battle or a siege, they slaughtered, butchered, anyone whose ransom wouldn't be high enough. Chaucer's 'perfekt gentile knight' was a real whitewash job. The closest we'll see is Sir Harold. He doesn't go out of his way to be cruel, but he does have some real rough edges."

"What's different, Rick? In our day the titles are different and it looks a bit more civilised, but the ones on top still do as they damn well please. Did you ever think about the ones below you? Sure we look after Todd, but what about the other stinking brats around the town and castle? What we spend on him would keep dozens of those other kids. Todd takes it all as his right and looks down on the likes of Robert and the slaveys."

"Shit, Dennis. I don't see you and Arthur spreading much of your smokies loot around and you've both signed up with Sir Harold. You even more than Arthur."

"I wasn't preaching at you Rick. I know which side is up. I've been below stairs and I'm not going back down if I can help it. Anyway, I shook on a deal with Sir Harold. As you say, he's the best there is for us and I do my best for him."

They rode for some miles before Rick said: "Don't you think it odd that Gerald and Lady Gwenne have no children? He's not homosexual, bisexual maybe, but he has had bastards by other women."

"Yes, I wondered about that. Perhaps Malcolm will have some answers for us when we meet up. About the package, I mean."

At that Todd dropped back.

"Sir Gerald asks that you join him, Master Rick."

"Todd is intelligent, Master Richard. Sharp, alert, pert, a shade too forward mayhap. I would beat him soundly. Nine or ten you say?"

Still in the saddle, they munched on the bread and cheese and the chunks of cold fowl and meat that Lord Thomas's servants had packed in their saddlebags.

Mid-afternoon found them in sight of a small hamlet. At its centre was a tiny church and a small manor house surrounded by a stout wooden palisade. They had obviously been seen. On their approach, a man dressed in the style Sir Harold usually wore, but somehow more rustic, appeared at the gate, and buckled on a sword belt. Some villeins ran to join him and stood at the gate, uncertain what to do.

"They fear we may be robbers," Gerald laughed. "A high state of preparedness, I must say."

They continued their leisurely approach and within hailing distance of the gate stopped.

"I am Sir Gerald Fitzwilliam, brother to Sir Harold, neighbour to your lord, the Lord Thomas."

The man with the sword hurried forward.

"Edwin, My Lord." He bowed low. "Welcome to my humble holding. All I have is yours."

"Yes," Gerald said. He swung off his horse and threw the reins to Todd. "Yes. We will sup with you and pass the night here. Does Lord Thomas hunt this way often?"

"Fowl in season, there is little larger here on the fens."

"Good, the maids should be fresh and well rested. I am in need of diversion."

Gerald strode off.

Edwin nodded. At his signal, servants led the horses in. Rick and the others dismounted and slowly followed Sir Gerald.

The manor house had a very small great hall.

"It's tiny," Todd said. "It's smaller than half the solar at home. It doesn't even have a proper fireplace."

"You're a snob," Rick said.

"What's a snob?"

Before Rick could reply, a lady entered the hall ushering before her two little girls and a boy. She was red-faced and breathless, and her hands darted from the shoulders of the children to her hair and back.

"Master Edwin. There is a stranger in the solar bussing one of our serving wenches. I removed the children when he threw her on the bed and leapt on her."

She quivered and Edwin, with a rather lopsided smile at Rick, drew her through the rood screen. Rick could hear a low voiced and obviously heated exchange.

Supper was rather strained, Rick felt, but Gerald was oblivious to the atmosphere. He had reappeared after about an hour, complimented Edwin on the quality of his bed, graciously permitted Martha, Sir Edwin's wife, and the children to be presented to him, and announced he would sleep in the solar that night.

After the meal, they adjourned to the solar. There, Gerald said: "How old is your boy, madam?"

"Eleven, Sir Gerald. Twelve come Michaelmas."

"He is a well-grown, sturdy, handsome boy. I congratulate you. Come boy, stand by me."

The boy moved slowly, hesitantly, to stand beside Gerald. "Why is the boy still at home? Why not a page at some noble house?"

"I be not a knight," Edwin said. "A lowly squire..."

"Given the care and charge of this manor for services to Lord Thomas," Martha said.

"You hold the manor under one of Lord Thomas's underlings?"

"Indeed no," Martha said, "in direct fealty to Lord Thomas himself for personal services rendered."

"I cannot afford the fee for him to become a squire-in-training and I would not have him a mere servant at the great house," Edwin said.

"What is your name, boy?"

"Adam, My Lord."

"Can you read?"

"I know my letters, Sir Knight. The priest teaches me."

"Would you like to be a page in a great house and perhaps someday a squire?"

"Oh yes."

"Is it fair to raise the boy's hopes?" Rick said.

"Silence, Sirrah. Would you like to be my page?"

Adam looked at his parents. They both looked torn between the advantage they could see and uncertainty about Gerald.

"Well, Adam?"

"Yes, My Lord, if my parents permit."

"It is late. We have had a tiring day," Gerald said. "You may withdraw. Adam, you will stay, my page for this night. If you suit me, you will leave with us tomorrow."

Rick hardly knew where to look when they withdrew to the great hall. Once there, Martha dispatched some of the servants to sleep in the barn and after she checked there was enough straw for Rick, Dennis and Todd, ushered the girls into a corner. They could hear her low insistent voice and the deeper rumble of Edwin's while they argued about the events.

The door to the solar opened and Gerald stepped out.

"A call of nature. Pray do not disturb yourselves," he said, and passed through. Minutes later he passed back again with one of the serving wenches grasped by the wrist and pulled the giggling girl after him.

"At least Adam's safe for the moment," Rick whispered to Dennis over Todd's head.

"Safe, but having his education broadened?"

Chapter Seventeen

At dawn the usual stir and bustle of servants preparing for a new day roused Rick. He had relieved himself and splashed water from the trough on his face when Todd approached.

Todd yawned and scratched sleepily.

"Sir Gerald says you are to come at once," he said.

Rick shook his hands more or less dry while he waited for Todd to finish and adjust his dress.

"Lady Jo will kill you if she sees you pee against the wall again."

Todd grinned. "Where did you go?"

In the solar, Gerald drummed his fingers on the window ledge. Edwin and Martha stood together and talked in low voices on the other side of the bed. Adam was on his knees beside a wooden chest on the floor.

"At last." Gerald scowled.

Rick opened his mouth to reply and Gerald waved towards the table and a stool.

"Sit, write."

"What shall I write?"

"I, Sir Gerald Fitzwilliam, hereby declare I will indemnify Edwin, father of Adam, of any penalty imposed by Lord Thomas as a consequence of the said Adam parting Lord Thomas's domain without prior consent and approval to serve as my page. Should

Adam prove suitable I will at an appropriate time engage to have him trained as a squire in all the gentlemanly arts of war. In token of which I hereby affix my seal."

Rick finished the parchment and sanded it carefully. He handed it to Gerald and whispered: "Is this wise? Sir Harold..."

"I am my own master, Sirrah. Here, seal it with my ring."

"Don't you wish to read it first?"

"I have not read such chicken scratchings since I became a knight. Read it to us."

"Todd," Rick said, "you read it aloud to check what I have written."

In a high, clear voice Todd read out the document and, at Gerald's nod, Rick sealed it. As an afterthought he picked up the quill again and wrote quickly.

"Read it out, Todd."

"Written in the presence of Sir Gerald and Edwin, father of Adam, by Richard, Secretary to Sir Harold Fitzwilliam.

"Hereto, affixed their marks."

Rick signed the document with a flourish and handed the quill to Gerald who scrawled his name. When he handed the document and the quill to Edwin, Rick said: "Just make your mark, Master Edwin."

Martha glared at Rick. "My Goodman Edwin can read and write."

"Now, madam, I have enjoyed your hospitality, but we must ride."

Martha wept and clung to Adam.

"God's Blood. He is not going to his death. We have other pages. Master Richard will care for him," Rick groaned, "and see to his schooling. He will be better schooled thus than he would be here."

In the courtyard, Dennis waited beside their saddled horses.

"How is Adam to travel?" Rick said.

Gerald shrugged.

"The two boys can ride together."

When Todd opened his mouth to protest, Rick said in a low voice: "Shut up, Todd, or I'll beat you so hard you'll be glad to walk."

About an hour out, Rick suggested to Todd that he and Adam should swap places, but after he looked at them, said: "There's room on the saddle for both of you. I'm sure you'd be more comfortable that way than bouncing about on the rump behind the saddle."

Adam slid down. With Rick's help he climbed back up in front of Todd who held grimly onto the reins and kept both feet tight in the stirrups. A short time later, Rick noticed both boys giggled and laughed together.

They rode most of the day; again they ate in the saddle. Shortly before dusk Gerald said: "There should be an inn close by. We will sup and stop for the night there. It should only be a morning's ride to my brother's summer manor.

The inn was small and, Rick thought, not very clean even by the standards of the day. Other inns Rick had seen, though dark and dingy to his eye, had the rushes changed fairly frequently – if only to the extent of sweeping out the rushes from the common area, stained with spilt beer and food, and replacing them with the rushes swept off the sleeping ledges that edged the room. Here the rushes smelled of stale beer, and long ago consumed meals. With no sleeping ledge, guests in the common room slept on these same rushes adding the aroma of unwashed humanity to the smell of tallow candles and the smoke from the fire as it drifted towards the hole in the roof.

Gerald refused to sleep in the common area, and insisted on the only room. After a quick inspection of the room, Gerald had them stack their packs and saddlebags on the side of the bed away from the door.

Chapter Eighteen

Next morning was dull, almost dark, with a fine drizzle. The night had been uneventful, if not exactly restful, with both Todd and Adam tossing and turning.

When they rode out Rick noticed that Gerald checked the draw of his sword and, with an oath and a glare at the lead-grey sky, pulled off his riding cloak to drape it over the horse's neck. When Rick spurred to ride beside him, Gerald growled: "Single file. Me, the boys, you, then Dennis. Keep your eyes open and your sword hand free."

Almost half the morning had passed when they crossed an open space, and forded a steep-sided stream in the centre. Gerald raised his hand and beckoned them to close up on him.

"Look. There ahead. There is a tree fallen across the trail where it turns. If we advance to it, we will have no room to manoeuvre. We could be trapped."

"It could simply be a fallen tree," Rick said.

"Yes, go forward to check on foot."

Rick dismounted and walked along the narrow trail to the tree. It had been cut.

"It's very heavy. We'll need to force our way through the bush on either side."

He drew his sword to slash at the undergrowth. At his first attempt a man with a short sword appeared on the other side of the bush. Rick shouted and raced back to the others. Men appeared from nowhere.

"Back to the stream," Dennis shouted.

They raced back to the ford. Without time to remount, Rick hung onto his horse's stirrups. Across the ford, they stopped and dismounted barely ahead of their pursuers. At a hand signal from one man, some went upstream and others downstream.

"Damn, we should have kept going. They'll outflank us," Rick said.

"Save your breath, Rick," Dennis said. "Watch our back."

Dennis and Gerald faced the ford and three men started across. The clash of steel on steel rang out. Gerald's sword sliced across one man's face and neck. The second hesitated and Dennis lunged, twisted, and pulled. The man dropped face down into the stream. The third pressed his attack on Gerald who slipped on the muddy bank and left himself exposed for an instant. With a shout, the man thrust. The sword glanced off the chain mail shirt and Dennis's blade swung down to sever the hand at the wrist.

Rick, Adam and Todd had been so engrossed in the struggle at the ford, they had not watched behind them.

Adam shouted when someone grabbed him. Todd raised his hands and turned. The man who jumped on Todd bear-hugged him, but the boy's hands were free and they scrabbled at his attacker's face and eyes. The fingers gouged at his eyes, and the man screamed and dropped Todd.

Another man with a quarterstaff slowed when Todd crouched, a dagger now in his hand. He feinted with the staff and, on Todd's response, reversed his swing to bring it up towards Todd's groin. At the last minute, Todd twisted and the staff hit his outer thigh with a sickening thud. Todd dropped. Rick plunged his sword into the foe's side when he prepared to pound Todd's head. The man's fall wrenched the blade out of Rick's grasp and he stood weaponless.

Adam's captor slackened his grip ready to throw the boy aside and attack Rick. When the hand passed in front of him, Adam grabbed and bit hard. He was shaken off, but fell to one side of the man and promptly sank his teeth into the bare calf beside him. With his free hand, he drew his dagger and plunged it into the thigh above him, simultaneously with Rick's fist connecting in an uppercut. The man fell and lay still.

The four on the other side of the stream were still there, weapons in hand.

A standoff, Rick thought, they're afraid to attack across the ford now, and we'll lose our advantage if we start over the stream.

I'd better see to Todd.

When Rick turned back, Todd had staggered to his feet, his face fish-belly white. Rick watched speechless and horrified while Todd lurched over to the man Rick had knocked out, pulled the head back by the hair and cut the carotid artery. Todd's first attacker sat on the ground, his face in his hands. Blood dripped between his fingers and he moaned. Steadier now, on cat feet Todd stepped in front of him. He tossed a pebble to the man's left. The head swivelled left, the chin up, and Todd's dagger darted in and out, the neck spurted blood and the body fell back.

God, Rick thought, this is the child I threatened to beat this morning. Shit. Hoof-beats. They've got reinforcements.

He and Todd turned to look past Gerald and Dennis. The four remaining attackers split into pairs and ran, one pair upstream and the other down. They were ridden down rapidly and dragged back to be thrown to their knees before Gerald.

"Sir Harold's men," Rick sighed with relief when he saw the uniform of one of the horsemen.

"Master Gerald, your brother sent us to meet you."

"Well met. We will return to the inn. I have a score to settle. Bring those with you." Gerald indicated those of the group who were still alive. He turned to look at Rick and nodded grim approval at the carnage.

"Well done."

Rick, who now felt sick, nodded and put his hand on Todd's shoulder.

"I'm fine, Master Rick. I've had worse beatings," Todd said, but Rick saw him wince when Dennis helped him into his saddle.

"One of you take Adam," Rick instructed the soldiers.

Chapter Nineteen

When they clattered into the inn courtyard the innkeeper emerged. He stopped when he saw Gerald. The smile of greeting froze on his face.

"We have returned to settle our account innkeeper, but it is late. We will dine first. Dennis, go with him."

The innkeeper scurried off, Dennis and Adam at his heels.

Gerald turned to the soldier in charge.

"Hang those two."

He pointed.

"Should we not question them first?" Rick said.

"No, they are brigands. Proceed."

Rick recognised the two remaining bandits. They had been at the inn the night before.

Gerald placed his dagger point against the bare chest of one of them. "What did you intend for us?"

The man tried to pull back when Gerald pressed the point in. "Simple murder and robbery? Hold me to ransom? What for the boys? A quick death? Or did your men plan to have some amusement first?"

With each question Gerald either pressed or twisted the blade and the man squirmed.

"Are those dead? Fine, hang these. Damn the man. Where's my dinner? I'm hungry."

The innkeeper appeared and announced that the meal was ready. He became even whiter when he saw the heads of the first two bandits on poles beside the barn while the others twisted in the air, feet barly inches above the ground.

All the others ate heartily and drank copious draughts of ale, but Rick felt sick. Todd noticed Rick was not eating.

"I'm sorry," Todd said. "I shouldn't be seated till you have eaten."

The effort was rather spoilt by the speech being mumbled through a mouth stuffed with stew and black bread. Rick laughed and Todd went on: "Sir Gerald did say we were all to sit at once. Can I get you anything?"

"No, Todd. You have done enough today."

"That was an excellent meal innkeeper and very quickly prepared." Gerald smiled and the man trembled. "You anticipated a large company for dinner today?"

"There were two caldrons of stew almost ready, and fresh ale from the storeroom," Dennis said.

"Where are the scullions and his wife?"

"I have them locked in the storeroom."

"Good. Sergeant."

The soldier in charge stood.

"My Lord?"

"I saw a loose hayloft ladder outside. Have it brought in here."

Gerald sipped his ale and smiled at the innkeeper.

"Some more wood for the fire. No, no. One of my men will fetch it. I would not have you tire too early."

The ladder consisted of two poles about nine feet long tied together at the top and about two feet apart at the bottom with shorter poles as cross pieces.

"Excellent. Tie him to it."

In a short time, they tied the innkeeper with his hands stretched above his head towards the apex and feet tightly attached to the poles about a foot from the bottom.

"The top should reach the edge of the smoke hole if we place the legs a little away from the fire," Gerald said and the soldiers positioned the ladder as instructed.

"I am sorry the fire is a little smoky with the new wood," Gerald said, "but it should become less smoky as it heats. Place the fire irons in the fire."

Todd, edging forward for a better view, collided with one of the soldiers and his thigh bumped against the table. He gave a half-scream half-shout and fell in a faint.

"Clumsy oaf. I'll have you flogged."

"No, Sir Gerald," Rick said. "Todd was hurt at the fight. It wasn't the soldier's fault."

The soldier involved flashed Rick a look of gratitude and gently lifted Todd onto the table while someone else swept the dishes clear.

Rick pulled up Todd's tunic, undid the ties, and peeled his left hose down. The left thigh from above the knee was a purple black mass.

"God. What a mess," Rick said.

"That should be bled," Dennis said. "Poor little bugger. He rode all the way back like that."

One of the soldiers sharpened a dagger that Rick insisted be boiled before he would use it. Todd was fully conscious again and wanted to sit up. Dennis pushed him back down. Rick explained what he intended to do.

Todd, his eyes enormous, bit his lip and said: "You will do it?"

"Yes, Todd. I'll do it."

Rick closed his eyes for a minute, and thought, God, I hope I don't hit a blood vessel. Now, parallel to the long muscle and not deep enough to touch bone.

"Dennis hold his shoulders tight. My Lord, would you hold his thigh? No, Sir Gerald, from the other side of the table. One hand from groin to outer hip, the other at the knee."

Rick crossed himself, held the leg with one hand and made an incision about one and a half inches long with the other. Dark bruised blood began to flow at once. Rick hoped desperately his treatment was correct and gently kneaded the leg from the edge of the bruise towards his incision. Immediately, the swelling reduced and the leg became more normal in shape and colour. The mark of where the quarterstaff had hit the leg was now clearly visible. When the colour of the blood began to change, Rick asked for clean linen and linen binding strips.

"You can let go now, My Lord," Rick said, and Gerald removed his hand.

With a pad bound tightly over the wound, Rick helped Todd pull his hose back up. When he stood, Todd staggered and Rick steadied him.

"I'll get him out to the air," Rick said. "Would someone bring him some ale…"

"And some bread and stew?" Todd said.

The soldiers laughed and one or two patted Todd on the shoulder while he hobbled to the door.

It was Dennis and Adam who brought out the supplies, and Adam looked at Todd with gleaming eyes.

The two boys laughed and giggled, but Rick found himself focused on the two heads on poles and the two figures that still hung from the trees. A vision of Todd cutting the two throats flashed before him and he was promptly sick.

While he leaned over the fence retching, he felt an arm round his waist and Todd's voice said: "Master Rick, what's wrong? Here, wipe your face."

The boy handed him a damp cloth. After he had wiped his face and rubbed the cloth round his neck, Rick felt better.

"You should rest Todd. Adam, come help him. Here, let's sit in the sun."

The three of them sat. Rick between the two boys.

"Todd fought well today, did he not?" Adam said, and Todd glowed. "Did you see him slit their throats?"

Rick tensed. He could still see it.

"It was easy. I used to watch them kill the pigs," Todd said.

Adam laughed. "You didn't have time to hang them by the heels first."

Shit, I'm going to be sick again. These kids are centuries older than me. God, I've nothing to be sick on.

"Master Rick, are you ill?" Todd said. "Were you wounded in the fight?"

"No, no. I'm fine. Adam fought well too; but for him, I would not have been able to bring down the last man."

Adam beamed and ducked his head shyly.

"Should I fetch you some stew and bread?" Adam asked. "You lost yours."

"No, Adam. Some ale perhaps."

Adam ran back out with a jug of ale.

"We are missing everything," he said. "Sir Gerald is about to torture the innkeeper."

"Can we?"

"Yes, Todd," Rick sighed, "if you wish. Help him, Adam, I'll stay here for a while."

The boys went towards the inn and Rick heard: "Is he really your master? He is more like a priest or a monk. When he tended you, he was as gentle as a maid."

"He killed one of the men, didn't he? He knocked down another without a weapon. If I need it, he beats me and he will you too."

God, what an age.

Rick wondered how Jo was. She had told him to look after Todd ... Rick drifted off into a sleep in the warm sun, the ale heavy on his empty stomach.

He awoke with a start when someone sat beside him and touched his knee.

"That was well done with Todd," Gerald said and Rick struggled into a more upright position. "Relax, Todd said you had no interest in our simple methods of questioning. We must talk about such matters later."

Damn Todd, Rick thought. What the hell had he landed me in now?

"Dennis fought well," Gerald went on, "as did you."

"Todd killed two of the men."

"Yes, Adam told me. Todd is very loyal to you."

Rick realised that considerable time must have passed. The sun was much lower in the sky.

"We will overnight here," Gerald said, "and reach my brother by mid-afternoon tomorrow. Come, I need your opinion on the condition of the innkeeper."

Stalling for time Rick said: "Has he given you any information?"

"Yes, some. The eleven we encountered may not be all of them, but for sure most. Such leadership as they had was those two."

He waved at the two bodies that still hung in the courtyard.

"They came in sometime after All Hallows last year. Their captain died of a flux some weeks ago. Some were strangers. They had a paymaster, but either the innkeeper does not know who, or he is incredibly courageous and foolish. He rambles a little now."

In the inn, Rick thought someone had burnt some meat. He was almost sick again when he realised that it was the smell of human flesh seared with a red-hot iron. The innkeeper was still on the ladder, but was now naked, his head lolled to one side. The ladder leaned against a wall on the other side of the room from the fire.

Rick looked at him, shocked, revolted. The skin had a very unpleasant, unhealthy pallor. It was cold and clammy to the touch, but there was profuse sweating. The pulse, when Rick found it, was weak and rapid. The breathing was fast and shallow. Burns could be seen on the chest and in one armpit. The man had obviously been flogged.

Rick leaned closer to the face.

"Can you hear me?"

There was no response, but when Rick pinched an earlobe hard the eyes flickered open and the man mumbled incoherently.

"He is in shock," Rick said. "It would be pointless to question him further now. He could die of shock. Have him untied and lay him down. Feet slightly higher than his head. Wrap him in a blanket."

Chapter Twenty

It was a miserable night for Rick. Every time he did drop off, he had visions of armies of small boys slitting throats. Most terrifying was that the boys did not look evil or malevolent: they looked like Todd at his innocent best. Each time, Rick woke in a cold sweat. Each time, he felt a flush of relief that it was all a dream. Each time, the relief evaporated quickly when he realised he was still in 1380.

Nor did it help that Todd, sound asleep, followed him round the bed like a puppy seeking warmth. He moaned when he lay on his injured leg or when Rick touched it on their travels.

Finally he fell into an exhausted sleep, and felt he had only closed his eyes when Todd's voice nagged at him.

"Master Rick. Master Rick. It's dawn. Everyone is on the move."

When he and Todd entered the main room of the inn after he had checked Todd's leg, Gerald's civil greeting and his concern over Todd's wound pleased Rick.

The innkeeper was nowhere in sight and Rick thought with relief that they had released him. When they emerged to mount, Rick noticed there were now three bodies where there had previously been two.

In an aggrieved voice, Todd said: "I told you, Master Rick, we shouldn't have wasted time with my leg. We've missed the hanging."

Dennis intercepted Rick's second slap at Todd's head and Gerald looked on with amusement.

Todd's voice cut through Rick's reverie and he looked up to see that they were at the open space where they had been attacked.

The group wheeled towards the edge of the open area and Todd started to swing down off his saddle.

Gerald called: "Todd, stay mounted. Sergeant, see what we have here."

They all loosed their swords in their scabbards and the sergeant advanced, sword in hand.

"A dead man, My Lord. Lacking his right hand. He must have bled to death."

Todd and Adam slid down and ran over to look, and Dennis and Gerald joined them.

"It is the varlet who almost stabbed me. Interesting."

"Come and see, Master Rick," Todd called, but Rick simply shook his head.

They rode past the ford where they had fought the day before and Rick shuddered.

Todd and Adam rode together and chattered and laughed. The sun shone brilliantly and felt warm. It should have been a very pleasant morning.

They cleared the wood and rode out onto the heath, but Rick still rode slightly apart from the others.

"Men on horseback," the sergeant shouted.

Again everyone shifted in the saddle and checked weapons. Rick followed the example of the others. The two groups slowly approached and Gerald dropped back to ride beside Rick.

"You fought well," Gerald said, "and I see you are prepared to fight again. In some ways you are like a clerk in orders, but you have too much spirit for that. Todd is like all boys, interested in all things, why does he anger you so?"

"It's Martin, Sir Harold's sergeant, and Arthur," Dennis shouted across the boys and he and the boys spurred forward to meet them.

"We expected you yesterday," Martin said.

"Doubtless, Arthur, you were concerned for my safety," Gerald said.

Arthur grinned and bowed in his saddle.

"Indeed I was, Master Gerald. I would never have another easy minute if anyone else killed you."

Chapter Twenty-One

Sir Harold's summer manor was smaller than Lord Thomas's mansion, but it was still impressive.

To Rick's surprise, Sir Harold, with Chris and Henry at his heels, cantered out to meet them.

"No ceremony, brother," Sir Harold said and dismounted.

He embraced Gerald and nodded to Dennis.

"I'll get your report later, Dennis."

Todd bowed. "My Lord, we have had an adventure."

"I am glad to see you well. The Lady Jo worried about you."

He turned to Rick who started to bow and found himself embraced and thumped on the back.

In the courtyard Jo crushed Todd to her, and kissed the squirming boy.

Arthur laughed. "He's collected another frigging boy, Jo."

"He's Gerald's page," Rick said. "I didn't pick him up."

"Relax Rick," Jo whispered. "Arthur's teasing. I'm glad to see you back safe and sound, even with another small boy."

She kissed him and struggled when Rick kissed back enthusiastically and hugged hard.

"You all need to wash. Todd for one hasn't been near water since you left us." Jo pulled back. "You are to sleep in the antechamber to Sir Harold's chamber. I have had servants set a tub there for you and heat water. See that Todd washes before supper."

"He is your page, Jo."

"Not till he's clean."

With a sigh, Rick put a hand on Todd's shoulder.

"Lead on, Henry. My Lady Jo has decreed a bath. Malcolm, I would like you to look at Todd please."

"Is Todd hurt? Let me look at him."

"Not till he's clean, Jo. Come on, let's go."

Chris grinned when Sir Harold said he should go with Rick and Todd. In the antechamber was a great wooden tub; even larger than the one Sir Harold used at the castle. Rick stripped and stepped in while Malcolm examined Todd's leg.

"Not a bad job at all. A good, clean cut with no sign of infection, but quite a bruise."

Nosy, Chris pushed forward to see and gulped.

"Wow, what happened?"

"Right, Todd, into the tub with you," Malcolm said.

Rick protested. "I'm just in."

"There's plenty of room for both of you. In you get, Todd."

Rick dried himself and Chris bustled forward with fresh clothes.

"Sir Harold said to get these out for you," he said. "There's clean stuff for Todd too."

Malcolm and Chris listened to Todd's excited account of their adventure.

"You boys can go," Rick said. "I've got some writing to do before dinner."

Todd's voice faded into the distance, still chattering on about the hangings to Chris.

"We'll meet later," Malcolm said, "to pool our information, but I've some patients to see to now."

Engrossed in his writing, Rick did not hear the very tentative knock at the door, and jumped at a touch on his arm.

"Henry."

"Sorry, Master. The Lady Jo sent me. I did knock."

Henry bowed and smiled.

"Has the Lady Jo been working you hard?"

"Oh no, master. The Lady Jo is very kind. She talks of you all the time."

"Does she now?"

"Todd is in trouble for telling tall tales. He came to see the Lady Jo with Chris after his bath. He told Chris you had killed a man and he killed two, as good a score as Master Dennis and Master Gerald."

"That annoyed Lady Jo? It's true."

Wide eyed, Henry grinned. "Then Lady Jo will be even more angry."

Jo burst in, Todd's right ear held in a firm grip.

"My Lady. Please. That ear will be twice the size of the other."

"Rick, what's this nonsense I hear from Todd?"

"Jo..."

"He says you allowed him to take part in a fight and he and you killed three men."

"Jo. I didn't allow him. We were attacked. It was kill or be killed."

"You allowed him to watch the hangings and the torture of the innkeeper."

"Christ, Jo..."

"Don't swear."

"Shut up long enough to listen. We were attacked. Todd did well, better than me. I was in shock. How the hell could I stop him seeing the hangings? They happened before I was aware of them. Gerald was in charge, not me."

"But the torture of the innkeeper..."

"Todd missed some important details to protect me. I was outside, sick. After, I was asleep. By the time I got in, the innkeeper was unconscious and Gerald was bellowing for his dinner. Have you seen Todd's leg?"

"Yes, I have. And if you think that will distract me, it won't work. How could you let that happen to him?"

"God, you're impossible. We're alive and they're dead. It's that simple in this time. Would you rather it was the other way round?"

Jo opened her mouth to retort, but Henry blurted out: "Are you two betrothed? Or brother and sister?"

Both Rick and Jo turned to look at him and Henry blushed, poised to flee. Jo laughed.

"Why did you say that?" Jo said and Henry blushed an even deeper shade of red, looked down and shuffled.

"You always quarrel, but you don't keep out of each other's way. Master Rick does not like the Lady Gwenne nor she him. So they bow when they meet and are very civil about nothing till they part."

"A very astute observation, Henry," Rick said.

Henry smiled rather uncertainly and looked from one to the other.

"Well, I suppose I was perhaps a little hard on both of you." Jo smiled. "It was too much to expect that you two could keep out of mischief.

"Sir Harold instructs that you are to sit at high table tonight. Come, Todd, we have to attend on the Lady Eleanor."

Chapter Twenty-Two

When they entered the great hall for dinner, Rick stopped and stood a little uncertain.

"The Lady Jo said we were to sit at the high table," Henry said and proudly led the way to the dais.

"Ah, Master Secretary. Come, sit at my right, between my brother and myself," Sir Harold said before he nodded to the major-domo who brought the assembly to order. Grace said, the hall erupted into the usual Babel of noise.

"My brother says you handled yourself well, most unlike a secretary."

"I did what I could. Todd did well."

"Indeed he did, I hear." Sir Harold positively glowed. "It was as well that he was with you and not Henry. My former secretaries would have been on their knees in prayer, not sword in hand. Much good would it have done them in this world. We will hear your tale later. I have already heard from Dennis and my brother."

Rick thought Chris and Henry served well during the meal, but Adam was more than a little clumsy at times. After one near disaster, Rick happened to look up and catch Sir Harold's scowl in Adam's direction.

"I don't know why you permitted my brother to acquire another boy."

"Surely, it was not my place to say yea or nay. I doubt if

Master Gerald would have paid much heed to any strictures on my part."

"Perhaps not, but now that he is here, I intend to place him in your care."

"Oh, My Lord."

"No thanks are necessary. You have made a good job of Christopher, who will be a most satisfactory page and squire. Todd has blossomed under your tutelage and Henry is delighted to have you back. Is that not so?" Henry squealed when Sir Harold reached back and slapped his rump. "The Lady Jo worried about your safety. Most concerned for you and Todd."

Chapter Twenty-Three

Several days after Rick rejoined the group, Malcolm finally interpreted the prescription from Andrew the Physician. Rick had almost forgotten about it.

When Malcolm asked for a private audience, Rick assumed it concerned some minor health problem at the manor and arranged it for Sir Harold's bedchamber. The business of the day virtually over, Sir Harold offered wine. When Malcolm refused, Sir Harold nodded at Rick who became recording secretary again.

With a glance at Henry, Malcolm said: "It concerns a certain doctor and a prescription."

"Henry, you may leave us," Sir Harold said. "Well, Master Physician?"

"I had some difficulty assessing it…"

"Obviously. It took you long enough. It is fortunate I am a man of vast patience."

Chris grinned but, when Sir Harold scowled, became very busy with Sir Harold's belt and sword at the sideboard.

"It's a mixture of several plant extracts."

"Which do what? God's Blood man, you try my patience."

"Some of the ingredients are reputed to cause spontaneous abortions in early pregnancy."

"Reputed? Do they do so?"

"Well, apothecaries in France, Italy, and the Low Countries sell them for such purposes."

"To whom do they sell? No Christian would ever consider such an abomination."

Malcolm shuffled and cleared his throat. "Ahem, perhaps so, but some ladies of great houses who may have been indiscreet have been known to purchase such."

Sir Harold flushed and crossed himself. "God's wounds. None of my household had better try such tricks."

"Then what would happen to the mother?" Rick said.

"I'd see her sequestered all her life or dispatched to a nunnery."

"Perhaps that's why a woman might resort to such medicine. In any case, I've heard use of such a cure is not unheard of even in a nunnery."

Sir Harold paled and looked at them. "You two have heard of evils I would not dream of. Be glad we talk in private. Get to our point, the potion."

"It is a potent mixture of several such reputed extracts. That's unusual, as any one would be enough. There is also an ingredient that could well be fatal."

"Who benefits if you have no more children, no male heir?" Rick said.

Sir Harold slumped onto his bed.

"Christopher, pour some wine. For the masters too, you dolt."

Chris was over his extreme nervousness of Sir Harold. Rick could have sworn his cousin's tongue flickered out for an instant before he turned away from Sir Harold to wink at Rick and go for the wine.

"Now, Master Secretary, do you have an answer the equal of your question?"

"Unfortunately, I do not."

Chapter Twenty-Four

The group met in the garden next morning to discuss Malcolm's news.

"Let's try to summarise what we know," Rick said. "Gerald and Andrew were both in on the attempt on Malcolm's life, but each for his own reasons. An alliance of convenience, nothing more. I'm sure. Gerald has added men in his pay to Sir Harold's soldiers in the past and those two men were to be an addition to this group. Gerald had been trying to build a power base, common in this age, but there's no evidence he had any knowledge of the potion."

Jo scowled. "You're all miles off the mark. All this talk about convoluted plots. Look closer to home, closer to human nature."

"Well, don't stop there," Malcolm said.

"Mary, Gwenne's lady-in-waiting, she's in love with Gerald. Apparently, she was to be betrothed to Gerald, but somehow Gwenne's family came up with a better contract. So Mary became lady-in-waiting to her cousin Gwenne instead of the other way round."

"I thought Mary always defended Gwenne against the other ladies," Rick said.

"You're a twit." Rick winced. He wished Jo wouldn't talk to him like that, especially in front of Arthur. "What better way to split Gwenne off from the other ladies than to leap to her defence at every slight, imagined or otherwise? Soon Gwenne would have no one to depend on but Mary, and that puts Mary in control."

"If Mary has achieved that, what would she need the potion for?"

"Don't you know anything about women?" Jo said, and Arthur laughed. "Oh shut up, Arthur. You're all blind and stupid. Mary wants Gerald for herself."

"She's very welcome to him, provided she doesn't kill the frigging bastard. I intend to do that."

"Be serious. Mary wants Gerald and I think she is capable of killing to get him. Even perhaps plotting to remove Sir Harold to give Gerald pride of place."

"Malcolm, a thought," Rick said. "Are we dealing with one potion or prescription, only one? Or is it possible that there are several?"

"Well, the prescription was a list of names of ingredients. Dennis and Arthur copied them down, remember? I suppose, I just assumed it was one prescription for a potion. It was odd there were several different extracts, each of which would supposedly work on its own. Remember I did say that. What's the point?"

"The point is, the one you said could be fatal, who is it for?"

"How would you give these to someone, Doc? I don't see any of these frigging gentry holding her bloody nose while someone pours poison down."

"Probably in wine, mulled wine, maybe, or mixed in a sauce, even a pottage. The herbs and so on would hide any bitter taste."

"Then it's one of the servants, a slavey. These nobs don't cook for themselves."

"Lady Mary has special sauces made to her own recipe, My Lady," Todd said. "She keeps them 'specially for the Lady Gwenne and the Lady Eleanor. When I was in the kitchens she used to come down sometimes to make them. She had me beaten once because she caught me watching when she added herbs from a big chest."

"God, the ladies say she's famous for a pottage she makes. A family recipe apparently," Jo said. "She makes special possets for Lady Eleanor and Lady Gwenne quite regularly, at least two, three times a month. Sir Harold said the other day that Mary hadn't made a pottage for all of them for over a year."

"This is all pure speculation," Rick said.

Jo frowned at him. "Margaret commented that the last time Mary had made her pottage was before Sir Harold's son died. The whole family were sick that spring, and Mary nursed the boy."

"Todd, do you remember last spring when Sir Harold's son died, were many at the castle ill?"

"I don't know," Todd shrugged. "Wait, I think that was when My Lord's physician died. Cook made a joke about it being a good time since no one else needed his services. Shortly after that My Lord and his family fell ill. I think."

"The doctor and the boy, what did they die of?" Malcolm said.

"A flux, people say."

"Yes, Jo, I remember that, but they call any of the dysentery-like conditions endemic in this time a flux. Nausea, vomiting, uncontrollable diarrhoea, these would all be symptoms of the poison on the list too."

"Have you talked to Lady Eleanor about the potion?" Rick said.

"No. I started to ask her about some of the extracts that could cause abortions. My interest in such materials shocked her, so I dropped the subject."

"Sir Harold must hear this," Dennis said. "Master Rick, you tell him. I'll come with you."

"Master Rick! Master Rick?" Arthur laughed. "Since when do we call him Master Rick?"

"He is secretary and friend to our lord, Sir Harold. I have sworn fealty to Sir Harold, as have you, Arthur, and this is business."

Arthur snorted.

"Is that it?" Malcolm said. "I can't spend all day here gossiping. I've patients to see."

"All right. Keep your hair on, Malcolm," Rick said.

The tentative conclusions did not please Sir Harold, but he agreed there were grounds for further investigation and that Mary should be watched.

The serving wenches Arthur slept with confirmed that Mary had already prepared the ingredients of some of her special sauces and possets. She kept them ready, in dry form, in little earthenware pots.

After supper, while Arthur dallied with two serving wenches, Chris and Todd sneaked into the pantry and emptied all of Mary's pots, and refilled them with a herbal mixture provided by Malcolm.

Now Jo had brought it to Rick's attention, he could see Mary doted on Gerald and he more or less ignored her.

Like Jo and I in reverse, Rick thought.

Rick was afraid that Mary would notice a change in Sir Harold's manner. He now watched her with suspicion and, Rick thought, loathing. Jo assured him that Mary saw no change.

Chapter Twenty-Five

Several weeks later, Sir Harold commented that both Gwenne and Eleanor were in remarkably good health.

"Positively glowing. The air must suit them."

Arthur's wenches told him that Mary had been in to check her pots, and she looked puzzled after she tasted a pinch of each.

That evening, in the solar, Mary poured wine for the gentlemen, but before she had the pages pass it to their masters, Todd capered, bumped her, and turned her round. Chris rearranged the goblets on the sideboard.

Todd apologised before he handed the goblets to Adam, Chris and Henry for their masters. Mary, her face red, peered at the goblets. When she looked at the one Adam was about to hand to Gerald, she paled and told Adam he had the wrong goblet. Gerald smiled, and reached for the goblet.

"They were all fresh set out, Mistress Mary. Wine poured for my brother would surely not harm me."

Mary tripped on the hem of her gown, stumbled forward and knocked the goblet out of Adam's hand, and turned to call Todd a venomous toad.

In an icy voice, Sir Harold said: "You are over-wrought, Mistress Mary. My ward can be a little high spirited at times, but he has done nothing to merit such an attack. You have my permission to withdraw. Todd was clumsy and over boisterous. I shall correct him later in my chamber."

Todd bowed, face impassive.

When Sir Harold withdrew from the solar, Todd bowed to Jo and followed Sir Harold and Chris. Henry and Rick detoured past the garde-robe and Henry was yawning when they reached the anteroom. After telling the boy to go to sleep, Rick entered Sir Harold's chamber.

Todd fidgeted while Chris helped Sir Harold undress. Sir Harold sighed, stretched and scratched.

"Will you beat him, Master Richard, or shall I?"

Before Rick could answer, Chris handed Sir Harold the birch rod. They all jumped when Sir Harold brought it down hard on his bed and repeated the blow five more times.

"Now, master page, you will mind your manners," he said aloud, and lowered his voice. "What did you see?"

When Todd reported he had seen Mary put a powder in one goblet, Sir Harold scowled.

"You would have let my brother drink it?"

Todd and Chris looked at each other, and both flushed.

"He knew Mistress Mary would stop him," Rick said.

"Did he now? How? I will believe that for the moment. I have a large capacity for belief. At any rate, you stopped it getting to me."

Both boys looked really shocked and almost in chorus said:

"We would not see you poisoned."

"We could not have you harmed."

At a gesture from Sir Harold, Chris poured wine for Sir Harold and Rick.

"Sit, Master Richard. I must think."

Sir Harold stared at the empty fireplace.

The boys withdrew to a corner and had a whispered argument. Rick glanced at them from time to time, afraid they would disturb Sir Harold. Before Rick realised exactly what was about to happen, Chris knelt before Sir Harold and tugged at Sir Harold's sleeve.

At Sir Harold's: "What is it now?" Chris looked ready to flee, but Todd kicked his thigh and in a stage whisper said: "Go on!"

Red-faced, Chris started to stumble through the oath of fealty. He stopped short and scowled at Todd when Sir Harold snapped: "Don't mumble, boy. Kneel up straight. This is a serious matter. Start again."

After an initial fumble, Chris said the oath in a loud, clear voice without error.

"This is your coaching, Master Richard?"

"No. I was not aware that Chris intended this."

Standing in front of Chris, Sir Harold placed both hands on Chris's head and accepted his oath. He turned away, wiped his eye on his sleeve, and cleared his throat noisily.

Chapter Twenty-Six

Sir Harold called a council of war next morning to discuss Mary. All of Rick's group was present plus the sergeant.

Rick reviewed the evidence and the various theories to date. After he had listened to everyone again, Sir Harold ruled that Mary had acted on her own, motivated by jealousy and ambition. Gerald, he was sure, was blameless.

There was a general consensus that Sir Harold was probably right, but much less agreement on what should be done. Discussion went on for some time.

"I do not wish a scandal to disrupt this very pleasant stay," Sir Harold said. "However, I do not intend to allow any further possible harm done."

The arrival of a courier ended the meeting and Sir Harold and Rick turned to other business.

Shortly before dinner, Rick and Sir Harold went to Lady Eleanor's chamber. After the usual courtesies, Sir Harold, his face solemn, cleared his throat.

"I have some sad news, Mistress Mary. I fear your father is dying. The courier recently come brought me these tidings. Catch her someone."

When Mary recovered from her faint, Sir Harold went on: "You ride within the hour. Master Dennis will go with you to command your escort. Take your serving woman. My sympathy, mistress."

They left during dinner. No one gave any sign of concern or upset. Gwenne made no comment when servants removed Mary's chest to storage.

The next day, Malcolm emptied the chest. He discovered little packets and containers, carefully labelled, one for each ingredient of the prescription. A roll of parchment found with the packets he turned over to Rick since it was in French.

Rick examined Mary's log: a list of dates with initials and numbers. The numbers corresponded to those on the packets. Very abbreviated comments in French apparently described the effect of the potion. One, around the time Sir Harold's previous physician died, had initials Rick didn't recognise, and several days later the same initials with a cross. A second, several days later, was simply "S.H., L.E., et enfants', and again some days farther on: "fils de S.H." In general Eleanor's initials appeared monthly, as did Gwenne's. When he reread, Rick noticed immediately before the entry he assumed was the physician was '…suspicious of why I need the potions…'

Malcolm and Rick presented their findings to Sir Harold. He simply nodded until Rick reached the entry that referred to his son.

"Let me see that."

He snatched the parchment from Rick's hand and stared at it intently. All colour drained from his face.

"My son, she murdered my only son."

Rick stood, unsure how to react.

"Should we send a courier after Dennis," Malcolm said, "and have Mistress Mary arrested?"

With a glance at Rick, Sir Harold laughed. "She is safe in Master Dennis's hands. Never fear."

"But…"

"I am not a simpleton. I sent her back to the castle under arrest. She will know that when she arrives. Had I known this earlier, I would have given her over to my brother to be put to the question."

Chapter Twenty-Seven

Rick and Sir Harold were seated quietly in the solar before dinner when Gerald burst in unannounced. The boys were playing chess in one alcove.

"Dismiss these peasants. I need to speak with you."

Sir Harold raised his eyebrows.

"I see no serfs here, brother; only my secretary and pages. You may speak freely."

"It is what one page has heard that concerns me."

The brothers stared at each other for some time before Gerald finally said: "Why do I hear from my page, through a turnspit, that my lady's lady-in-waiting is under arrest and not gone on a visit to her ailing father?"

"Ah, yes," Sir Harold looked at Rick. "Yes, we should speak. From whom did you say you had this intelligence? A turnspit? No kitchen skivvy was privy to this."

"Todd told my page Adam…"

"Todd is page to the Lady Jo, and my ward. As I remember, you praised him highly for his conduct on your recent travels."

Gerald struggled visibly not to lose his temper.

"Is the information true?"

Sir Harold nodded and turned to Rick.

"Tell my brother our evidence in detail."

Gerald listened, his fingers clasped tight on his dagger hilt.

"She was poisoning our wives? Do these potions work?"

"You and your lady have no children. My lady has not quickened with child since Mistress Mary arrived. I don't know about you, but there is no reason why it should be so with my lady."

Gerald flushed an angry red.

"You should not have sent her away. You should have informed me. I would have put her to the question."

"Here? I think not. Master Dennis has her safely lodged in a tower chamber. Well out of harm's way."

"She killed your son."

Sir Harold paled. "And I would know her co-conspirators."

They stared at each other, both pairs of eyes cold and calculating.

Abruptly Gerald's expression changed.

"My Lord, you cannot suspect that I would be party to such a scheme."

Sir Harold continued to stare at his brother. Gerald, chalk white now, advanced and dropped to his knees in front of Sir Harold. He presented his dagger, hilt first.

"If you truly believe that, kill me now with my own dagger."

He grabbed Sir Harold's wrist and pulled the dagger point toward his own breast.

The scene held for a moment before Sir Harold with a shudder moved back. He dropped the dagger and pulled Gerald to his feet.

"Rise, brother, I freely absolve you of that intention."

They embraced.

"Christopher, wine for Master Gerald," Sir Harold bellowed. He looked critically at Gerald. "Let us sit in the window niche. Had I believed you a party to my son's murder, the Lady Gwenne would now be several days a widow. You did conspire with Master Andrew, Sir William's physician."

"He knew of some mercenaries for hire. Nothing more."

Gerald shrugged.

"They were to be added quietly to my garrison, but answerable to you?"

Again Gerald shrugged and gave a disarming smile.

"The attempt on Malcolm's life," Rick blurted. "You knew of that."

"A miscalculation on my part. I am not answerable to servants, no matter how learned."

To Rick's horror, Sir Harold laughed. "Touché, but brother, in future, keep in mind that these are my people, under my protection."

Gerald smiled. "I will observe the niceties."

"We will arrest Master Andrew on our way back to the castle," Sir Harold said. "In the meantime, we will keep this information privily among us only. None of the servants are to know anything of this. Agreed? You brother, Martin, my sergeant, Master Richard's people and none other?"

Chapter Twenty-Eight

The summer days flew past, at least for Sir Harold's immediate household. Even Gerald relaxed.

Rick was aware from the correspondence he dealt with and from talking to couriers there was unrest elsewhere, particularly to the South. One focus was on the taxes and the arbitrary actions of the tax collectors, and a second was a growing resentment of the landed gentry. He heard from time to time of the movements and the preaching of the hedge priest, John Ball, whose sermons advocating priestly poverty upset the rich clerics, and his stress on social equality greatly angered the ruling upper classes.

Some time after Dennis's return from his escort duties with Mary, Sir Harold sent him and Arthur out to travel through the countryside, to observe and report.

In Sir Harold's manors, people were reasonably content and happy.

"They're too frigging ignorant to know any better," was Arthur's comment.

Only the artisan and merchant classes in the town and at the castle were restive.

"They don't want to help those on the bottom. They only want to use the serfs so they can claw up a bloody rung or so."

When sorting through correspondence just arrived, Rick recognised the writing of Wycliffe on one parchment. Later when he and Sir Harold met in the solar for routine business, he placed that letter right on top, unopened.

Sir Harold read it and handed the letter to Rick.

"Master Wycliffe is coming here," Rick said. "He follows directly the courier who brought this."

"Why so excited? We have had other, more important guests."

"Never in my wildest dreams did I ever imagine actually meeting Wycliffe. I have known of him, of course, for the longest time, since I was about eleven or twelve I think. He is a most significant historical figure."

Sir Harold was amused, but pleased at Rick's enthusiasm. The others were more or less indifferent to the news. After questioning the courier closely as to where and when he had last seen Wycliffe, and how he travelled, Sir Harold announced his intention to ride out next morning to meet his friend.

Shortly after first light, Sir Harold, Rick and their pages set out with an escort commanded by Dennis.

After several hours of riding, Chris asked rather plaintively if they would eat soon.

Dennis, glancing at the position of the sun, laughed and said: "Soon, Chris, soon."

Shortly after, riders were seen. Rick noted the change in alertness he had seen before, weapons were checked, and ranks were closed. Two snapped orders and the march order changed. Dennis at point with Sir Harold to his left, Rick and the boys in the middle, escort all round them.

They had obviously been seen. The other group slowed, stopped, and after a pause moved slowly forward again.

"I thought we would charge, swords waving," Chris grumbled at the continuation of the same stately walk that had been their pace most of the morning.

"Horses tire, as we do," Sir Harold said, but didn't take his eyes from the other group. "Until we know if they be friendly or hostile, we walk the horses. All the readier to fight, or run as may be the case."

Chris snorted. "It's like a game of chicken at home between two gangs of boys. No. More like two dogs sniffing each other out."

"I like your comparison," Sir Harold said, "but the time for caution is past."

"Are they wolves's heads? Are we going to fight?" Henry said.

Sir Harold shouted: "I can see Master Wycliffe. It is my friend."

He spurred forward, followed by Rick and the boys, and the escort dropped back. When they reached the other group, he swung out of his saddle and ran forward to embrace the frail, white-bearded man in sombre clothing who had already dismounted.

"He's small," Chris whispered. "Smaller than me. He hardly comes to Sir Harold's shoulders."

"Quick, Chris. My Lord's horse," Rick said, and dismounted.

Rick stood respectfully, a few paces from Sir Harold and Wycliffe, while Henry and Chris held the horses.

Sir Harold motioned Rick forward.

"Master Wycliffe, may I present my secretary, Master Richard."

With a deep bow, Rick said: "I am indeed honoured to meet you, sir. I have read and heard much about you."

"He has read and considered *De Civili Dominis*," Sir Harold said.

Wycliffe looked at Rick. A look that Rick felt bored right through him. Confused, he realised he had missed Wycliffe's question.

Patiently, Wycliffe repeated the question in Latin: a question about *De Civili Dominus*, and Rick replied.

Wycliffe smiled.

"We must talk later." He turned to Sir Harold. "A most unusual secretary, Sir Harold, as you write."

They rode a short way before Sir Harold suggested that they eat. The soldiers unstrapped the panniers from a pack horse, and, helped by the pages, unloaded them onto a canvas cloth spread on the ground.

"My Lord, Master Wycliffe." Dennis waved his hands towards the wicker baskets now placed upside down beside the cloth, and Sir Harold and his guest sat.

"Join us, Master Richard," Sir Harold said, and Chris and Henry presented bread, cheese, and cold cuts of fowl. "There is enough for all, Master Dennis. You and your men may partake."

Chris paused, mouth open inches from a chicken leg, when he saw Sir Harold scowl at him. With a sigh he replaced the leg. Sir Harold smiled, and cuffed Henry's ear when he bit into a chunk of meat.

"You are a page, Sirrah, and pages wait on their masters before they eat."

With a yelp, Henry replaced the meat, minus the bite, and Sir Harold turned to Wycliffe.

"A new page, master. Recently come from the nursery." He scowled at Rick. "His master does not beat him enough."

Wycliffe smiled. "They are only boys, Master Harold."

Rick, Chris and Henry started at the unexpected familiarity.

At Sir Harold's nod, both boys fell to.

While Sir Harold and Wycliffe talked of mutual friends and events of the day, Rick stood spellbound. Some of the events and people were familiar, but somehow subtly different. Rick's view of Wycliffe and the events of this time were, he supposed, coloured by the detractors and enemies of the Lollards.

They set out again, at an even slower pace than before. The two boys rode off on side trips occasionally pursued by Dennis or Sir Harold, but always accompanied by at least one trooper. Rick rode sedately with Wycliffe, who gave Rick a searching look: "Sir Harold has written to me, in his own hand no less, of your arrival, Master Richard. An interesting tale indeed, if true. I would hear it from your own lips."

Again Rick told the story of their arrival. Wycliffe heard him in silence and when he had finished commented: "Sir Harold can think of no other way of explaining your sudden appearance. It is known that the circles of standing stones are mysterious both in their origins and their properties. I am loathe to think your story is a miracle without any apparent Godly purpose, but like Sir Harold I feel I must accept it since there seems no other explanation. By your actions here you are shown to be good, not evil, regardless of your manner of arrival. I will pray for your group and for guidance for all."

Wycliffe, despite his frail appearance, sat his horse well. From time to time while they talked, he turned deep set eyes on Rick, eyes that sometimes flashed with indignation when he talked of abuses of the powers of the church, but were always bright with intelligence. Their talk ranged over most of the matters dealt with in Wycliffe's treatise and touched on the state of the serfs since the Death and the current unrest.

Wycliffe turned in his saddle to face Rick and looked him up and down.

"Why do you think My Lord of Lancaster supports me?"

Rick thought hard and shifted uncomfortably in his saddle. Wycliffe didn't give him time to reply.

"Is it out of great love he bears me personally? Is it out of a steady belief that I am right and Holy Mother Church of Rome is wrong?"

"I would not presume to question the motives of my Lord of Lancaster," Rick said.

"Nonsense, your voice and bearing betray you. You know, as well as I, he supports me because my reforms would see the nobles and the crown able to regain land and power ceded to the church in past ages."

"Your treatise is philosophical and theological, not political."

"It was and is, so intended, but many see political implications. Particularly so, since I am known to oppose the practice of appointing foreign priests and prelates to important and lucrative English positions. The church in England should be English."

"And should restrict itself to the cure of souls," Rick said.

"Yes."

"Why does Sir Harold support you? He is a devout man."

"And I am not?"

"Oh, no. That is not what I meant."

"I am devout in my allegiance to God. Venial priests disgrace themselves and the Church. They do not represent God."

Wycliffe looked at Rick, his eyes glowed.

"Man needs not a priest to stand between him and God."

Rick nodded. "When each man can read the Bible in his own tongue, he will not need an interpreter."

"You know of my translation?"

"Yes. A noble and monumental task, but a controversial one, I fear."

"I digress. Sir Harold is a loyal man. He holds his fief from My Lord of Lancaster."

"His greeting was not that of a tenant meeting someone supported by his feudal superior."

"Sir Harold did say you were perceptive. I have known him since he was a child. I knew his mother. A good Saxon lady. Sir Harold favours her."

Again they rode quietly, but it was a companionable silence.

"What do you make of this passage?"

Wycliffe quoted a portion in Latin from the missal and Rick translated: "This is my body which is given for you. Take, eat in remembrance of me."

"Nicely translated. I wonder if Sir Harold would release you to work with me? No matter. Are you familiar with the remainder of the passage?"

"Yes, Master Wycliffe."

"Do you find anything in it that says the bread actually becomes the true, the very flesh of Our Lord? Anything that supports this doctrine of Transubstantiation?"

"No, but the Church teaches…"

"Do you find anything in it that says that a priest has the power to effect such a transformation?"

"No, but it is heresy in this day and age to say so."

"I am not trying to trap you. This is a passage I have pondered on for a long time. This is a rare opportunity to have the view of a fresh mind. What do you think Our Lord meant?"

"Do ye this as remembrance of me."

"Remembrance, commemoration only? If so, what need is there of a priest?"

"Master Wycliffe, have a care. If you renounce Transubstantiation, you will lose many of your noble followers. Even, I think, John of Gaunt."

Wycliffe shifted in his saddle to look again directly at Rick.

"Do you know this? Or do you speculate this might be so?"

Rick squirmed. "I know it … I think … but if I do, nothing we do now matters. Everything is predestined."

"Not so. Many things are known to God. You have changed Todd's life. Sir Harold tells me so. In any case, I must act as my conscience dictates and speak as I see truth. We will talk later."

Chapter Twenty-Nine

They rode steadily all afternoon. Wycliffe spoke to each of the boys and to Dennis, but did not say anything further to Rick.

Close to supper they arrived at the manor. Eleanor and her entourage greeted them in the courtyard. Rick noticed Gerald's greeting was polite, but perfunctory.

Wycliffe staggered slightly walking to the solar and Sir Harold suggested he might wish to retire immediately after supper and not wait for the entertainment.

"Where are they putting him, Jo?" Rick said in her ear when their group walked to the walled garden.

"Sir Harold left word to have his chamber prepared for his guest."

"Where will Sir Harold sleep?"

"With Lady Eleanor in her chamber, idiot," Jo said, but she took his arm to stroll.

"It's funny, but I've never really thought of it before. The arrangements here are different from what I'd have expected in a minor manor."

"Christ. Here we go again."

"Shut up, Arthur," Dennis said. "If it doesn't interest you, shove off."

"Gone all high and mighty since we became Harold's frigging top watchdog, haven't we?"

"Stow it, Arthur," Dennis said.

When Arthur opened his mouth, Dennis scowled. With a grin Arthur held up both hands, palms towards Dennis, and walked away.

"Go on, Rick. What's different?" Dennis said.

"Well, in this time only the very wealthy families had separate rooms for My Lord and My Lady. In most manors the lord and his family slept in the solar. Usually on the only real bed. Everyone else slept where they could. One step up, there might be one or two rooms that could be set up for really important guests."

"So what's the point?" Malcolm said. "Sir Harold's loaded. We know that."

"Malcolm, you may be a good doctor," Dennis said. "But politically you're as thick as two short planks. So where does Sir Harold fit in, Rick?"

"Both here and at the castle he and Lady Eleanor have separate chambers…"

"But he doesn't always sleep in his own chamber," Todd said, and he and Chris giggled.

"That will do, Todd," Jo said.

"What have I done now?" Todd said. "You and Lady Margaret the other night…"

At Jo's glare his voice trailed off and he backed off a few steps.

"As I was saying," Rick said, "at the castle, even Gerald and Lady Gwenne have separate chambers…" He scowled at Todd when he and Chris giggled again. "There's a room for the ladies-in-waiting. We know Sir Harold has several manors. He has the right of high justice. His holdings are directly from John of Gaunt, not through any other intermediary."

"So?" Malcolm said.

"I don't know if I'm making too much of it. Have I misremembered, or were the books I read wrong? Sir Harold has to be more than a simple knight."

"Rick," Jo said, "I'd never really thought of it before, but the style of address, is that how a knight is addressed?"

"How did people address Sir William, Henry's father?" Rick said. "Anyone notice?"

"Not, My Lord, anyway," Dennis said. "But he called Sir Harold, My Lord."

"I still don't see what it matters," Malcolm said. "We're well set."

"This is 1380, Malcolm. Surely even you remember what happens in 1381?"

"No, Rick. What?"

"Oh, for God's sake, Malcolm. Don't play the buffoon. The Peasants' Revolt."

Todd, wide eyed, stared at Rick.

"You can remember the future?" He crossed himself.

"If you breathe a word of what you hear with us to anyone, I'll have your tongue torn out and send you as a slavey to Lord Thomas's kitchen."

"Dennis. There's no need to frighten the child," Jo said, and put a protective arm round Todd's shoulders. Todd shook himself free indignantly.

"I would not betray Master Rick. Anyway, he is the Lord of the Stones. He has the right to high justice for us, not Master Dennis."

Jo started to laugh and Malcolm grinned, but both stopped at the expression on Dennis's face.

"Yes, Todd," Dennis said. "You're right."

"What's all the bother about anyway?" Todd said. "All know, Sir Harold is a baron."

They all laughed, and Todd, not sure at first if they were laughing at him, joined in when Dennis slapped his back.

"I don't know what we'd do without you, Todd. Todd the Pragmatist."

"Will the revolt affect us much here?" Jo said.

"Well, there wasn't too much action around here," Rick said. "We're well away from major centres, but Norwich and Yarmouth had bloody riots. Some individual landholders were badly treated in rural areas. I don't remember anything about Sir Harold at all. That's why I wonder if we're missing some detail, some other name or title."

Chapter Thirty

Next morning, Wycliffe asked to meet the group in the walled garden.

"Todd, I wish to speak privately with the masters from the Circle." At Todd's crestfallen look, Wycliffe smiled at the boy. "Could you take the place of the page Chris that he may join us here? We will have a chance to talk later."

Todd smiled back and bowed.

Henry grumbled and went with Todd, but only after Rick repeated the instruction.

"The child needs discipline," Wycliffe said.

"Spare the rod and spoil the child," Dennis said grinning.

"You are familiar with Proverbs, master? In the vernacular?"

Dennis looked at Rick.

"Sir Harold was right," Wycliffe said. "You, Master Secretary, are the key, the leader. Will you tell me your story?"

Wycliffe listened patiently while Rick retold the events that lead to their arrival.

"A wondrous tale indeed. You are right to keep your own counsel in this. It would smack of witchcraft to simple men."

"To many not so simple men too."

"True, and many would seize on it as a pretext to destroy you," Wycliffe said. "You have all read the Bible? In English?"

Malcolm laughed. "Yes, but not since I was child like Chris

here."

"Dennis will have read it," Arthur said. "He reads frigging bus tickets if there's nothing else."

"And you, Master Arthur, Man of the People, Stalwart Son of the Soil, have you read the Bible?"

Rick turned red, choked on the piece of fruit in his mouth and coughed.

"You should do something for his lordship's cough, Malcolm," Arthur said. "Only what I had to as a child. My mother and father did not agree on religion. He held it was all stuff and nonsense. She tried to be a good Catholic, against the odds.

"What are you lot all staring at? I was baptised a Catholic. Pop allowed that, but till I got here I hadn't been in a church since Ma's funeral."

"In your time, is the church still ruled from Rome?"

"No…" Rick said.

"Yes…" Jo said, at the same time.

They both laughed.

"Hers is, sort of," Rick said.

Jo said: "His isn't."

As best he could, Rick explained how the Church of England was governed, and how the Roman Church had reformed.

"Cardinals hold their appointments from the Pope in Rome, but in each country the upper echelon are nationals of that country."

"Except in England, where they're all Irish," Arthur said.

With a small gesture of impatience, Wycliffe turned to Rick.

"There have been reforms? There is a national church? Man does not need an advocate between him and God."

Rick was not sure whether the last part was a question or a statement.

"A national church is long established and many of the abuses of this time resolved. Some men still feel the need for a mediator and some churches still teach this is so."

Wycliffe sighed. "However, a thinking, devout man may choose? The King and the priests would not coerce him?"

Rick nodded. He could not trust himself to speak; to tell this gentle man of the centuries of wars and persecutions to come; to tell him his detractors would exhume his body, years after his death, and burn it; to tell him his followers, the Lollards, would suffer persecution and, some, death by burning at the stake.

"My questions sadden you," Wycliffe said. "I will ask you no more. You come from a time of what might be, not what will be."

"An alternate universe." Rick barely breathed the words.

"All things are possible to God. He did give man free will. The power to chose, but man must accept the consequences of choice. Better we simply accept and bow to the will of the Lord."

"How goes your translation?" Rick said.

Eyes twinkling, Wycliffe said: "Well enough. I return directly to Lutterworth from here. It is my most important contribution. Man cannot govern himself in accordance with the Word of God if he cannot read it in his own tongue. Read and digest. Read and think, without an intermediary to interpret it for him."

"This bible is for the Government of the People, by the People, and for the People," Rick said.

"Exactly so, exactly so."

"Surely Lincoln said that, or something like it," Jo objected.

"Master Wycliffe said it first in his introduction to his bible," Rick said.

"Where do I sign up?" Arthur asked.

Chapter Thirty-One

In the days that followed, Wycliffe had several private meetings with Sir Harold. He observed Rick's classes in the church, and strolled one day with Rick when he dismissed the boys.

"Education is the key, education is the key. I dream of a time when each man can read the Word of God for himself and decide for himself what he believes."

"What if he chooses not to believe?"

"Then I would grieve for him, but belief is an act of faith, not intellect. God's will is inscrutable and his power infinite. By His Grace and with His help we will live right. We must not be arrogant and stupidly proud of man's free will which is itself a Gift of God."

"Aren't you afraid that without direction, the Church will splinter, form factions, and end up fighting?"

"No, there would be no Church as we now know it. Each man would be his own priest. No hierarchy. Such priests as continued would be pastors: wise, compassionate men to whom others would turn for advice, and perhaps leadership, but who would not impose their views."

"A noble vision, but one that must make the Church now very nervous; and the nobility."

Wycliffe shrugged.

"The nobility who are truly noble in God's eyes have nothing to fear. The lawful exercise of lordship or dominion over men depends on Grace and the righteousness of the person who exercises it. God will remove unfit nobles when He sees fit and when it suits His purpose."

"You don't trust Him to reform the Church?"

"Secular lordship is the natural order – God has placed every man in his rightful position; Kings, Lords and commoners. The Church made a mistake when it organised itself in a like manner, with bishops and abbots ruling over property like lords of the manor and becoming wealthy on the sweat of others. It must return to its original path. It must return to what Our Lord intended. It must return to the cure of souls, with priestly poverty for all priests, with no worldly goods, lands and possessions to defend."

This would attract the support of the anti-clerical party, Rick thought. It would be very much to their advantage to see clergy banned from holding lucrative crown offices. As clearly stated as this, it simply did not tie in with the teachings of the hedge priests. With a start Rick realised Wycliffe had spoken again.

"You and your group have had a very real influence on Sir Harold. He has always been a kindly and compassionate lord. Too lenient and considerate of his people in the minds of many."

Rick laughed.

"Arthur would not agree with that."

"Under lords like Sir Harold, wages have risen faster than prices. Even landless labourers earn good pay. Many villeins even own property." Wycliffe paused.

"There's a lot of real anger at the wealth and worldliness of the higher clergy," Rick said. "Many villeins hate the landlord class for the Statute of Labourers."

"Surely if enough men like Sir Harold can be persuaded that change must come, it will come – if slowly?"

"Amen to that. But history shows that revolts and revolutions come when conditions are improving, when oppression is decreasing, like taking the lid off a boiling pot. The rising expectation leads to anger at the slowness with which the old order is reforming itself."

"We must pray I am right, Master Richard, that you come from an else-when of what might be, and not what will be or must be from this time on. Arthur, I think, wishes to believe this. Dennis is already rooted in this time. You are the key. Where you lead, your group will follow. So will Todd."

"Todd is one of us," Rick said absently, his thoughts on what Wycliffe had said.

"Just so, just so, but only because you have accepted him. He loves the Lady Jo and would die for her. He admires and respects you."

"What of Henry?"

"He is a small boy spoilt by over-indulgence living with his mother and her ladies. You also spoil him. He must be beaten when he is rude and disobedient, which is often, I fear."

"I don't approve of beating, not as a regular practice."

"Your age must be strange indeed. Here, now, Henry thinks you are soft and pliable, and that you do not care enough about him to discipline him."

"How can he believe that?" Rick was shocked and deeply offended.

"I do not believe so. I respect your views. I do not suggest he be beaten for your amusement or pleasure. That would be evil and sinful, but he expects correction when he needs it from those he loves and who love him. You may think it wrong, but it is what he sees all round him, what he hears of. Don't expect too much of the child. He cannot leap to your level. It is only natural he take advantage of what he sees as weakness."

After a short silence, Wycliffe went on: "I did not mean to preach a sermon. Perhaps you should do as Sir Harold suggests. You take Todd, and let Henry page to the Lady Jo. She will beat him if required. She beats Todd."

"Oh, surely not."

"Yes, but with love. Marry the Lady Jo d'Arcy of Oxford. You would make a powerful alliance. I have already said so to Master Harold."

Chapter Thirty-Two

"Jo," Rick said. "My Lady Jo d'Arcy of Oxford, I have a bone to pick with you."

Jo looked startled at Rick's tone and his grip on her arm when they left the great hall after supper. He steered her towards the walled garden ahead of the group.

"You beat Todd."

"That's none of your business," Jo said. "How do you know anyway?"

She turned and beckoned to Todd to come closer. When he did so, her hand shot out to grip his ear.

"Aow. What have I done now?"

"Todd didn't tell me. Let him go. Wycliffe told me."

"He must have told Wycliffe."

"My Lady, please. That ear is already two sizes bigger."

"Then it's true," Rick said.

"I discipline Todd when he needs it. That's all. With a peeled willow branch no thicker than my little finger."

"You were the one who raised hell when we were about to beat him for stabbing Dennis."

"That was different, Rick, and you know it. Anyway, that was then, when we'd only arrived, other times, other customs."

"If it's all so open and above board, why were you so annoyed when you thought he told me. Why are you still twisting his ear?"

"I'm not twisting it, just holding it," Jo said, but she did let go. Todd rubbed his ear and grimaced at Rick. "It's not a question of hiding anything. It surprised me that Todd discussed private matters."

"With me? Come off it, Jo, he's family."

Todd grinned and nodded.

"We're not family, Rick. Not by a long shot…"

Jo caught sight of Todd's forlorn expression and snapped: "Look what you've done now. Of course, you're family, Todd."

"It doesn't really hurt. Not like cook or the others in the kitchen," Todd said, and hurried on, "but enough, My Lady, enough to keep me right."

Both Rick and Jo laughed, and Todd, his face a mixture of pleasure and relief, grinned at them.

"Have you thought any more about marrying me, Jo?"

"God, you have a weird sense of timing and no romance in your soul."

Jo strode off to join the others. Todd trotted behind her.

Rick looked at their retreating backs.

"Jo, Barkus is willing."

Arthur and Malcolm looked quite blank, but Dennis laughed and gave him the thumbs up sign.

Chapter Thirty-Three

When Wycliffe left, Sir Harold sent Dennis with him as escort. To Rick's surprise, Arthur formally requested, and was given permission, to travel with Wycliffe to Lutterworth.

A considerable amount of assorted manor business had accumulated over Wycliffe's visit. Sir Harold was irritable and snapped at Rick while they worked.

"Have I somehow offended?" Rick said.

"What? We have no time to gossip. Tend your business."

"Yes, My Lord."

Rick worked silently while Sir Harold scowled and drummed his fingers on the table.

"God's wounds, we must talk. Christopher. Wine for Master Richard and myself, then you and Henry may leave us."

"You are aware of what my friend proposes?"

"His translation?"

"Don't fence with me, Sirrah. His views on Transubstantiation. Having spoken at length with you and your group, he proposes to deny it publicly."

"We spoke of it, but I did warn him against speaking publicly."

"Why? You agree with his views, is that not so?"

"Yes, I do, but his denial of the doctrine will lose him important support; my Lord of Lancaster for one, and other members of the nobility."

"So, what did you recommend?"

"A man may believe what he wishes. It's not always advisable to speak out."

"Master Wycliffe would never agree to lie. He lives his beliefs."

"It's not necessary to lie, merely to refrain from speech."

Sir Harold did not reply at first. He stared at the ground for some time, then looked at his empty goblet.

Rick stood. "Permit me, My Lord."

He filled the goblet, and, after a short wait, turned.

"Oh, pour for yourself, and sit. Here, in private at least, we can dispense with ceremony. Master Wycliffe says I should treat you as a man of rank."

"From him, I'm not sure that's a compliment."

For an instant, Rick thought his attempt at humour had misfired. Sir Harold flushed before he roared with laughter.

"By *Corpus Dominus*, Master Wycliffe is right. You *are* a man of substance, but you mistake Master Wycliffe's views if you think that."

"Will he be circumspect?" Rick said. "Or will he speak as his conscience dictates?"

"Nay, you tell me. My friend says you know."

"I'm afraid he'll speak out. Some, whom many will call the Hatted Knights, will follow him, but he'll lose much of his noble support."

"Our friend said I should seek and follow your advice."

"Did you discuss the political and social scene at all? I'm afraid there'll be a lot of unrest. Even strife and death."

Sir Harold nodded.

"The Hedge Priests have seized on our friend's ideas. They preach equality for all, and so disturb the peace of the realm. They would see all men reduced to the level of the common herd. God placed each man in his place and station for His own purposes. It is our duty to do our best in the station in which we find ourselves."

"Some say a mere accident of birth," Rick said.

"I say without doubt, if all men became equal tomorrow, by the day after there would be wealthy men and paupers, the day after that, kings, barons, knights, freemen, and serfs."

"But would they be the same men in the same stations?"

Sir Harold stared at Rick, but Rick stared back unblinking, and Sir Harold finally laughed.

"No, perhaps not. All the more reason to maintain the status quo."

"All the more reason for slow gradual change. Sudden changes bring violence. Attempts at sudden change that fail, result in much harsher conditions for the defeated than they suffered before."

"Tell that to your hedge priests."

"They are not *my* hedge priests."

"No, I believe not. Arthur's maybe?"

"The apathy of the serfs appals Arthur. He may see the hedge priests as the most likely way to arouse them, but he sees the burghers and petty tradesmen as greedy and no better than the aristocracy."

Chapter Thirty-Four

"Well, Arthur," Malcolm said. "How was your holiday? A nice jaunt?"

The group strolled in the garden after Arthur and Dennis's return from escort duties with Wycliffe.

"Very instructive, Medicine Man. Wycliffe might look like he has one foot in the grave, but he's sharp – sharp as a bloody tack."

"Converted you, has he?"

"To what, Doc? If you take out all the mumbo jumbo about God, the old boy could almost have written the Young Communist's Handbook. The Manifesto, even."

"I was afraid of that." Rick groaned. "You've picked up exactly the message Wycliffe doesn't want to send."

"Look. Have I got it right? He says, since Christians hold all property of God under a contract to be virtuous, sin violates this contract and destroys title to goods and offices."

"Yes, Arthur, you've got the words right, but it's your interpretation, not Wycliffe's."

"Christ. If it becomes popular, it would be open season on frigging idiots like Gerald. No wonder he doesn't like Wycliffe."

"Sir Harold would be all right," Dennis said. "He respects his people."

Rick expected Arthur to argue. Instead he nodded, and said: "If Wycliffe's right, as lords go now, Harold's pretty fair. His serfs are better off with him than most others. At least he feels some obligations of his station, even if he is bloody autocratic."

"Amazing, Arthur," Jo said. "I never thought I'd ever hear you say anything like that."

"We heard one of the hedge priests on our way back," Dennis said. "He made a speech, a sermon I suppose, in which he linked the behaviour of the lords somehow with Transubstantiation. It was a bit over the heads of the serfs."

Rick closed his eyes for a moment,

"Lords devour poor men's goods in gluttony and waste and pride, and they perish for mischief and thirst and cold, and their children also ... And so in a manner they eat and drink poor men's flesh and blood."

"Christ," Arthur said, "you make my blood run cold. That's word for word what he said. How the hell did you know it?"

"It's a quote attributed to Wycliffe," Rick said. "Since I met and talked to him, I don't believe it's really his." He shivered. "We might be in an alternate universe, but so far it's hellish like our own real past."

"So what it boils down to is that we're back to square one. Not a damned thing we can do. Just wait for the tide to sweep us along."

"No," Rick said. "We stick together and do what we think or feel right and proper. We've got to feel we're here for some reason. Not simply blind chance."

"You mean the daft bugger was acting on divine inspiration when he set those bloody charges off that night at the Circle? The blast that sent us here?"

Arthur laughed, and Malcolm scowled.

"Let's not start that all over," Rick said. "I mean we're here to help."

Interlude Four

Lady Jo's Reverie

Summer has passed. Within a fortnight we'll be back in residence at the castle.

Last autumn, Pete, I would have cried if someone had told me I'd be so happy this summer. Such a pleasant summer, even the servants are relaxed. Todd is brown and healthy, and has grown by inches. His arm is still a little bent, but Malcolm says the growth plates weren't damaged. He learns so quickly. I'm afraid that all too soon he'll be much too big and knowing for a lady's personal page.

The others still believe that someday we'll return to our own time. I doubt it. Whatever brought us here was blind to us and to our needs. If it was rational, it's on a plane beyond our understanding. The Circle, or one like it, might move us once again, but what the trigger is or where we'd go, who knows?

Rick wrote a poem about it, and gave it to me. Arthur scoffed, but Dennis had a copy made. Malcolm looked thoughtful when he heard it. Perhaps Rick has it right.

STONE CIRCLES

The Stones of Time, sentries at the Gateway stand,
Worn with age and strife some lean, some lie,
Some gone forever to a mundane task for Man.
The Gateways wait. Way stations in a vast network
Of space and time. Their purpose long forgotten,
If ever known, by Man.
The coin to bring to life the silent, lonely station,
Does it still exist, unknown, unrecognised?
Do unwary and unwitting travellers, depart by chance?
Their coin relating to a schedule lost for eons,
In a system long unused?
No helpful staff to point the way,
The coin paid is all?
Or is Man's span too feeble to grasp the whole?
And what he takes for travel far and time immeasurable
But the rearrangement of the dust
As greater beings journey through?

Sir Harold is what Father would have been had he lived now: an autocrat, sure of his rightful place. He takes it for granted that everyone jumps at his commands, his every whim an order. The servants and the serfs respect him. Arthur says they only fear him, but concedes they fear and hate his brother Gerald. If they lose their fear, Gerald would be dead, not so Sir Harold. Dear Pete, you would have respected him, but you would have quarrelled as you did with Father. Your feelings for the great unwashed, equally needless and strange to Sir Harold as they were to Father.

Of all of us, Dennis has changed the most. He's still quiet and unassuming, but now has a quiet self-confidence, and even, at times, an air of menace. Arthur and he aren't as close, since Dennis takes his oath and duty to Sir Harold very seriously. Sir Harold trusts him and he shares the post of bodyguard, and confidant of sorts, with Martin the sergeant. Dennis fits this time and place better than the rest of us.

Malcolm chafes at being here on holiday when people need him in the town. In his own way he has accepted this time and place. His skills are much admired and he really enjoys that.

Sir Harold again recently mentioned finding me a husband. He and Lady Eleanor have treated me like a daughter here. My lack of dower and family, they'll make up, at least enough for some low-ranking client knight of Sir Harold's. Oh, Pete, I don't want to be married off, traded as a pledge of future favours from Sir Harold.

Rick proposes every day. I really like him, but do I love him enough to think of marriage in the time we came from? Still, he's better than those chinless wonders our parents picked out for me. He'd surely be better than a total stranger or ending up in a nunnery, but would that be fair to Rick?

Book Three

Chapter One

"We shall soon return to the castle. Autumn approaches," Sir Harold said. "This has been an excellent summer."

Rick agreed absently, busy with accounts.

"I cannot recall when I enjoyed this manor so. My lady has found it pleasant to have you and Lady Jo to converse and read with."

"I shall be finished presently, and we can review the accounts."

"God's Blood. Put the accounts aside. When I wish to review them, we will."

Chris looked up from the chessboard and grinned at Rick. He rose and bowed.

"Wine, My Lord?"

"Yes, an excellent suggestion. Master Richard?"

Rick nodded and Chris whispered: "He's in a really good mood. Don't annoy him."

Chris poured at the sideboard, and Henry picked up one goblet and carried it carefully to Sir Harold. He bowed.

"Todd has his Lady's permission to fish in the mill lake. May we go and fish too, My Lord, Master Rick?"

"Yes, boys," Sir Harold said. "We shall not have need of you till dinner."

He smiled when the boys whooped and ran.

"Christopher has grown. We must have new clothes made for him on our return. For Todd too."

They sipped and Rick glanced back at his accounts.

"Leave them. Leave be. What remains can be seen to by your clerks. Henry has improved these past weeks. I told you beating would be good for him."

Rick sighed. Henry was more alert, attentive to his duties, and less inclined to mouth off as Dennis said. But it had been hard. Harder on me than on Henry, Rick thought.

Obviously Sir Harold and Dennis approved. Malcolm was largely indifferent, but Arthur ribbed him endlessly about it, and accused him of enjoying his role. Jo was just Jo.

With a start, Rick realised Sir Harold had spoken.

"Pardon, my mind was elsewhere. You were speaking of the boys."

"I was not. I thought we were discussing your future. A subject in which I would have expected you to have some interest."

"Yes, of course."

"I have a small manor, not a day's ride from the castle, deserted, abandoned, since an outbreak of the Death. The manor house is small, but in fair repair, or can be made perfect. The other manor buildings were also repairable when last I was there. Can the place be cleansed, think you?"

"It is fleas from rats that carry the Death."

"So you and Malcolm say. Are you still paying the bounty on rat's tails?"

"Yes, we are. I think after all this time that there would be little danger at the manor you speak of."

"Is this an end that you, Arthur, Dennis and Malcolm might achieve? Given some able bodied serfs, of course."

"I think so. You wish to reclaim the manor? There have been no revenues from it for a long time."

"When we return, you will examine the buildings."

"If you offer life tenancy, inheritable, to some landless serfs and labourers, I'm sure we would have willing helpers, and less afraid of the Death, too."

With a smile Sir Harold said: "If you wish, it could be done that way. I intend to give the manor to you. After all, you and the Lady Jo will require a home when you marry."

"But ... but ... Jo has not accepted."

"Some time in October, I think my lady suggested. Lady Margaret also thought that it would be suitable."

"Please. Has anyone spoken to Jo?"

"The Lady Jo is well aware I am considering suitable matches for her. October is a year from her brother's death, more than adequate time to grieve."

"Has she agreed?"

"Does the prospect not please you? Do you, after all, prefer boys?"

"Damn it ... yes! ... I mean ... I want to marry Jo, if she'll have me. And no ... I don't prefer boys."

"Good. It's settled."

"Can I at least talk to Lady Jo before anyone tells her?"

"What strange ideas you have. It is my place, as her guardian, to tell her what arrangements I have made for her..." At the expression on Rick's face, Sir Harold held up his hands. "Yes, out of the feelings I have for both of you, you may tell her, within a day."

"Thank you," Rick said. His stomach churned.

God. What would Jo say and do?

"I have decided, by the way, after tomorrow, that Henry will be Lady Jo's page. You will take Todd. I shall announce that at supper."

Oh, Christ, I'll be eaten alive for sure.

"Come, pour some more wine and we will seal the contract."

Chapter Two

At dinner Rick ate almost nothing. Henry in his new found attentiveness noticed and commented in a loud voice.

"Shut up, Henry, and take this note to Lady Jo. Quietly."

After she read the note, Jo looked over at Rick with a puzzled frown and nodded.

In the chapel Rick paced nervously. He had cancelled the class for the day and hoped Todd had got word to the other boys.

The door opened and Jo came in.

"Todd, you and Henry play quietly by the door, please," Rick said. "Come down to near the altar, Jo."

"What's all this about? Your note sounded urgent."

"It is."

At a loss how to start, Rick stood silent.

"Spit it out. We can't stay here alone long. Someone will notice and talk."

"Shut up, please."

Taking both of Jo's hands in his, Rick sank to his knees.

"Oh, for God's sake, get up. You look ridiculous."

"Christ. For once shut up and listen. I love you. I think I've loved you since the night we slept together." Jo snatched her hands back and Rick grabbed for them and hung on. "You know what I mean. Please will you marry me?"

"Yes."

"Please think, don't answer like before. Think."

"I said, yes."

"Consider before you say no again. ... What?"

"I said, yes. Oh, get up for heaven's sake."

With a jerk, Jo pulled Rick to his feet. He promptly threw his arms round her, and kissed her. When she actually kissed him back, he almost dropped.

"Rick," Jo pushed him back a little. "Rick, please. I've got to tell you this."

He still held her, unable to believe this was this was not a dream.

"Margaret told me that Harold will marry me off by October. He'd let it be you, but if not, he has other likelies lined up. I had to tell you. It's only fair to you."

"What if you refuse?"

"Then he'll send me to a convent."

Jo kissed him again.

She kissed me, Rick thought, and Henry's voice piped up from the other side of the chapel.

"Shall I ask if we can go out? We could play pitch and toss. Better than watching them."

Rick laughed. Jo pulled back, took his arm and walked back to the door. There, she reached out and ruffled Henry's hair.

"We have to talk, my boy, if you are to be my page. Come," she said, and moved off. "Rick, tell Sir Harold, yes. Let him make any announcements."

Todd bowed. A huge grin split his face.

"So it is true, Master Rick. I am to be your page. It was all the ladies talked of last night. They forget sometimes that I'm there."

"Henry will need to learn to keep his mouth shut about anything he hears," Rick said.

Todd rubbed his ear and laughed.

"He will. I expect to see his ear grow. My lady, the Lady Jo, can fairly make you dance."

"Yes," Rick said, "she can."

Chapter Three

Preparations for the return were almost complete. The servants had removed and crated the windows, everything was set, when Sir Harold started to fuss about a second wagon for the ladies.

Rick could not understand the problem. On the way to the summer manor only Gwenne and her lady-in-waiting had travelled in a wagon. All the other ladies had ridden horseback. He commented on this while Chris prepared his master for bed. Sir Harold scratched and stretched.

"Wine, Todd. Join me, Master Richard."

Rick wondered why the good humour.

"My lady is with child." Sir Harold grinned.

"Congratulations. Couldn't Lady Gwenne ride horseback?"

Sir Harold laughed and slapped Rick's back.

"She is also with child. A splendid summer for the Fitzgerald's."

With Sir Harold in high good humour, the ride to Sir William's manor was quick and pleasant. In the last few miles, Sir Harold grew solemn. He flagged Rick, Arthur, and Dennis to ride close to him, at some distance from the others.

"I intend to arrest Andrew the Physician and have him taken to the castle for questioning," he said. "Dennis, you and Arthur will lodge with him tonight, with Malcolm."

"When do you wish the arrest to be?" Dennis said.

"I will advise Sir William after supper, shortly before we retire, after Andrew and you have withdrawn. Have three good men wait with four horses saddled in Andrew's paddock. Arrest Andrew when you return to his house."

"Is Malcolm to know?" Rick said.

"Not until the moment of arrest. After that, hold Andrew's servants till dawn. Search the house thoroughly. When we ride out, bring his strong box and any papers you may find in the house."

The reception at Sir William's was cordial. Henry, permission granted, visited with his mother and her ladies before supper and spoke briefly with his father after supper. His father was a little surprised that Henry was now Jo's page, but was well pleased with his manners and general deportment.

From their arrival, Rick watched Andrew. When Eleanor and Gwenne emerged from their wagons, he looked surprised, but commented to one of Sir William's people on how well they looked. "…but I do not see Lady Mary, Lady Gwenne's lady-in-waiting…" Rick caught.

Andrew was less than enthusiastic that Dennis, Arthur and Malcolm were to lodge with him, but he smiled and bowed to them.

When the entertainment finished, Rick saw Sir Harold glance at Dennis, who nodded. Sir Harold spoke quietly to Sir William when they rose to leave and motioned Rick to follow them.

When informed of the impending arrest, Sir William claimed his physician could not possibly be involved in such a murderous plot, and said he was sure on investigation that Master Andrew would be seen to be innocent of all evil intent.

Sir Harold closed the discussion, saying: "I take it, Sir William, that you find no objection to my proceedings and your sole interest now lies in the outcome?"

"Indeed, My Lord. I submit willingly to your wisdom and justice, as do all of my people."

When they rode out next morning, Malcolm was angry. At first he spoke to no one, but later, he spurred his horse close to Rick.

"Those two hoodlums behaved disgracefully last night."

"Sir Harold told them to arrest Andrew and hand him over to an escort to be taken to the castle."

"Then they might have had the courtesy to tell me, instead of simply pushing me out of the way. They were quite unnecessarily rough, and they tied him."

"Sir Harold said he was to be tied to his horse."

"They attacked his apprentice and his page, and ransacked the house."

"Cool it, Malcolm. Sir Harold told them to turn over the house, to look for evidence. I really don't see either of them really hurting the page. Dennis wouldn't let Arthur do anything to the apprentice beyond making sure he didn't interfere with their work."

Malcolm brooded in silence.

"Remember, Andrew tried to have you killed," Rick said.

"But last night, guests in a fellow's home and all that. He is a doctor, a professional man."

"Come off it. God, you can be stuffy and pompous. You're miffed because we didn't tell you ahead of time."

"Not at all, but you should have. You would think I was untrustworthy."

"Well, you have been known to spout off after a jar or two, haven't you? Anyway, only Arthur, Dennis and I knew, apart from Sir Harold, of course."

Malcolm rode in silence, a scowl on his face, but after a while, he grinned.

"In retrospect, I suppose it did have its comical aspects."

"Our brave doctor telling you how he tried to save his frigging colleague?" Arthur's mocking voice came from behind them. "Go on, Doc, tell him how you slithered across the floor on your bum and ended up under the table. Not the first time, I know, but the first time it was food that did it."

Chapter Four

At the castle, life resumed as before, except that Rick and Chris no longer lived at the house with the others. Chris now slept on a trestle bed in Sir Harold's chamber, and Rick and Todd slept in the antechamber.

Mary, the servant girl they had left at the house, was pregnant. Much to Rick's surprise, Arthur was ecstatic. He was adamant the child was his. The girl had been faithful to him, he was sure, since the big row with Malcolm in the autumn.

The trio, Arthur, Dennis and Malcolm went out to celebrate. When Sir Harold heard of their escapade he roared with laughter, but Jo was furious.

"Mary's got all the work," she said to Rick. "She's got to carry the child, and those three louts go out and get drunk. To celebrate! You'd think they'd been clever. If Malcolm wasn't Sir Harold's doctor, he'd be in the stocks for last night's carry-on."

She was slightly mollified next day when Arthur asked her help to find a nice clean, fresh girl to do the heavy work for Mary. Rick was not quite so sure of Arthur's motives.

On the first Sunday after their return, Sir Harold had the banns called for Rick and Jo, with the intention of having their wedding in mid- or late-October. It created little stir or interest beyond their immediate circle.

Andrew's strong box and the documents seized from his house

produced nothing more than they already had from the previous search in the spring.

"I have decided," Sir Harold said to Rick, "to have Andrew put to the question. My brother will question him. You will observe and record."

When Rick tried to argue that torture was not necessary, Sir Harold turned a stony, ice cold face at him.

"My son is dead. My wife endangered. My line in question because he supplied potions to Lady Mary. I must have answers. You will do as I tell you."

"Couldn't someone else observe and record?"

"No. You, I trust. I wish you present at all times when Master Gerald is with Andrew. Every question, every answer, I want to know, and every nuance of both."

Chapter Five

In the early dawn light Rick shivered. He looked round the cell. Rough bare walls and two high, slit windows gave little comfort. The centre of the room was taken up with a rack, a brazier glowed sullenly to one side, and cast iron tools hung on the wall behind. Rick did not even want to guess at the use of each. He almost sat on the one chair before he realised it had leather belts to hold anyone seated in position.

"Ah. Master Richard. Good morning," Gerald said. "I had hoped to see you here under somewhat different conditions. Pray, place yourself by the lectern. You can view the proceedings from there, and it is at a good height to make notes."

The door opened and Andrew came in with two guards. His garments were stained and dirty, his hair unkempt, his eyes wild. This was not the sleek, well-dressed, confident physician of former days.

"I trust you are well," Gerald said. "Your accommodations on this visit are, I'm afraid, less salubrious than when you were last here."

"Sir Gerald, I must protest. Ruffians seized me at knifepoint in my own home and brought me here."

"They arrested you on Sir Harold's orders, with Sir William's knowledge."

"Might I speak with Sir Harold…"

"No, you may not. You are charged with supplying the Lady Mary, lady-in-waiting to my wife, with poisonous substances and counselling her in her evil purposes."

The colour drained from Andrew's face and he stammered: "No ... no ... I barely know the Lady Mary!"

"You are further suspected of complicity in the death of John, physician to my Lord Brother, and in the death of My Lord's only son and heir."

Face grey, Andrew turned to Rick.

"Master, I am innocent of all these matters. I beseech you, intercede with Sir Harold for me."

"Strip him," Gerald said.

Naked, Andrew trembled before Gerald.

"Show him the implements."

At Gerald's words, two more men came into the cell. One used a pair of leather bellows to blow the almost dormant fire in the brazier to a white heat, while the other placed one of the cast iron implements in the coals. When the brand glowed white, the man stepped towards Andrew who tried to step back. Two guards pinioned his arms behind him, gripped his hair tightly, and held his head still.

The stench of burning hair filled the room.

"No doubt you can feel the heat on your face behind the beard. Think of it on your flesh. There are many sensitive places. We have pincers that can nibble at your flesh..." Laying the brand down, the guard moved another implement slowly before Andrew's eyes. "These are used white hot, so they cauterise as they nibble. Cold pincers might let you bleed too quickly and become weak from loss of blood. But, of course, as a physician you know that."

Gerald nodded and the two men who held Andrew walked him to the rack.

If it had been me, Rick thought, I'd have screamed out

anything I thought might please Gerald. They make them tougher or a lot more insensitive now.

"How say you? You've seen what's in store."

"I have done nothing. When the Lady Mary returns from her father's sick bed she will bear me out."

Gerald nodded and the two guards stretched Andrew on the bed of the rack.

"Take up the slack. Now a quarter turn."

"Master Andrew," Rick blurted out, "save yourself much pain. We have your diaries, your records. We have the Lady Mary…"

"Silence, Sirrah," Gerald shouted. "I will ask the questions here, and in my own time. You may observe and record only."

He smiled at Andrew and Rick shuddered.

"Another quarter turn and lower the bed."

The centre portion of the rack dropped about six inches and left Andrew suspended by his wrists and ankles. He groaned loudly. Without further instructions the guard placed a wedge shaped board under Andrew's back at about kidney level and cranked the bed back up till Andrew stretched across the board like a violin string over its bridge. They placed weights on his knees and chest.

"A little refinement of my own invention, based on observations abroad. Come, Master Richard, we will leave our guest to his thoughts for a little," Gerald said.

To the guards he added: "If the tension slackens, you may tighten a tooth or two of the ratchet, but I wish him in tune, not unconscious."

Gerald led the way to the outer wall walk. Quite how it came about, Rick was not really sure, but he heard himself describe modern brainwashing techniques.

"The boy Todd did say you were familiar with methods of extracting information. You are full of surprises. I have seen what you call sleep deprivation used. They pushed a bodkin through the gristle from one side of the nose to the other and threaded a piece of rawhide through. From time to time a guard would tweak the rawhide. Guards changed every two hours and the prisoner had to stand with them. Three days was very effective and not the mark of a blow."

Rick shivered, although it was not really cold, and jumped when Gerald took his arm like an old friend while they strolled.

"Interesting you should know of such techniques," Gerald said. "We shall have whatever truth there is to Master Andrew out of him before supper. Plenty of time after that for experiment and amusement. I have not had such an opportunity since my brother returned. Come, we must get back. He should be in a very pleasant state of anticipation."

At Gerald's insistence, they broke for dinner, although Rick could eat nothing. Gerald was in high spirits and in reply to a question from Sir Harold said: "We shall have the truth by mid-afternoon, My Lord Brother. Your secretary is very knowledgeable in these matters."

Todd grinned at Rick, and Rick scowled back.

By mid-afternoon, Gerald sent for Sir Harold. While they waited, a guard poured a bucket of cold water over Andrew, and Gerald had wine fetched for himself and Rick.

"You may tell My Lord what you have told us," Gerald said when Sir Harold arrived.

Andrew's correspondent was a minor functionary at court in Arundel's service. A man he had met when serving as physician to a previous employer. Sir William knew nothing of the correspondence. Whether Arundel and Courtney ever actually heard of anything he wrote, Andrew did not know. He had never received any recompense. He had written to his friend initially in reply to a letter from him.

Mary, he had met before she came to serve with Lady Gwenne, and before he joined Sir William. They had discussed various simples and potions. He was aware that at one time Mary was to have been Gerald's wife. He had met her again when he visited Sir Harold's physician. She proposed a scheme for her to become Gerald's wife and Gerald to become the Baron. In his greed, he had supplied her with the needed materials. The death of the physician and Sir Harold's son had frightened him, but by then it was too late to back out.

"Have the priest fetched," Sir Harold said. "Let Master Andrew sign in his presence. Let the priest shrive him. Hang him tomorrow at first light."

When Rick joined Sir Harold with the signed document he felt queasy. Todd, who had been playing chess with Chris, leapt to his feet and without instruction poured wine. He carried one goblet to Rick and pushed him to sit in the window alcove before he handed the other goblet and the document to Sir Harold.

"You are convinced," Sir Harold said, "that this is all? There are no others involved?"

Rick sighed. "Yes, I'm convinced. There is no grand plot. Those two acted on their own for greedy, selfish motives. Observe the addendum. Andrew hired the two mercenaries for Sir Gerald and instructed them to attempt to kill Malcolm. He thought he could become your physician and help Lady Mary in her plans. Gerald knew of the attempt on Malcolm, but nothing else. I would swear Andrew has told us all he knows."

"Good. I will inform Lady Mary's family," Sir Harold said. "She may remain here, with one lady-in-waiting, sequestered in the tower, or they may arrange to have her sequestered for life in some convent. Gerald may tell Lady Mary."

"Andrew is still with Sir Gerald."

"Possibly, but we need nothing further. You say we have all there is."

"Sir Gerald intends to continue with the torture. Not for information, but for sport."

"Can we go and watch?" Todd said, and Rick knocked him off his feet with a backhanded slap.

"This man caused the death of my only son. He conspired to kill me. I will not interfere with Gerald in this. Andrew hangs tomorrow in any case."

Rick had pulled Todd to his feet.

With a grin, Todd asked: "Can we watch the hanging?"

Todd got to watch despite Rick's revulsion, since Sir Harold insisted on being present, accompanied by his secretary.

Andrew, to Rick's surprise, was able to walk with the support of two soldiers. He was fully conscious, and the long white shift he wore covered any marks on his body. The priest walked with him, and Andrew was most attentive. On the outer wall walk, to one side of the gate, they stopped.

"The hook's on the outside of the wall," Todd whispered. "They'll stand him in the arrow slot and push him off."

"No, boy." Rick jumped when Gerald spoke. "This time we use the beam."

He pointed to a massive beam, with a pulley, that projected from the top of the wall. When one of the soldiers crawled along the beam to thread the rope through the pulley, Rick realised the noose had been round Andrew's neck since he left the cell. Gerald examined it carefully and adjusted it, before he nodded to the soldiers who held Andrew. Instead of simply pushing Andrew off, they tied his legs together at the knees and the ankles, and bound his arms by his side, before they pulled the rope tight, and lowered him gently.

"God, he'll strangle slowly," Rick said. "He can't even kick his legs to speed it up."

They watched until the last quiver.

"Good, leave him there, for all to see," Sir Harold said. "Let us repair to the solar. Todd, you can mull ale for us. It is a cool morning."

Chapter Six

Two days after the hanging, Rick set out for the manor Sir Harold had pledged him. Dennis, Arthur, Todd, Chris and twenty men accompanied him. The men were older on average than Rick had expected. He had hoped for younger sons of serfs from Sir Harold's other manors. The ever-present escort of six men was under Dennis's command.

They reached the manor after a very comfortable day's ride at a pace suitable to the wagons and pack animals, and spent the night in the manor house.

"It's not big is it?" Todd said. "About the size of the one Adam's parents have."

In daylight, Rick surveyed the property. The manor house had one large room. A wood screen at one end made a passageway from one side of the house to the other. The buttery, pantry, and kitchen lay on the far side of the passage. Outside, attached to the first building at right angles, was a second smaller structure. Steps led down to a cellar below, and a second set of rickety steps led up to a smaller hall or room with a southern exposure.

"The solar," Rick said.

The solar formed with the great hall, two sides of a small courtyard. The third side consisted of a stable-barn combination, and on the fourth the remains of a wooden palisade could be seen.

At the front of the great hall there was a small courtyard with the ruins of a palisade that ran along the inner side of a small ditch.

Other small, single room buildings clustered round the manor house in varying states of repair. The manor house itself was a post and beam structure with wattle-and-daub walls. The smaller structures were A-frames, again with wattle-and-daub walls.

One surly giant touched his forelock.

"Where shall us start, Master? Best get the manor house in order first, I reckons."

"No. We'll start with the village houses," Rick said. "They're in worse shape, and they'll be occupied first."

The men fell to work with a will, but they muttered to each other and darted sideways glances under frowning eyebrows at Dennis, Arthur, and Rick when they helped unload the two supply wagons. They all looked away when Arthur, impatient of Rick's clumsiness at weaving wattles, said: "Christ, Rick, if you can't help, don't frigging hinder."

Around ten, Rick and Todd began to set out the bread, cheese, and ale they had brought. The serfs shuffled nervously before they slowly found places to sit when Rick announced everyone would eat together.

After dinner, the two boys were given leave to hunt and turned up later with two brace of rabbits.

One of the serfs ducked his head and said shyly: "Us knows how to cook them a treat, Master. Shall us do them for Your Lordship's supper?"

"No, you're all too busy. Todd will help me make a stew. Four rabbits won't go far among this lot."

They all stared at him.

Todd had set snares for next day, so Rick cooked all four rabbits and used smokies they had brought with them to augment the meal.

In three days they had repaired the existing A-frames and built four more, to bring the number up to twenty. They still looked very primitive and makeshift to Rick, but the serfs were pleased with them. They assured Rick that the buildings would "fair keep out wind and water, and what owt else could a man desire?"

To decide who got which hut, Rick had them draw lots, and each, delighted, set about putting some distinctive mark above his entrance. Rick expected they would sleep in their own huts, but with the dark they all drifted in to sleep in the great hall.

When Rick suggested on the fifth day that half of them could return to their villages and bring back their wives and families, the serfs were silent and Rick wondered if he had made some sort of blunder.

The surly giant spoke again.

"It is true then, what Squire's steward told us. Us were not lied to. Us can live here?"

"Of course you can, man. You're a tithing now," Rick said, and they all stood a little straighter. "Unless the tithing rejects one of you now, this is your home. You will have title as life tenants, which you can pass on to your sons, with a rent payable to me or my heirs. Elect one of your number as my reeve."

At a signal from Rick the soldiers moved out of the great hall and Rick's companions followed. Rick stood in the doorway and saw the serfs look round them at the empty great hall before a babble of conversation erupted.

Some time later the largest of the serfs appeared at the door and approached Rick, who stood with the others beside the small stream.

"I be Dicken, Master," he said and touched his forelock. "Can you come back in, please?"

The nineteen seated in a circle started to stand when Rick came in. He waved them down.

"This is your council. I am here as your guest."

There was a rumble of low voices.

Dicken indicated a gap in the ring and Rick sat cross-legged.

"Us cannot pick a reeve," Dicken said. "Us cannot agree. Will you accept election by lot?"

"If it is agreeable to you, yes."

Dicken handed each man a straw, and solemnly threw away the rest of the handful, save one. He collected the straws, and in front of Rick cut all but one to the same length. The last he trimmed with his knife a full two inches shorter than the others. This done, he handed all twenty straws to Rick, who, taking ten in each hand, pushed the free ends level with the back of his other hand.

"Mary, Mother of God guide this choice," a voice said, and several crossed themselves.

A deeper voice said: "Lord of the Forest and the Stones choose for us," and several voices said, "Sh," but Rick was sure he saw nods in the gloom.

Dicken looked at Rick, and picked a straw. Each man took a straw in turn as the group slowly filed past Rick. When Rick's hands were empty, they lined up in front of Rick to hand back the straws. They all watched Rick compare each straw with the first one handed back. More than half the group had passed when Dicken stood in front of Rick. The straw looked short in Dicken's large hand. When Rick placed it alongside his test piece, a sigh went up from the group.

"Congratulations, Dicken," Rick said.

"You will allow the election?" Dicken said.

"Yes, I will. If Mary, Mother of Our Lord, and the Lord of the Forest and the Stones chose you, who am I to disagree?"

Rick laughed, but no one else did.

Chapter Seven

Next day, Dicken told Rick which ten men would go back to collect their families and, with a tug at his forelock, he turned to go.

"Wait, I want to talk to you," Rick said. "Yesterday, you marked the short straw, didn't you? Both ends with your thumbnail? You knew which one to pick." Dicken shrugged. "You questioned if I would allow your election. Why?"

"Us thought you noticed the marks."

"I did, but you are still reeve. I need someone with some initiative, but if you cheat me in any other way, I'll have you hanged. You doubted the promise of a life tenancy. Why?"

When Dicken shuffled and stared at the ground, Rick grew impatient.

"Answer me, man. You are my reeve now. I depend on you."

"Squire's reeve picked us to come to rid himself of a troublemaker, as he thought. From the others it was the same for most."

"What sort of troublemakers? Thieves, drunks, work shy? What? I must know."

"No. Us been whipped for insolence, for disobedience. Put in stocks too, for talking out against the reeve and the master. Why should squire's crop come before mine? If he loses some of hisn he eats his share of mine anyway. If us loses mine, me and mine starve."

"But isn't Sir Harold a good master? I've heard that."

Dicken shrugged.

"Yes, some say so. In those manors he oversees himself, it is said all men are fairly treated. But he doesn't know all that his squire tenants do. Not all lords feel like Sir Harold does."

"I don't mind such troublemakers," Rick said.

"Can us build a church?"

"Yes, if the tithing wish it. I'll have Master Wycliffe find a priest for us."

Dicken nodded and grinned.

"Us told the others, from the first day, you be different. Master Arthur surely is agin the high nobles and their priests."

Rick laughed. "Master Arthur is agin most everything, except Master Arthur."

Chapter Eight

Work progressed so smoothly at the manor that Rick decided to ride back to the castle with Chris to report progress.

"I am glad to see you, Master Richard, you too Chris," sergeant Martin greeted them when they rode in. "My Lord has been in a rare temper these last days."

"Why? What's the problem?" Rick said.

"The clerk you left to do your work has had a pot of ink dumped on his head, Henry has been beaten, the Lady Jo and My Lord are not speaking."

"Maybe we'd better go back to the manor?" Chris said.

Rick sighed. "No, let's dust off and present ourselves to Sir Harold."

Moments later they paused in the passage outside the anteroom to Sir Harold's chamber. Rick knocked, waited, and pushed open the outer door and walked to the chamber door. They heard the rumble of Sir Harold's voice, followed by a clang, and a string of oaths, coincident with the sound of a blow and a shriek.

At the risk of a reprimand, Rick pushed open the door and entered with Chris close on his heels.

With his back to the door Sir Harold shook Henry by the shoulders. He heard the door open and the footsteps.

"God's wounds," he bellowed and turned, "this is intolerable. Await permission before..." His voice faded when he saw Rick and Chris. He beamed. "Master Richard. Christopher. By *Corpus Christi*, a welcome sight indeed."

Henry ran to hide behind Rick, and Chris, after a bow, moved to the sideboard and poured a goblet of wine.

"A soothing goblet, My Lord?" Chris said and presented it to Sir Harold.

"I am in no need of soothing, Sirrah. I am the most patient of men and equitable of temper."

Chris stood impassive, the goblet held out before him. Sir Harold smiled and took it. Chris stooped and picked up Sir Harold's broad belt, dagger and scabbard.

"Where are your manners? A goblet for my secretary. Come, Master Richard, join me."

They sipped, and Henry carefully kept Rick between himself and Sir Harold.

"The knave tried to boil me in my bath one day and freeze my marrow the next. He burnt my best shift. Today, he almost deprived me of my manhood with my own dagger, before he dropped it on my toe. He has learnt nothing."

He reached behind Rick, grabbed Henry by the back of the neck, and forced him to his knees.

"It is lucky for him, I am patient man."

Sir Harold turned to glare at Chris. His grin vanished instantly.

"And why are you grinning like a jack-a-nape, Sirrah?"

"Me, Sire?" Chris said, wide-eyed innocence.

"Return to your Mistress," Sir Harold said. "Christopher is back. My belt and dagger."

"We are only back tonight to report," Rick said, "and return to the manor tomorrow."

"I will decide when you return to the manor. We will talk after supper. There is much work to be done."

"Alfred should be able to handle most things."

"The man is a dolt. He cannot keep up with me. The fool

stopped me to ask questions. I almost lost my train of thought."

"I've heard of fright turning someone white overnight," Chris said, and grinned. "But Alfred must be the first to go streaky black from blond."

Sir Harold turned an icy stare on Chris for a moment before he laughed aloud.

"By Our Lady, it is good to have you two back."

At supper Rick sat with Jo.

"Todd did not return with you, Master Richard?" Henry said.

"No, so you'll have to serve both of us. Right, Jo? That'll keep you busy."

"Not half as busy as paging to only Sir Harold."

Henry grinned and Rick laughed.

"Come on, Jo, laugh. Henry's making a joke of it."

"It's fine for you, you weren't here to hear him scream."

"I'm fine, My Lady. Really. Sir Harold hurts less than you do when you beat me..."

When Henry saw Jo's expression change, he stopped and smiled from Jo to Rick. He shrugged and fluttered his hands.

"But you don't make such a noise with me," Jo said.

For a moment Henry made no answer. He shifted from foot to foot. With a placatory smile, he said: "Not after the first time, My Lady. You don't stop when I scream. Sir Harold does, and so did Master Rick."

Rick laughed out loud, and pulled Henry to him while Jo stared.

"You cunning little devil," she said and rose. "Come with me."

She led him to where Sir Harold sat. Jo curtsied.

"My Lord. I have been out of sorts and in ill humour with you these past days..."

"No matter," he said. "We have all missed Master Richard. You most of all, I'm sure."

Jo blushed.

"Should my – our – page need correction in future, let me know. I will beat him. Right, Sirrah?"

Jo shook Henry by the ear, and he grimaced.

"He does learn," Sir Harold said. "You have made a good start with him. He must be less careless and clumsy. That is all."

"He only seemed careless and clumsy with you because he was frightened," Jo said a little sharply.

"Of me! Of me? Why should that be? I am..." he caught Chris's fleeting grin, "the most gentle of men. Am I not, Christopher?"

"Oh, yes, My Lord, of a surety."

"We should not quarrel, daughter." Both Jo and Rick were startled at this. "Let us be at peace."

He offered his cheek to Jo.

In the solar after supper Sir Harold steered Rick to a window alcove. Rick told him of their progress at the manor. When he had finished, Sir Harold questioned him closely on the men he had been given and how satisfactory they had been.

"I fear some of my people have been less than co-operative. Martin has heard that some stewards have taken the chance to rid themselves of outspoken troublemakers."

"Yes, I know, but they have worked well. I am content with them."

"Are you sure? If these stewards have made trouble for you knowingly, I will have them flogged."

"No, I assure you. They may unwittingly have done me a favour in giving me men of some spirit. Arthur thinks so."

"Ah, yes. Our Man of the People."

Rick could feel himself flush, but pressed on.

"Arthur worked very co-operatively with them and they with him. I think we have the nucleus of a very good group. A 'collective,' Arthur calls it."

"A strange concept indeed, co-operation between lord and serf.

I say do this and it is done, or someone is flogged."

"But as I see it, you are reasonable in your demands. We have simply gone a step further. Co-operation has to come. About Chris and I returning to the manor tomorrow…"

"No. Not tomorrow. I need you here. Two or three days perhaps."

"But, when Jo and I marry, will we not live at our manor?"

Sir Harold looked at him in surprise.

"Certainly not. I gave you the manor that you might have some standing and an income. You will remain my secretary, and My Lady requires Lady Jo's services."

"But the manor…"

"Your income will be secure. We will find a good strong steward to run the manor. Someone who can handle the villeins."

"No, My Lord. You gave me the manor. Chance or fate gave me the men I have. I will not have them cowed by some steward. Jo and I can visit the manor from time to time?"

"Certainly. I shall not interfere in your manor, provided your duties here for me are performed."

Chapter Nine

It was four days later before Rick and Chris returned to the manor, with strict instructions to be back at the castle within the week.

The village had changed. Rick saw at least two pigs rooting around the huts, and there were small children everywhere, plus dogs and chickens. When he and Chris came in sight of the village, a horn sounded and men appeared. Todd ran out of the manor house courtyard and trotted over to hold Rick's horse.

"What kept you? I have been keeping watch from the tower since you left."

"A good excuse to get out of work," Arthur said, and swung at Todd.

"Welcome home, Master." Dicken bowed and touched his forelock.

"Thank you. I see our people have moved in. The village looks good."

"Wait till you see the manor," Todd said. "We've been hard at work on it."

"We? That's good. Todd the Straw Boss," Arthur said.

Dennis put an arm round Todd's shoulder. "He's been helping me. Haven't you, Todd?"

"Why the tower," Rick said. "That's new."

The tower stood inside the ruins of the palisade. It consisted of three poles, forming an equilateral triangle four feet on a side, with a square platform at the top, about twenty-five feet above the ground. A rope ladder dangled to within two feet of the dirt.

"You can see almost all the manor from up there, and all of the approaches," Dennis said.

"We really built it for some place to put Todd where he wouldn't get in the bloody way. You two can have your office up there."

Dicken looked shocked, and Rick said: "Someone mentioned the manor house?"

"Yes, master. Us have cleaned and repaired it."

"But what about the village and the fields?"

"Us is used to doing the lord's work, master, as well as everything else. Us met and talked and agreed to do the manor house now. First time nobody told us we had to."

"Well, thank you. You all agreed?"

One of the villagers ducked his head and muttered: "Dicken promised to break heads if us didn't."

The other villagers laughed, but Dicken scowled.

"You, Willum, is no brother to me. Us helps you, don't us?"

"Let's go into the manor house," Rick said.

The main building had been swept clean and fresh rushes placed in the great hall. Daylight was no longer visible through any of the walls and shutters hung folded back at the windows. Under the solar, the cellar had been emptied and cleaned and their new supplies neatly stacked. The staircase up to the solar no longer creaked and swayed when it was climbed. Inside, Rick looked around in surprise. It was clean and sweet smelling. Oiled skin or parchment had been stretched across the openings in the shutters, so that even closed, they let some light in.

Rick walked round and the village men watched him. When he stepped out of the solar, he glanced at the outhouses.

"Nothing has been done there yet, master."

"Dicken. Men of D'Arcy. I thank you for your gift. I am

delighted with the work on the manor house. The pack animals that came with me today have supplies for the coming winter. We will store these in the village granary, when it's finished. These are for all equally. Tomorrow, we'll have a feast at supper in the great hall for all."

Their own supper that night was plain, but very satisfactory. Dicken had organised some of the village wives to take turns as cook in the manor, and some girls to serve.

Over supper, Rick told them of Sir Harold's plans, and offered the stewardship of the manor to Arthur. There was a startled silence. Arthur flushed.

"Pull the other leg."

"No, Arthur, think about it. I don't want some stranger here lording it over the villagers when I'm not here. You teach them how to run the village; how to govern themselves. Your only duty to me is to make sure this works, and collect the rents."

"A rent collector. A frigging rent collector."

"Shut up and think for God's sake," Dennis said. "It's an ideal chance for you. You don't mind collecting the loot from the smokies for doing damn all, do you? Give Rick his due; but for him, these poor bastards would live out their lives as serfs. Here they achieve more, if they want to. That should be worth at least the piddling rent they'll pay him."

"We'll bring Margaret and Robert out to you," Rick said.

"Where would we live? I don't fancy being heaved out when the bloody Lord of the Manor pays a call."

"We can build you a house. There's a good spot outside the palisade," Dennis said. "Chris and I will help you put a fireplace in."

"Okay. Done. Where do I sign, My Lord?" Arthur said, and Rick stuck out his hand.

"Between gentlemen."

"Don't be frigging insulting," Arthur said, but he grasped

Rick's hand firmly.

Next day Rick inspected the whole manor. Because they had no crops to harvest, the villagers were clearing the fields of the scrub that had grown over them while the manor had been abandoned. Obviously hard, back-breaking work, but everyone waved cheerfully at them, even Willum.

The village was alive with young children. Most were under five, but one or two could be as old as eleven or twelve and they worked in the fields with the adults.

"What would you think are the ages of our men?" Rick said.

"Difficult to say," Arthur said. "People look older now, somehow, but I think our oldest is probably about thirty. Dicken maybe twenty-five. The youngest is barely nineteen. All the others tease him because his wife is expecting their second child."

"About two thirds of the population now is under fifteen. Anybody over forty-five is ancient. In 1376, six of the nine members of the Privy Council were under thirty-four, William Courtney, Bishop of London, certainly was. Gaunt himself was only thirty-six."

"Thanks, I've always wanted to know that," Arthur said. "Look at this stream here. If we put a weir or dam across just here, we could build up a big enough head for a mill wheel. Could we build a mill?"

"A mill would need a license or charter from Sir Harold. I don't know. Where's the nearest mill?"

"Dicken says two manors over. Two days there and back with wagons or pack animals. Go on, Rick. You're the blue eyed boy. Get us permission."

"Well, I'll try. What about a fish pond?"

"It shouldn't be a big deal digging one," Arthur said, "but stocking it and keeping it up ... I haven't the slightest."

"I'll see what I can find out. In the meantime, can we do anything about the middens?"

Rick gestured. Even in this short time, outside each hut there was a small collection of household refuse. While they walked, one of the pigs contentedly snuffled through a pile, scattering it.

"What about sanitation? I don't see any outhouses, except at the manor house."

"God, Rick. Instead of playing back your books in that weird head of yours, look round you. See for yourself. They piss behind a hedge, or a tree, or a bush, and have a crap at the edge of a field. Even if we built outhouses, they wouldn't use them. They think they're unhealthy."

Rick laughed.

"They said that about indoor plumbing, too, when it started. Well, do what you can. See if we can at least avoid the middens outside each house and the manure piles."

Chapter Ten

"Master Rick, are you awake?"

"Yes, Todd, but it's not dawn yet. Lie quiet."

"It is today, isn't it? The wedding?"

"You know perfectly well it is."

It was almost dawn. Rick could barely make out Todd's outline on the other trestle bed in the anteroom. He sighed.

"Don't you want to get married?"

"Yes, of course, but I could do without all the fuss."

Arthur and Dennis had arrived back at the castle the previous evening, and Rick still cringed at the comments.

Jo took them better than I did, Rick thought.

"The result of a sound education in an all girls boarding school, my boy," Jo had said. "Any of the girls could embarrass the pants off the likes of Arthur without really trying."

"Sir Harold has had the tower guest chamber aired these last two days," Todd said. "The one really important visitors can sleep in. There's to be a fire in it all day, and warming pans. I heard the servants talk, you know."

"Yes, I *do* know. Shut up."

Rick sighed again. When Sir Harold had told him about the guestroom he had mistakenly assumed it was to be a permanent, or at least a semi-permanent arrangement.

"By *Corpus Dominus*," Sir Harold had said, "you live like a monk this last year, and now you expect to tup your lady every night?"

The early part of the morning passed as in a dream for Rick. Sir Harold's barber trimmed his hair and he allowed himself to be bathed in perfumed water and dressed in his new clothes, a gift from Sir Harold.

Finally it was time for the ceremony. Malcolm stood with Rick at the altar rail.

"Who would have guessed a year ago, you'd be here today waiting to marry Pete's brother ... er ... sister?" Malcolm whispered and laughed. "Well, Arthur beat you to it, and I'll not be long behind. The next mayor has consented to let his daughter marry me."

Rick was surprised. With Arthur at the manor, and Dennis splitting his time between the manor and the castle, Malcolm had been on his own at the house in town. Jo had found replacements for Margaret and Robert, but Rick had been so busy with his own affairs he had rather lost touch with Malcolm, even though he saw him every day.

"Congratulations," he said. "But isn't that the girl you said looked like a horse?"

Malcolm laughed.

"The dowry is good. He thinks he's doing well marrying her to Sir Harold's physician. A doctor should be married. Anyway, all cats look grey in the dark."

Rick opened his mouth to reply, but Jo and Sir Harold arrived at the rail. Rick glanced quickly at Jo and smiled.

"I thought you'd be at Pete's requiem," Jo hissed at him. "Even Dennis and Arthur remembered."

Oh, shit, Rick thought, a great start. How could I forget a year ago today?

However, Jo smiled at him and looked radiant.

"I'm sure Pete approves," she said. "Where is the fool of a

priest? Let's get on with it."

The nuptial mass over, Sir Harold led the way to the great hall, seating Rick on his right and Jo on his left.

"Just a simple repast," Sir Harold said. "Master Richard wanted no great ceremony."

"The big feast will be at supper tonight," Todd said and ducked to avoid Sir Harold's hand.

"We already know," Jo said. "No one could miss the preparations."

"I didn't know," Rick said, and they all laughed.

"No, I expect you didn't," Jo said.

After dinner Jo announced she wished to visit the circle. Rick was doubtful if they should, but Jo was adamant. The group would visit the circle, and that was that.

At Jo's insistence they rode to the far side of the ford, where they left the horses and Henry with a groom.

They walked in silence up the hill through the wood to the circle. There they stopped, and Jo turned away to wipe her eyes.

"Remember coming down that day?" Chris said. "We stopped, and your shirt was all untucked. You were a boy then."

"Shut up, Chris," Rick said.

"No, it's all right," Jo said.

This was their first time at the circle since Pete's funeral. Jo went to where the pole had been and knelt. The others glanced at Rick who shook his head and moved to kneel beside Jo. Todd stood uncertainly for a moment, moved towards Jo, but stopped and knelt with Rick.

After some time Jo crossed herself, rose, blew her nose, pulled Todd to his feet and hugged him.

"Come, Rick," she said, "on your feet. We can't spend the rest of our lives on our knees. It's over."

She took Rick's arm and squeezed it while they walked to join the others outside the circle.

"Let's go down," she said. "Pete's gone. He won't be alive again for six centuries. We have our lives to live here."

They laughed and joked on their way back down, and Henry was perplexed at the change.

Chapter Eleven

The supper was riotous. Wine and beer flowed freely, and as the evening progressed the songs and comments became increasingly bawdy. Rick, who drank very little, became more and more embarrassed. At one point the major-domo banged for silence with very little effect, and Sir Harold himself bellowed. When some semblance of order was established, Todd stepped forward. He bowed to Sir Harold, to Rick, and to Jo, then, to Rick's squirming embarrassment, declaimed Rick's poem:

My Lady of the Raven Locks
The moonlight slowly crept across the floor
My Lady of the Raven Locks was there.
Her skin like alabaster made me soar
An eagle, wings ecstatic in the air.
I was in an enchanted land of hill
And valley, soft, rounded, wherein I lost
My soul. My Lady has my soul in thrall
Her every wish commands – my will a ghost.
Yet in the day she knows me not.
Her smile which pierces to my very heart is cool.
Hands which lightly touch her page without guile.
Have me roasting in fires of hell.
A fool to so love one who is beyond my reach My Lady of My

Dreams, your mercy I beseech.

"I'll kill the little bugger," Rick said. "He had no right to read my journal."

Jo leaned forward to look at Rick past Sir Harold. She smiled.

"That was charming. Why didn't you let me see it?"

At that, Lady Eleanor rose, and she and her ladies left, with Jo in the centre. Henry rose to follow his mistress, but Sir Harold caught his wrist and pulled him back.

"The Lady Jo goes to be prepared for her marriage bed. She needs not her page for this. Come, Master Richard, you are not drinking. Christopher, see to his goblet."

Rick had thought the proceedings to this point ribald, but the withdrawal of Lady Eleanor and her ladies saw a sudden escalation of the bawdy humour. The mummers reappeared. To the uproarious approval of the audience they mimed the wooing of an unbelievably buxom woman by a timid inexperienced young man. They ended with the wedding night, at which the young man swooned, and his place was taken enthusiastically by a plump leering priest, who had lurked in the background throughout.

"Time we moved," Sir Harold said. "We would not wish to keep the Lady Jo waiting."

For a horrified moment Rick thought the entire company was to accompany them, but only Sir Harold's immediate entourage and Rick's people followed them out of the great hall.

Rick started to struggle but resigned himself to the inevitable. He was stripped, sprinkled with rose water, thrust into a long shift, and thus prepared, he found himself carried through the passages to the tower chamber.

There, Lady Eleanor and her ladies waited. She curtsied to Sir Harold.

"The Lady Jo awaits her lord," she said, and waved her hand towards the bed.

The bed curtain was drawn and Rick, the shift pulled off, was pushed into the bed beside Jo.

"Embrace your Lady," Sir Harold said, and Rick wondered how long the show was expected to go on. Could he perform before an audience without expiring of embarrassment? Could he perform at all?

He turned to Jo, clasped her to him, and kissed her. There was applause, and Sir Harold said: "Draw the curtain and withdraw, masters, ladies."

At last, Rick was alone with Jo.

"I thought we'd never get rid of them," Rick whispered and embraced Jo.

"Well, I see Barkus really is willing," Jo murmured.

Chapter Twelve

Rick wakened with a start.

God. What a dream, he thought, and stretched. His hand touched the figure on the bed beside him.

Christ. It wasn't a dream. Jo and I are married.

"You awake, Rick?"

"Yes, is it morning?"

"No," Jo laughed. "You dozed off. You've been asleep for about half an hour or so."

They lay cradled in each other's arms.

"You all right?" Rick said.

"Just great."

Rick sighed, but with contentment this time.

"I was really scared they would stay," he said. "You know, till…"

"We made love?" Jo finished for him.

"I don't think I could have. Not in front of a crowd."

"We could have faked it."

"Jo!"

"God, Rick, you are a prude. We could have faked it to let them have their jollies and they'd have gone."

"But…"

Jo kissed him and, aroused again, he kissed her back.

Later, they lay side by side, but Rick tensed.

"There's someone out there." He sat up.

Jo giggled.

"It can't be anyone meaning any harm. Sir Harold will have guards posted. Lie down."

The curtains at Rick's side of the bed parted. Todd's grinning face appeared. He held out a gown to Rick.

"I warmed it at the fire, master."

Todd yelped when Rick grabbed the gown in one hand, and with the other pushed Todd's face back through the curtain.

"I'll kill the little bugger this time. Sneaking round spying on us." Rick spluttered and struggled into the robe.

"He's your page. Of course he'd be there." Jo grabbed Rick's arm when he tried to get up. "Henry will be there too. He's my page remember?"

When Rick parted the curtain and stood up, Todd dashed forward.

"Does Our Lady rise too?"

Todd dashed back to the fire, and ran with a robe for Jo to the other side of the bed.

When Jo emerged, Rick was seated in the only chair in the room in front of the fire. She looked at him and laughed.

"Master Rick doesn't know whether to beat you or hug you," she said.

Todd looked from one to the other with a puzzled frown.

"Why? Didn't you enjoy it? Would you rather beat me?" Todd grinned. "Sir Harold said to keep the fire well, and to mull wine when I heard talking: that you might need refreshment and to have robes ready lest you catch a chill after being overheated." Rick squirmed, but said nothing. "I did mull wine, the first time I heard you talk, but it has grown cold. Shall I mull some more?"

"No," Rick said.

Jo said: "Yes, thank you. Really, Rick. It's the bride who is supposed to be coy and blushing. Todd is only being a good page.

You didn't answer him. Didn't you enjoy it?"

She laughed when Rick pulled her round and kissed her again.

"Make three goblets. Join us," Jo said. "Where's Henry?"

"Master Sleepyhead is doing what he does best." Todd pointed to a figure curled up on the rushes on the other side of the fire.

"Let's get to bed, Jo. Todd, you get some sleep. We won't need you again tonight."

In bed, Rick drew the curtains.

"Christ, what a time. We have a ten-year-old for a servant, who slits throats without batting an eyelid, and he sits out there with all the aplomb of a brothel keeper…"

"If that's what you think of me, you can just get back out and sleep with him." Jo laughed, and pulled Rick down.

Chapter Thirteen

Jo and Rick returned to the castle after a happy week at the manor, to find plans for the parliament had changed. London was in the grip of more unrest than usual: one John Kirkeby, leader of a group of London traders, had murdered a Genoese commercial envoy, and despite much support for Kirkeby in London, the authorities were about to try him. Parliament was now to be in Northampton. Sir Harold had intended to travel with his usual large retinue to London, but was now drastically reducing the numbers.

"What is there in Northampton worth travelling for?" he snapped when Rick suggested that rather than upset those now to be left behind, they should all go.

"There is no great house large enough to take the whole of our party," Sir Harold said. "We shall be meanly lodged, at great expense. In London, Lady Eleanor and I would have been welcome at the Savoy Palace."

"I would have liked to see the Savoy in all its glory," Rick said, "but you are right, Northampton in the rain is a sorry replacement."

"We will visit London again. You will see the Savoy. Now, what is this talk of rain? This has been a fair autumn. The roads hereabouts are dry and hard."

Next morning, rain poured down from a leaden sky, and Sir

Harold scowled suspiciously at Rick.

"How long will this last, Sirrah?"

Rick spread his hands palms up.

"Really, I'm not responsible."

"I did not say you were, but you knew it would come. How long will it last?"

"Long enough, I'm afraid, for the roads to become quagmires, and it will rain while parliament sits."

The journey to Northampton was as miserable as Rick had predicted. They squelched slowly through deep soft mud. At times they had to dismount and men struggled mid-calf deep in mud to help their horses through. Some fords were impassable and long detours were forced on them.

It took three days longer than Sir Harold had intended to reach Northampton, and, by then, the few lodgings in the small town were already taken.

Tired and bad tempered, they trudged through the town. At one house sharp words from a retainer of the knight already in possession provoked a blow from one of Sir Harold's men. Instantly daggers were out and swords drawn. A man slashed at Todd, and Dennis barked an order. It was immediately obvious his were trained, disciplined fighting men, while their opponents were servants. There would have been a massacre, but the knight appeared and bellowed at his men to put up their arms. He turned to Sir Harold, who had remained mounted.

"My Lord Baron," he said and bowed, "might I offer to share this humble lodging?"

"Sir Simon, is it not? You have holdings in Kent?"

"Yes, My Lord. We did meet at a previous parliament."

Sir Harold swung out of his saddle. "Dine with me."

"I fear the provisions are as mean as the accommodation. The town is poorly prepared for this gathering."

"No matter. My secretary foresaw this problem and we have

some supplies with us. Master Dennis, have your men see to our mounts. They can sleep with the horses, or in whatever shelter they can find, but post a guard. You will sleep in my chamber."

Sir Harold turned. "Now, where is my room? The ride has chilled me to the bone. Christopher, I need a tub and hot water."

"There is but one bed..." Sir Simon said.

"Fine. Show us to it."

In the room, Sir Harold nodded approval when he saw the large bed and the fireplace.

"This will be suitable. Have the servants remove these belongings. Master Richard, you, Todd and Christopher will sleep here with me. Thank you, Sir Simon."

When Sir Simon had gone, Rick said: "I don't think this is exactly what Sir Simon had in mind when he offered to share the lodging. We have evicted him. Where will he sleep?"

"We? Master Richard, we? No matter. He can sleep in the common chamber with my gentlemen."

He shivered, scowled, and strode to the door.

"Christopher, Todd, Master Dennis," he bellowed. "By Our Lady, where is everybody? I need a fire and a tub. Christopher!"

At his call, Chris ran in with an armful of wood.

"The servants are heating water and looking for a tub."

He busied himself with the fire.

"That is not work for my page. We are not on campaign. Why is Todd not here? This disorder is intolerable."

"I can manage," Chris said. "Some of the servants fled when it looked as if there was to be fighting. Our men are looking for them. I thought it best if those still here saw to your bath. Master Dennis is dressing Todd's arm."

"What's wrong with Todd's arm?" Sir Harold said.

"It got cut right at the start," Chris said, over his shoulder.

"Why was I not informed at once? What varlet did this? By *Corpus Dominus*, I will have him flogged."

"He's dead," Dennis said from the door. "Here's Todd."

Rick started for the doorway toward Todd, but Sir Harold shouldered him aside.

"A flesh wound, nothing more," Dennis said, when Sir Harold tried to look at the already blood-soaked linen cloth wrapped round Todd's upper left arm. "Leave the pad, please. The pressure will soon stop the bleeding."

"The dead man, how did that happen? I saw no real fighting."

"No," Dennis said, "only two blows were struck. The one that wounded Todd, and the one that killed Sir Simon's servant."

"Most unfortunate. Master Richard, find Sir Simon. Let a mass be said for the man. I will pay, and for ale that his fellows may drink to his passage."

Rick stopped to ask Todd how he was and Sir Harold bellowed: "Now, Master Secretary. I shall not beat him for not being where he should have been till you return. I leave that to you."

When Rick got back after settling with the disgruntled Sir Simon, Sir Harold was in a wooden tub in front of the fire. Chris looked up from rubbing Sir Harold's back with a cloth and winked.

"What delayed you?" Sir Harold said. "Is all arranged?"

"Yes, My Lord."

"Dry me, Christopher. My clothes, Todd. Do you wish the tub now, Master Richard? It is still pleasantly warm."

Richard shook his head.

"Then you boys may use it. Master Richard, help me dress."

Todd cleared his throat. "My Lord."

Sir Harold merely raised his eyebrows.

"Since I am to be beaten, could it be now, before our bath?"

"Master Richard?" Sir Harold said.

"Oh, surely that was a joke. The boy was wounded. Isn't that enough?"

"A man is dead. That is no jest. Todd had no right to be where he was and dismounted. His actions were the direct cause of the man's death as surely as if he had struck the actual blow."

Rick suddenly felt cold and sick. Who had killed the servant? He looked at Todd, and Todd stared impassively back.

"Todd, did you stab him?"

"Yes, Master Rick."

In a daze, Rick took the rod Sir Harold handed him, and bent Todd over the wooden chest at the foot of the bed.

Damn this time. Damn Todd for accepting so casually the need – the right – to kill. Why can't he be the simple child he looks?

In a red haze, Rick saw Todd slit throats at the ford, with a look of innocence on his face.

"Stop, Rick. Stop."

Chris's shout came through to Rick at the same time he felt his wrist seized and the rod torn from his grip. He turned, and Dennis hit him, hard, on the side of the jaw.

From the floor, Rick looked up to see Todd, naked, leap at Dennis and pummel him. Chris jumped forward to hold Todd.

Sir Harold's shout froze them all in position.

"Todd, move away from Dennis. Now! Christopher, help Master Richard to his feet. Dennis, step to the other side of the chamber."

They followed his instructions in silence. Dazed, Rick shook his head. He could not remember beating Todd, only a red hot anger at the whole situation; the whole bloody mess of being here at all; of fright that Todd had put himself in this dangerous situation. Todd? Had he really hurt the boy?

Rick moved towards Todd, and Sir Harold said: "Enough chastisement for now."

"God, what got into you?" Chris said. "I thought you would kill Todd."

Chris was in tears and shook, while Todd appeared more

confused than hurt. Dennis was upset and concerned.

"I shall consider this a family squabble," Sir Harold said, "otherwise, I would have to have Dennis flogged for his attack on my secretary, and Todd flogged for his assault on my master-at-arms. We are all tired and out of temper with the journey and the rain. Master Richard? Do you think otherwise?"

Still too shaken to talk, Rick shook his head.

"If we are quite finished," Sir Harold said, "you boys get into the tub before it freezes over. Master Richard, Master Dennis, remove your outer clothing and spread it out to dry before the fire."

While they followed his orders, Sir Harold walked to the door and shouted for wine or ale.

"What the hell was all that about?" Dennis whispered. "When I came in, Todd was yelling his head off. You could hear him all over the house, all over town probably, and you looked like a zombie. I was afraid you'd kill the little bugger if I didn't stop you."

"Thanks. You took the right action for all of us."

A servant entered with a jug and pewter mugs.

"Ale, My Lord," he said, and darted a frightened glance round the room.

"Master Dennis, mull some ale for us. For the boys too, if you will, although Todd, for one, is hot enough, I think." Sir Harold roared with laughter. "My brother Gerald is right. I doubted him, but that beating was well done. Each blow timed for best effect, enough time between to allow pain to build to a peak before the next. Masterly indeed."

Rick muttered under his breath, lurched to his feet, and stumbled over to the window where he leaned his forehead against the cool wall. He felt thoroughly ashamed and alarmed. When a hand touched his arm gently, he jumped.

"Are you all right?" Todd sounded genuinely concerned.

"I should be asking you."

Rick put an arm around Todd's shoulder, and to his surprise the boy did not flinch. They rejoined the others at the fire.

"We shall be comfortable enough here," Sir Harold said. "Not grand, but snug enough." He looked from one to another. "Tell me, Christopher, would you defend me equally valiantly, if Master Dennis attacked me while I beat you?"

"My Lord, who would dare attack you?"

Sir Harold laughed. "Your cousin is a diplomat."

"If it had been cook I'd knocked down," Dennis said, "would you still have jumped me, Todd?"

While Todd considered the question seriously, Rick sagged. Why should Todd feel any affection for him, or loyalty to him? Wasn't Rick simply one more stranger who beat him, in a life full of strangers?

"No," Todd said. "Cook beat me for no reason, or because he felt like it. Master Rick never does. Our lord said I was to be beaten. It could have been you, or Chris, or a servant beating me. It wasn't right Master Rick got hit because it was him."

Todd paused for breath and Chris said: "Lucky you didn't have a dagger handy…"

"If I'd wanted to, I could have pulled Master Dennis's, quicker than he could stop me. I only wanted him not to hit Master Rick again."

"I've still got the scar from last time," Dennis growled and shook Todd by the neck.

Todd shrieked, and giggled, a boy again, when he grabbed at the blanket slipping from his shoulders.

"Here, I'm roasted," Dennis said. "You mull some more ale, little brother."

Chapter Fourteen

Next morning, Rick ached and felt desperately tired.

He and Sir Harold had shared the large bed with Chris and Todd, while Dennis slept on the rushes in front of the fire. Todd, next to Rick, had been restless, and moaned in his sleep. Rick in his guilt had been aware of every toss and turn. Sometime before dawn, Todd wakened and wriggled restlessly.

"Oh, lie still for God's sake," Rick said.

"Master Rick?" Todd said. "Am I family, as Sir Harold said? Master Dennis called me brother."

"Yes, Todd, you're family. You know that."

With a sigh, Todd turned his back to Rick, wriggled closer to him and pulled Rick's arm round him, to hang on to it with both hands. Soon he was snoring gently, and Rick lay exhausted, but wide-awake. How easy it was at times to forget Todd was only an eleven-year-old boy, and at others to forget he had killed at least three men.

"Come, Master Richard, it's past dawn. Bestir yourself."

Rick heard Sir Harold's voice, as if from a great distance. What was he doing in their bedchamber?

"That's not your lady you have there," Sir Harold said, and sounded much closer. With a start Rick realised where he was, and that Todd lay beside him nestled in his arms.

Chris was already up and dressed, and setting the fire. Todd scrambled to the foot of the bed, and relieved himself into the earthenware chamber pot, before he ran to the window and dumped the contents out.

Todd was obviously sore and stiff, but otherwise in fine spirits. He frowned when Rick coughed and shivered, though he sat close to the fire. Impatiently, Rick tried to brush aside Todd's hand when the boy touched his forehead.

"Master Rick is unwell," Todd said. "He burns with fever."

In a dream, Rick found himself back in bed; his clothing removed and bedclothes piled up on him.

"Master Dennis and Christopher can tend me at the meetings," Sir Harold said. "Todd, see to it that Master Richard stays warm."

For the next few days, Rick did little else but sleep. From time to time, Todd plied him with bread and hot soup. He was aware of Todd imperiously ordering the house servants around, and that Sir Harold was displeased with the proceedings at parliament, but in general Rick felt detached; an observer.

One afternoon, Rick felt wide-awake and alert. He sat up in bed and saw Todd doze before the fire.

"My clothes, please."

"Master. You're better?"

"Yes, I think I am. See if you can get me some food."

When Sir Harold returned that evening, Rick asked: "Do we leave for home tomorrow?"

"Why so, Master Richard?"

"The issue is decided, isn't it? Parliament has passed the Poll Tax and adjourned."

Sir Harold stared at Rick.

"How could you know that? We have come straight here from the session. No one could be here before us."

Rick shrugged. "Sudbury and Hales have admitted they mismanaged the finances of the realm."

"I said as much two nights ago. I thought you were asleep, but you might have heard."

"They borrowed massively, even pawned the King's jewels. Yet the Army in France is three months in arrears with its pay."

Sir Harold nodded. "Go on."

"Lords and commons argued and grumbled all day," Rick said. " '…money had been badly and deceitfully used and nothing done for the profit of the realm…' "

"By Our Lady," Sir Harold said, "you might have been there."

"But they didn't insist that the war end," Rick said. "They crumbled. They agreed to yet another poll tax – a tax per head just for existing – the third in as many years, '…for the safety of the kingdom and the keeping of the sea…' "

"God's Blood. Word for word. Do you by any chance know the amount of the tax?"

"Yes, three groats for every person over fifteen, three weeks wages for the average labourer."

"Oh, come, Sirrah, the lords and commons agreed, if men of property and money pay more than their share, the burden on the villeins will not be severe."

"Nonsense, how many lords and lordlings will willingly pay more than they absolutely need to?"

Sir Harold grew red and scowled. There was a tense silence, before he laughed.

"I'd as lief have you with me as against me."

"I said Master Rick remembers the future," Todd said, proudly.

"What a way to curse a man: to tell him the manner of his death, to tell him the year, the month, the day, the hour of his death." Sir Harold shuddered. "You know such matters?"

"For some," Rick said, "but not for any, except Master Wycliffe, that I have met in your company."

"What of Sudbury and Hales? You mentioned them by name."

Rick considered in silence. In a low voice he said: "On June 14, 1381, the rabble seize Sir Simon Sudbury, Archbishop of

Canterbury, Chancellor of England, in the Tower Chapel. They drag him beyond the gates on Tower Hill, and there, behead him. It is clumsily done, taking a full eight strokes of a sword, after which they nail the Archbishop's red mitre to his head. They also kill there a second knight, Robert Hale, Treasurer of England. The mob carry the heads mounted on poles to the gates of London Bridge."

Sir Harold crossed himself. "God's wounds, enough. I wish to know no more. It does you credit that you could not meet these gentlemen. Later, we will talk further about what could bring these abominations about."

Chapter Fifteen

Next morning they left for home. Sir Harold instructed Rick to ride with him and the others to remain at a distance.

"Todd has said on several occasions that you remember the future. It strikes me that your memories are very selective."

"Not so. At least, I would say patchy rather than deliberately selective. I do not choose what I remember."

"How so? Is not what went before your time known, recorded?"

"Yes, My Lord, but think about it. Do you remember all that happened around here in 780?"

Sir Harold laughed. "I know the tales of hereabout, as do most folk."

"The tales concern only important men caught up in great deeds. Isn't that so?"

"Yes, but some sing of lesser men like Rob-in-a-Hood, an outlaw in the days King John, brother of Richard the Lion Heart."

"Quite so," Rick said, "but his time is less than two hundred years ago, not six hundred. Some of your minstrels might know details of men others have forgotten. What I remember is what I have read. Not everything is written. Not everything that was written is in agreement. The high nobles, the great heroes, the great despoilers, their names and deeds are recorded, and sometimes lesser folk who crossed their paths.

"What is written depends on who wrote it. Two accounts of the same event can differ vastly. Where there is unanimity, I would suspect the reports of one side have been suppressed."

"So, I am of no consequence."

"No, I don't say that. I haven't read everything, but from what I have, I surmise that you are not a major player."

"Hmm. I suppose we must all accept the station assigned to us by God."

"Master Wycliffe talks of lords who observe the contract with God and are thereby confirmed in their place and holdings. I see you as one of those."

"But you are aware that many lords consider me to be in error?" Sir Harold said.

"Yes. There was a Bertram de Born, of the time of Richard I, who wrote of the peasants:

...For swine they are and swine remain,
All decency they find a strain...

and of the lords who treat the peasants as human he said:

... Hold fast the serf, or you will find
The treason growing on his face.
That Lord deserves to meet disgrace
Who, with the chance to crush, stands by.
For peasants are a rebel race.
When sheltered in a strong-walled place,
Their hearts grow insolently high,
Exposed as treacherous and base...

The fact he wrote that implies there are other lords who think as you do."

After a long silence, Sir Harold said: "How am I best to protect my people? The high and the low. I have no desire to see them rise in revolt, only to suffer punishment and even death."

"If I knew how to prevent the coming trouble, I would do everything I could to stop it. It's like trying to halt a flood tide.

The best we can do is build a dyke round our people."

"We? Our?" Sir Harold said, and, as Rick made to speak, waved him down. "No matter. How do we build such a dyke?"

"You've already done a lot in your treatment of your serfs, but that may not be enough. Can we afford to pay the poll tax for our people?"

"We? Our? Again?" Sir Harold laughed. "I have become used to it, but it would greatly anger my brother Gerald. But, to your question, no, we could not afford to pay the tax for all our people. We simply do not have so much money available."

"Ah. A cash flow problem. Could we pay over a period of time?"

"Well, two thirds are to be paid when called for before the end of February, the balance by June, but…"

"No, My Lord, that was the intention, but I'm afraid we'll find it all called for by March."

Sir Harold was thoughtful for a short time.

"You can pay for D'Arcy, as I can pay for the manors directly under my control. My knight tenants must make up their own minds. I shall advise them of what I intend and of my wish that they should do likewise as far as they are able."

"What of the townspeople?"

"They are in the main freemen and must fend for themselves. Some merchants and guild masters are wealthy. They can well afford to pay the tax, both for themselves and for their journeymen and apprentices."

"You'll be at the summer manor at the height of the revolt," Rick said. "If the castle is well manned, and you have a loyal troupe of men-at-arms with you, all should be over by autumn."

"Do I do this to save myself? I have fought. I am not afraid to fight again."

"The revolt will fail. Reasonable lords like yourself will be essential to moderate the backlash. You save yourself, and thus your people."

Sir Harold sighed.

He turned in his saddle. "Christopher. Todd. Come, let us race. I am tired of Master Sober-sides. There are cobwebs to blow away."

Chapter Sixteen

Life at the castle returned to normal. Rick resumed classes for the boys, and some of the town merchants sought Sir Harold's permission to have their sons attend. Although Rick said he would take them with the others for no charge, Jo objected furiously, and even Sir Harold laughed at him.

Rick bought the vacant house next to Malcolm's, outside the castle gates, and used the ground floor as his school and office. When they could, he and Jo used the sleeping loft as a private retreat from the very public life at the castle.

At Christmas, Sir Harold refused to let Rick and Jo celebrate at D'Arcy. There was the same round of feasts as the year before, with equally many guests crammed into the castle.

Even Malcolm admitted he missed Arthur.

After New Year, Sir Harold announced he would visit D'Arcy. Jo insisted that she and Rick be permitted to go on two days early, and take with them a cook and several servants.

Since Rick and Jo had been at D'Arcy on their honeymoon, Arthur and the villagers had built a tiny rubble-wall church with thatch roof, and an A-frame beside it to house the priest. The church was scarcely big enough to accommodate the villagers, standing.

Dicken was very proud of the addition, and himself introduced the priest. Wycliffe had found them the ideal man. The priest had helped build the church, and had his own strip of land that he proposed to work himself. Since his arrival, he had toiled alongside the villagers.

Sir Harold came accompanied by the usual entourage of gentlemen, and a sizeable escort. When Rick expressed some disappointment that Lady Eleanor had not come, Sir Harold reminded him that both she and Lady Gwenne were pregnant, and would not travel, even this far, in the winter.

After the tour of the manor, Sir Harold said he was well pleased with the progress. Naturally, he took over the bed in the solar and displaced Rick and Jo to the trestle beds and the three boys to the rushes on the floor. His gentlemen bedded down in the great hall. One or two hinted that Arthur and Margaret should vacate the very comfortable steward's house Arthur had built. Arthur glared at Rick, daring him to give the order. He grinned when Rick allocated Malcolm, Dennis, and Martin to his main room, and Sir Harold nodded.

The banquet went well, although some of Sir Harold's gentlemen grumbled about the lack of entertainment and the bucolic setting. Malcolm, who had, as usual on such occasions, drunk deeply, challenged any bored gentleman to single combat with any weapon of the gentleman's choice. There were no takers at first, but Dicken, who, as reeve, was present, lurched to his feet and accepted the challenge, and chose to wrestle.

They looked evenly matched, and soon wagers were placed all round the hall. Dicken won by two falls to one, and he and Malcolm left for more beer, arms round each other.

Next morning, Sir Harold announced to Rick he wanted to meet with Arthur and Dicken, away from his gentlemen, to discuss their administration of the manor. Dicken was obviously hung over, but, when he had recovered from his nervousness at being included in a private conference with Sir Harold, spoke well and enthusiastically about the manor. Malcolm, who had not been seen since the night before, wobbled out of Dicken's hut. Sir Harold saw him and bellowed with laughter.

"Come join our conference, Master Physician. I would appreciate your diagnosis of this manor."

By the time Sir Harold and his entourage left, Sir Harold had seen everything about the village, and had talked to all the villagers.

"Join us in two days," Sir Harold said to Rick. "We have much to discuss. This manor is well run and fair set to be prosperous. The people are happy with their lot. Yes, we have much to discuss."

Chapter Seventeen

"How does D'Arcy differ from my other manors?" Sir Harold asked, after they had finished the correspondence for the day. "These men were notorious malcontents in their previous villages. Dicken, your reeve, had been flogged and fined, heavily, several times, for insolence, as had most of the others."

"Then that must make the other villages quieter now," Rick said, and Chris laughed. He busied himself with the carafe when Sir Harold scowled.

"For now, yes, perhaps. News travels slowly between villages. The atmosphere in D'Arcy was of quiet contentment. What have you and Arthur done?"

"They are no longer serfs."

"By *Corpus Dominus*. I gave no such authority. You overreach yourself."

"You gave me the manor and its people. I have done only what you have done in some manors."

"However, without my direct consent, by Our Lady."

"They pay me rent for the land, and will perform services for the manor for wages. Are there likely to be any problems with the Statute of Labourers?"

Sir Harold stared at the ceiling.

"No, I think not, as long as you have only the men from your own village. Lord Thomas is the Justice charged with enforcing the Statute of Labourers in this area. He imprisons, orders placed in stocks – even orders branded – anyone who demands higher wages. He has been known to outlaw peasants who have fled their manors to escape the effects of the statute."

"Some lords pay more than the statute permits to their own villagers or serfs."

"The village serfs must perform the services for their lord. His word against them to Lord Thomas could have them imprisoned, fined, and flogged."

"You forget I keep the books of account for your manors."

Sir Harold smiled. "You intend to inform Lord Thomas?"

"What happens to the lord who overpays?"

"Why should anything happen to the lord?" Sir Harold said. "The statute is to control those who would demand excessive wages. The statute is silent on voluntary overpayment by the lords."

"However, it is discouraged as we discussed earlier?"

"Yes, it is. I am tired of this conversation. The tax assessors and collectors will be here before month end."

"Yes, My Lord, I do see your correspondence."

"I meant, what arrangements have you made at D'Arcy?"

"Arthur has made the proper count and collected one groat for every person over fifteen."

"I thought you had decided to pay it all."

"We decided to set up a village fund. The villagers can sell any future surpluses. A tithe of that surplus, in money or kind, comes to me, and a tithe to the village fund, to be used as the reeve and the village council see fit. The money Arthur has collected will start the fund. The villagers will clearly see it is their fund."

"And the poll tax?"

"Arthur has the three groats per person for the collectors. We have taken the money from our fish smoking profits, since I have no rents yet, from D'Arcy."

"You still work as a group? The fish smoking income, how is it divided?"

"Two thirds go to the co-operative; those who actually work the process and provide the fish. The balance goes to Arthur, Dennis, Chris, and myself. I have a smaller share than the others. I keep their books."

"It is profitable still?"

"Yes, indeed. Even after paying your rent and your license. I can see why the Fishmongers Guild opposed us so. Their monopoly must be very lucrative."

Sir Harold waved Chris away, and he and Todd moved off to play chess.

"Your priest at D'Arcy. He is from Master Wycliffe?"

"Yes. I did show you the correspondence."

"Hmm. I remember now," Sir Harold said. "But Gerald says a priest of that name was a hedge priest, and a known associate of John Ball."

"He is a working priest … You approved the fish pond?"

"I did, but it was much larger than the size of the village would need."

Rick laughed.

"I think Arthur intends to smoke any surplus and sell them … Would you consider allowing a mill at D'Arcy?"

"Apart from the town, the nearest mill is in Gerald's village," Sir Harold said, thoughtfully. "Yes, I might consider granting a charter. One sack of flour in thirty to me."

"One in sixty, My Lord."

"One in thirty-five."

"One in forty and you pay half the cost of building the mill."

"Robber, thief, scoundrel. Whose secretary are you? Quarter the cost!"

"One third of the cost."

"Done. With Arthur in charge and you reviewing accounts it is sure to prosper. See to the necessary papers."

Chapter Eighteen

The winter months passed quickly; Rick was very busy. Between his duties as Sir Harold's secretary, his school, monitoring the accounts of the fish smoking enterprise, and the occasional visit to D'Arcy to see how the mill was progressing, he had little leisure.

Jo announced she was pregnant. By her calculation: "We must have caught on first go." Rick was delighted with the news, but irked at her crudity.

Arthur had congratulated Jo. "Our Lord of the Circle has some lead in his pencil after all."

Much to Gerald's vocal displeasure, Sir Harold said that he would stand godfather to his ward's child.

In February, Sir Harold's correspondence began to indicate an alarming shortfall in the expected revenue from the poll tax. On February 22, the Government demanded the immediate collection of the entire sum due and sent out instructions to that effect.

Minor riots occurred in the town, and there were reports of villages hiding unmarried women and other dependants. Sir Harold's own manors and D'Arcy were free of such problems, but the villages of some of Sir Harold's tenant knights and Gerald's villagers were among those reported deficient.

On March 16, the Government decided that there was clear evidence most collectors had been negligent, and some corrupt. Within seven days, instructions came from Lord Thomas for Sir

Harold to nominate fresh commissioners to revise the lists of those liable to tax. Sir Harold could see no way out. The tax was the law of the land, he told Rick. When none of the commoners Sir Harold nominated would serve, he jumped at Rick's suggestion to appoint Master Gerald and make him responsible for his own commissioners.

On April 7, Lady Eleanor gave birth to a healthy boy. Sir Harold had all the town churches ring their bells, and had banners flown from all the castle towers. For the evening, Sir Harold paid for drink served in the town alehouses, and the town watch carried Malcolm home. Arthur, who was in town on business, grumbled that there had been no such celebrations when his son was born.

Six days later, Lady Gwenne gave birth, also to a healthy boy. Sir Harold had the banners flown and the bells rung, but declined to order celebrations in town. Gerald was away from the castle with his tax commissioners.

"Now the births are past, we can plan to move to the summer manor," Sir Harold said. "But the Lady Jo cannot travel in her condition."

"I'm fine," Jo said. "I am at closest three months from giving birth, perhaps four. Malcolm will be with us. Rick," she threw a crust at him, "speak up. We're going."

It was mid-May before all was ready for the move. Arthur did not go with them because he thought the first summer at D'Arcy was critical, and Sir Harold agreed. Gerald also stayed behind because he still had work to do with the tax commissioners. Rick had no choice. Jo was going, and anyway, Sir Harold insisted his secretary and his physician travel with him.

From Sir Harold's correspondence, he and Rick were well aware of the unrest and disturbances, particularly South and West of London. But in some ways the time passed for Rick like a dream, a dream in which some dreadful monster lurks unseen in the dark, known to be there, but the dreamer is powerless to act before it becomes a nightmare.

The day they reached Sir William's manor, Gerald rode in at dusk. He strode into the great hall, with Adam mere steps behind him, then bowed briefly to Sir William, and to Sir Harold.

"I must speak to you, My Lord Brother. I will await you in your room. Adam, bring me food and drink. I am weary. We have ridden far."

When Sir Harold joined Gerald, all the hostility Rick had felt when they first arrived was back. Gerald scowled.

"Dismiss these," Gerald said and gestured at Rick and the pages. "What I have to say is for your ears only."

At Sir Harold's nod, Rick bowed and indicated to Chris and Todd they should leave with him.

"Leave us, Adam," Gerald said. "I won't need you again tonight. Tell the Lady Gwenne that I will join her later."

"We haven't seen you for ages," Todd said to Adam. "Has it been exciting, riding with Master Gerald?"

Adam looked warily at Rick and nodded.

"If you boys want to talk," Rick said, "why don't you go outside for a while. Rejoin me in the solar later. Don't get up to any mischief."

That night Todd, Rick and Chris lay together on the rushes in Sir Harold's room.

"Master Rick. Master Rick, are you awake?" Todd whispered.

"What? God, it's night-time, Todd."

"Can we go outside? Please. I must talk to you."

Rick sat up and grumbled at Todd.

"Quietly," Todd whispered. "Don't wake Sir Harold."

Outside the room, the guard stirred and Todd whispered to him. He grinned at Rick in the gloom and nodded.

"What did you tell him?" Rick said.

"That you were restless and we seek a serving wench."

"God, he'll think I'm after you," Rick blurted out.

"Oh, no, if that were so, why would we need to leave our room?"

Rick followed Todd out to the walled garden. He looked round and jumped.

"There's someone there," he said. "Over in the corner, a shadow moved."

"It's Adam, he's waiting for us."

"Master Richard."

Adam bowed. He tensed when Rick gripped his wrist and drew him back into the shadows.

"It's all right," Todd said. "He won't beat you for nothing. Tell Master Rick what you told Chris and me."

"When we started to redo the rolls and collect taxes, Master Gerald would pick someone in the village to beat, a beardless youth. He had him beaten in front of the other villagers, not much, only enough to make him squeal. Master Gerald threatened to have him flogged dead if the count wasn't right, then to start on someone else."

"Did it work?" Todd said.

"Yes, I think so. At least, the rolls were closer to the last tax rolls, or so the clerk said."

"What can I do?" Rick said. "We've heard about his tax collecting methods, but Sir Harold either cannot or will not interfere."

"Adam's not finished," Todd said, and impatiently punched Adam's arm. "Get on."

"One morning, after he'd had a youth with him, Master Gerald was pleased and excited. He didn't even beat me. We had to saddle up and ride back to the villages we'd already been to. Master Gerald questioned villagers, tortured two. Master Arthur had been in most villages, and talked about the preachings of John Ball. Some men went back to D'Arcy with him."

"God. We don't need that. This is the wrong time."

"Master Gerald told the clerk that he had them now. He had the damned Masters of the Circle. His Lord Brother couldn't shield them now. He went on about, 'devisers of false news and reporters...' "

" '...reporters of horrible and false lies concerning prelates, dukes, earls, barons and other nobles and great men of the realm... Hereof great peril and mischief might come to all the realm and quick subversion and destruction of the said realm if due remedy is not provided.' ... That's from a statute of 1379. Gerald could nail Arthur to the wall with that. It's the basis for the arrest of John Ball. Arthur could simply vanish once Gerald gets Lord Thomas to arrest him. Did you hear anything else?"

"No, when Master Gerald saw me come in, he stopped."

Next morning, by the time Sir Harold's party was ready to leave, Gerald had already ridden out. Several times Rick tried to get Sir Harold on his own to talk, but from first light, his gentlemen were admitted to the chamber and a private conversation was simply not possible.

It was fully two hours before Chris cantered back from his place immediately behind Sir Harold.

"Hi, Rick," he said. "His Nibs wants you. Boy, is he all steamed up. Is it about what Adam said last night? I got a swat just because I was there. I hadn't even opened my mouth."

"Shut up."

"God's blood, you too. Sorry I spoke."

"Stay with Todd," Rick snapped, and he kicked his horse to a trot.

"What kept you, Sirrah?" Sir Harold said.

"How have I offended, My Lord?"

"You are followers of the hedge priests."

"No, My Lord. We are not."

"You have broken bread with me, and eaten of my salt, and you betray me."

"My Lord, you are mistaken."

With a glare at Rick, Sir Harold spurred his horse, and Rick galloped in pursuit. His dagger almost jolted free, and Rick's hand flew to the hilt. Almost instantly there were men round him, and Dennis was between Rick and Sir Harold. Blades flashed in the sun. Out of the corner of his eye Rick saw Todd, dagger in hand, spur forward, Chris at his side. Horrified and confused, Rick bellowed: "No, Todd. Chris," and raised both hands. Rick, now a much better rider, was still not up to riding with no hands. He fell off his horse. Winded, Rick lay on his back and stared up at a circle of men, blades in hand, who scowled down at him.

"Hold. Put up your blades," Sir Harold shouted. "I'll hang anyone who draws blood."

Sir Harold shouldered his way through his courtiers, laughed and put out his hand.

"Come, Master Secretary, friend, rise. You look ridiculous. Martin, I will eat here with the Masters from the Circle. We must meet."

He turned to the men who still stood swords in hand.

"Sheathe your weapons. If Master Richard wished to kill me, he has had many chances in my chamber at night."

Sir Harold sat on one of the panniers, and Rick and the group stood round him. Chris, Todd, and Henry rushed to serve the cold meat, cheese, bread, and wine.

Chris grinned at Sir Harold.

"Is Master Rick to be your jester?"

Sir Harold scowled at him.

"You and Todd rode in, daggers drawn. Whom did you intend to defend, me or Master Richard?"

Solemnly, Todd said: "Master Rick, of course, but not against you."

Chris looked decidedly uncomfortable, but said: "Rick is my cousin."

"As Gerald is my brother," Sir Harold said with a frown.

"He is no longer your male heir," Dennis said, quietly.

Sir Harold turned to look at Dennis appraisingly.

"An apt thought. And you, on whose side were you prepared do battle?"

Dennis bowed.

"I gave you a soldier's oath of fealty. You will not find me wanting."

"You would have killed Master Richard?"

Jo flushed and stared at Dennis, while Todd moved closer, between him and Rick. Chris looked from Dennis to Rick, alarm and uncertainty on his face.

"You were in no danger from Master Rick, Sire," Dennis said. "Some of your gentlemen are jealous of him, and listen too readily to Master Gerald. They mistook Rick's intentions, possibly."

"You prevaricate, Sirrah. Answer me directly. You would have killed Master Richard?"

"I see no conflict. Would Martin kill you to defend Our Lord of Lancaster?"

Rick thought Sir Harold was about to explode. His face purpled and he clenched his fists.

"By the Body of Christ, you go too far, Sirrah. I am Lord John's man as Martin is mine. No such defence would ever be needed."

Jo smiled. "Touché, My Lord."

"What? Be silent. This is not woman's business, mistress."

"My husband's life is very much my business. You yourself have said it best. Rick is your man. Have you ever had cause to doubt it?"

"Martin," Sir Harold said, "you have heard all. What do you think?"

"The Masters of the Circle defend each other as the wolverine defends her young. They are a group that acts as one, but it is your group. I would trust my life, and yours, to them."

"Then is my brother lying?"

"It would not be the first time," Martin said. "As we both well know."

"Might I speak?" Rick said, and at Sir Harold's nod went on. "I don't know, of course, what Master Gerald said to you. I do know from his page that Arthur has been reported speaking in some villages in support of John Ball's ideas."

"This is the very treason of which Gerald spoke."

"I did try to speak with you earlier, but you surrounded yourself with your gentlemen and excluded me."

"Martin says you are a group. Do you support Arthur? Agree with him? Does he speak for you?" Sir Harold turned to Malcolm. "Master Physician, you are unusually silent. What say you?"

Malcolm looked as if he was about to speak, but after a glance at Rick, shrugged.

"So, Master Richard, it is once again you."

"My Lord, do I speak for you?"

"Only when I authorise you to do so."

"So, at other times I speak my own mind and anyone who ascribes my words or actions to you is wrong, or at best misguided?"

"I take your point. You disown Arthur? You dissociate your group from him?"

"No, at least not yet. If an enemy of mine reported to you treasonous words or acts on my part, would you disown me without inquiry or without seeking some explanation?"

"If I did, Sirrah, you would, at this moment, be on your way back to the castle to await my brother's pleasure, or hanging from Sir William's gibbet."

Rick paled and swallowed, and Jo pulled him and Todd closer to her.

Sir Harold smiled grimly.

"I was never nearer to calling my guard, than when you and Todd rose in the night. Despite my brother's urging, I trusted you. I trust you still."

"Thank you." Rick bowed. "We deeply appreciate your confidence and thank you for your generosity to us."

"Arthur is less appreciative."

"Arthur is Arthur. He is not about to lead the people of D'Arcy astray into any wild adventure that could hurt them."

"What shall we do, My Lord of the Circle?" Sir Harold said. "My brother left, much out of temper, this morning, because I would not permit him to arrest you and your people. You and Christopher, next to Arthur, are the ones he would most wish to question personally. I fear Adam will have an uncomfortable day or so."

"I'm sure Arthur is trying to improve the lot of our people, working within the system," Rick said. "He will not incite disobedience or rebellion, at least not intentionally. May I ride to D'Arcy to warn him?"

"No. You may not. Had I wished you hanged, I would have done it at Sir William's or here today. Despite my lack of permission, if Gerald finds you away from me before he has time to cool, you are dead. And where would I find another such page?" Sir Harold gave Chris an almost affectionate one-arm hug. He scowled. "I might even have to take Henry back."

Henry retreated to stand beside Jo.

"Might I write to Arthur and send one of your men-at-arms to him?"

"Yes, I will permit that. Warn him to guard his tongue. To stay close to D'Arcy. And above all to avoid any confrontation with Gerald. I have forbidden him to arrest Arthur without my express consent, but I cannot answer for Gerald's actions if there is further provocation."

Chapter Nineteen

"If Chris doesn't come soon can we have a holiday?" Henry glanced up from his work at Rick when he paced the chapel yet again.

"You have plenty to do. Get on with it."

With a sigh and a pout, Henry turned back to his work.

The door opened and Chris bounced in. Henry promptly put down his pen and sat back.

"Finished, Henry?" Rick said.

"No, Master Rick, but..." With a sigh, Henry picked up his pen again.

"His Nibs wants you, Rick. Now."

"Chris, that's not a proper way to refer to Our Lord, Sir Harold," Rick said.

"Oh, it's only us here."

Rick nodded towards Henry. "Small pitchers, and all that..."

When Rick and Chris approached the solar, they could hear Sir Harold's angry voice.

"No, you may not suggest anything of the kind. Master Richard is my secretary and my friend. He has proved himself many times."

There was a low rumble of another voice, followed by Sir Harold's again.

"Damn my brother and his suspicions. I rule here, not him. If that is not to your liking, you may withdraw to your manor, this very day."

Rick coughed loudly and banged the solar door before he entered.

"Ah, Master Richard," Sir Harold said, "we have some work to do. Thank you for being so prompt to our call, but first, a dish of wine between friends."

Chris bustled over to pour and Sir Harold turned a stony face on one of his gentlemen.

"You have other business? No? You may leave us."

His face red, the man bowed at Sir Harold's waved dismissal. When he turned away, a voice said quietly: "A gentleman is not to be dismissed like some servant, especially before a servant."

Purple, Sir Harold turned back to face his court.

"Master Richard of D'Arcy is my secretary, a servant, yes, as you are all my servants. A true friend, as some of you are not."

Sir Harold glared at them, and there was sudden shuffling. Three gentlemen found themselves front and centre, when the others moved back discreetly.

"He has a longer lineage than all of you, and he will be known, when you and I have crumbled to dust and are long forgotten. It doesn't matter who his father is, except to his father, and he knows and is proud even if he cannot acknowledge him to us now."

In the silence that followed, Sir Harold stared at each of the three gentlemen in turn, and each looked down.

"If you are still here at dawn tomorrow, I assume your support and loyalty. I will act appropriately if you disappoint me."

Sir Harold linked arms with Rick and walked him to one end of the solar, while Chris trotted after them with the wine.

"My Lord, I have no wish to cause any problems between you and your gentlemen."

"You do not cause the problem. They and my brother create their own problems. You are merely a convenient rallying point."

"You sent for me? I usually teach at this hour."

"Yes, read these."

Rick barely glanced at the first piece of parchment before he looked up. "You have read these through, My Lord?"

Sir Harold smiled faintly and nodded. "And you, Master Richard, know what they contain without reading further?"

Rick closed his eyes, and after a short pause recited:

"*One Thomas Bampton, Commissioner of the Poll Tax, accompanied by three clerks and two sergeants-at-arms, ordered the Hundred of Barnstaple to appear before him for a revision of the tax rolls. On May thirtieth the men of Fobbing, Corringham, and Stanford-le-Hope did appear, but under arms and they put Bampton and his men to flight.*"

"You have more detail than the dispatch," Sir Harold said. "What further?"

"When was the dispatch sent?"

"On June fourth."

Rick again closed his eyes and recited:

"*Bampton reported to the King's Council. They sent to Brentwood, Sir Robert Belknap, a chief justice of the common pleas. He was to punish the rioters. When Belknap arrived, he was seized. He had with him only a small retinue. His captors made him divulge the names of local justices who had already convicted tax defaulters, then let him return to London. The three clerks were not so lucky. They were the same ones who had come with Bampton, and they were beheaded as traitors to the people. Three of Belknap's jurors were found and also beheaded. The six heads were carried on poles through Brentwood and other villages.*"

"By now, the peasantry round London is in arms," Rick concluded.

"You have the dispatch exactly and more," Sir Harold said. "If I ever doubted you, I doubt no more. Are we safe here?"

"I don't know. I don't know what will happen locally. I know

Our Lord of Lancaster is in Scotland, in Edinburgh, and his wife in Spain." Sir Harold raised his eyebrows. "I hope my lack of knowledge of what happens, or happened, here, means nothing happens. Your people think well of you. They may not rise to the call. Many didn't. However, peasants fear and loathe Lord Thomas. Savage acts of vengeance do happen on both sides."

They stood in silence, and Chris approached with more wine, but Sir Harold waved him away.

"You do not conceal knowledge of danger to Gerald, do you?" Sir Harold asked, and immediately added: "No. No, of course you do not. Arthur would, and Dennis, or even the Lady Jo, might, but you would not."

He gnawed on his lower lip.

"I must warn him, and Lord Thomas. I owe them that. Come. Let's go to my room. We must write."

Rick wrote the two letters and sanded them. Sir Harold stared at them in his hand.

"Now, to find a messenger. He must be known to Gerald and Lord Henry as being in my confidence. Who?"

"I'll go."

"You! You?" Sir Harold laughed. "Gerald would have you hanged on sight despite my instructions."

"If you were Gerald that might well be a problem, but Gerald could not deny himself the pleasure of killing me slowly, of playing with me. If I have a *laissez-passez* from you, there will be time to present it."

"You would risk this for Gerald?"

"No, not for him, but it is important to you, isn't it? I may also be able to protect Arthur. I have a responsibility to him."

"I will write your *laissez-passez* in my own hand. Both Gerald and Lord Henry know it. You will leave tomorrow?"

"At dawn."

"I will alert Martin to provide an escort."

"No, by your leave, I'll take Todd, and we'll travel alone, in simple clothing. Don't let the Lady Jo know till we're well gone."

"I still say you should have an escort."

"We'll be less conspicuous without an escort. Anyway, I would rather Martin and Dennis were both here, should the need arise."

Chapter Twenty

"What will Lady Jo say when she finds us gone?" Todd said some hours into their ride.

"I think we've got the safest part." Rick grinned. "Sir Harold's sure to get a real earful."

They rode hard, and for the most part in silence, and saw little sign of life. By nightfall they reached Sir William's manor. The servant who admitted them recognised Rick as Sir Harold's secretary and showed them into the anteroom.

"Sir William, your servant, sir," Rick said, and bowed when Henry's father strode in. "Might I have a word in private?"

The servant left and Sir William looked hard at Rick.

"What bad news brings you here in such a hurry?"

"The peasants have revolted in the South," Rick said. "Even now a peasant army is in London, and risings have taken place in many other areas."

"This comes of being over-gentle with the swine. I have often told Sir Harold so. He should listen more to his brother, he has the right idea."

Sir William bellowed for a servant.

"Fetch the Master-at-arms, Sirrah. Now!"

Later, when they lay in the straw together in the great hall, Todd whispered to Rick.

"Which side are we on, master?"

"Christ, Todd. I don't want to be on any side. The peasants will lose and there'll be horrible repercussions. Sir William is wrong, but if having a messenger arrested stops his people from rising and giving him an excuse to punish them, it's worthwhile."

"What if Sir William has the messenger tortured?"

Rick shuddered. "One death to prevent many? I don't know, Todd. I'm not God. You've lived at the bottom. Would you want to go back?"

"God's wounds no, Master."

"The revolt won't improve life for the serfs. For many, for some time to come, it will be even worse. I couldn't stop it, Todd. The best I could do was to try to shelter us and some of the serfs. Would stopping it have been right anyway? Some say life changed gradually in England instead of catastrophically, as in the French Revolution, because of this revolt."

Todd snored, and Rick laughed.

Next morning, Sir William stood at Rick's saddle before they left.

"Tell Sir Gerald I shall hang any peasant impudent enough to attempt a revolt in my demesne. I am glad to see you have come to your senses. Good hunting."

"Where should we seek Master Gerald?" Todd said. "Should we not have gone first to Lord Thomas's? He could well be there."

"We ride first to D'Arcy to warn Arthur and our people there. After that, we'll ride for Lord Thomas's and home."

"Three sides of a square, Master." Todd laughed and spurred his horse out of Rick's range.

Unencumbered by a pack train or slow-moving carts, they ate in the saddle and made excellent time. They reached town shortly before the gates closed for the night. Rick's servants at the town house quickly prepared a meal, while Todd caught up on the gossip.

"Master Gerald is at his own manor near D'Arcy," Todd said.

"He has had some men arrested in town as runaway serfs."

"Ask Mathilde to come here."

Mathilde bowed to Rick and rubbed her hands in her apron.

"Todd tells me there have been arrests in town."

"Yes, Master Richard. Thirteen men who had been here more than a year and a day, living free, were taken at Master Gerald's orders, and sent under escort to Lord Henry for sentencing."

"Law and custom says they're free. Did no one object?"

"Oh, yes, but Master Gerald seized and tore the town charter when the mayor and some burghers met with him. He wounded one townsman who drew on him, then had him hanged. Then the 'prentice boys rioted, and Master Gerald had four flogged. One died, and one he took with him when he withdrew to his manor."

"The castle garrison, what did they do?" Rick said.

"They shut the gate and raised the drawbridge."

Todd laughed, and Rick scowled at him.

"How many men has Gerald with him?"

"Six men went with the serfs to Lord Henry's, Master. Master Gerald now has two clerks and two men."

"Todd, run to the Mayor's house and ask him if he and two senior burghers can come here tonight. He knows you by sight."

Mathilde began to clean, and grumbled about the short notice, until Rick lost his temper and told her not to raise any more dust.

The mayor and the mayor designate, Malcolm's father-in-law to be, arrived together, followed almost immediately by another burgher. They were, by now, used to seeing Rick, one step behind and to the right of Sir Harold at most meetings.

"Masters," Rick said, and he and they bowed to each other. "I understand there has been some unrest in the town since Sir Harold's departure."

All three started to talk at once, and Rick raised his hand.

"Peace, Masters, peace. I know what happened, and I assure you that your charter will be inviolate. Sir Gerald was wrong. He did not act with Sir Harold's knowledge or blessing."

"We know that, Master Secretary," one said, and the others nodded. "Sir Gerald said his writ from Lord Thomas over-rode Sir Harold's charter. We have a petition here from our Council for Sir Harold. Will you take it back with you?"

"Sir Harold holds these lands from My Lord of Lancaster, John of Gaunt, the King's Uncle," Rick said. "Lord Thomas cannot dispossess or override him."

"So Roger of the Wool merchants Guild said, and Sir Gerald hanged him."

The other two nodded agreement with the mayor's words, and the mayor designate said: "Sir Gerald hinted that Lancaster would soon not be so powerful, and that he, Gerald, could soon be Baron and master here."

"Not so, Masters. Not so." Rick told them of the events in the South. "By now, the King will have met at Mile End with the rebels and Wat Tyler, the man from Kent who led the rebels to London, is dead. There will be messengers sent to say that all are free; that the King has granted all. Other messengers will follow with news of Tyler's death and all is denied, so rise and fight, there is nothing to lose. Can you keep the town quiet, more or less, so Sir Harold can justify lenience?"

"I understand this not at all," the mayor said. "How can you know this? No one can know today what has only happened in London, today. News of the capital usually takes three days or more."

"Do you trust me?" Rick said.

"Yes, but..."

"Then for God's sake do what I ask. Keep all quiet for the next two weeks. Now, can you open the town gate for me? Todd and I ride for D'Arcy this night."

"Why must we ride at night?" Todd said, after some time. "There are demons abroad in the dark and the night air is bad for you."

Rick swore when Todd bumped knees with him for the third time since they had left town.

"We can't ride side by side in the dark, Todd. It simply won't work."

"Can I ride with you and lead my horse?" Todd said, out of the dark.

Todd mounted behind Rick and held tight.

"Is that better, Todd?" Rick said.

Todd, for answer, simply clung more tightly.

God, he is only a child, Rick thought. I keep forgetting.

The short summer night was over when they came in sight of D'Arcy and Todd remounted his own horse.

"Now we can see clearly, I need not be so close to defend, if we are attacked," Todd said, and Rick solemnly agreed.

Rick pounded on the door to Arthur's house till a grumbling voice shouted: "Enough. Enough. I hear you. Leave the frigging door."

The door opened, and Arthur said: "Now, what's all the bloody fuss?" He rubbed his eyes and saw it was Rick.

"It's you! What the hell are you doing here? At this time of day? Come in. Come in. Robert. Up. Light the fire. The Lord of the Manor is here."

"Arthur, we're bushed. We rode all day yesterday, and all last night. Did you get my warning?"

"Yes. A bit bloody dramatic, weren't you?"

"Damn it, Arthur. When will you grow up? If Sir Harold hadn't intervened, you and I would both be dead now. If you don't care about yourself, think of Dennis, Jo, Malcolm, Chris, and Todd, think of your wife, your son, Robert, the people of D'Arcy."

"You really do think there is danger?"

"Christ. This is the Peasants' Revolt. It's not a Boy Scout jamboree. There have been some very nasty deaths already and more to come. Gerald doesn't need any excuses."

"How long does it last? Can I get in on the fighting? I might just make a difference."

"It's over, Arthur."

"You said it had just started."

"Yes, and it's over. In fourteen days, they rose, marched on London, and took it, burned the Savoy to the ground, beheaded landlords and unpopular crown ministers. Wat Tyler is dead now, the authorities are recovering from their shock."

"So we should be safe now?"

"No, Arthur. Sporadic outbreaks will take place for two weeks after the collapse of the revolt in London, in outlying shires like here. The authorities suppress these savagely. The executions will begin soon. I don't want our people hanging from trees like over-ripe fruit."

"Okay, okay. I get the picture. What do you want me to do?"

"Nothing. Absolutely nothing. Keep our people home. Work the land. Lie low. Prepare them to survive. That's your revolution. That's your protest. A village, run by its people, that works without threatening anyone."

"Shit, Rick. Didn't I always say you should be a politician? I could get you a booking to speak anywhere … in our own time that is."

"We'll sleep for a while. I've got to find Gerald and give him Sir Harold's letter, but later – in this time."

Chapter Twenty-One

Roused from a deep sleep, Rick heard Arthur's voice raised in anger, and Gerald's unmistakable tones. He had barely sat up and rubbed the sleep out of his eyes when the solar door was thrown open and Gerald strode in.

"This is not your manor, Sirrah. Nor does it belong to your lordling, regardless of whose bastard he is," Gerald shouted. "I shall reclaim all when I take possession from my brother, and that, mayhap, soon."

He stopped at the foot of the bed.

"Your lackey tells me you have a letter from my brother, and a *laissez-passez* no less. Give them here."

Todd scurried out of bed to where they had piled their clothes and saddlebags, and carried a pouch back to Rick. Gerald took the proffered letters and scowled while he read them slowly.

"These are in my brother's own hand," he said. "Do you know the content?"

"Not in specifics, Sir Gerald, but in general, yes."

Gerald snorted. "My brother was ever too trusting, too gentle, with everyone but me."

"He did send me to warn you, Sir Gerald, didn't he?"

"Hah. I am in need of no such warning. He should look to his own safety. By dealing over-gently with the swine he has given many cause to suspect and distrust him. This letter condemns him.

He knows of impending insurrections, but does nothing to prevent them."

"Sir Gerald, London fell to the mob. The Savoy was fired. The peasant leader, Wat Tyler, is already dead. How could Sir…"

"The Savoy burned you say? Were Mistress Swineford and her brood there?"

"They escaped harm."

"Enough. I must ride to Lord Thomas. I have arrested a man known to you, one Willum, who claims to be of this village. He is on his way to trial to join the other runaway serfs."

"He hasn't run from here," Arthur said. "I sent him from D'Arcy on an errand."

"I did not say he had run from here, Sirrah," Gerald said with a smile. "He is from my manor. Missing since last autumn."

"He is one of the serfs granted to D'Arcy by Sir Harold himself," Rick said.

"Indeed. You have documents, no doubt? You are going to Lord Thomas, I understand. We should ride together. You can speak for Willum before we brand him."

"I'll come too," Arthur said.

Gerald raised his eyebrows. "You have leave to wander from the manor at will. Interesting."

"Arthur has my permission to accompany us," Rick said. "We should go now. There are still several hours of daylight. Perhaps we'll catch up with Willum and your men."

Arthur left to tell Margaret and have the horses saddled, while Todd and Rick dressed.

Gerald eyed Todd.

"You have grown since our adventure last year. Yes indeed. You will be an interesting youth in a year or so. Perhaps when Master Richard is no longer with us, I will take you over. Adam has been somewhat of a disappointment."

Chapter Twenty-Two

"You have no escort, Sir Gerald?" Rick said in surprise when they assembled in the courtyard.

Gerald shrugged. "Only Adam and I. I can move more quickly thus. The vermin would not dare meddle with me."

"What about me or Rick?" Arthur said.

"Hah. You, I can handle. When I fight, I fight to kill, without passion. You only think you can. As for Master Richard, he would not dare offend My Lord Brother by allowing any harm to come to me."

Christ, Rick thought, he's got us pegged.

"Todd now," Gerald went on, and turned in the saddle to look at the boy. "There's a different matter, but I am safe while his Master Rick says so. It will be an interesting and a dangerous challenge to tame Todd. Could I ever trust him, I wonder, with anything sharp close to me?"

"No, My Lord, never," Todd said, quietly. "If you harm Master Rick, I will kill you."

Gerald laughed. "We'll see. We'll see."

They bypassed the town and Sir William's manor, spent two nights in small manors, and rode hard with few rests during daylight.

On the third night, Arthur, Todd and Rick lay in the barn. Gerald had as usual taken over the solar for himself and evicted the landholders.

"I don't like this," Arthur said. "It feels like a trap. Gerald is just too frigging cheery and cocky."

"What else can we do?" Rick said. "He has Willum and those other free serfs from town. Their only chance is for us to speak up for them before Lord Thomas."

"If we get the chance. What's to stop him arresting us when he has enough men?"

"I have Sir Harold's *laissez-passez*."

"A lot of bloody good that'll do us when we're dangling at the end of a rope. The only reason we're not under arrest now is he has no men, and he conned us into going with him. I'll say this for him, he has guts.

"And what about the straw-boss here?" Arthur said, and tickled Todd. "I don't like what I think Gerald has in mind for him. Maybe Todd should lie low around here, till we see how the winds blows."

"No, Master Arthur, leave me be." Todd pushed Arthur's hands away. "This is serious. I'll fight. I can. Master Rick needs someone to protect him."

Arthur laughed. "The Lord Protector Todd."

He again reached for Todd to tickle him. Rick pulled Todd away from Arthur, and the boy tensed and lashed out with his fist. There was a crack, and Todd scrambled over Rick away from Arthur.

"Christ. I'll kill the little bugger. Oh, my eye."

"I'm not a baby for you to play with," Todd said out of the darkness. "I'm a man. This is serious talk. What you said about the Lord Protector, we've been talking, Adam and me…"

"The Lord Protector," Rick said. "That was a title Lancaster used, Gaunt, Sir Harold's feudal superior."

"Adam says Master Gerald and Lord Thomas talked about the Lord Protector last time they met," Todd said. "They knew about the troubles with the poll tax. This Lord Protector would get blamed by both sides. It's his bad handling of the war in France and his support for Wycliffe that's to blame."

"Can you remember anything else?"

"Well, Adam has seen dispatches, letters from Lord Thomas to Master Gerald and Master Gerald's replies. You taught him to read remember? They think this Lord Protector might be so out of favour he'll have to go into exile."

"And if he does," Rick said, "they could pull Sir Harold and his other supporters down after him, and Gerald would get to take over. No wonder he's so cock-a-hoop."

"Have we backed the wrong frigging horse? If so, I'd just as soon kill Gerald here and now, and take our chances."

"No, strangely enough, Lancaster becomes more popular, well less unpopular, with the peasants," Rick said. "Remember he's in Scotland now and takes no part in the suppression. The really nasty stuff stops when he gets back. A coincidence, I think, but it does none-the-less. And he keeps control of all his lands. They've backed the wrong horse."

Chapter Twenty-Three

Shortly before noon they reached a small hamlet. Where the cultivated land started, Gerald reined his horse in.

"There's no one to be seen in the fields. Odd."

"And no one around the houses either," Rick said.

They walked the horses along the path and through the hamlet to a small copse beyond.

"Look." Todd pointed.

A head on a pike.

"God. It's here," Rick said.

"That's one of my clerks," Gerald shouted.

Slowly out of the brush five bedraggled men appeared. Finally, one bowed, and the others touched their forelocks.

"Sir Gerald," someone said.

"What has happened here?" Gerald said. "You are five of the runaways I was sending to Lord Thomas."

"We stopped here last night, My Lord," one said. "The soldiers were set upon by a crowd."

"There were six of them, well-armed and experienced men," Gerald said and the man shrugged.

"There was a fight." He nodded towards the copse. "The other prisoners have gone with the villagers and those who attacked. We were afraid and didn't know what to do."

"How could my soldiers be overcome by peasant swine?"

"My Lord, come into the copse, if you please," Todd said.

The headless body lay inside and three other naked, bloody bodies hung from trees. Two bodies dressed in rags and tatters lay to one side.

"Oh, Christ. Look at that," Rick said.

"It's the guard commander," Adam said. "He's tied with his back to the trunk by his hands and feet."

Todd shook Rick's hands off and ran forward. "Someone's pulled his guts out through a hole in his belly, and piled them up in front of him. Both ends are still attached."

The man groaned and Todd jumped.

"He's still alive."

The peasant, who had spoken before said: "The one they called Barber knocked him out, and had the others strip him and tie him. He waited till they had a fire going, then Barber cut him open and staunched the bleeding with hot irons. Barber pulled the guts out without cutting them. He laughed and asked him how it felt to be at the other end of torture."

Rick shuddered. "Can we do anything for him?"

"Kill him quickly and cleanly," Arthur and Gerald said together, and looked at each other in surprise.

When they stood outside the copse, Todd moved closer to Rick, whose hands shook when he placed them on Todd's shoulders.

"Why did you have to do it, Todd?" Rick said. "Why? Why you?"

"I was closest, Master, and it had to be done."

"We will move on to Lord Thomas's manor," Gerald said. "Todd, tie these swine. Adam, help him."

"You are not in a position to decide, Master Gerald," Rick said. "You're outnumbered."

"By sheep. Todd, do as I tell you."

"Sheep didn't do that," Rick said, and nodded towards the

copse.

"No, by God, they didn't. I'll see these hanged, drawn, and quartered. Slowly."

Rick turned to the peasants.

"Go back to town, and stay quietly there. You're free. Nothing more will be done to you."

"I will have them slowly strangled."

"No," Rick said. "We passed no disturbances on our way here. Whoever did this came from the direction of Lord Thomas's and have returned there.

"Do you recognise me?" Rick asked the peasants, and, when they nodded, held out his hand to show them a ring.

"That is my brother's ring, varlet. How came you by it?"

"Honestly, Master Gerald. I speak with Sir Harold's authority in this. Return to town. You are safe if you don't encourage further rebellion. If I'm wrong in this, I'll hang with you. Now go."

"Forward to Lord Thomas's," Gerald said. "Walter is there."

"And Willum," Arthur said. "Let's get him out of it before the axe falls."

Chapter Twenty-Four

They exchanged clothes with the townsmen to be less conspicuous, and moved on. Adam and Todd dressed in bits and pieces of ragged clothing found in several huts.

Before they reached the cultivated lands round Lord Thomas's domain they hid the horses and walked. In the distance a smudge of smoke hovered and no serfs worked the fields.

At the gate in the palisade round the manor house itself, they stopped by a peasant who slouched there. Todd spat on the ground and grinned at the man.

"We heard of great doings here. My father's a minstrel. We can brighten any feast. He's a peddler," Todd pointed to Gerald. "But someone stole his mule and goods. He has nought left but his boy. Arthur's a soldier back from France seeking work."

"I'm no gateman," the man said. "Go on in if you want to."

In the courtyard small groups of men sat around fires and looked curiously at them when they walked in.

The heads of Lord Thomas and his captain were on two poles in the centre of the yard.

No one stopped them from walking into the manor house itself.

Outside the great hall, one peasant grabbed Arthur's arm. "You are still sober friend. Help me stop this. This is not what we march for. Rape, pillage, murder, drunkenness. We have lost. We shall all be swept away."

Without answer Arthur shook him off.

At the head table a huge peasant sat in Lord Thomas's chair, his feet on the table. He banged down his pewter mug and shouted: "Food."

Dishevelled ladies and gentlemen of Lord Thomas's court served the meal. Those in attendance on the head table crawled on their knees. In some ways, Rick thought, this was no worse than official revels in the past.

A group of battered young men were led in, linked by a rope tied to each neck. Amid ribald jeers and cheers they untied the end youth and pushed him into the centre of the hall.

"It's Walter," Todd whispered.

A young peasant wrestled with Walter who had grown in the year and was better built and fed than the peasant. He threw the boy, but instead of following up, he raced for the head table and grabbed a dagger from it and threw himself towards the leader of the peasants. One blow of the peasant's tankard knocked Walter out.

The leader sent for an A-frame ladder and had Walter stripped and tied to it. A dish of water was thrown in his face, and the peasant leader started to flog him.

"I must help Walter." Gerald tried to move. Arthur knocked him out with a billet of wood. Rick and Arthur half carried, half-dragged Gerald out of the hall.

"Too much fine wine and beer, brother," Arthur said to the world in general, and there was laughter.

"It might have been simpler to let him go and get himself killed," Rick said.

"And let someone else have the frigging pleasure?" Arthur said. "Not bloody likely. Anyway he'd have attracted attention to us. Where did those two damned boys go?"

"You stay with Gerald," Rick said. "I'll look for them."

Inside again, glassy eyed peasants sat slumped against the

walls, items they had looted clutched to them. Others, not so drunk, attempted to steal from their fellows. Fights erupted and died down equally quickly.

Several peasants desperately tried to control the mob.

"Brothers," one shouted, "the tyrant Lord Thomas is dead. We have released his prisoners from his cellars. We must march for truth and justice tomorrow. Let us leave this evil place. Let us not become the lords we displace."

"Tomorrow, friend, tomorrow," another called. "Let us live like lords for one night."

Rick spotted Adam and Todd as a peasant grabbed Adam by the arm.

"This is no potboy," he shouted. "These hands haven't worked as we work. He does not smell like one of us."

The man peered at Adam.

"Where are his lice? Let me see his body."

When the man began to tear off Adam's clothes, Todd stumbled against him, tripped him, and pulled Adam free.

"He is too drunk to know what we are, masters," Todd said to a cluster of peasants. "Not all slaveys in a great house are turnspits. There are many jobs for peasant boys here."

"Some very soft ones, by the looks of it," someone said, but he laughed and men drifted away.

Todd spotted Rick and dragged Adam after him.

"Father," he said, aloud, and added quietly, "let's get out of here before they notice he's not moving."

"Todd. You didn't?"

"You'd rather they killed Adam like they did Walter?"

Rick hustled them back to where he had left Arthur and Gerald.

"Tell this varlet to untie me, Sirrah," Gerald said when Rick appeared.

"Why did you tie him, Arthur?"

"So he wouldn't trot back in and commit suicide for all of us."

"I'll have Arthur untie you if I can have your word as a gentleman," Arthur snorted, "your word you'll lie low with us till we can leave safely."

"But Walter..."

"Walter's dead," Todd said. "When the big one got tired, they took turns flogging him. One was careless and the whip got round Walter's neck and drawn tight. I felt him, he's dead all right."

"We may all be needed to help protect Sir Harold," Rick said.

"You have my word, Sirrah. Untie me."

That night they slept in the hayloft with one adult awake at all times. At first light peasants began to move out with their loot. From the loft Rick saw the giant argue with one of the sober ones from the night before. The giant seemed to want to stay at the manor while the other wanted them to march on. While they debated, much of their army walked away.

"The main group isn't headed toward our horses," Rick said. "We can slide out and make for Adam's parents' place."

To Rick's surprise their horses were still there, and they mounted and rode out.

At Adam's manor there was no sign of life, and Adam, after he had run through the manor, stood disconsolate in the yard.

"If they'd been killed we'd have seen the bodies," Rick said.

"Unless they've been hidden," Todd said.

"There's been no attempt at hiding bodies so far," Rick insisted.

He turned when Adam shouted: "Mother, Father," and started to run towards the wood lot.

Adam's parents had been drawn out by the sound of Adam's voice and he greeted them enthusiastically.

"It all happened so suddenly," Adam's mother said. "One of our serfs, who ran away more than a year ago, arrived one morning some hours after dawn..."

"And all of our village men went with him," Adam's father

continued. "There were no threats, no fighting, no violence against us, they simply went. When one of the village children saw riders today my wife thought it safer to hide. Just in case. The village women and children ran off to hide on the heath."

"Father. Andrew the big serf, the lazy one who ran away; he was there, at Lord Thomas's."

"Yes, Adam, that's the one."

"You mean that pig of a peasant was one of yours?" Gerald bellowed. "You could have stopped him here. Walter need not have died."

Gerald drew his sword and advanced on Adam's father, who stumbled back.

"Sir Gerald, he's unarmed," Rick shouted.

"I would not deign to fight him. Vermin like this I exterminate." Gerald slashed at Edwin, and opened a gash in his arm. "You will die slowly, not cleanly by the sword," Gerald said, and stalked him.

Arthur leapt in, sword in hand, and pushed Adam's father to one side.

"You'll have to kill me first."

"My pleasure, dog. What will it be? A belly slash?"

He feinted, slashed, and cut Arthur's tunic across his abdomen.

Obviously, Gerald was a skilled, aggressive swordsman, and Arthur was at best a reasonably competent amateur, and no match for Gerald.

"He's only playing with him, Todd." Rick groaned.

Todd picked up a pole, the handle of some farm implement, and darted forward. He swung the pole with all his weight to connect behind Gerald's knees. Gerald fell, and his sword slipped from his grasp. Todd picked it up and ran off with it.

Arthur stepped back, threw his sword to one side, and drew his dagger. The underhand grip and the easy swaying style telegraphed to Gerald his opponent was more comfortable and skilled with a knife than he was with a sword.

"Leave him, Todd. Thanks. He's mine."

Arthur watched Gerald get to his feet and draw his dagger.

They circled in a half-crouch, testing each other out. Now Arthur was the aggressor and Gerald wary. Finally, close to the wooden barn, they grappled; each held the other's knife wrist. With a rush, Arthur pushed Gerald against the wall. He banged Gerald's hand repeatedly on the rough boards. When Gerald's knife fell, Rick yelled: "Enough, Arthur. Back off."

Instead, Arthur wrenched his own knife hand free and pressed his blade to Gerald's chest.

"I'll see you hang, dog," Gerald said. "I'll see you all hang."

Arthur pressed.

"You haven't the stomach for it, peasant. I'll enjoy the boys first. Perhaps impale one for you to see, before I deal with you."

"Back off, Arthur," Rick said. "Sir Harold wouldn't let him."

"Either do it, or drop your weapon, pig."

Gerald smiled when Arthur drew back slightly, but his eyes widened at the renewed pressure of the blade between two ribs.

"This is for Pete, Sir Gerald, and for any other poor bastard you've murdered."

He pressed harder.

"And even for Walter. He might have been a half-decent kid but for you."

"A priest, Master Arthur, you would not kill an unshriven man."

"To be absolved? No frigging way. Rot in hell forever."

Arthur gave a last thrust, let go, and stepped back. For an instant Gerald stood, eyes wide, mouth open. Both hands grasped the hilt of the knife, before his body went limp and crumpled to a heap against the wall.

"God. What now?" Rick said.

"We should bury him," Todd said. "But see to Arthur and

Adam's father first, they're hurt."

"Well done, little brother. You may be as useless as tits on a bull for any honest work, but it's good to have you on my side in a fight."

"Did you hear him, Master Rick? Master Arthur called me brother."

Adam had remained motionless, white faced, while Arthur and Gerald fought. Now when his mother rushed to dress his father's wound, Adam moved to stand beside Gerald's body. After a moment he knelt, rolled the body onto its back, and folded the hands across the abdomen. He grasped the knife hilt in both hands and pulled, grunted and pulled again. This time he freed the blade. With one hand he closed Gerald's eyes.

While Adam knelt and stared at the body, Rick stood beside him, and put a hand on his shoulder. Angrily, Adam shook off Rick's hand.

"It's all right to cry, Adam," Rick said.

The boy stood up slowly, looked at Rick with an unreadable expression on his face. He turned to spit on the body, and threw himself into Rick's arms.

Chapter Twenty-Five

"An excellent meal, Mistress," Rick said. "Thank you."

Arthur quaffed his ale and burped. "We haven't eaten properly for two days."

Adam's father nodded his head to Rick.

"What happens now, Master Richard? Sir Gerald was Sir Harold's brother and well known to Lord Thomas."

He shivered.

"We needn't worry too much about Lord Thomas. He's dead." Rick described what they had seen at Lord Thomas's manor.

Horrified, Adam's father crossed himself.

"Lord have mercy, Christ have mercy, Lord have mercy."

"I hope he will," Rick said, "because the judges with soldiers won't and they'll be here soon."

"They will hang Master Arthur?" Adam said.

"They'll need to catch me first."

Arthur grinned, but Adam and Todd both still looked frightened.

"I think your men will begin to reappear over the next few days," Rick said. "Accept them back. They've done nothing against you. Try to get village life back to normal as quickly as possible. Don't attempt any retribution. But if Andrew should appear, tell him to flee. He'll hang when they find him."

"What of Gerald and Arthur?" Todd said.

"Gerald became separated from us, and we don't know where he went," Rick said. Arthur laughed. "Does that contain a lie? Where's the lie?"

"He is certainly separated from us," Adam's father said.

"But we do know where he's gone. Straight to hell," Arthur said.

"He was distracted over Walter's death and was not in full control of himself when we last saw him."

"That is true," Adam's mother said. "We could all swear to that on the Holy Bible itself."

"And we must do so, unless we wish to see Arthur hang," Rick said.

Next morning, Rick and Todd started for the summer manor, and Arthur left to return to D'Arcy.

"Why isn't Adam coming with us?" Todd said.

"He was Master Gerald's page. We have no place for him now, and anyway, I think he'll be happier with his parents."

"What will Sir Harold do?"

"I don't know, Todd. Shut up and let me think. I haven't even decided what to tell him."

"The Lady Jo will be angry at us, won't she?"

"Yes, I expect she will," Rick said. "But she will be pleased to see us back in one piece, at first anyway."

By mid-afternoon next day, they reached the outlying fields of the summer manor. All looked normal, with peasants peacefully at work in the fields, but when they approached closer to the manor itself they saw soldiers on patrol. One man came forward to meet them while the other watched.

"Master Richard? It is Master Richard. I almost didn't know you, dressed in crude homespun. Welcome, Master." The man bowed. "Sir Harold will be in the solar. I cannot perform the usual courtesy of escorting you. Master Dennis has given very firm orders."

"No need, Mark," Rick said, and the man beamed at Rick's recognition. "Master Dennis is right to be cautious."

"We'll go to Sir Harold's chamber," Rick said to Todd. "Find Chris for me."

"God, Rick, we were worried," Chris said. "Jo's been like a cat on hot bricks, and Sir Harold's been even more bloody minded than usual."

"Go to Sir Harold and tell him quietly I'm here, nothing else mind."

"I don't know anything else, do I?" Chris grumbled. "Todd wouldn't tell me."

"Good. For once he's done what he was told."

Rick paced the room while he waited, unsure of how Sir Harold would take his news.

"I hope, Todd, I'm right in thinking they don't kill bearers of bad tidings any more."

"Master Richard, Todd. You are safe. Praise be to God." Sir Harold strode in and embraced them both.

"My Lord." Rick coughed. "I fear I bear ill news. Master Gerald, your brother, is dead."

"Murdered by the rebels?"

"No, My Lord," Rick hesitated, "in a fight with Arthur."

"And you dare tell me so."

"I could have chosen not to tell you. You would never have known."

"Then, why have you told me? I must hang Arthur now."

"Please, listen first." Rick told him of the events at Lord Thomas's manor.

Sir Harold stroked his beard.

"Gerald was prepared to try to rescue Walter you say?"

"Yes, My Lord, and would have run in, had Arthur not knocked him out."

"Would he have succeeded?" Sir Harold smiled at Rick. "You

are not a fighting man to judge such. Todd, did he have a chance?"

Todd flushed bright red, and paused for a moment.

"No, My Lord, they were wild and drunk and there was enough of them to kill any who interfered with their sport. He would have been taken and killed."

"So my calculating brother would have given his life in an obviously hopeless attempt."

"He may have thought he could succeed. Some were very drunk."

"May have been prideful enough, you mean, Master Richard. No. Todd's assessment is what Gerald would see were he not blinded by emotion. The boy must have meant more to him than I had supposed. Strange, I would not have seen Gerald give his life for any other. And Arthur denied him that valiant end? He would be bitterly resentful to owe his life to Arthur, especially under such circumstances."

They stood for some time.

"He and Arthur fought, you say?"

"Yes, My Lord," Rick said. "Master Gerald was about to kill Adam's father, who was unarmed, and Arthur intervened."

"And Arthur won?"

"Master Gerald lost his sword," Todd said, "and Master Arthur laid his aside to fight with daggers."

"Ah. I have seen Arthur with a dagger."

"You won't hang Arthur, Sire, will you?" Chris said.

"Who knows of this?"

"Adam and his parents, you, Chris, Todd, and myself ... Arthur, of course," Rick said.

"Has Arthur fled from my justice?"

"No. My Lord, he has returned to D'Arcy, with my permission, to await your justice."

"Hmm. He should remain there. I do not wish to see him."

"What will you announce to your people?"

"That Gerald has died in the revolt, nothing more. Masses will be said for the repose of his soul. Arthur will pay."

"I'm afraid Arthur would rather hang."

"Don't tempt me, Sirrah."

"I'll pay for masses, for a year and a day."

"Then you shall have the wardship of Gerald's son and the boy's manors till he is of age."

"What will the Lady Gwenne say?"

"What should she say but: 'Yes, My Lord. Thank you, My Lord.'?"

God, Rick thought, Jo would have hell of a lot more to say than that.

"Thank you, I will do my utmost to deserve the trust you place in me."

"I wish the boy to grow up as Todd and Christopher have, with no resemblance whatever to my brother in character."

Sir Harold turned away, and said over his shoulder: "I will inform the Lady Gwenne and my people now, of both the death and my decision on the wardship. I'll not give anyone time to hatch any scheme. Have Todd fetch the Lady Jo to meet you here."

"Rick, what on earth were you thinking of? To rush off without a word to anyone," Jo dashed in and turned to Todd, "and where were your brains to let him go and not tell me. I should take a switch to you."

"It's nice to be home, isn't it, Todd?" Rick said, and Jo threw her arms round him, to kiss and hug him.

"Anyway, I'm glad to have you back in one piece."

She turned and held her arms out to Todd.

Chapter Twenty-Six

To Rick's surprise, life continued much as the year before at the summer manor. Lady Gwenne calmly accepted her loss, and was even gracious to Rick when he formally met with her to assume the wardship of her son and his estates.

Letters came to Sir Harold with accounts of the brutal repercussions that followed the suppression of the revolt. There had been no actual risings on Sir Harold's holdings, and, on Rick's earnest advice, those who had slipped away to join the rebels were allowed to return home quietly without comment.

A judge of assizes arrived with a large escort and soon Todd and Henry were agog with stories of floggings and hangings. The judges hanged many peasants, particularly in the South of England, but now in the outlying shires, heavy fines and even property confiscation were more common. The landowners simply did not wish to lose productive labourers, except when they proved to have taken part in actual atrocities against nobles or landowners.

Next afternoon, while Jo and Rick talked to the judge, Todd and Henry rushed in.

"They caught Andrew and the one they called Barber," Todd said. "You remember, Master Rick?"

Rick nodded and shuddered.

"They hanged both of them, but cut them down when they were only unconscious to bring them round before their bellies were slit and their guts pulled out."

"Todd. I don't want to hear the rest," Jo said.

"They flogged each twice before they hanged them," Henry said, "and again between hanging and drawing."

"Henry. When I told Todd to stop, I did not mean for you to carry on."

Jo walked to the far end of the solar, and Todd, after a cautious glance, said quietly: "They've got the heads in sacks in the barn. Want to see, Chris? The sergeant let me look."

Chris shook his head.

"Young man," the judge said, "such matters should not be talked of before a lady in your mistress's delicate condition. It could well affect the child she carries."

"Old wives' tale," Malcolm said. But Todd, contrite, followed Jo to the end of the solar.

"Those swine deserve their fate," the judge said, and accepted the goblet of wine offered by Chris. "But it was too quick. One justice I heard of hanged a peasant twenty times. Once in each of the towns, villages and hamlets he visited. Before death, the pig was cut down and revived and kept healthy for the next occasion. By the last time, his neck was so stretched and weak he could not hold up his head. It flopped about like a straw doll."

Todd rejoined them. "Did the last hanging kill him, sir?"

"Your pages are too forward, Sir Harold," the judge said. "I did not address the boy. I would relish the beating of him."

He stared hard at Todd, who stared back unblinking. The judge roared with laughter.

"No, boy. You have the point of my story exactly. When they cut him down, one of the men was careless and dropped the swine. His neck broke. The justice was furious. He had intended the wretch to last till they reached London. He had even stopped the daily flogging and had a collar of leather made to support the neck and head on their travels. Out of his own pocket."

While the judge laughed at his own story, Rick muttered: "And you're surprised the peasants revolted; you're surprised they behaved as they did with such sadistic justices."

"What? I did not catch that."

"A prayer for the dead, My Lord," Chris said, quickly. "More wine?"

"Those two, whose heads you saw, boy, beheaded Lord Thomas and his Captain."

"Were many others killed there?" Malcolm said.

"Several of the squires-in-training died. One they found strangled with a whip, still tied to a flogging frame."

"Walter," Rick said, and Todd nodded.

"Others died of ill humours when their wounds festered."

"Septicaemia," Malcolm said. "If they had wounds from pitchforks and the like, no wonder."

"I would say," Rick said, "that under the circumstances, the peasants behaved no worse than they had seen their betters behave. They treated their enemies no worse than their enemies treated them, no better, alas, but surely no worse."

The judge looked hard at him.

"A man is assigned his station in life by God. It is not up to him to question the wisdom of the Almighty. He must perform the offices of his station as best he can. His reward is in the hereafter. He who revolts against the status quo here on earth, revolts against God, and the hand of every man should be against him."

Chapter Twenty-Seven

After the judge left, word came that John Ball had been captured in Coventry and sent to London. On July thirteenth, he was sentenced to be hanged, drawn, and quartered. On the morning of July fifteenth the sentence had been carried out.

"Snap out of it, Rick," Jo said. "There's no point in you mooning around like a dying duck over this."

"But…"

"No buts. We're safe, all of us. Even Arthur and Todd. Gerald is dead. Sir Harold and his family are as safe and secure as anyone is at this time."

"You don't understand."

"What's to understand? We're here. Our child is shortly to be born here. We're better off than I ever dared hope we'd be when we first got here."

"I know all that, but knowing what will happen in some places doesn't help. I had hoped somehow I'd – we'd – make some difference."

"How do you know we haven't? Todd's life is changed because of us. Gerald is dead because of us. Arthur's administration of D'Arcy has changed the lives of at least the people of D'Arcy. You and Malcolm have influenced Sir Harold. So the big events are unchanged. You've rambled on often enough about inertia. Maybe the best we could hope is some small local changes."

"Enough. As Arthur says, 'hoist the lecture warning cone.' "

"The *frigging* lecture warning cone."

"Jo. Really."

"Cheer up. Let's make the best of it and do what we can. Come here. Quick. Put your hand here and feel the baby kick. That's reality. This isn't some minstrel's romance ... this is true reality!"

Chapter Twenty-Eight

A healthy baby boy was born in the last week of July. Sir Harold declared a holiday in the manor village and held a rowdy feast. Malcolm was drunk for two days and swayed ominously when he stood in church for the boy's baptism as Peter Richard Harold D'Arcy.

Todd was disappointed at the choice of names, but brightened when Jo said: "We'll name the next one after you, Todd."

"When, My Lady? Soon? And what about one for Chris?"

"I would dearly like to hear Arthur's comment on that," Sir Harold said.

There was a silence before Rick laughed, and Sir Harold nodded rather grimly at Rick, before he too laughed.

The return to the castle was uneventful, and life resumed its regular course. Rick had the Town Charter redrafted, and Sir Harold held a feast for its presentation to the Mayor and burghers. It was an especially festive occasion for the town, since many towns, like St Albans in the South, had their charters withdrawn or suspended for their part in the revolt.

The townspeople clearly credited Rick with their good fortune. Sir Harold in his presentation speech praised Rick highly. To everyone's surprise, he announced his intention of gifting to Rick, his heirs and successors, in perpetuity, the manor next to the town, the manor in which the circle of stones stood.

Malcolm's father-in-law to be announced the November marriage of his eldest daughter to: "...the learned, skilled, Master Malcolm, Physician to our most gracious and generous lord, Sir Harold, and friend to Master Richard, who is in every way a most worthy Lord of the Stones."

Loud drunken snores from Malcolm somewhat marred the effect, as did his immediate challenge to fight any present when prodded awake by Chris.

Richard was sorry Arthur could not be at the feast. He was still not welcome at the castle, although Sir Harold did now talk of him quite freely and without apparent rancour.

"For heaven's sake," Jo said, when Rick voiced his concern, "when he is here, he's nothing but an embarrassment to you. Leave well enough alone."

"He's still one of us," Rick persisted.

"I don't see his friend Dennis worries overmuch about him."

"He's safe and well, and that's fine for Dennis. I don't know that they were ever really close friends. Arthur doesn't think or understand Dennis at all well."

"What will happen to us? Have you any clues at all?"

"We don't appear in any history book or written record I've ever heard of, so we're not major players. My guess is Arthur will manage the manors for me, and skim off enough to become a rich freeman. His family will rise. Dennis will take over from Martin as Sir Harold's de facto military commander. He'll always be there when needed, but he'll always be an enigma. Malcolm will get fat and very rich: a much loved, if rather irascible, physician. Chris will become Sir Harold's son's chief factotum, his guide and mentor, and eventually his right hand man when the son takes over from Sir Harold."

"Chris? You've got to be joking."

"No, why? Chris is doing nicely. He's bright and loyal."

"What about us? And Todd?"

"We'll do fine. I'll keep on as Sir Harold's secretary, and run my school. We have the income from the manors. If we can pry you loose from Lady Eleanor, you could even teach in our school. If you're not too busy with the babies; the boys you've promised Todd and Chris."

Jo grimaced at him.

"My teaching would set tongues wagging. A *woman* teaching?"

"They'd get used to it."

"Perhaps we could take in some girls too."

"And why not?"

"My Todd, what will become of him?"

"He could stay with us and prosper. He really is a bright little devil. However, in this time, the road up for someone like Todd, with no family connections at all, is the Church."

"Todd a priest?" Jo said, scarcely able to breathe for laughing.

"Why not? He is as devout as many, more than most in these times. His Latin is good, better than mine soon. Didn't you see how he hero-worshipped Wycliffe? He really latched onto him when he was here."

"But Todd a priest," Jo said.

With the approach of the second anniversary of their arrival and Pete's death, Jo began to suggest some sort of ceremony, for them alone, at the circle. At first, there was no particular enthusiasm, but by the day she had them persuaded.

Shortly before dusk, they left their horses with a groom on the circle side of the ford. Jo knelt in prayer where Pete died, while Rick held the baby Peter.

Afterwards, they sat at sunset, and looked out towards the town.

"It's still spooky," Chris said, but his voice had deepened in the two years and it no longer sounded childish.

"A pity Arthur couldn't be here," Rick said. At that there was a scuffle in the brush. Arthur appeared, and dragged Todd by the arm after him.

"Arthur," Jo said.

"Todd," Rick said, "you were to stay at the castle. You said the stones after dark frightened you."

Todd wedged himself between Rick and Jo and scowled at Arthur.

"Found him skulking up the hill," Arthur said. "This the kid? Peter isn't it?"

He looked and laughed.

"Todd tells me you've got another bun in the oven. To be called Todd this time?"

"I did not, Master Rick, My Lady."

"Anyway," Arthur said, "we're all here, even Pete in a sense. Who has the frigging fireworks this time? That's the token, isn't it, My Lord of the Stones? Strange, it looks like a storm. It was clear earlier."

They sat while lightning flashes lit the sky. The flickering light made some stones lean drunkenly, while others faded in and out of view.

The End

Epilogue

Unlike others caught in the twisted circle of the Möbius Loop (that undeniable quirk of time and space) one group got home only six hundred-plus years later ... as newborn babies.

They had, long since, lived out their lives and died of age, disease or violence in fourteenth century Europe, leaving children and corpses in their wake.

Generations later not one reborn of the group remembered his future past. Innocently they played their roles again from childhood through high school and college to the brutal castles and revolts of their own past futures ... and nothing in The Loop changed.

Even Peter got home to live his youth up until that fatal night in The Circle of Stones on the hill.

This will not be the last time they'll play their roles, caught in the never-ending, never-beginning Loop – would anything be different had they not made their protests? Of course not.

There is nothing new under the sun.

Also Available from BeWrite Books

Crime
Sweet Molly Maguire – Terry Houston

The surreal world of a mean city newspaper swallowed the very toughest or spat them out. This circus of hopeless drunks and heartless back-stabbers was no place for Sweet Molly Maguire. She died, raped and pregnant, and didn't merit a single line of print. But for one reporter, her death wasn't the end of just another story. It was the opening sentence in a search for something rare in the news room ... the bitter truth.

Paperback ISBN 1-904224-05-9
 $13.50 US/ £9.80 UK/ $21.24 Canada/ €15.55 Europe
Ebook ISBN 1-904224-01-6
 $6.55 US/ £4.80 UK/ $10.40 Canada/ €7.65 Europe
CD – Rom ISBN 1-904224-06-7
 $10.25 US/ £7.50 UK/ $16.25 Canada/ €11.90 Europe

Horror
Chill – Terri Pine, Peter Lee, Andrew Müller

Dim the lights. Tug up the quilt so that only your eyes are visible. Now, slip into the dark, dark night of this world's greatest masters of macabre. Try not to sleep. Watch for moving shadows. And – whatever happens – *don't* get out of bed ... you may catch your very death ...

Paperback ISBN 1-904224-08-3
 $13.50 US/ £9.80 UK/ $21.24 Canada/ €15.55 Europe
Ebook ISBN 1-904224-03-2
 $6.55 US/ £4.80 UK/ $10.40 Canada/ €7.65 Europe
CD – Rom ISBN 1-904224-11-3
 $10.25 US/ £7.50 UK/ $16.25 Canada/ €11.90 Europe

Crime
The Knotted Cord – Alistair Kinnon

The body of a naked young boy hanging in a dusty barn stirs sickening feelings of déjà vu in the detective. As he untangles each knot in the tangled cord of his investigation, he uncovers a murderous thread ... and police prejudices which may have allowed previous killings to happen ... not to mention his own guilt! **Alistair Kinnon** has written much more than a tense, psychological crime novel -- his twisting plot takes the reader into the murky world of child sex-for-sale ... the parent's darkest nightmare and the child's greatest threat.

Paperback   ISBN 1-904224-12-1
             $13.50 US/ £9.80 UK/ $21.24 Canada/ €15.55 Europe
Ebook   ISBN 1-904224-04-1
             $6.55 US/ £4.80 UK/ $10.40 Canada/ €7.65 Europe
CD – Rom   ISBN 1-904224-13-X
             $10.25 US/ £7.50 UK/ $16.25 Canada/ €11.90 Europe

Fantasy Humour
Zolin – A Rockin' Good Wizard – Barry Ireland

Worlds go along happily side-by-side in their own dimensiverses ... until they accidentally bump into each other. Then a wild Glasgow rock band, randy witches, dragons for hire and kings and queens end up rocking where they should have been rolling. And bewildered apprentice wizard, Zolin, is piggy in the middle. **Barry Ireland's** book is to Fantasy what The Hitchhiker's Guide to the Galaxy was to Sci Fi. An adult fairy tale!

Paperback   ISBN 1-904224-19-9
             $13.50 US/ £9.80 UK/ $21.24 Canada/ €15.55 Europe
Ebook   ISBN 1-904224-18-0
             $6.55 US/ £4.80 UK/ $10.40 Canada/ €7.65 Europe
CD – Rom   ISBN 1-904224-20-2
             $10.25 US/ £7.50 UK/ $16.25 Canada/ €11.90 Europe

Thriller
Blood Money – Azam Gill

A starkly realistic novel of love and hate in the murky world of international terrorism, mercenary soldiering, dirty banking and underground government agencies. Gill, with the skill of a master story teller and the authority of an actual former insider, writes a gritty story of star-crossed love against a scenario strikingly close to that which may have led up to the attack on the Twin Towers ... and a war far from over.

Paperback   ISBN 1-904224-91-1
           $13.50 US/ £9.80 UK/ $21.24 Canada/ €15.55 Europe
Ebook   ISBN 1-904224-90-3
           $6.55 US/ £4.80 UK/ $10.40 Canada/ €7.65 Europe
CD – Rom   ISBN 1-904224-92-X
           $10.25 US/ £7.50 UK/ $16.25 Canada/ €11.90 Europe

Crime
Porlock Counterpoint – Sam Smith

Sam Smith goes one step beyond the psychological crime novel when he places cynical cops to, like the reader, observe the counterpoint between two levels of criminal. The middle-aged, middle-class couple smuggling hard drugs for their avaricious dreams and the desperate young couple who 'borrow' their car simply to get to hospital in time for the birth of their baby. The quartet may never meet ... but their lives, worlds apart in terms of social rank and the definition of 'crime', collide with shattering results.

Paperback   ISBN 1-904224-15-6
           $13.50 US/ £9.80 UK/ $21.24 Canada/ €15.55 Europe
Ebook   ISBN 1-904224-14-8
           $6.55 US/ £4.80 UK/ $10.40 Canada/ €7.65 Europe
CD – Rom   ISBN 1-904224-16-4
           $10.25 US/ £7.50 UK/ $16.25 Canada/ €11.90 Europe

Short Stories
The Miller Moth – Mike Broemmel
The miller moth flutters through Mike Broemmel's pages like a phantom - sometimes benevolent, sometimes threatening. A shade of human life itself. Characters you'll meet are ordinary people in ordinary situations -- made extraordinary with the touch of a modern Steinbeck. You will recognize yourself, family and neighbours in this collection of deceptively simple stories crafted with the intricacy, delicacy and humanity of a master wordsmith.

Paperback ISBN 1-904224-15-6
$13.50 US/ £9.80 UK/ $21.24 Canada/ €15.55 Europe
Ebook ISBN 1-904224-14-8
$6.55 US/ £4.80 UK/ $10.40 Canada/ €7.65 Europe
CD – Rom ISBN 1-904224-16-4
$10.25 US/ £7.50 UK/ $16.25 Canada/ €11.90 Europe

N.B The price for paperback and CD-Rom excludes postage and packaging. Prices correct at time of press.

Coming soon: *Vera & Eddy's War by Sam Smith*
The Care Vortex by Sam Smith
The Dandelion Clock by Jay Mandal
Someplace Like Home by Terrence Moore
A Stranger and Afraid by Arthur Allwright

All the above titles are available from

www.bewrite.net

Printed in the United Kingdom by
Lightning Source UK Ltd., Milton Keynes
137230UK00001B/7/A